"Christy."

And she let out a gentle gasp.

"What?" he asked in response to her reaction. "What is it?"

She struggled to swallow back all the inexplicable emotion assaulting her. She just hadn't accurately envisioned what it would be like to be alone with him like this. Or . . . how it would feel to hear him say her name. "You've never called me Christy before."

He blinked, clearly not having realized that. And those blue eyes stayed locked on her as he said, "I guess . . . I feel like I know you now."

And then his warm hand closed over hers where it rested on her thigh, and she looked down, took in the sight of their fingers together, on her leg, and felt the touch moving all through her like some kind of hot, sweet drug coursing through her veins.

And that was when he leaned over and kissed her.

By Toni Blake

TONI BLAKE

ALL I WANT IS YOU

A CORAL COVE NOVEL

AVON

An Imprint of HarperCollins*Publishers*

AVON BOOKS
An Imprint of HarperCollins*Publishers*
195 Broadway
New York, New York 10007

Copyright © 2014 by Toni Herzog
ISBN 978-0-06-222952-6
www.avonromance.com

First Avon Books mass market printing: June 2014

Avon Trademark Reg. U.S. Pat. Off. and in Other Countries, Marca Registrada, Hecho en U.S.A.
HarperCollins® is a registered trademark of HarperCollins Publishers.

Printed in the U.S.A.

10 9 8 7 6 5 4 3 2 1

To Robin Zentmeyer,
with whom I shared my first apartment—
who was there with me when the door was kicked in,
when the light fixture came crashing down,
and when the potted plants were thrown.
All these years later, life becomes art.

Acknowledgments

All I Want Is You is a book that's been a long time in the making. I first conceived the story idea, and many of the details about it, nearly fifteen years ago. And much of the inspiration came from personal life experiences and travels that have been percolating inside me for nearly thirty. It's so fun to finally see this particular story come to fruition.

Thanks to the incomparable Lindsey Faber for endless brainstorming help and plot problem solving as this story took shape. I couldn't ask for a better, smarter, or more helpful friend.

Thanks to my first reader, Renee Norris, not only for reading this book in record time, but for helping me see shining bits of light in it that had escaped me until she pointed them out.

Thanks, as always, to Meg Ruley, Christina Hogrebe, and the rest of my fabulous agenting team at the Rotrosen Agency for all your support, guidance, and cheerleading on my behalf.

Thanks to the amazing folks at Avon Books for finding new and wonderful ways to sell my books, and for being a super warm and supportive environment in which to write and publish.

And special thanks to my fabulous editor, May Chen, for being so amazingly kind, patient, and understanding during the writing of this book—and when I kept missing deadlines. Your support is truly and deeply appreciated!

ALL I WANT
IS YOU

Down, down, down.
Would the fall never come to an end?

Lewis Carroll, *Alice in Wonderland*

Prologue

CHRISTY KNIGHT sat in an old, comfy easy chair in Under the Covers, the bookstore on Destiny's quaint town square, cradling a large mug of hot chocolate between her palms, surrounded by hometown friends. The wintry February wind outside whistled, but the cozy bookshop felt warm. Almost safe even. And it had been a while since she'd felt safe.

The past few years had been rough—far rougher than life had prepared her for—and mostly, she tried to deal with that by putting on a brave face. But as she looked to the friendly expressions of Amy Bright and Sue Ann Simpkins, who she'd known her whole life, and Anna Romo, a more recent friend, she knew she could open up to them and be honest. Especially when Amy said, "Whatever's going on, you can tell us. You know that, right?"

Christy nodded, then let out the breath she hadn't quite realized she'd been holding. "Well, the truth is . . . maybe my life in the city is harder than I've made it out to be. Not many people know this, but . . . when Mom and Dad died, I discovered they'd been having financial trouble, and that they'd let their insurance policies lapse."

She sensed shock blanketing the room, heard the gasps the others so valiantly tried to hold in—and pressed onward. "Ultimately, I was left with . . . nothing. So it's been . . . difficult."

Christy had kept all that quiet after her parents' tragic death in a house fire here three years earlier—both to protect their good names and because she didn't want pity. Surviving it all had been hard *enough* without pity heaped on top of it.

Sitting in the easy chair next to hers, Amy reached over to touch her arm. "Christy, I'm so sorry."

"But I guess this explains why you left school," Sue Ann said from the overstuffed chair across from her. Christy had dropped out of the University of Cincinnati—a two-hour drive from Destiny—just one semester shy of receiving her bachelor's degree. "That never made sense to me—but now . . . I guess it was a money thing."

Christy confirmed it with a nod. "I had no choice. I had to move into an apartment and work full-time to keep afloat."

"Well," said Anna, perched on the arm of Sue Ann's chair, "I think it's amazing that you've handled this completely on your own. That's not easy. You should be proud of yourself." Christy valued

Anna's opinion, as she'd been through some tough times, too—but now came the *really* hard part. Admitting that . . . maybe she *couldn't* handle it anymore. That she was tired. That she wanted to make a change, find an easier way to live.

She swallowed back her discomfort and told them why she'd driven back to her hometown this weekend. "I kept thinking life would get easier, that I'd make more money somehow. But it hasn't. And so . . . I'm wondering if maybe I should throw in the towel and come home. To Destiny."

When her friends' eyes all lit up, it restored in her a long lost sense of security, of being welcomed, and encouraged her to go on. "I've always dreamed of making a living selling my jewelry, but I work so much that there's no time to explore that." Christy created custom jewelry from inexpensive vintage pieces in her spare time. "And I just thought . . . if I come home, maybe I can finally, somehow, find a way to make that happen—and find a way to feel at peace in my own life again."

"You should *totally* come home," Anna encouraged her warmly. "Even though I almost fought it at first when I moved to Destiny, people here are so caring that it's hard *not* to feel at peace."

Except . . . why had Sue Ann's expression filled with doubt? "Though as beautiful as your jewelry is," she said, "I'm not sure Destiny is the place to make a living selling it."

"I'm afraid I have to agree," Amy added, though she appeared surprisingly cheery and wide-eyed about it. Then she pointed upward. "But you could live in my old apartment above the store for free."

She owned Under the Covers and had resided upstairs until she'd married Logan Whitaker last summer—now she made her home with him in his cottage on Blue Valley Lake.

"And you could work in the bookstore," Anna added, motioning around them. "I love my part-time job here, but the bed-and-breakfast is really keeping me busy these days and I've told Amy she needs to find someone to replace me."

"And you could adopt a cat!" Amy said.

Suddenly a little overwhelmed, Christy blinked. "A cat?"

Anna met her gaze matter-of-factly. "It's become a big thing in Destiny. Everyone adopts a cat. Even me. Even though I thought I didn't like cats."

"A lot of strays show up here," Amy explained. "And I let them live in the store for as long as they need to, but I also make it a mission to find good homes for them. We don't have a cat on hand right now . . ."

"But one will show up soon," Sue Ann said. "Trust me on this. They always do."

"And a cat will make your life in Destiny complete," Amy said sweetly. "And before you know it, you'll be as happy as all of *us* are."

Christy let out another breath as she looked around at the faces of her friends. They were all so nice. And so caring. And coming home would give her that ease of instantly belonging, of having people to turn to. And the truth was, she yearned for that. It was one of those things she'd never fully appreciated until it was gone.

But Amy, Anna, and Sue Ann were all older

than her—in their thirties. They all had significant others—strong, reliable guys to share the struggles of everyday life with. They were all much further along in their journey through adulthood. It made sense that they were happy and at peace.

At twenty-four, though, Christy didn't have a significant other—or anyone else—to rely on. And as kind an offer as it was, the idea of working day in and day out in this tiny bookstore—no matter how cute it was—just didn't appeal. And she was not—and perhaps would never be—at a place in life where she'd believe a cat would complete her. Even now, she realized—after all she'd been through, all the loss and all the struggles—her dreams were still bigger than that.

She loved Destiny, and she loved the kind people here. But the moment forced her to face something that, deep down, she'd probably known all along, or she would have come back much sooner. Destiny, for all its many charms, would never let her evolve into who she was supposed to be, and she just didn't belong here anymore. It was a wonderful little town, but it was also the place where her parents had died and her childhood home had burned to the ground.

She was tired. She often felt beaten. And it had been tempting to consider retreating to a safer place than she'd managed to carve out for herself in the city.

But the reality was . . . her life in Destiny was over.

She generally gave herself very good advice,
(though she very seldom followed it).

Lewis Carroll, *Alice in Wonderland*

Chapter 1

CHRISTY PUSHED the key into the old lock on her front door and turned it. Nothing. She repeated the motion, twisting the doorknob and pushing inward. Still nothing.

"Howdy do, neighbor."

Crap, I almost made it. She looked up to see Mrs. Hart, the old woman who lived below her. "Hi," she said, glancing up only briefly in hopes of not inviting conversation. When she'd first met Mrs. Hart, she'd thought: How nice, a sweet little old lady to talk to. The notion had made her think of Destiny and decide that even in the city maybe she could find people who reminded her of home. Only it turned out that Mrs. Hart was mostly an irritating gossip whose lengthy meanderings were hard to escape once she got started.

"The Harringtons were at it again last night, did you hear?"

Christy tried to answer shortly. "Yep, sure did." The Harringtons lived across the street in a house laden with potted plants. Terra-cotta and ceramic pots of all shapes and sizes filled the ledges of the large covered porch and lined the front walk. And they argued a lot. More and more lately, it seemed.

"I worry for her. Do you know what I heard him say to her when they were fighting in the front yard night before last?"

One more try with the key and . . . click—the door unlocked. *Third time's the charm.* It usually was. *One day I'm going to get this door open on the first try.* But for now she just said, "I'm so sorry, Mrs. Hart, I have to run," and trundled forward, two plastic grocery bags looped over one wrist, and started up the old wooden stairs that led to her second floor apartment in a rundown Cincinnati neighborhood.

She lived in an old two-story home of dark brick that had been divided into a duplex complete with a second door added on to the front. The house, with its high ceilings and dark wood moldings, had clearly seen better days. But she tried to be thankful for the touches that reminded her the place had once been more elegant.

"Son of a bitch."

Of course, walking in to find her roommate, Bethany, cussing, put a damper on the elegance she was trying to appreciate.

"What's wrong?" Christy asked as she entered the living room.

Bethany, an aspiring artist, stood behind her easel, but rather than a paintbrush she held a cell phone. "That bastard cut my hours again this week."

Christy sighed. It was an ongoing drama, for both of them—trying to put in enough hours at low-paying jobs to make the rent. Bethany worked at a local fresh food market—which at least came with the perk of free fruit just before it went bad—and Christy at a chain fashion store in the mall. Which didn't come with many perks, but at least she was surrounded by pretty things.

"Oh, and I brought those home for you," Bethany said, suddenly calmer now as she pointed to an old strand of fake pearls on the circa 1980 coffee table. Bethany was good at compartmentalizing, which Christy had learned was a valuable skill of the broke and poor, even if she hadn't quite yet mastered it herself. "They've been in the lost and found bin at work for over thirty days, so they're yours."

Christy lowered her grocery bags to the table and bent to pick up the pearls. "These are great—thanks!" Since Christy's particular art—and art was the thing she and Bethany had most in common—required old costume jewelry, little made her happier these days than getting materials for free.

After putting away the milk and other groceries, Christy eased her aching feet out of the heels she'd worn to work, then changed into sweats. It was April—two months had passed since her realization that she couldn't return home to Destiny. The good thing about spring was that she and Bethany didn't have to walk around the apartment freezing because they couldn't afford to turn the heat up. But the bad thing was that soon it would be sweltering hot in a place with no air-conditioning.

On this warm April day, Bethany had opened a few windows and Christy could smell the city scents wafting their way inside. The house sat just blocks from a distillery on one side and a flavor-making factory on the other. She decided to name today's scent "vanilla whiskey."

"You know what you need to do," Bethany said from behind her as Christy stood at the window peering out on the cracked sidewalk below.

Christy guessed her expression must have led Bethany to read her thoughts. After realizing she couldn't go home, she'd had no choice but to continue facing her troubles head-on—but it was hard to keep her chin up all the time in the midst of poverty, whether it came in the form of heat, cold, bad smells, or trouble paying the rent. Even so, she told Bethany, "Don't say it."

But Bethany said it anyway—the same way she always did. "You need to find yourself a rich man to take you away from all this."

Bethany was like a broken record on this topic lately. And Christy raised a challenging gaze as it occurred to her for the first time ever to say, "Why do *I* need a rich man and you don't?"

Yet her roommate only shrugged. "Oh, I'd take one if he came along. But it's different for me because I chose this. I knew the road I was traveling and I went down it anyway. You didn't have the same choice."

True enough. Bethany came from a happy middle class family to whom she could go home if she ever got that desperate. Never quite feeling she fit in to their mainstream world, she'd chosen the risky path of art as a lifestyle. And though Christy felt that following one's heart was the noblest path, it was definitely her parents' deaths that had determined her current fate—it had never been a decision.

Still, she simply replied as she always did when Bethany brought this up. "I am *not* going out chasing rich guys. Because I'm not the gold digger type. That's just so yucky." She gave a slight shiver. "If I ever get married, it'll be because I fall madly, desperately in love with someone."

She'd been in love once before—a boy named Kyle during her first year of college—and though their relationship had eventually fizzled, she remembered love being a wonderful thing. And she had no intention of settling for less.

"I didn't say you couldn't fall in love with them," Bethany pointed out with a dramatic head tilt, her dark brown locks swaying. "I'm just saying it should be a guy with assets, and that it should be, like, now." She stepped closer to where Christy still stood by the window, leaning against the wall, and let her voice go lower. "I worry about you. You weren't cut out for this."

Christy raised her eyebrows. "And you were?"

Another shrug from her friend. "I pull off the starving artist thing better than you—I look good skinny. And I'm less idealistic—I don't believe in rainbows and unicorns, or in falling madly, desperately in love—so I'm able to be more practical when things don't turn out like I want. And we both know that if things ever get really, really bad, I won't starve. I always have the option of giving up and going home. So it's different for me. I have a fallback position. You don't."

"Thanks for the reminder," Christy said with an eye roll and a sigh. Then she caught sight of Mrs. Harrington watering her plants. The woman clearly loved them—Christy had seen her pot and repot things on her front porch in almost all seasons. She took them all inside for winter and Christy had been happy to notice her putting them back on the porch one day last week. She found a certain comfort in watching the woman with her plants and flowers, even from a distance. "They're what keeps her going," she mused.

"Huh?" Bethany asked.

"The plants. They're what keeps her moving forward in life. They give her hope, take away her stress. They are to her what my jewelry is to me and your art is to you."

"Plants and art and jewelry," Bethany said softly, now peering out the window, too. "Such small, fragile things to hold such weight."

They both stayed quiet for a moment, perhaps letting the observation sink in.

But then Bethany added another big dose of pragmatism. "I still say you need to seriously start looking for a rich man. The ideas of love and romance are great—but there are other good things in life that are just as important, Christy. And a lot more practical."

LATER that night, Christy sat on the couch, a felt-lined jewelry tray in her lap, incorporating an old brooch into a heavy, draping, multi-strand necklace of fake pearls and a few delicate pale pink ceramic rose-shaped beads. Curled up in an adjacent easy chair, Bethany perused local gallery websites, dreaming of getting her first showing. A reality dating show droned on their old TV as if to remind Christy how manufactured and plastic relationships could be—whether or not she wanted to believe that.

When Christy's cell phone rang, Bethany grabbed the remote to reduce the volume. And Christy glanced down to see her grandpa Charlie's smiling face come up on the screen. Although he'd resided in a rest home in Florida since her high school days, he was her only remaining relative with whom she stayed in contact—he'd still lived in Destiny with her late grandmother during Christy's growing up years and she'd been close to both.

"Hi, Grandpa," she said merrily.

"How's my sweet grandbaby tonight?" he asked.

"Doing just great," she said, telling herself it wasn't really a lie since hearing from him definitely lifted her spirits. "How's life in the land of sunshine? Have you been out picking up chicks in bikinis on your surfboard?"

"No, afraid not," he said plainly. Which meant something was wrong. Normally, a little banter about bikini chicks or surfing would make him laugh and then he'd concoct a wild tale about gallivanting up and down the beach attracting girls with his fine physique.

So she didn't bother beating around the bush. "What's up, Grandpa?"

And his answering sigh worried her even more. This just wasn't like him. "Well, damn the luck—called you up just to chat, thinkin' it would cheer me up, but you saw straight through me. I must be losin' my touch."

"So what's wrong? What do you need cheered up about?"

"Oh, I don't wanna trouble you, darlin'. Let's just talk about *your* day."

"My day wasn't particularly cheerful, either," she admitted, deciding to be more honest now. "And it's going to get even worse if you don't come clean and tell me what's bothering you."

When he didn't reply, Christy's throat tightened. This was starting to seem serious.

"Grandpa Charlie? What's wrong? Tell me," she demanded.

"You might end up sorry you asked."

"No, I won't," she insisted. "In fact, I won't sleep tonight if I don't know. So spill."

"Well, my grandgirl, it's like this," he began—and then her grandpa proceeded to tell her he was out of money. All the air left Christy's lungs as he explained that if he didn't come up with a hefty amount in the next six months, he'd be shipped out of the pleasant, friendly place he now thought of as home and shoved into a state run facility not of his choosing.

And while his health was not as bad as that

of some of the residents where he lived, he did require daily medical care. He was diabetic. He moved slowly with the aid of a walker or scooter. He often required oxygen, and he'd had enough minor "heart episodes" that the nurses kept a close eye on him. Christy knew he'd always been happy with the care he received, that it was a top-notch facility. "But you see now why I didn't want to dump that on you," he concluded.

Yes, she definitely did. Her heart sank as she absorbed the almost paralyzing news. "But I'm still glad you told me," she said, trying to sound as if she had some control—over anything. "It's better that I at least know the situation. And you have no idea how badly I wish I could help. If I had the money, I'd give it to you in a heartbeat, but as it is, I can barely . . ."

Oh crap. She was tired and, that quickly, had said more than she'd meant to. Her grandfather was among the masses to whom she'd never confessed her money woes. Since he was a thousand miles away and living on a fixed income himself, it had seemed pointless to give him something extra to fret about, especially when he'd been mourning the death of her father, his only child.

"That's sweet, my girl," he said after she trailed off, "but you can barely what?"

And now *she* was the one sighing and not answering. Finally, she said, "You have enough to worry about without me adding to it, so let's just focus on—"

He interrupted her. "You can barely what, darlin'?"

Christy struggled to take a breath. Stark concern had thickened his voice. And while she'd never wanted to trouble him with this—ugh—she supposed she had no choice now but to be honest, even if the timing seemed beyond rotten. "Well, Grandpa, the truth is . . ."

And then she told him. All of it. The lapsed homeowner's insurance policy—she'd gotten nothing for the house and belongings, all of which had been reduced to black rubble and ash. The lapsed life insurance policy—she'd still not paid for her parents' funerals, though she sent the funeral home in Destiny a few dollars as often as she could and the owners were kind about it. And then there were the student loans and other bills she struggled to pay each month. "But . . . we'll figure something out," she concluded, trying to stay positive. "For both of us."

"Whoa, whoa, whoa there, darlin'," Grandpa Charlie said then, his tone admonishing her. "My predicament isn't your problem to take on. And now that I hear what *you've* been goin' through, I regret dumpin' this on you even more. Shouldn't have called when I was in a low mood—and I shoulda kept my big trap shut."

But she protested. "No, your predicament *is* my problem, I'm *making* it my problem, and I'm going to find a way to fix it." Though even as the words left her mouth, she had no idea how. She only knew that she loved her Grandpa, and that they'd both suffered enough the past few years, and that she wasn't going to let him suffer further. It was one thing for her own security to be at risk—but when it was her Grandpa's health and comfort at stake . . . it instilled in her an instant resolve to somehow—*somehow*—repair the situation.

When she disconnected with him a few stressful minutes later, her heart pounded too hard in her chest. The last time she'd gotten a phone call that brought bad family news, she'd found out her parents were dead. This wasn't that—far from it, thank God—and yet as she tried to slow her breathing, she found herself yanked back in time, reliving the devastation.

"Um, everything okay?" Bethany asked doubtfully.

"No," Christy said. "In fact, right when I thought things couldn't get much worse, they did. In a huge way." And maybe offering to take on her grandpa's money problem at the same time she had plenty of her own was crazy, but how could she do anything else?

With the TV still on mute, both girls stayed silent and Christy realized the house had begun to shake slightly—from a train passing by on the tracks at the end of the street. She mostly didn't even notice the subtle vibrations anymore, or the sound, but right now it felt like a tiny little earthquake rocking her already delicate world. She'd experienced such a lack of control ever since her parents' deaths, a sense of not being able to save anyone, including herself—and if she could just find a way to help her grandpa keep his life the way he wanted it, she already knew it would help *her* life make some kind of sense again.

And that's when the old frosted glass light fixture suspended from the ceiling above came crashing down onto the coffee table, exploding into a million slivers of glass. Neither girl jumped or screamed—they both simply flinched, stayed still, then looked at each other. Christy supposed it took a lot to shock either of them now.

"From the vibrations," Christy said. "From the trains. It must have been working its way loose little by little, every time a train went by, all this time, for who knows how many years."

"And tonight it reached its breaking point," Bethany said.

"It could have seriously injured one of us," Christy observed.

"It still could," Bethany replied, surveying the bits of glass all around them. "But we'll just move slowly, be careful. It'll be fine."

Christy nodded. Yes, it would be fine. It was only a broken light.

But some things *wouldn't* be fine. Some things weren't so easy to fix or clean up.

"Maybe that was a sign," she murmured.

"What kind of a sign?"

"Maybe I've reached a breaking point, too," Christy said.

Bethany just blinked. "What do you mean?"

And Christy could barely believe the words that were about to leave her lips—but she said them anyway. "Maybe you're right. Maybe the time has come to give up and give in. Maybe I do need to find a rich man."

> There were doors all round the hall,
> but they were all locked.
>
> Lewis Carroll, *Alice in Wonderland*

Chapter 2

"Now, I don't mean it could be just anyone," she was quick to add. "And I wouldn't ever marry someone I don't care about. But . . . maybe it's time to . . . narrow my dating pool to financially solvent men and start going to more upscale places."

She went on to explain about her grandpa's situation. "He has six months, so maybe that's enough time to find a guy who fits the bill and will be so crazy about me that he won't mind bailing Grandpa Charlie out."

"And if it makes your own life a little easier in the bargain, that's good, too," Bethany pointed out.

Christy let a tired sigh escape her as she admitted, "It *would* be a relief not to feel so on edge and worried all the time." So even if she didn't feel a hundred percent great about this change of heart . . . well, at least it brought with it the idea of hope, for her and her grandfather both.

"Though . . . I think you might have to do more than just narrow your dating pool." Bethany set her laptop aside. "If you're serious about this, you're going to have to be more aggressive about dating than you usually are."

Yet Christy rolled her eyes. "Who has time to be aggressive about dating? I barely have time to brush my teeth some days." She purposely worked long shifts at the mall—it was the only way to make enough to get by.

"I'm saying you'll have to *make* the time," Bethany told her. "You might have to set your jewelry aside for a while. I know working on it makes you happy, but right now is about . . . survival."

Christy swallowed, practically gulping. She wanted to accuse her friend of being overly dramatic, but this *was* about survival. For Grandpa Charlie anyway.

So they spent the rest of the evening brainstorming what Bethany started calling Operation: Rich Dude. They sat on the old couch, legs crossed, facing each other, and came up with plans for putting Christy's quest into action. And to her surprise, as they talked and strategized, Christy even began to feel energized by the idea, the same way she felt energized by making jewelry and dreaming of becoming successful with it.

And Bethany was a great cheerleader. "You can do this!" she said with the enthusiasm of a coach about to send her team out onto the field.

So Christy nodded her agreement.

But Bethany looked disappointed. "Repeat it," she instructed. "Tell me you can do this."

"Oh—okay," Christy said, catching on. "I can do this!"

Bethany smiled. "That's better."

Yet then an old feeling of sentimentality crept into Christy's bones—along with the imagined bliss of how it would feel to find that *real, perfect* Mr. Right, that guy who so gets you, that guy who makes your heart flutter and turns everything inside you soft and warm. And this new plan was a pretty far cry from that, no matter how they tried to spin it.

And as was so often the case, her feelings must have shown on her face because that's when Bethany said, "What's wrong?"

Christy sighed. Met Bethany's eyes with her own. And asked, "What about falling in love? Where is love in all this?"

"Eh, love," Bethany replied with a characteristic shrug of her thin shoulders. "Love is . . . a chemical reaction. It's like a drug—it makes you lose control. It doesn't sound that great to me, frankly. And like I said earlier, I'm not sure falling in love is even real."

"Oh, it's real," Christy said quietly. "I've seen it. In my parents. And my friends in Destiny. My friend Amy is so in love with her husband, Logan. And my friend Anna nearly swoons when she talks about Duke."

"Duke?" Bethany balked.

"He used to be a biker," Christy explained.

Bethany, for a moment, looked intrigued. Almost fascinated. But then she came back down to earth. "No money in being a biker. Unless it's the illegal kind."

"No, he's not rich," Christy confirmed with a shake of her head. "But he's *hot*. And he loves her. And he makes her crazy happy."

Yet again Bethany just shrugged it off. "Lotta different ways to be happy. And I'm guessing your friend didn't start out broke or have a grandpa in need. And besides, I told you earlier, it's not like you can't love the guy. You just need to find an upwardly mobile one to be all gaga over, that's all."

"And I need to find him in the next six months," Christy reminded her.

Bethany nodded, her more resolute expression returning. "So you really can't afford to be overly picky," she pointed out, ever practical. "But we just won't worry about that yet. Now back to the plan."

HAVING decided Christy should start hanging out in some classier places, the next night they dressed up and went to a ritzy bar downtown and ordered expensive Cokes—because they were cheaper than expensive mixed drinks or expensive beer. The following night they drove to Hyde Park, a better suburb than the one where they lived, and repeated the process. When guys approached them, Bethany pretended to be shy and let Christy do most of the talking.

Each night, Christy chatted with a few different contenders—some handsome, others not so much, but all of whom gave the impression of being well off. And though she found herself generally uncomfortable flirting with guys for whom she felt no real *zing* or attraction, she did it anyway—especially when Bethany's kick under the table reminded her she had to.

Before the second night came to a close, she'd given out her social media contact info to three guys—deciding to keep her phone number to herself for now since they were, all, in fact, strangers "and could still be ax murderers for all we know," she pointed out to Bethany. "You don't have to be poor to be a serial killer."

Another part of their plan involved the mall where Christy worked. Before and after shifts, and on breaks, they'd decided she should hang out near jewelry stores. She was supposed to approach any wealthy-looking male shoppers by asking them if they knew where Victoria's Secret was.

"What if that just makes them think I have a boyfriend?" she'd asked Bethany.

"If they're interested, they'll ask. And you'll say no."

"Then why I am buying something at Victoria's Secret? That would make me appear to be a girl who *plans* on casual sex."

Bethany gave her typical shrug. "I'm not sure the average man would find that an undesirable trait, at least at the first-meeting stage. But if you feel the need to explain, just . . . say you like the feel of nice things against your skin."

Christy had cringed slightly—fearing that was pretty much synonymous with saying she liked casual sex—but when the time came to enact the plan, none of the men she spoke to took the bait. And she soon realized that men in nice jewelry stores were there shopping for their wives or girl-friends.

Having discovered the big flaw in the plan, she then switched her attention to men's suit depart-ments and before her first break there had passed, she'd had a pleasant conversation with a guy who told her he'd just passed the bar exam. And she didn't even have to bring up Victoria's Secret—instead *he* had asked *her* for an opinion on which suit to buy. His name was Jared and he was actu-ally pretty cute, and it wasn't difficult to flirt with him. And as she told him how to find her online, she began to think maybe this really was going to work out.

I can do this. I can do this. I can do this.

AFTER a week of friendly discussions and strate-gic online banter, Jared invited Christy to a com-pany dinner for his law firm at a fancy restaurant the following Wednesday night. She got off work at five thirty and he was picking her up at seven. With rush hour traffic, that would cut it close, but she could make it. She also had plans to meet a guy named Tim for drinks on Friday. Bethany was proud of her, and she was pretty proud of her-self, as well. *I really* can *do this. I can save Grandpa Charlie—and me, too. And there's nothing wrong with it—I will totally fall for one of these guys and that'll make it all okay.*

When Wednesday rolled around, though,

work was hectic. A co-worker called in sick, they were uncharacteristically busy, her boss was in a snippy mood, and she cracked a heel on her only pair of black pumps, leaving her to spend the last few hours limping around lopsided.

Worse yet, the shoes were an integral part of her dressy date outfit! So despite not having time, as soon as she clocked out, she limped speedily to a discount shoe store on the mall's lower level, just praying they'd have a cheap, attractive pair she could replace hers with. The good news: They did. The bad: They hurt like hell to wear.

Frazzled and running late, she bought them anyway. *After all, what's a little more suffering on top of the rest?* Surely, after everything else she'd managed the last few years, she could handle a pair of uncomfortable shoes.

Bad traffic slowed her down getting home—of all the days for a wreck on the interstate—and by the time she found a spot to park on the street a few doors up from her house, she had less than forty minutes before Jared arrived. *But that's okay—that's plenty of time.*

Blessedly, there was no sign of Mrs. Hart. And Bethany was working 'til nine tonight, which meant she'd have no distractions getting ready. She smiled as she climbed the concrete steps that led onto the front porch, convincing herself that everything would go her way from this moment forward.

Which was when she slid her key into the lock, turned it to the left—and nothing happened. As was often the case. But she was used to this—it was no biggie—so she jiggled the doorknob, jiggled the key, twisted it with a little oomph . . . and still nothing. And weirdly, it felt different than usual; the part of the door where the lock was located felt . . . loose, almost as if the lock wasn't, in fact, locked at all. So why wasn't the door opening?

She repeated the process twice more—and got the same result. Which left her staring down at the doorknob, perplexed. Okay, what the hell was this about?

But stay cool. Nothing's wrong here. Everything's fine. Everything's going your way—starting now.

She tried the key in the lock yet again, willing it with all her mental might to work this time.

But it still didn't.

Jiggling and pushing harder still, Christy slowly but surely began to draw an odd conclusion. She'd gotten a text from Bethany today saying the landlord had finally come to do repairs they'd requested two months ago. Bethany had been on her way out, but the landlord had assured her he'd lock up when he left. And the entire time they'd lived here, Christy had been aware there were other locks on the door, higher up, that they didn't use and which she'd never been given a key for. As she'd suspected, their usual lock *wasn't* locked. And she could lean the door inward just enough to determine that one of those other locks *had* been locked—by the landlord obviously. Who apparently did have a key.

All of which meant . . . she couldn't get into her own apartment. Forty minutes before her big, potentially life-altering, disaster-deterring date, and she couldn't get in!

Yanking out her cell phone, she called Bethany. Two minutes later, she'd found out her friend didn't have a key to those other locks, either. But she did have the landlord's number.

Five minutes after that, Christy had finished a frustrating conversation with the landlord's wife, who explained that he was still out for the day and he'd forgotten his cell phone this morning and couldn't be reached—but that Christy should feel free to call a locksmith.

Christy hung up five *more* minutes later, nearly hyperventilating now, after talking with a locksmith who'd informed her he could have someone there in about two hours.

It was less than half an hour before Jared was scheduled to arrive. And lord, what if he was five or ten minutes early? The truth was, she didn't even really like the idea of Jared seeing where she lived, but he'd insisted on picking her up—so she simply *couldn't* have him showing up to find her locked out of her own house, looking bedraggled from a rough day at work and clearly having no control over her life. On top of everything else, she'd worn her new shoes home and her toes were already pinched in agony.

She needed a plan. She needed to think outside the box. She couldn't blow this opportunity. Because sure, maybe he would understand—but he might also get a bad impression of her, and she simply couldn't let that happen. Too much was riding on this.

I have to get in this house. I have to. In fact, I'm going to. No matter what it takes.

Beginning to look around for ideas, she spotted the house directly across the street, two doors up from the Harringtons. She'd never talked to the guy who'd moved in just a few months ago, but she'd seen him plenty of times in passing, and he'd looked kind of rugged, at least from a distance, which probably also meant he was strong. She'd seen him carrying around toolboxes and two-by-fours, too. And maybe the idea that had just popped into her head would sound crazy, but she just didn't have time to worry about that right now. Precious seconds were ticking away.

Without giving it another thought, she marched across the street on her aching feet, climbed the few steps to his wide, awning-covered front porch, and rang the bell. *Please be home, please be home.*

A few seconds later, the door opened—and a surprisingly handsome guy stood on the other side. Having never seen him close up, the sight of him actually stole her breath. He looked a little scruffy in a zip-up hoodie over a T-shirt and slightly paint-spattered jeans, but his thick dark hair and piercing blue eyes made up for it.

"Hi," he said uncertainly when she managed to say nothing at all.

"I'm your neighbor," she blurted awkwardly then, pointing across the street.

"Oh. Yeah. Think I've seen you before."

She nodded. Still struggled to breathe. And wished he weren't so good-looking. It was a very inconvenient distraction. "I need a favor," she said, still not quite able to speak in any clear way.

"Um, okay," he replied. But he still sounded a little wary—understandably.

"I'm locked out of my house," she explained, "and I need you to kick down the door."

He just looked at her like he couldn't have possibly heard her correctly—which was, again, perfectly understandable. But it still made her feel a little crazy. Or like she *appeared* to be crazy anyway. Maybe both. Finally he said, "You want me to kick down your door? Is that what you said?"

She pursed her lips, sighed. She had so little time. And he was almost unbearably attractive in his unshaven, needs-a-haircut way. "I realize that probably sounds nutty," she offered.

"Yeah, it kinda does," he replied.

Crap. She took a breath, tried again. "And I wish I had time to explain—but I don't. Will you do it?"

He lowered his chin, hesitating. "Sorry, but you're gonna have to give me a little more to go on. Some kind of reason. I can't just go kicking down a door without one."

Okay, she supposed she could get that. But she didn't have time to mince words. "I'm late. And I have a date, a very important date."

"So I've got Alice in Wonderland at my door," he muttered beneath his breath.

She sighed once more, fully embarrassed now. He thought she was some kind of whack job. And for some reason, despite everything, she felt the need to correct him. "It was actually the White Rabbit who was late for the very important date."

"Whatever," he said. "Go on."

"Well, my landlord accidentally locked me out today when he came to do repairs. There's a second lock on the door, you see. Well, more than one actually. And I don't have a key for it, but apparently the landlord does." As she babbled on, it struck her how much her life did sound just as non-sensical as *Alice in Wonderland*.

"And he can't just come give you a key?"

"His wife can't reach him. And the locksmith can't come for hours. And it's"—she dropped her gaze to her watch—"oh God, only a little more than twenty minutes until my date."

She watched impatiently as her scruffy, handsome neighbor shifted his weight from one work boot to the other. "What's so important about this date?"

This time her sigh came out exasperated. How much did he need to know already? He was starting to seem pretty nosy. "Look, I know it sounds weird, but I don't have time to explain. So will you help me or not?"

Meeting his eyes again, she found it hard to keep their gazes connected—because he was just too handsome and something intense shone in his stare. But she persevered, because this was all so vital and even seemed to grow more imperative with each passing moment.

He stood there hesitating—for an agonizingly long moment—before finally saying, "All right, Alice, sure—I'll kick down your door."

Relief rushed through her as she said, "Thank you! Thank you so, so much!" Though as she spoke, she spontaneously reached out to grab his hand—and then a tingle ran up her arm as she realized what she'd done and that they were both suddenly frozen in place by the touch, so she dropped it just as quickly. "Come on, let's go." She turned to head down the steps, thankful to no longer be peering into those eyes of his and just hoping he followed her.

"Gonna tell me about this date of yours?" he asked from behind as they crossed the narrow street, stepping between two parked cars.

"Why are you so interested?" she asked without looking at him.

"Just not sure what makes any date important enough to kick down a door, that's all."

"Maybe I'm just . . . tired of letting circumstances beyond my control rule my life," she said. *But God, that was a little personal. Spill your guts to the guy, why don't you.* She decided to keep talking before he had time to analyze that too much. "Or maybe I just value keeping my commitments. There's nothing wrong with thinking *any* date is important."

As they reached the opposite curb, he said, "You realize it's probably gonna damage the door or the frame, right? Maybe both?"

"I don't care," she told him, recognizing that her gut-spilling comment *was* part of what drove her. She was sick of fate dealing her a crappy hand. She was tired of feeling out of control. She was taking control *back*. "Though if I seem a little crazy, I'm really not."

As they climbed the steps to her porch, he

glanced over at her. "You do. Just a little." Though the twinkle in his eye made her think he was kidding. Or she hoped so anyway.

As they approached the door, Christy's heartbeat sped up. It had already been working overtime, ever since she'd left work, but now her adrenaline was in serious overdrive. It was fifteen minutes 'til Jared was due. And she had just asked someone to kick down her door. Yet she also couldn't see any other way at the moment but to press forward.

She watched as her neighbor pushed and leaned against the door, testing its strength against his own.

"Think you can do it?" she asked softly, the gravity of the decision settling around her.

"Yep," he said. "Probably." He stood back then, studying the door as if it were an adversary, clearly planning his attack. Then he shifted that penetrating blue gaze to hers. "You're sure you want me to do this, right? You really want me to kick it down."

"Yes." No hesitation. "And hurry. I'm *so* late."

"For your very important date," he replied.

"Yes," she said again. Though this time the word came out more quietly and she sounded annoyingly sheepish to herself.

Silence blanketed the porch for a few long seconds in which she could feel them both weighing the craziness of this, and it didn't help that they were complete strangers. Until finally he said, "Okay, here goes."

And with that, he lifted one leg, bending his

knee, and punched his work boot toward the door, landing a hard blow just above the knob. The harsh sound of cracking wood split the spring air and a slow motion second later, the old door fell neatly inward, having come completely unhinged—as well as broken at the lock—landing flat in the little hall that led to the stairs. He'd done it as neatly and efficiently as any TV cop.

They both stayed quiet, kind of amazed, then looked at each other.

"I did it," he said, as if surprised that he really had.

"You did. Thank you!"

"That's what you wanted, right? You really wanted me to kick down the door."

She understood his confusion over it, even now. "Yes." Though for the first time, she began to wonder . . . "How am I gonna leave now, though? How am I gonna lock the door when I go?" Oh no—how had she not considered that part?

"That's a pretty good question, Alice," he said. "One I wish you'd thought of a minute ago."

But she merely released a sigh, determined to stay positive about this. "It's okay. It'll be fine. I'll figure something out." She stopped then, blinked, bunched up her lips. "Unless . . . unless *you* can figure something out. While I'm getting ready. You seem like the kind of guy who . . . fixes stuff."

Just then, the door next to hers opened and old Mrs. Hart stepped out. "Lordy bee, what was that racket?" Then her eyes squared on the empty doorway where Christy's door used to stand. "What in heaven's name happened?"

"I . . . was locked out," she explained.

"So I kicked her door in," her scruffy neighbor said.

She flashed him a look. Maybe it would have become obvious anyway, but she didn't really need him advertising it.

"Well, that was an extreme thing to do," Mrs. Hart said critically, sounding all too sensible at the moment.

"You broke down the door? You couldn't wait 'til I got here? You broke it down? You're gonna have to pay for that, you know."

They all turned to see a heavyset man Christy had never met before, and she said, "You must be my landlord."

"I can't believe you broke down the door!" he said in reply. And she realized he was looking at her like she was crazy—which was beginning to seem like a trend—and that maybe he had every right to. But he just didn't know all she'd been through, and all that was at stake here.

That was when her handsome neighbor threw up his hands to declare his blamelessness. "She asked me to. I'm just an innocent bystander here."

Her only defense was to say, "Your wife couldn't reach you. And the locksmith couldn't come. And I had to get in. It's important." She checked her watch again. Ugh. Ten 'til seven. Jared could be here any moment.

"What the hell was so important that you broke down the door?" the still clearly astonished landlord asked.

"She has a date," her neighbor replied for her.

"A date," the landlord repeated.

God, this was a nightmare. Like the rest of her life. "I—I'll pay for the door," she said. "Not that I know how," she added under her breath. "Or . . . I'll figure out a way to fix it."

Her words hung quietly in the air for a moment before her neighbor quietly suggested, "*I* can probably fix it," and she and the landlord and Mrs. Hart all looked at him.

"You can?" Christy asked in a softer tone than she'd intended.

"I'll see what I can do," he offered. "Just let me go grab my toolbox."

"I—I—really have to go get ready," she said to the porch's inhabitants at large. "I promise I'll deal with the fallout of this, but I can't right now. It's important," she claimed again.

"An important date," the landlord said dryly.

"Yes," she whispered, then vacated the porch and literally ran up the stairs, as much to escape the ridiculous situation she'd created as to get ready for her "very important date."

And a part of her knew she should probably just throw in the towel at this point and accept that she couldn't go out tonight, important or not—yet that desperate, determined part of her remained committed to saving the evening somehow. *This can all be okay. I can save it. I can make it worth all the madness.*

Bounding into her bedroom, she began stripping down, tossing the day's work clothes wherever they fell. She rifled through her small, tightly packed closet for the skirt she'd planned to wear.

Yanking it from a hanger, she hurried into it. Then scoured the closet again—this time in search of the cute top she'd planned to put with it. *Crap. Where was it?*

From downstairs, noises. The mutterings of the landlord to Mrs. Hart. Then Mrs. Hart's reply. "All I know is I heard a loud bang, came out, and found it this way. That's when the fella across the street said he'd kicked it down." *Yes, great, let's keep repeating the really crazy-sounding part.*

Feeling downright frantic, she began yanking out handfuls of hangers, inspecting what hung on them, then throwing them on the bed. *Where's that top?* She'd gotten it on clearance at work and she'd thought it was perfect for a romantic first date.

All was quiet downstairs now, so hopefully that meant the landlord was gone. With any luck, Mrs. Hart had gone back inside, too. Then the *plunk* of metal against wood told her the neighbor had just lowered his toolbox to the porch. *Where on earth can that top be?*

And how am I going to explain this door situation to my date?

That's when she stopped, took a deep breath. *Maybe he'll be late.* Not a great attribute, but right now, she'd find it totally forgivable. She resumed looking for the feminine top.

And then, from outside, amid the general muffled noise of the city, she heard the neat, clean slam of a car door and, despite that it could be anyone, she somehow knew . . . Jared wasn't late. *Crap. Okay, find something else to wear. And hurry.*

Surveying the pile of clothes now strewn across

her bed, she grabbed up the first dressy-enough top she saw—actually a short-sleeved sweater. Then she caught sight of herself in the mirror. *Oh Lord, I'm a disaster!* Her hair was messy and her face far too shiny! Dropping the sweater, she reached for a tissue to blot her skin, and as for her hair—she reached for a hairbrush, but this seemed more like a curling iron situation.

"Um, Alice? I think your very important date is here."

She flinched. Her neighbor's deep voice had come from just outside her open bedroom door, and here she stood in her bra only a few feet away! She hurriedly snatched up the sweater that now lay in a heap, struggled to straighten it out and throw it on, then marched into the living room to, indeed, find Mr. Hot-and-Scruffy had just walked right up the stairs into her apartment!

"What are you doing up here?" she spat.

He blinked, apparently not having expected her reprimand. "Well, I thought I should let you know he was here. Since there isn't exactly a door for him to knock on." He held up his hands in defense once again. "And I didn't want to be the one to try to explain that."

Ugh, he was right. He was only trying to be helpful and she was snapping at him.

That was when, from downstairs, a male voice called, "Um, hello? Is anyone here? I'm looking for Christy . . . but maybe I have the wrong place."

"Crap," she whispered.

"Better not just stand there," her neighbor said,

and a mere glance into his eyes, even now, made her breath go shallow. *But don't give him so much credit—maybe it's* all of this *making you feel unable to breathe.*

Regardless, she looked back and forth between him and the sound of Jared's voice, then gave him a rough shove toward the bedroom. "Get in there," she said under her breath. "And be quiet. I don't want him getting the wrong idea."

Then she rushed toward the stairs in bare feet and bad hair. She was far from ready, but she had no choice. She didn't want Jared to leave, after all.

Reaching the head of the stairs, she peered down to find him staring up, looking all clean-cut and well-dressed—and also perplexed. "Hey, hi!" she said, pasting on a smile. "I'm so sorry about the mess down there. Minor disaster when I got home today." She forced a laugh. "And I'm running a little late, but I'll be down in just a minute, okay?"

That's when she realized he actually looked a little surprised to see her—like maybe he was *hoping* he had the wrong place. At the moment, she couldn't blame him. "So . . . what happened to your door? Did someone break in or something?"

It was tempting to say yes—that would be a good reason, after all, for a door to be off its hinges. But that would only lead to further lies and make a bad situation worse, so she just said, "No, nothing like that." Then she tried to laugh again, more lightheartedly this time—but it came out sounding as fake as it was.

He looked back at the door. "Then what happened?"

Sheesh, what was his obsession with her door? Even if it *was* weird—couldn't he just go with the flow here a little?

"It's the funniest story," she claimed, trying to blow off his concern. "I'll tell you over dinner."

That was when he narrowed his gaze on her, or more precisely, it seemed, on her sweater. Was he staring at her chest? "What?" she said, blinking.

"Is your sweater inside out?"

She glanced down. Looked at the sleeve. Saw the thick seam running up to her shoulder. Oh God. Another laugh echoed automatically from her throat. It sounded a little maniacal to her this time. "Oh wow, looks like it is." Then she rolled her eyes. "You won't believe what a crazy day I've had."

By now, Jared had begun to look a little skeptical—about everything. "I'm . . . not sure I really want to know."

"Huh?" she asked, the confidence she'd so desperately tried to keep afloat beginning to waver.

His expression turned dark, disappointed, judgmental. "And did I hear a guy's voice up there with you just now?"

She tried to breathe. "Yes, but that's just my neighbor."

And now it was Jared throwing up his hands, clearly ready to back away from this situation. "You know what? I'm not sure what's going on here, but I'm starting to think this was a bad idea."

And as he turned to walk away—stepping

awkwardly past the fallen front door—Christy said, "Jared, wait—I can explain. Really!"

But Jared didn't wait. He just kept working his way past the door, until he stepped out into the evening sun now hitting the front porch, then disappeared from view.

And her heart dropped.

She couldn't believe it. All she'd done to try to pull off this date. And it ended like this? And he'd seemed like a really good guy, too—the kind who *would* maybe be wild about her and want to help her. And the kind who—perhaps wisely—steered clear of wild people. Her hopes plummeted as she stared at the spot he'd just vacated.

"That's a shame," her neighbor said from behind her.

Turning dejectedly, in her inside-out sweater and bad hair, to find him standing just outside the bedroom door, she numbly said, "You have no idea."

"He drove a Jag, too," the neighbor informed her. "A nice one."

And Christy's jaw dropped. She'd realized Jared had money, though she hadn't actually known how much. But to be driving a Jaguar at his age—late twenties she guessed—that said a lot. "Oh God—really?" she replied, feeling the full potential of what she'd just lost.

In response, Mr. Hot-and-Scruffy lowered his chin and said, "I think I get it now."

"Get what?" she asked, mentally exhausted.

"Why that date was so important."

And on top of every other letdown of the last

few hours—and the last few years—it stung to realize her neighbor thought she was the one thing that she so, so desperately didn't want to be: a woman who wanted a man only for his money.

Alice soon came to the conclusion
that it was a very difficult game indeed.

Lewis Carroll, *Alice in Wonderland*

Chapter 3

"IT'S NOT like that," she said quietly.

"What's it like then?" he asked.

She shook her head. "It's complicated. But . . .
not like it probably seems to you."

Jack DuVall stood looking at the pretty girl who
had just come dropping unexpectedly into his life
like Alice falling down the rabbit hole. Her eyes
had grown unaccountably sad and the moment
turned awkward. His fault, he supposed. He'd just
gotten too personal. "Look," he said, "it's none of
my business anyway." Then he stepped forward,
ready to move past her, down the stairs. "I should
get to work on your door."

Somehow he almost *felt* how pretty she was as
he brushed past her—and his nose picked up a
trace of . . . perfume maybe; something nice, feminine. Something stirred in his chest in response,
and he realized for the first time that maybe he'd

been a little disappointed to discover Alice hadn't come knocking on his door for *him*—but to instead get his help catching another guy. Not that it mattered. After all, this chick clearly had way too much going on for him to want to get involved in any of it.

He'd reached the bottom of the stairs before he realized she'd followed him. He pulled up short upon reaching the fallen door and so she did, too, but not before ending up on the very last step, just an inch or two behind where he stood—the nearness creating some sort of invisible force field between them, a connection that felt physical even though their bodies weren't actually touching. "Sorry," she whispered near his ear after not quite colliding with him.

"No problem," he murmured in reply. Then he went about lifting up the heavy old door to clear the walking path.

"I still can't believe you had me kick this thing down," he added, thinking aloud as he leaned it against one of the interior walls of the short hall that led from the entrance to the steps.

"I can't, either," she said. He glanced over in time to see her shake her head, suddenly seeming a lot less crazy than she had just a couple of minutes ago. "What was I thinking?"

Turning to study the broken door frame, he sized up how to best repair it for now. "That you were pretty damn desperate to make this date happen," he said without really weighing it.

He was trying to avoid looking at her—trying to keep this a light conversation, especially since they didn't even know each other—but when she stayed quiet, he found himself peeking over, his gaze rising to her eyes. In the dimly lit hall, he could make out that they were a kaleidoscope version of hazel that held him in their grip for just a second before he forced himself free of it.

"Could . . . could I explain? About the date? About why it was so important?"

He looked back to the door frame. Decided to saw out the edges where the wood had split and replace that section with some of the scrap wood he'd carried over. He could probably use the same strike plate once he freed it from the part of the frame that had broken off and was still attached to the lock, and the door. "It's none of my business, like I said. I should have kept my mouth shut upstairs." He focused on the busted wood the whole time.

"But . . . since you didn't—and since I kind of dragged you into this—I'd . . . *like* to explain. Maybe it won't make a difference, but I guess I just don't want you to think I'm awful."

This caught him off guard. Alice in Wonderland hadn't seemed too worried about his perception of her up to now. And he didn't really want to get any more close-up and personal with whatever was going on here. "Not necessary," he told her to let them both off the hook.

"For me it is."

Crap. He knelt down to flip up the lid on his red toolbox. Then he looked to the short sections of two-by-fours he'd brought along as well, thinking through his next moves—both in terms of the repair and what he was going to say. Finally, he settled on, "Okay then, I guess. If you really want to tell me. But don't do it on my account. I don't even know you—ya know?"

She sighed, appeared a little discombobulated. But not in the crazy way this time. That was when he realized he was looking at her again. He drew his eyes quickly back to his tools, reaching for a small saw.

"The thing is . . . okay, yes, I was interested in that guy based on . . . money." She sounded pained saying it and he could understand why—it was a pretty rotten thing to admit. And so far, he couldn't decide if he admired her honesty or was bothered by the blunt, ugly truth behind it.

"But I also actually liked him. And I know the money thing sounds despicable—but . . . it's about survival. And not just for me. It's about my grandpa."

Oh boy. This was getting way too involved for him, that fast. He already regretted letting her start to explain. "You really don't have to tell me this," he assured her again. But he'd stopped looking at her, instead refocusing on his work. To his surprise, the hinges and bolts were intact, so he could easily reattach the door and just tighten them up.

"God, you're right," she said on a sigh, then shifted her weight from one foot to the other. "I won't dump this on you. I don't even know why I started to. Well—okay, yes I do . . . I'm embarrassed. And I'm usually a lot more normal than I probably seem to you. It's just that ever since my parents died . . ."

Everything in Jack stiffened. Shit. Talk about something he hadn't seen coming. And his natural inclination was to say something comforting . . . but he stopped himself. This was already way, way more than he'd bargained for when he'd answered the door a little while ago.

Now she stopped, stiffening a little herself. "Crap, there I go again—dumping. Forget I said that last part. Or any of this."

He looked up at her, unable to avoid seeing the loss in her pretty eyes. "That might be a tall order." But just as quickly, he looked back to the work before him. It seemed a much more sensible thing to concentrate on. And still, he heard himself asking, "I guess you have other family, though. Brothers and sisters?"

"No, there's no one else really. Other than my Grandpa. But he's in Florida, in a rest home." Her voice sounded small, a little fragile. Yet then she toughened up again, seemed a lot more like the taking-care-of-business girl who'd come knocking on his door. "But it's fine—I can handle it. It's only because my grandpa needs help that I'm feeling a little . . . well, desperate, I guess—like you said. Even if I don't love that word."

"Sorry about that," he said, and he meant it. "But having me kick down your door instead of just waiting for someone to unlock it . . . well, just *seemed* kinda desperate."

"I can see that now. But at the time . . . it just seemed so unfair. To be locked out of my own house on top of everything else. And on the one night when I had this important date."

She sounded so deflated that it almost made him wonder what all she'd been through. And again, what had happened to her parents and what kind of help her grandpa in Florida needed from her so badly. Almost. But he wasn't going to ask. He didn't want to get sucked into this girl's drama.

Of course he didn't want to be an ogre, either—so he just decided to change the subject. "Don't know if it'll suit the landlord or not, but I can probably find some stain to match this door frame, and do as good a job on it as he would pay somebody for. The old lock and these others can still be used—but I might add a deadbolt for good measure."

"That would be great. How much?"

"How much what?" he asked.

"How much will you charge me?"

He glanced at her only briefly, then looked back to the work before him. "You've had a rough day, so it's on me."

He heard her soft intake of breath—and felt it, too, almost as if it echoed through his own body. "That's so nice. Thank you."

He just gave his head a short shake as if it say it was nothing. And in fact, it was something—but not a lot. He enjoyed working with his hands, doing home repair and refurbishment. And he wouldn't have felt right to charge her when she was already going through a tough time—it was only a small time investment for him plus the price of a deadbolt lock. "Just give him a call, ask him if it's okay if you take care of it on your end. He can inspect it when I'm done if he wants."

"He won't. It took two months to get him to come fix things here today, and from what my roommate tells me, we'll probably find out he only fixed half the stuff we called about. He's kind of a clod."

Heading back out onto the porch, Jack knelt to put himself at eye level with the broken part of the door, then picked up his saw and began removing the rough edges of broken wood left behind. It was a shame in a way—it was a thick old door frame, probably original to the house, which he knew from researching the history of his own had probably been built in the 1930s. But on the other hand, nothing lasted forever. And some things didn't last very long at all, so maybe the best way to look at it was to figure this door frame had had a good long life before getting broken a little.

They mostly quit talking then, and at some point Alice sat down on the steps and quietly watched him work, seeming undaunted by the fact that she still wore an inside out sweater and no shoes. Or maybe she just didn't care. Interesting girl, Alice.

"You don't have to stay here with me," he finally told her. "If you have other stuff to do."

"I don't, really," she said. "I expected to be on a date right now. And besides, I kinda like watching you work. I like watching things . . . come together."

"Why's that?"

"I don't know. Maybe," she mused, "because it's better than watching things fall apart."

So Jack kept working—slowly and methodically measuring, sawing, and hammering in bare new wood where the old had given way. After that, he used a key left behind by the landlord to open the lock that had caused all this trouble, then detached the strike plate from the old wood. With Alice's help balancing the door, he reaffixed it to the hinges, changing out a few screws for heavier ones to make sure it would hold tight. Then finally he put the old strike plate on the new section of door frame he'd just installed, testing it afterward to make sure everything lined up.

When he was done, he said, "I'll take a piece of this broken wood and get some matching stain. I'll be back over in a couple days to finish the job."

"Thank you again," she said, getting to her feet. "I really appreciate the help—more than I can say."

He shrugged it off. "It's not a big thing."

"Yes it is. To me anyway."

Aware that his heart was beating a little faster than usual, he chose not to reply to that, and instead just picked up his toolbox and turned to go.

"Um, hey," she said, stopping him in his tracks before he reached the edge of the porch, "what's your name?"

"Jack," he told her.

"I'm Christy," she said. "Christy Knight."

Yeah, he'd heard her "very important date" say her name earlier—but for some reason he asked, "Mind if I just keep calling you Alice?"

She cast him a sideways glance, looking understandably suspicious. "Um, why?"

"Maybe I think it suits you," he said.

Though perhaps there was another underlying

reason. Maybe it would be a reminder to him that she was . . . a little lost, struggling, grasping for answers and help, just like the girl in the story. And that even as appealing as she was in some ways, he'd be wise to keep his distance.

CHRISTY was already tired of trying to catch a rich man, especially given how crappy she'd felt attempting to explain it to Jack, but Bethany wouldn't let her give up that easily. "Grandpa Charlie's rest home bill isn't going to pay itself," she promptly reminded Christy the night after what, between them, became known as "the great Jared debacle."

And the very mention of her grandpa's name refueled her, relit the fire inside her to do whatever it took to save his home, to make sure neither of them lost anything else. "You're right," she conceded. The two girls sat in their living room, Christy piecing together a new bracelet on her jewelry tray.

She still couldn't help questioning, though, if this was the only way. "But look at the message fate sent me," she said, lifting her gaze to her roommate, "when I tried to go after a rich guy."

This, however, merely produced one of Bethany's usual shrugs. "Maybe fate's message was: 'This isn't the right one, so you don't have to waste your time on him.' It doesn't mean fate is against the whole idea."

Christy didn't like to admit it, but her friend made a good point. Maybe she spent too much time thinking the universe was conspiring against her and not enough time expecting it to help her out and lead her in the right direction. "Okay then," she said on a sigh, "back to the drawing board, I guess. What's next?"

"Why don't we go drink some expensive Cokes in another nice place downtown. On me. And we can dress up and pretend we have tickets to see whatever's playing at the Aronoff. I think *Phantom* is in town."

The mention of *The Phantom of the Opera* made her think of her friend Anna, back in Destiny. Anna's cat, Erik, had been named after the phantom himself and she owned a cool, old edition of the original novel the musical was based on. Christy had never seen the show, but she wished she had, or that she could—and how wonderful it would be to have enough money to just jaunt off to the theater on a typical Thursday night. "Okay, I'm in," she said. "But what if we're drinking our Cokes and we meet guys who are going to see *Phantom* and they want to walk us over there?"

"If we meet guys without dates going to see Phantom, they're gay, so it doesn't matter. Now come on, let's get dressed!"

As Jack painted dark wood stain onto the new section of door frame two evenings after kicking down the attached door, he realized why he liked working with his hands so much. It required focus, and it was the perfect distraction. From whatever a guy needed distraction from at any particular moment. And right now, what he needed distraction from was the cute blonde upstairs. The one with all the problems he had no interest in getting involved in. Other than door repair. Door repair he could handle. Why on earth was she on his mind *that* way?

The sound of Aerosmith echoed from somewhere up the street as he worked, Steven Tyler's gravelly voice singing about being jaded. The weather was fair and came with a breeze, which was good since the door would need to stay propped open until the new wood dried. But otherwise, the job was quick—the one-step stain he'd selected covered easily in a single coat and matched the older part of the frame well.

When he was done, he stood back to admire his handiwork. At a glance, most people wouldn't notice the door had ever been damaged. And he'd definitely made it stronger—he hadn't wanted to point this out to his pretty little neighbor, but the fact that he'd busted in the door so easily meant that pretty much anyone could. So at least there was an upside to all this, which was that she and her roommate would be safer now.

"Hey Alice," he called up the stairs, "I'm done. Just need to leave the door open a few hours so this can dry."

She appeared at the top of the stairs, smiling. "Thank you again, Jack. This is so nice of you." Then she glanced over her shoulder and pointed vaguely behind her. "Would you like a glass of iced tea? I just made it."

Jack weighed his options. He liked iced tea. But he probably should just go. "Thanks, but—"

"If you say no, I'll feel bad." Her face took on

an adorable pout he found surprisingly sexy. "It's really the only way I have to thank you."

Aw hell. He held in a sigh and said, "Okay, sure, I'll have a glass."

And her smile returned—just before she disappeared from the landing, the words, "Great, come on up," echoing down to him.

This time he let *out* the sigh since she wasn't there to see—then stooped to balance the brush he'd just dipped in a jar of paint thinner atop the closed can of stain before climbing the stairs.

He stepped into the living room where he'd been a couple of nights ago, and while he waited, he took in details about the room he hadn't caught the first time. Furniture that had seen better days. A colorful cityscape painting on the mantel that topped an old, no-longer-functional fireplace, signed by Bethany Wills, who he guessed might be the roommate, especially since an easel and some blank canvases stood in one corner. Near the mantel sat an analog television set with a converter box on top. And on the couch, a velvety sort of tray that held a bunch of loose pearls and crystally-looking beads. Next to it, some old necklaces that made him think of his grandmother lay stretched across one cushion, for some reason drawing his attention more than the other things in the room.

So much that when Alice came back in with two tall glasses of iced tea, he pointed down at the jewelry. "Those look like things my grandma used to wear."

She nodded easily, replying, "And I'm going to

turn them into things that girls *my* age want to wear."

Curious, he met her gaze. "What do you mean?"

"I upcycle old jewelry. You know, take something old and make it new again, give it a new life." He must have looked perplexed—and he kind of was—since she went on to say, "Here, I'll show you what I mean," and lowered her glass to the coffee table before starting across the room toward some shelves.

A moment later, she'd opened an old multi-tiered jewelry box and returned carrying more jewelry. But only as she stretched out the necklaces, then extracted one from the rest, could he see what she'd created. She'd taken a bunch of glass beads and fake pearls and strung them together on three strands that twisted slightly around one another to make a thick necklace that, even to his uneducated eye, looked much more modern and stylish than the original pieces could have.

His first thought: He was mildly surprised to discover a deeper, more creative side to the sweet but money-driven Alice. His second? Remembering her watching him work and telling him she liked seeing things come together. That made more sense to him now. And almost led him to think they might have a little something in common.

"That's really cool," he told her. Then wondered aloud, "What made you think to start doing that, taking old jewelry apart and making new stuff from it?"

"My love of old jewelry stretches back to my

childhood, to time spent with my *own* grandma. She wore that kind of jewelry, too," she added with a cute wink. "Grandma Livvy let me play with her jewelry when I was little, and then she started giving me older pieces she didn't want anymore, and as I grew up, reworking them became a hobby."

"Do you give some of the new pieces to Grandma Livvy?" he asked.

"I used to," she said. "She died right after I graduated from high school."

Damn—how quickly he'd forgotten that she had no family except her grandpa. Or maybe he'd *chosen* to forget. That she was alone. And that, really, she seemed pretty darn brave. Well, brave if he forgot about her trying to bag a rich man. "Sorry," he said, feeling sorry for far more than just his forgetting, or her loss.

"I wish she could see the pieces I'm turning out now—I've gotten better at it over time and I like to think she'd be impressed."

"I'm sure she would," he replied. "What do you do with the pieces you make now?"

She lowered her chin, her expression going surprisingly timid. "So far I give them to friends. I'd love to be able to sell them someday, but . . ."

"But?"

She sighed, then turned away, walking back to the jewelry chest and lowering the pieces inside. As she closed the lid, he got the odd sensation that she was closing *herself* up at the same time. She still faced away from him as she said, "I guess I haven't had the time or energy to pursue that since my parents died. I'm not even sure how I'd go about it."

Jack suffered the urge to respond in lots of different ways. He wanted to tell her to *make* the time, and to follow her dreams. He wanted to tell her about the dreams *he'd* followed. He wanted to ask how her parents had died. And he also kind of wanted to give her a hug. But he didn't do any of those things. Because he barely knew her, after all. And she wasn't the only one who could close herself up. In fact, for him it probably came even easier.

Though he wished she'd stop seeming so damn sweet now. Resisting his attraction to her had felt simpler back when she'd seemed crazy and reckless. But maybe this would get back to being simpler if he returned his focus to the one thing about her that still silently said: Keep away! "So . . . you still on the quest to find a rich dude?"

Although—shit—it was a pretty inappropriate, not to mention harsh, response to what she'd last said, and he regretted the question as soon as it spilled out of his mouth.

When she turned back toward him, her eyes had taken on the look of a kicked puppy. Or hell, maybe it was shame he saw there. His chest tightened. *But don't beat yourself up. She's the one who admitted what she was doing.*

"Um . . . yes," she said softly, the sound a gentle hiss. "I mean, I guess. Because I don't know what else to do right now. The thing is, my grandpa is going to get kicked out of his rest home in six months if he can't come up with the money to stay there. And he has health issues and they take good care of him there. It's important."

Aw hell. "Um, what happened to you not explaining this to me because it's none of my business?"

"I felt criticized by your question," she answered bluntly.

And he sighed. Fair enough. It had been a lousy thing to ask. And he wasn't even sure why he had. Knee-jerk reaction maybe. Old wounds. But he shook it off.

None of this matters. You can be friendly with her, be her helpful neighbor, without getting anymore involved here.

It was a damn shame, though, in ways. Because as he stood there scrambling for a reply, he found himself even more aware than usual of her simple beauty—straight silky blond hair fell to the middle of her back, those hazel eyes lit up her face, and he finally understood what the term heart-shaped lips meant. But shit. Stop thinking about her like that. "Sorry," he finally managed. "I, uh, hope you figure out a way to help your grandpa." And then he looked away, to the painting on the mantel, just to make sure she couldn't see the attraction that might be lurking in his eyes. "As for how you do it, like I said the other night, it's none of my business. I shouldn't have brought it up."

"I'm not a bad person," she insisted quietly. And that tugged at his heart, made him feel as if he'd been mean. But he shoved the spark of emotion away.

"I'm sure you're not. But for what it's worth," he

added, still focusing on the painting, "I think you could do something with that jewelry of yours. I think you could sell it if you tried."

"Maybe eventually," she said, her tone rife with doubt. "But not enough of it, not fast enough. And I could never make the kind of money I need to help my grandpa."

He only shrugged, drank his tea. It was actually the first sip he'd taken and it was cool and sweet in his throat, a pleasant distraction from the awkward conversation.

"Mind if I ask," she said when he didn't respond, "what you do for a living that makes my dating choices an issue for you?"

He couldn't help being happy about the change in topic—though in another way, not so much. "It's not an issue for me at all," he assured her, then answered, "and you're looking at it." He opened his arms slightly to draw attention to his thin flannel shirt and the tool belt fastened around his hips. "Just your general handyman and fix-it guy."

But he still didn't let his gaze connect with hers. Since it was probably the biggest lie he'd ever told.

"Where do you come from?" said the
Red Queen. "And where are you going?"

Lewis Carroll, *Through the Looking Glass*

Chapter 4

"WELL, THEN guess that makes it extra nice of
you to help me out for free," she said.

"And I flip houses on the side," he heard himself add. Maybe because that part was a lot truer
and saying it made him feel better.

"Yeah?" she asked, sounding interested.

He nodded. "I buy one, live in it while I fix it up,
and then I sell it for a good profit."

"That's kind of cool," she replied.

And, that fast, he knew she meant it. Because of
how she liked watching things come together. Plus
he could just see it in her eyes. There was something real there, something open—something he
wouldn't have expected from the kind of girl who
went after a guy for money.

And maybe that openness—if he hadn't known
better he might even have described it as a type
of innocence—was why he felt like a piece of shit.

Because he didn't want her to know the truth—which was that he had exactly what she was looking for in a man. Probably just as much as Jared in the Jaguar—or more.

"Thanks," he said, though it came out quick and low. Because she wouldn't be so quick to compliment him if she knew the rest of his story.

Jack had earned a bachelor's degree in finance with a minor in business from the University of Pennsylvania, which happened to rank first in the nation for both curriculums. After coming home to Cincinnati and spending a year doing the suit-and-tie thing as a junior investment advisor at a downtown firm, he'd thrown caution to the wind and started his own investment advisory company online at the age of twenty-three—and he'd been making a killing at it ever since, for seven years now. As CEO of The DuVall Group, he employed advisors all over the country, all of whose analysis and customer interaction took place via the Internet. As someone who'd tried the corporate life and didn't like the atmosphere, it worked for him—turned out you could be a whiz at investing and still be a down to earth guy who lived casually, liked simple things, and didn't feel the need to flaunt his wealth. Part of his success could be attributed to the low overhead—no offices, no suits, no wining and dining the clients—and the rest to the fact that Jack was just damn good at what he did.

But he didn't want Alice to find out about any of that. Though he hadn't quite known that until he'd actually heard himself lying about it, holding back. Another sign of those old wounds, he guessed.

"Are you flipping the house you live in now?" she asked him.

"That's the plan. Was in rough shape when I bought it, but I use my free time to fix it up, bit by bit." He didn't *have* to refurbish old homes, of course—to the contrary, he could easily afford to buy a large, lavish house anywhere in the city—but his parents had taught him a strong work ethic, and like his dad, he enjoyed working with his hands. His father had been a carpenter his whole life and taught Jack everything he knew. Now Jack was fortunate enough to be able to help his parents out financially. His dad still insisted on working, but at least the lean winters in the construction trade didn't hurt as much anymore.

The topic of renovating the house reminded him to ask Christy, "Did you call the landlord?"

"Yes," she said, "I left him a message and he didn't call me back. But that's his usual way and I'm pretty sure it means he's happy to let you patch it up without dragging him into it."

"Did he fix everything he was supposed to the other day?" he inquired, remembering she'd thought it unlikely.

And she sighed. "No. He managed to repair a leaky faucet and replace a light fixture that had broken, but the toilet still isn't working right, and there's some drywall falling down in my bedroom. Oh, and there's a damaged baseboard where I think mice are getting in." She shuddered. "We've caught two so far. It's horrible. Poor little mice. But we can't just let them run around loose, you know?"

Jack shifted his weight from one work boot to the other. And even as he heard the next words leave his mouth, he thought he should have considered them more carefully. "If you want, I can take a look at that stuff."

In response, Alice tilted her lovely blond head, her look almost skeptical. "Why are you being so nice to me?"

He thought it over and was completely honest. "You seem like you could use the help. And I'm a nice guy."

"Well . . . thank you," she said, suddenly appearing a little bashful . . . or maybe the expression on that pretty face was more like sheepishness. And that was when he realized he was trying his damnedest to size her up, to get behind those hazel eyes and see the truth.

He didn't want to care. He didn't want to give a damn. And he still wasn't sure why he did. After all, what was it to him if she found some guy with money to bankroll her grandpa's rest home care? Maybe he just found her . . . intriguing. A gold digger with a heart of gold? Could such a thing exist?

"You're welcome," he finally said, telling himself to forget the questions in his head. The answers didn't matter. He could look out for this girl a little without it leading anywhere. He could keep his attraction in check, a distant thing, better unexplored.

And as for those questions, he supposed it only

made sense he would ask them. It was hard to avoid certain parallels, after all. But avoid them he would. Since he'd already been down that road, and it had been the worst disaster of his life.

"ARE you sure you really have a roommate?" Jack asked Christy with a wink two days later when he came back to do her repairs and found her, once again, alone.

"Bethany works a lot," she said. "And dates a lot. And she's an artist, so she's out networking a lot." *And good Lord, she suddenly sounds so much more interesting than me, even if just as poor.* The very idea made her feel even worse than usual. Or . . . maybe it was just being with Jack and having him know her biggest problems and the possibly less-than-honorable way she was trying to fix them.

After all, before all that had started, she'd been stressed and poverty-stricken, but she'd felt . . . well, at least noble about it, like someone who was out there surviving, finding ways to deal with the unpleasant circumstances that had befallen her. And now, when she thought about her big plan to catch a rich man . . . it felt a lot more like giving up, taking the coward's way out. And having a really likable—not to mention hot—guy know about it only seemed to heap that feeling onto her even more.

"I noticed the paintings last time," he said, motioning to Bethany's cityscape on the mantel. "She's talented."

"She's hoping to get a showing at one of the local galleries soon," Christy replied.

He held up his toolbox. "So what's first on the fix-it list?"

"Um, how about the toilet?"

He gave a short nod. "Toilets are easy. Lead the way."

For the next hour, they made small talk while he worked—first fixing the badly flushing toilet and then sealing up the infamous mouse hole, a repair which flooded Christy with an even bigger sense of relief than she'd expected.

Though in all honesty, she was thinking about Jack a lot more than she was thinking about mice. She was noticing the way his dark hair peeked and poked from beneath the old baseball cap he wore backwards on his head today. She was watching his hands as they labored, the way they maneuvered various tools. She thought they didn't look as hard and calloused as she might expect for a guy who made a living working with them. Which kind of made her wonder how they'd feel on *her*.

But yikes, stop.

Not that it was easy to do. She couldn't help being attracted to him, even now, despite it having been obvious the other night that it would be in her best interest to get past that.

Then he turned to look at her from where he stood on a small step stool, inspecting the drywall problem in her bedroom. "Can you hand me that little plastic tub in my toolbox?" He was pointing at the red metal box but looking at her. And wow—she'd simply never had so much trouble maintaining eye contact with anyone as she repeatedly did with Jack. His gaze was just so blue and intense—she made eye contact with other people all the time, but something about looking into *his* eyes felt . . . intimate.

Yet she knew nothing would happen between them. Because besides not meeting her current requirements, she could tell he didn't like her motives. Even if he kept claiming he didn't care.

And it was still *so* embarrassing to have anyone but Bethany know about that. But she couldn't put that ugly secret about herself back into the bottle she'd so carelessly spilled it from. All she could do was be grateful for his help—and okay, maybe also enjoy the electrical charge she experienced in his presence, especially when they happened to touch.

Which was exactly what occurred when she passed him the little tub of spackle he'd asked for—their fingers brushed, and hot sparks raced up her arm. Oh, if only he'd entered her life at some other time—and for some different purpose other than breaking down her door so she could go on a date with a rich man. Ugh—talk about bad timing.

The same grazing of fingertips happened again when she passed him the spackling knife he next requested. And she wondered if he felt it, too. Surely he had. How could he *not* feel so much crackling electricity?

But stop—you can't want him. You seriously can't. Because he surely doesn't have a great impression of you, even if he's being nice. And then there was that other more shameful reason, too. The one about him not having the important thing she really needed right now to help Grandpa Charlie. The reason that really did make her a fairly despicable girl in ways. Maybe. She was getting more confused on that by the hour. But she pushed the thoughts from her head as best she could as she watched him smudge a clay-like goop over her wall with the straight-edged spackling knife.

Just like when he'd been repairing her door, she enjoyed watching him work. She liked the smooth, fluid movements of his arms, the shift of his broad shoulders, the way he used his hands. Which again made her speculate about other ways he might be good with his hands, too.

It was jarring to suddenly find herself having such a strong sexual response to someone because . . . well, she usually didn't. Not this much anyway. She'd dated in high school and college; she knew what it was to tingle from a kiss or a touch and to yearn for more. And there'd been Kyle, of course, her first love, to whom she'd given her virginity. But her response to Jack was different—stronger. And ridiculously inconvenient. *Now? My body and brain have to team up to scheme against me this way now? When it makes the least sense ever? When I can't act on it?*

"We'll need to remount these brackets," he said.

"Huh?" The sound echoed from her throat soft and confused-sounding—because he'd caught her off guard by speaking, because she'd been so caught up in the simple maleness of him.

And as a few more minutes passed, she discovered his butt looked all too nice in the faded blue jeans he wore. Since his back was to her, it felt safe to let herself peek. And then she wondered what his butt looked like *without* the jeans. And what kind of underwear he wore.

When he turned toward her from his spot on the step stool, she jerked her eyes upward, to his handsome face. Then she blinked, trying to look natural.

"The mudding I'm doing here is more of a cosmetic fix," he explained. "Not really strong enough to screw something into it that's gonna hold any weight. So it'll be better if I relocate the brackets for your curtain rods a little. Just enough to make 'em hold better, but you won't even notice the difference."

"Oh," she replied softly, "okay." Though she still sounded far too spacy for her own liking.

"You all right?" he asked with a slight tilt of his head.

Oh good—she sounded spacy to him, too. "Um, yeah—fine." She spoke more boldly, normally, now. "I'm sure they'll look great, wherever you put them."

After that, Jack went back to work and Christy resumed watching his hands, and his shoulders, and his butt. And then she decided it would be wise to stop watching him altogether, and she was just about to excuse herself and go find something more productive to do—when he said, "This is gonna take more than two hands—can you climb up here beside me and hold this in place?"

He held one of the metal brackets against the wall with one hand, wielding an electric screwdriver with the other.

And Christy heard her voice go all whispery and light again as she said, "Yeah, sure," and stepped up beside him on the stool that was really only meant for one person. Their hips and outer thighs pressed together.

"Tight fit," he said, his voice going a little softer, deeper. But he kept his eyes from meeting hers and that suited her just fine since every molecule of her body rippled with electricity now. Even more so when she lifted her hands over her head to hold the bracket, giving her the sensation of thrusting her breasts none too modestly in his direction.

As he reached up to twist a large screw into the wall, his arms brushed warmly against her, and their hands touched a little due to close proximity. She held very still, uncertain if what she experienced was closer to pleasure or torture. But she was pretty sure she'd never been more conscious of a man's body. Even guys she'd gotten much more personal with than this.

She grew startlingly aware of his face, the dark, unshaven stubble on his jaw, his mouth. At the same time, she felt the presence of his bigger more masculine hands near her smaller, softer fingers, the broadness of his shoulders, the hard muscles in his arms. Everything about him was just so very . . . male. So very different from everything about *her*.

She suffered the desire to lean in to him, to know that maleness more, to let it envelop her. And at the same time, she endured the awkwardness of fearing he felt her yearning—and maybe didn't feel it in return. Or even if he did, that he didn't like who he thought she was—in a girl/guy way—so no matter how she measured it, it came out feeling one-sided and embarrassing.

"Okay," he said a few agonizingly long seconds later, "now we just need to move the step stool over and do the other one."

"The other one," she repeated dumbly, a little horrified to find out this wasn't over, that there was more. And yet somehow, at the same time, she was secretly ecstatic inside. More closeness. More drinking in the musky male scent of him.

"The other bracket," he clarified, stepping down to the floor.

"Oh. Yeah," she replied, following suit.

And a short moment later, he was holding that second bracket in place, and she was rejoining him on that folding stool meant for one, and their bodies were brushing together again, and then— dear God—his forearm grazed her breast and sent a trail of fire blazing all through her. And if she wasn't dealing with enough physical assaults on her senses already, when he said, "Um, sorry," it came out all sexy and raspy, his hot breath warming her skin, and she looked up to see how close their faces, eyes, mouths, suddenly were—and surged with wetness in her panties.

After that, there was only just looking away, wondering if he'd seen the stark lust in her gaze, and waiting out the severe nearness that threatened to bury her.

"Okay," he said a minute later, "brackets are done." But his voice sounded as thick as her throat felt at the moment. And then they were both stepping down, and he was lifting the curtain rod back into place, telling her, "Curtains are fixed now," but in her mind she was still looking into his eyes, drinking in his warmth, wanting him to touch her—everywhere.

"Um, thanks." Another heated whisper on her part. Because he was just so beautiful in that rugged, manly way. And it had stolen her breath.

And she wished like mad that she didn't need money so badly. But she did. And he knew it. And that would forever taint everything between them, no matter what happened now.

So she took an additional step away, and she lowered her eyes, and then darted them up toward the curtain, where it would make more sense for them to be under normal circumstances. And she sensed him doing the same.

It was clearly the best move.

For both of them, it seemed.

JACK was glad the days were getting warmer, and the nights, too—warm enough to sit out on his front porch and watch the world go by. Well, maybe he couldn't see the whole world from this one little street, but he thought it was a fair representation of people. It was the kind of on-the-edge neighborhood that held both good and bad, and a lot of in between.

There were the kids in the big, run-down Victorian on the corner who broke bottles in the street, and flung obscenities at every person who passed by.

There were quiet couples like the Marches up the street, whom he knew only because they'd seen him doing some work on the exterior of his house one sunny winter day and Mr. March had asked for his help carrying in a heavy desk they'd picked up at a yard sale.

And there were louder couples like the Harringtons, whose snappish tones could be heard two doors away—as recently as an hour ago when they'd come home around dusk.

There was a little old man named Mr. Garver directly in the house to Jack's left who liked to walk to the corner market a few blocks away rather than drive, and who had fallen in the habit of stopping to chat if he saw Jack outside. He liked to tell stories about the Korean War, which Jack figured put him in his eighties.

Mr. Garver had also told him about his late wife, Margaret, who'd passed nearly ten years ago. "Miss her every day, even now," Mr. Garver had said, and it had filled Jack with sadness. He'd found himself wondering if it was worth it—to let your heart go that much, to invest that much love in someone—if, in the end, there was a pretty good chance you'd end up without them. Whether because they died or because they fell out of love with you. And he'd concluded that maybe life was easier if you just kept a certain distance from attachments that ran that deep. He didn't ever want to find himself still missing someone ten years after they'd gone.

And then there was Christy. Who he couldn't quite get a bead on. The money-chasing part of her just didn't mesh with the rest. He wasn't even sure why he'd helped her so much lately.

Well, wait—that wasn't true. He'd helped her because she'd seemed sweet, and because he genuinely liked her. And he also supposed he'd helped her because . . . hell, every time he was near her he felt a certain zing—something he hadn't experienced in a while, that excitement of new attraction, chemistry—and despite his best intentions, it drew him in.

It's okay, though. Her problems were *her* problems, not his. He wasn't getting any further enmeshed in her life. So it was no big deal.

Even if he kept thinking about her.

Even if his gaze drifted to her house, her windows, too often.

Even if he'd found himself keeping an eye out for her car, aware of when she came and went.

Since he'd done those repairs for her a week ago, they'd exchanged a few waves, and they'd had one brief conversation on the sidewalk during which he'd asked if everything he'd fixed was holding up. She'd said yes and thanked him again.

And hell if he didn't find himself wishing he had another reason to see her again now. Something else to fix.

Darkness had fallen when he looked up to see a late model BMW turn onto the city street, coming to a rough halt in front of Christy's house. He couldn't see into the car, but a few seconds later a door slammed and the Beamer accelerated roughly, screeching away. And then he made out her silhouette standing across the street from him, and though he couldn't see her face, something in her posture gave the impression she might be a little shaken up.

"Rough night?" he called.

"You could say that." Her voice sounded small. *Quit noticing that part.* "At least you don't have mice anymore," he reminded her matter-of-factly. "And your toilet works."

"You're right. Thank you." But she still sounded a little beaten, and—hell—it pulled at his heart more than he liked.

So as she turned to head inside, without planning it, he heard himself say, "Want some ice cream?"

She stopped, peered back toward him in the darkness. "Huh?"

"I said—do you want some ice cream? I was about to fix myself a bowl. Chocolate." It was the truth, about planning to fix himself some—but the sharing part came as a surprise, to him as much as her.

"Okay," she said, and it made him feel good that she sounded a little cheered by the invitation, reminding him that during life's rough spots, sometimes it was the little things that kept you going.

As he watched her walk toward him, he couldn't deny how pretty she looked—she wore a summery blue dress with white sandals and her cheeks appeared sun kissed, like maybe she'd been out in the bright, warm sun they'd had the last couple of days. A breeze lifted the blond locks from her shoulders as she ascended the steps onto his porch.

Though it was only as Jack stood up and opened his front screen door for her that he realized—she was coming into his house. Which contained an office filled with the latest, greatest computer and enough other high tech gadgetry and charts and paperwork that even a glimpse of it might tell her he was more than just a handyman.

"Kitchen's that way," he said, pointing and pretty much herding her in that direction before she could start sneaking peeks anywhere else.

As he grabbed the carton of ice cream from the freezer and started scooping from it into two glass bowls, she commented on the new sink and faucet he'd put in and asked what else he'd done in the room. He pointed out other changes he'd made in the kitchen, and as they passed back through the living room, he took pride in showing her the hardwood staircase he'd refinished, and some beams he'd exposed by removing a dropped ceiling someone had put in, probably during the seventies.

And he'd thought he'd done an admirable job of distracting her from the doorway to his office—when something even much more damning came into view: a picture of his wife.

> "Curiouser and curiouser!"
>
> Lewis Carroll, *Alice in Wonderland*

Chapter 5

$\mathcal{W}$ELL, SHE wasn't *still* his wife. And the picture shouldn't have been out, but his mother had unpacked it when helping him move—it was one she'd framed and given to him, of him and Candy on their honeymoon in Hawaii. When he'd spotted it, he'd picked it up and stuck it on the bottom shelf of a bookcase, figuring he'd put it away later. And he'd given it little thought since then.

Less than two years after that magical honeymoon, the bad parts had taken place—the gut-wrenching parts. To this day, he remained unsure how much of their relationship had been real and how much fabricated.

"Let's go back outside—it's still nice out," he told Christy, ready to usher her right back out the door before she spotted this other big thing he'd kept from her. Not that it was any of her business actually, not any more than who she dated was his. So it *wasn't* exactly like he'd *kept* it from her—but now he realized he preferred her not knowing.

Even though he knew he could just blow it off, just say, "Didn't work out," or "Got married too young," the fact was that he didn't want to talk about it *at all*, to her or anyone else. He didn't particularly like being reminded of his own pain, or that he'd failed at something that big.

Outside, they settled in the wooden swing he'd hung from the wide porch's awning a couple of months ago. It situated them closely together, reminding him of the day he'd moved her curtain rod. She smelled sweet, like something slightly flowery, slightly fruity, and he liked it too much. *Just be careful here, dude.*

He asked if she knew Mr. Garver, and she relayed some funny stories about her downstairs neighbor, Mrs. Hart, who he'd quickly figured out was a busybody. They talked about the odd combination of scents created by the distillery and the flavor factory nearby, and she declared the one floating through the air tonight "strawberry bourbon, I think." She asked him why on earth he'd chosen a house in this crazy, rundown neighborhood to refurbish, and he'd told her, "Price was right. And I think with a little positive attention, this neighborhood could turn around."

"You're very optimistic," she said skeptically.

About some *things.*

Just then, Mr. Harrington could be heard yelling, "You're fuckin' insane, Lori! Fuckin' insane!"

And they both let out a laugh at the absurd

irony—even if the laughter was tainted with a little sadness. "Yep, it's a great place," she quipped.

"Mr. Garver's cool, and the Marches are nice," he countered. "And you're not half bad, either." He found himself playfully nudging her bare ankle with his tennis shoe. "And who knows—maybe I can sell this place to a nice family who'll really tip the scales."

"If the kids on the corner don't beat them up and scare them away."

He laughed again, because he couldn't help seeing her point—but he also couldn't be sorry he'd chosen this particular house, for lots of reasons. It had character—and the people here had character. And the most compelling character of all was Alice herself.

When their bowls sat empty on the wood planks below their feet, she said, "Thanks for the ice cream, but I should go. Work in the morning, and . . . it's been a rough night, like you noticed." And as they both got to their feet, she added, "You made it better, though, so thanks."

"Don't worry about that guy," he told her easily. "You're better than him."

She peered up, looking all pretty and innocent as usual. "Am I?" she asked. "I'm not sure anymore."

And maybe he still wasn't entirely sure himself, either, despite having said so—yet as they stood face to face in the soft light of his front porch, the pungent aromas of strawberries and bourbon wrapping around them, he found himself . . . inexplicably leaning in, placing his hands on her shoulders, and lowering a soft kiss to her forehead.

She looked up, their gazes locking, her eyes as big as two bright round moons shining on him in the night. And he wanted to kiss her so badly— this time on the mouth—that he could taste it, could taste how hot and sweet it would be. His muscles ached with the wanting; his chest tightened.

But then he took a step back from her.

And he reached for the screen door handle.

And he said, " 'Night, Alice," just before stepping inside and quietly pushing the front door shut.

Despite himself, he was getting too close here. But no more. No more.

SOME days Christy didn't feel like she knew much. She didn't know how to help her grandpa—not to mention herself—with money problems. She didn't know how to date wealthy men with any success—every such endeavor so far had fallen somewhere in the range of quiet, lackluster failure to raging disaster. But the one thing she knew was that when she'd said goodnight to Jack two evenings earlier, he'd given her the best forehead kiss ever.

She'd felt it trickling down through her like soft, luscious raindrops that somehow seeped into each and every needy pore of her skin as he'd closed the door . . . and she'd nearly floated down the porch steps and across the street. In ways, she still felt it now—as if his lips had left some indelible mark there, tattooing her forehead with his gentle affection.

Why, oh why, oh why? Why did *he* have to make her feel that way? Why couldn't it be James, the banker she'd had the most boring dinner of her life with last week? Why not Brooks, who, like his name, had just been too yuppie and arrogant for her, forcing her to eventually tell him so? It had been Brooks who had raced off into the night while Jack had watched from his porch. Why had she met the one man who really melted her soul—that quickly—when she couldn't have him? And when she'd been in the midst of making herself look like a woman who was only after money.

Wait, you don't just look *like a woman after money—you* are *a woman after money.*

Ugh—what a sobering realization, and one she still hadn't gotten comfortable with.

She sat curled up in a baby-doll tee and Hello Kitty pajama bottoms, trying to watch TV. She wished she could talk to Bethany about all this right now, but she'd gotten a text earlier informing her that her roommate probably wouldn't be home tonight—she was with a hot guy she'd sold some fruit to at the market and things were going well.

She and Bethany were so different in ways— Bethany was cool with casual sex, Bethany was cool with being poor, Bethany was cool with . . . well, with most things, now that Christy thought about it. Christy envied her for being so laid-back and together.

When her cell phone rang, she was happy for the distraction from her troubles even before seeing who it was—until she glanced down to discover it was Grandpa Charlie calling. Not that she didn't like hearing from him—she just wasn't in the mood to be even more reminded of the current doom and gloom hanging over them both.

"Hey, Grandpa," she said, putting a smile into her voice as she answered.

"Hey there, darlin' girl, how are ya tonight?"

"Fine," she lied. "Just fine."

"Having a good spring?" he asked.

And . . . she could lie some more, but since Grandpa Charlie and she had always been close, she made the split-second decision to tell him the truth. Or at least part of it. "Well, Grandpa, just between you and me, things kinda suck." She let out a laugh at the end, though, trying to inject a little levity.

"What's so sucky, honey?" he asked. "I mean, besides the obvious." They both knew that neither of them had recovered from her parents' untimely deaths—and now they both shared the cash flow issue, too.

"Boys," she confided in him. "They're so . . . stupid." Which didn't entirely sum up her troubles—but in a way, it did. And sometimes it was best to just keep things simple.

Grandpa Charlie gave a good-hearted chuckle, the kind that made her miss being around him. "That they are, my girl. That they are." Then he added, "You know what you should do? Ditch 'em all for a while and head south. Come see your old grandpa and have yourself a vacation. I bet you could use one."

"Wow, could I ever!" The very thought of it— the beach, a getaway—sounded amazing. Albeit pretty unthinkable. Even though she hadn't seen him since the funerals and hadn't had anything resembling a vacation since her mom and dad had died. To dip her toes in the sand or feel the Florida sun on her face sounded beyond heavenly.

"Then come on down. Weather's beautiful here right now. And you sound too tense for someone so young."

She sucked in her breath, hating to remind him of the sad truth. "I'd love to, but . . . I don't see how I can. Money and all. You know the situation." And it was even much worse now, given *his* situation.

So it surprised the hell out of her when he said, "You know, every now and then in life the smartest thing you can do is just . . . do what you want to do. And trust fate to work things out."

Christy just sat there. She knew her Grandpa was in full possession of his faculties, but at the moment it sounded like he was giving her shockingly bad advice. "Um, Grandpa, saying I did this—saying I took off work for a week or two and spent money I don't have—how would I pay my bills next month?"

"Like I said," he told her, "just have faith it'll work out."

"Uh, while I appreciate the notion," she replied, "I think maybe that's how people end up homeless."

"Well, here's another angle, darlin'. If you need help afterward, you can let me know and I'll send you a little cash to help you get by."

"But you don't have any, either," she pointed out.

"I have enough to last me 'til fall," he said. "And if I end up getting kicked outta here a week or two earlier, what difference does it make in the big picture? Right now, I want my grandbaby to come see me and that's that."

They continued talking and soon, to Christy's astonishment, the idea actually began to seem almost feasible. Her boss was usually easygoing and would probably let her have the time. And it would be good for both of them to spend some together right now. And the last few weeks had left Christy pretty drained—the idea of basking in the sun and not chasing around rich guys or trying to solve massive money problems for a little while sounded kind of dreamy.

So by the time they hung up, they'd discussed a tentative plan. She would take off work, drive down to see him, and maybe the whole thing would end up just clearing her head, renewing her energy, and helping her find some answers.

She went to bed lulled to sleep by the scent of lemon gin thanks to an open window, and somehow already feeling refreshed. She might actually have something to look forward to, something that was actually relaxing and happy as opposed to stressful and pressure filled. She still wasn't sure how she would afford it, but the beach lured her.

And maybe getting away from Jack DuVall for a while would be wise, too. Maybe she'd get over this lustful little crush. Maybe she'd even meet some rich mogul type on the beach who wanted to take her away from it all. She couldn't help thinking it was a nice idea—even if, in actuality, the idea of being taken away from Jack made her a little sad inside.

She wasn't sure what time it was when she woke to noise—yelling and breaking glass—until a glimpse of the clock told her it was, yikes, just past two A.M. The Harringtons.

And she really didn't want to get out of bed and look out the window—but it was the repeated sounds of something crashing, breaking, that made her get up. She almost knew what the sound was, and she didn't want it to be true, yet she had to see for certain.

And sure enough, a glance out the window confirmed her fears. Mr. and Mrs. Harrington stood in their front yard throwing her potted plants at each another, one by one.

Some of the pots were glass, others simpler terra-cotta. And many were still intact, but others lay shattered in jagged bits on the front walk and littering the freshly mown yard, dark soil and roots spilling out.

Christy's heart broke a little at the sight. But another part of her just pushed that hurt aside— because she'd learned how to do that when she needed to.

After a few minutes at the window watching the surreal scene, something drew her down the stairs on bare feet. There wouldn't be any sleep until this was over, after all. And it was kind of like a wreck on the highway—she didn't *want* to look, but she couldn't quite stop herself. Stepping quietly outside, she took a seat on the cool concrete steps leading from the porch, realizing a few other neighbors were out quietly observing, as well.

The couple intermittently yelled at each other in between hurling Mrs. Harrington's beloved plants at each other. He called her a bitch. She called him a bastard. Someone from down the block yelled at them to shut up. Mr. Harrington threatened to kick the unseen neighbor's ass. It all struck Christy as obscenely sad and tragic and absurd.

That's when a dark shadow to the left caught her eye and she looked up to see Jack crossing the street toward her. He carried two small bowls, one in each hand. "Called the police," he told her matter-of-factly as he passed a bowl of chocolate ice cream down to her, complete with a spoon, then took a seat at her side. He wore a wrinkled white T-shirt and jeans she suspected he'd pulled from the dirty clothes, and his feet, like hers, were bare. "Probably a little melty," he said, "but seemed like we should at least have refreshments."

They sat observing it all in silence for a few moments, like watching a movie, and as the horrible mess in the yard got bigger, Christy couldn't help feeling how wasteful and destructive it was, and how it was ruining this wonderful thing Mrs. Harrington had put so much love and care—so much of *herself*—into. Until finally she said, "It's like watching them throwing little pieces of her soul back and forth, breaking it into more and more tiny bits. Soon there won't be anything left."

"That's deep," he commented.

"It *is* deep. It's the thing she loves. The thing she puts her heart into. And they're just throwing it away, just using it to wound each other, like it's nothing."

"I hate you, you son of a bitch!" Mrs. Harrington shouted.

"Go to hell, you stupid whore!" Mr. Harrington flung back.

God, this was just too ugly, too awful. Christy sighed. "My grandpa invited me to come visit him in Florida," she shared for no particular reason—maybe because the idea of escape suddenly sounded all the more appealing. "I can't afford to go, but I'm trying to figure out a way. I think I need to get away from this chaos for a while."

Just then, three cop cars came racing up the street, sirens quiet but the blue lights illuminating the darkness to leave it glowing and iridescent, making the night feel even more unreal.

"That sounds nice right about now," Jack said. "Maybe you can find some cheap airfare."

But she shook her head. "I'm going to drive. By the time I pay to rent a car there, it'll add up to just as much, and if I drive I can take all my jewelry and materials."

"Why do you need your jewelry stuff on vacation?"

"I thought it would be nice to show Grandpa Charlie what my grandma's jewelry ended up inspiring. And . . ."

When she trailed off, he prodded her. "And?"

The air continued to be tinted a shade of electric blue. "Well, I'm not sure, but I was thinking . . . maybe I could try to . . . sell some of it. At the beach. They have a thing there every night at sunset with street performers and vendors." The idea had just occurred to her while sitting and watching the Harringtons break all their pots. It had left her feeling the need to do something constructive, and this was what she'd come up with—though she had no idea if it was a viable plan.

"That's a nice thought," Jack replied, "but a long way to drive alone in a car that—don't take this the wrong way—looks like it's seen better days."

That part was true, but Christy just shrugged it off. She was trying to take Grandpa Charlie's attitude, just trusting things to work out. It felt naïve in a way—but she was tired of worrying and wanted to take a break from it. "I guess being on my own has made me brave. It'll be fine."

"Alice," he persisted, however, sounding downright adamant now, "it's dangerous."

And for the first time since he'd shown up, she drew her gaze from the drama across the street—the Harringtons were both yelling at the cops now, telling them to mind their own damn business—and looked at him. Even in the dark, his eyes sparkled warm and sexy, and the sight stole her breath. But then she got hold of herself and said, "Do you have any better ideas?"

He stayed silent a minute, during which a cop threatened to arrest Mr. Harrington if he refused to go inside and be quiet so his neighbors could sleep.

But then Jack said, "I could always go with you."

And Christy laughed, replying, "Good one."

Until he told her, "I'm serious. I could use a getaway myself. And call me a worry wart, Alice, but you haven't exactly struck me as someone who can completely take care of herself, brave or not."

At this, Christy gasped softly, offended—but then she remembered the history of their relationship so far and couldn't really think of a way to argue the point.

"And since you're, uh, not exactly rolling in dough right now," he added, "I'll even spring for the room."

"Room?" she asked, her eyebrows shooting up. "As in singular?"

He shrugged away her concerns. "They all come with two beds. And I'm . . . not exactly made of money, either."

She thought he'd sounded a bit uncertain when he said the last part, and she couldn't help thinking this all sounded like a terrible, hideous, horrendous idea. After all, traveling together? Sharing a room? With a man she barely knew? But was completely hot for? But who was also completely wrong for her at this pivotal time of her life? It was an absolutely *abominable* idea. Which could surely only lead to more of the very chaos she was trying to escape—well, even if it would probably be a very different kind of chaos. But chaos was chaos, and that wasn't what she needed right now.

And that was why it seemed so strange when she heard herself say, "Okay. Sounds like a plan."

They sat silently for a moment, both of them absorbing that, she supposed, and listening to the ruckus across the street—until Jack asked, "So where does your Grandpa live in Florida?"

And she told him, "A quaint little beach town called Coral Cove."

. . . If you drink from a bottled marked "poison,"
it is almost certain to disagree with you,
sooner or later.

Lewis Carroll, *Alice in Wonderland*

Chapter 6

As Jack had checked the oil in Christy's old
Toyota yesterday, he'd asked himself what the hell
he was doing. Going to Florida with her. A girl he
kept telling himself he should keep his distance
from.

As they'd talked last night about their travel
schedule over more ice cream on his front porch,
he'd asked himself the same question again.

And now, as he shoved a few pairs of khaki
shorts in a large duffel bag, he asked it one more
time. *What am I thinking? Why did I offer to go with
her, for God's sake?*

It had seemed like a sane enough suggestion at
the time. Like a compromise. It was a way of en-
suring her safety without letting on that he had
money and could easily have sprung for a plane
ticket and rental car for her. And a beach trip did

sound nice—he hadn't done anything fun for a while and some fun sounded healthy.

The problem was—he feared he might be starting to care for her.

Once upon a time, the answers here would have been easy. Once upon a time—not too long ago, actually—he would have just offered to help her out with travel expenses. In fact, he probably would have been dating her by now, and if things had progressed the way he thought they might have—he'd have been perfectly generous financially.

But the way things stood . . . if he started dating her now, and if he was honest about his financial situation, he'd never know for sure which interested her more: him or his bank account. There was no denying, after all, that the girl had dollar signs in her eyes right now, even if it wasn't her fault. No, it wasn't her fault she'd fallen on hard times, and it wasn't her fault her grandfather had, too. But it wasn't *his* fault he had reason to keep his guard up with women who needed money.

A few minutes later, he zipped the duffel shut and carried it downstairs, dropping it by the front door. Then he stepped into his office to finalize a few last business matters—he'd check in on his laptop while he was away, but as of noon today, he was officially on vacation. Something he hadn't taken since his honeymoon five years ago.

Powering down his desktop, he left the office, and as he passed through the living room, his eyes landed on that picture of him and Candy, the one he'd feared Christy might see. But this time he stopped, bent down, picked it up. He looked into the eyes of the two people staring back at him. And what he saw there was . . . innocence. In both of them.

Although he had no solid proof, he still believed in his heart that she hadn't been after his money in the beginning. Or . . . not consciously anyway. She'd been young. Sweet as the day was long. And mired in debt. He'd fallen in love and wanted to take care of her. And so that was what he'd done—he'd dived right into her life and bailed her out. It had all made sense because he'd had no doubt they'd be together forever.

But in the end it had turned out she was more in love with his money than with him. He was pretty sure she'd just been swept up in his knight-in-shining-armor routine, that she'd confused gratitude and relief with love. And then . . . a rainy afternoon, the shadowy curves of her naked body on top of another man.

But Jack pushed the image away as soon as it came. Damn, it had been a while since that particular memory had invaded his brain.

Mostly, Jack had ended up pretty confident in life. And he liked to think he was an easygoing guy. But his marriage at twenty-five—and subsequent divorce, only two years later—had left a raw spot inside him.

He'd tried dating after the divorce, at the insistence of friends. But with every woman, he couldn't shake the notion that his money was a part of the appeal, and he'd wondered: *If I didn't have it, would she still be hanging on my arm and sug-*

gesting we go back to my place after dinner? It had made him pull back, suggest a picnic instead of a five-star restaurant, or a movie instead of pricey theater tickets. And in the end, with three different girls, when it was just him and a bucket of chicken, or him and a DVD rental, it wasn't enough. But he pushed those thoughts aside, too. They were useless to think about, after all.

So he'd decided to go to Florida with Christy for a *lot* of reasons. He was long overdue for some relaxation—he'd been working in one way or another pretty much nonstop since splitting with Candy almost three years ago. And maybe he thought this would be a way to get to know Christy better without putting himself at risk.

But isn't this the same thing you did with Candy? Jumping in to take care of her? When she didn't even ask you to? The only thing Christy ever asked you to do, after all, was break down a door.

Yet . . . no, this is different. As long as she thinks we're on the same playing field financially, it's completely different. This is just . . . being a friend. This is getting to know someone. It's two totally different situations.

When he set the picture back on the low shelf, this time he turned the frame facedown. When he got home and had more time, he'd finally pack it away somewhere.

Despite all that, it still felt a little strange to carry his duffel bag outside, drop it on the porch, and lock the door behind him, knowing he was about to hit the road with this girl he'd only just recently met. He looked up to see her on her front porch, a wheeled suitcase by her side. She was talking on her cell phone, but waved to him, her smile as bright as the May sun shining brightly down on their city street today.

As he crossed the narrow thoroughfare toward her, though, a glance to his left drew his eyes to the chunks of shattered glass and clay rubble still littering the Harringtons' lawn almost a week after the incident. Spring green grass had rapidly grown up around it and needed to be mowed. The house had been quiet since that ugly night, so Jack had no idea if they'd gone their separate ways or quietly mended their fences. But he could see Christy's point about the pots—still lying there, all broken and ruined, they were a harsh reminder of how people could hurt each other so badly, how people who'd once loved each other could end up treating each other with such cold disregard.

Dropping his bag next to her car, he headed to the porch where she still stood talking. She pointed at her phone and mouthed, "Grandpa Charlie." He nodded.

"Yes, Jack and I are leaving right now. We'll stop in Georgia for the night, and I'll see you by dinnertime tomorrow."

Jack picked up her suitcase—which was girlishly pink but sported a few scuff marks and looked like something she'd owned since she was much younger—and carried it to the sidewalk, lowering it next to his own.

"No, I'm pretty sure he's not an ax murderer," she said to her grandfather, walking behind Jack, "or I'd probably be dead by now. He's really been a big help to me."

And when Jack turned to face her then, their eyes met, and she smiled at him and said into the phone, "He's a really great guy—I know you'll like him."

CHARLIE Knight hung up the phone, disconnecting from his granddaughter, and smiled up at Angie, one of his favorite nurses. "My grandbaby's coming tomorrow. Can't wait for you to meet her."

"Well, I'm sure I'll love her," Angie said, "as long as she's not half the handful you are." She added a wink.

Charlie sat in a wheelchair watching her walk about the room in the lavender scrubs she favored, checking the trash in his wastebasket, then picking up an empty soda can from a table near the window. He still wasn't used to that—not being able to pick up after himself with ease, not having any decent level of mobility. He could still get up on the walker when he needed to, but he'd found himself in the wheelchair and scooter more and more often lately.

"Wish you could have seen me when I was all young and fit," he told Angie. "Used to run, back in the day."

"Like, on a track team, in school?" she asked, glancing up from the chart she now made notes on.

"No, we didn't have a big enough school for track or cross country teams in Destiny then." He'd told her plenty about his hometown of Destiny, Ohio since coming here five years ago. "But we were poor and didn't have much in the way of vehicles. So if I wanted to get around very much, I had to do it on these two legs." He motioned vaguely down at them. "Running was faster than walking, and I never did like wasting time." Now it was *him* winking.

"And where did you run to?" Angie asked, lowering the chart back to the foot of his bed. "Chasing girls, I bet."

He laughed. And felt the fullness of a memory fill his chest. It was true what they said—youth was often wasted on the young. If only he could go back in time and appreciate what he'd had then more fully. Or even just feel it some more, bask in it. "Reckon you could say that," he told her.

"One girl in particular?" she asked. "Or were you the type to live up to your name—a good time Charlie?"

Another laugh escaped him. "Oh, I liked a lotta girls," he replied. "But . . . maybe there was one who was a little more special than the rest." A *lot* more. But somehow, even at his age, he still wasn't comfortable wearing his heart on his sleeve. "And her I didn't have to run to. My father was laid up that summer with a bad back, so I had a set of wheels—our old farm truck."

It surprised him when Angie tilted her head, looking a little sad. "Only a summer? With the special one?"

Even less. But he didn't want Angie to feel bad for him, so he kept it simple. "Only a summer." Then narrowed his gaze on the sweet nurse. "You look a little something like her," he confessed.

"Oh yeah?" Her eyebrows lifted, and the resemblance, which he'd noticed before, struck him fresh.

"Yep. Same dark hair, black as yours. Always thought it made her look sort of . . . exotic or somethin'. She wore it long like you do, too, with bangs. Her complexion was paler than yours, but she picked up a pretty tan come summer."

"Sounds like she was a looker," Angie teased.

But Charlie confirmed that part easily. "She was beautiful. Just like you."

Angie put her hands on her hips in accusation. "You're after extra pudding with dinner, aren't you?"

He let out a chuckle. "You're on to me. But reckon pudding's the next best thing to tryin' to get you to run away from that husband of yours with me."

"Well, I'll see what I can do about the pudding. And I hope that girl back in Destiny knew how lucky she was."

With that, Angie started toward the door—but Charlie held up a hand to stop her. "Angie?"

She looked back, hand on the doorknob.

"How's Mrs. Waters doing?" The woman down the hall from him had been in a coma since her arrival here four months ago. She had no family—even less than him—and he worried about her.

"No change," Angie said.

He just nodded. "Well, tell her Charlie asked about her."

She gave him the same skeptical look she did every time he suggested this.

"You know they say people in comas can some-times hear," he said in response to her expression. "And what with her bein' all alone, figure it couldn't hurt for her to think somebody cares."

Angie's expression softened. "You're right. And I'll tell her—I promise. You're a good egg, Charlie."

THEY were crossing the Ohio River on the Brent Spence Bridge leading from Cincinnati into Kentucky when Jack said from the passenger seat, "Let me know when you want me to drive."

Christy cast a dry look in his direction. "It's been fifteen minutes."

"Well, I'm just saying . . . whenever you want me to, I'm happy to take my turn. I like driving."

"So do I," she said pointedly. "So that makes you the co-pilot for now. If you're already bored, you can . . . pick some music for us to listen to or something."

"Now that you mention it, I figured your car probably didn't have an MP3 hookup, so I brought some CDs."

She slanted him another look. "You just have this all figured out, don't you?"

She put her eyes back on the road as they began winding their way up a large, twisting hill, but sensed his easy shrug next to her. "Just trying to be nice."

"Well, I'm just saying . . . don't think you can run the show here, okay?"

He held up his hands in defense. "No show running, Alice, I promise."

She had no idea why she was being so snippy

. . . except that maybe she was nervous. About traveling with him. About spending so much time so close to him. It would definitely change their relationship. But how? For the better or the worse? And what did she even want their relationship to be? All things considered, she had no idea. So if she was a little nervous, no wonder.

Watching Jack rummage in a small zipper bag at his feet, she asked, "What did you bring?"

She spotted a large bag of Fritos and—as he'd indicated—a stack of CDs. Plucking one out, he said, "How about Springsteen? *Born to Run*. Good road trip tunes."

Christy recognized the CD's cover—her parents had owned it. But like most everything, it had been lost in the fire. "Sure," she said quietly. And as Jack slid the CD into the player on the dash, it struck her that she hadn't heard any of these old songs since her parents had died.

She knew "Thunder Road" immediately by the first notes of the piano and the lonesome-sounding harmonica. And when Bruce sang the poignant first line, she felt it in her gut and understood in a whole new way why people loved these songs. Maybe it was something that had come with age, something she simply hadn't had the capacity to soak up when she'd been younger. Or maybe it was about experience—maybe you had to live long enough to lose something to really understand the quiet desperation in Bruce's voice.

"My dad loved this song," she heard herself share without quite planning it.

And though she continued watching the road

ahead, she sensed Jack's blue eyes upon her, felt the unanswered questions about her parents, felt his sympathy. She was almost sorry she'd spoken, put it out there, until he simply said, "It's a great song."

"Yeah," she agreed. "Thanks—for bringing it, playing it. And . . . well, thanks for coming with me."

As she'd wondered how this trip would go, she'd imagined it possibly being awkward—there was something almost personal about spending time in a car together, and with someone you didn't know well, it could be uncomfortable. But the truth was, even despite her nervous snipping, she didn't feel that way at all. And now that she let herself begin to relax, she realized that, already, they'd reached that place where some silence between them was okay.

So after he quietly said, "Happy to, Alice," they listened to the rest of "Thunder Road" without talking. And she found her thoughts settling into some old places that had to do with home and her dad, and her mom, and things that were gone— but also, at the same time, she felt a faint breath of hope and newness. And she wasn't sure where that had come from, but it was a completely different feeling than snagging a date with a rich guy because she thought he might rescue her.

IT was a few hours later as they neared the Kentucky/Tennessee border that a familiar old feeling struck Christy—a happy memory. "We're getting close to the Tennessee sign.

Makes me think of other trips to Florida, when I was younger, with my parents."

"Yeah?" Jack asked.

One thing she particularly liked about being behind the wheel right now was that it kept her from looking at him very much. Sometimes that was still difficult—and a quick glimpse just now reminded her why. Those eyes. And that strong jaw with the hint of stubble on it. He didn't seem to shave much. She liked it.

"Before my grandma died, she and Grandpa Charlie had a winter place in Coral Cove. We always used to drive down for a week every March, just before they packed up and came home for the summer. And somewhere around Tennessee was usually where it really started feeling like a real adventure—even though we were going to the same place every time. And if we were lucky, it was where the air started feeling warmer, where it started holding the promise of . . . summer. Even though it was still wintertime. When I was little, I thought Florida was a magic place where it was always summer." She hadn't exactly planned to start a share fest here, but talking to him had just gotten so easy over the short time they'd known each other that it had come out.

"That's nice," Jack said softly, sounding sincere. "My family didn't travel much when I was growing up—no money for it. But I've tried to make up for that some since then. And I took a few road trips to Florida myself back in my college days."

She looked over at him, a little surprised. "You acted like driving was such a crazy idea."

"No, I acted like driving was a crazy idea for a girl by herself in a car that"—he leaned over to look—"has over a hundred thousand miles on it. But I can appreciate a good road trip as much as the next guy."

Just then, they passed over the border into Tennessee, whizzing past the sign—and an unexpected recollection made Christy let out a laugh.

When she glanced over in time to see Jack raise his eyebrows at her like a silent question, she explained. "Dad used to stop at all the state signs and he and I would get out and take a picture of me with the sign. It never got old, I don't know why." Another soft trill of laughter escaped her as she went on. "Mom would be saying, 'I wish you two lunatics would get back in the car before you get run over,' but Dad would just laugh and we'd take our picture. Our albums were filled with the same pictures over and over again."

Jack smiled easily and said, "Maybe you can show me sometime."

Which was a lovely idea—but it forced Christy to bite her lower lip as the sad truth came hurtling back to her brain. "They're, um, gone," she told him, working to keep her gaze locked tight to the road ahead of her. The car currently ascended a steep incline, winding up into the northern Tennessee mountains, so it was a good time to watch where she was going, and a good time to have something to focus on besides Jack or the reason she couldn't show him the pictures.

"Oh—okay," he said softly, and she knew he'd

felt the weight in her words even though she'd tried to sound normal when she'd said them.

So she was thankful when he changed the subject. "I, uh, know a place in Georgia where we can stop for the night," he said. "Unless you have someplace special you usually stay when you're driving through."

She shook her head. "No, we always just played that part by ear. Where's your place?"

"Between Atlanta and Macon. A stop with a motel called the Colonial Inn."

"Sounds nice enough to me," she said.

THE drive with Christy was killing Jack. As in somehow making him even more attracted to her. There was something about the close quarters of her little Corolla, something about not being able to walk away from her. Usually, that was his saving grace—that their meetings were brief: an hour here, twenty minutes there. Maybe he hadn't really thought this trip thing through well enough. But it was too late now.

They hit a drive-thru for dinner just north of Atlanta and ate quickly in the parking lot. They shared a large order of fries and their fingers kept brushing together when they reached for one at the same time. And in every instance that they touched, his groin tightened a little further. From a damn graze of her fingers. Shit. He'd pretty much stopped dating altogether since the unpleasant post-divorce encounters—but at the moment he was regretting that. A guy had needs, after all.

Only . . . he hadn't quite realized how needy he was feeling. Up to now with Christy, yeah, sure, he'd experienced that almost visceral chemistry with her—when hanging curtains, when eating ice cream on his front porch, and on other occasions, too. But he'd had the situation completely under control. He'd felt fully able to back away from the temptation. Whereas this . . . hell, this felt different.

But don't sweat it. You can do this. After all, he'd feel like an ass to invite himself on her trip and then try to seduce her on the very first night. He'd *look* like an ass, too. And he worked pretty hard in life not to *be* an ass—so he didn't want to screw that up now.

You're lying to her. About your money. And not telling her about Candy—that's sort of like lying at this point, too. Doesn't that *make you an ass?*

But as he got out of the car a few minutes later to pump gas while Christy went to the restroom, he convinced himself it *didn't* make him an ass. He wasn't doing anything to hurt her, after all. He was just exercising a little self-preservation. Nothing wrong with that.

"Ready?"

Her voice came from behind him and he turned to see her looking ridiculously pretty for a girl who'd been on the road for seven hours. She wore a fitted pink tee that hugged her shape and offered just a hint of shadowy cleavage. Her eyes shone clear and bright, her smile cheerful. He suffered the urge to kiss the lush shadow that wanted to tug his eyes downward—but he forced himself to focus on her face. Her hair was drawn back into a ponytail today, giving him the impression of seeing more of her than usual—the curve of her neck, the soft blush high on her cheeks.

"Something wrong?" she asked when he didn't answer.

He just blinked. *Yes. I want you. I've been trying like hell not to—but I still want you.* "No," he finally said. Then gave his head a short shake. "Just tired, I guess. Let's hit the road."

THE sky stayed clear and blue through Atlanta, then night began to fall. And then it began to rain. In buckets. Before Christy knew it, the downpour plus the darkness had seriously decreased visibility. "Any chance your Colonial Inn is coming up soon?" she asked Jack.

She waited as he consulted his cell phone. "Yep—anytime now. Next exit, I think. Can you see okay to drive?"

"No one can see okay to drive in this," she told him. "But you don't need to white-knuckle the door handle or anything—I'm fine."

And even as she focused tightly on the road, Christy couldn't deny an unmistakable awareness . . . the sense, just since the downpour had started, of somehow being almost cocooned with Jack in the car. In a good way.

But that also made it kind of a *bad* way. It was just like the day he'd repaired her wall and rehung the curtain with her—except worse. Even if they weren't actually touching now.

"Here," Jack said when an expressway exit suddenly appeared out of nowhere in the night—she must have missed the signs leading up to it in the deluge. She veered onto the ramp, thankful they were about to stop, then followed Jack's directions to the Colonial Inn.

As they pulled in, Christy couldn't help thinking the weather must be making the place look . . . well, run down. It was an old single-story row motel that screamed 1950s and didn't look very Colonial, and some lights were out on the sign, leaving it to say: COLON L IN. "Um, no offense," she began softly as she slowed the car to a halt in the nearly empty parking lot, "but what is it you like about this place?"

"It's cheap," he said in his usual, easy way.

She tipped her head back slightly. "Ah." She couldn't argue with that.

"What is it you *don't* like?"

Looking through the still pouring rain, she offered an assessment. "Well, to be honest, it looks pretty beat-up and neglected. And the swimming pool"—which was empty and surrounded by a torn, rusty chain-link fence—"is shaped like a coffin. But . . . my apartment fits the same description—other than coffin-shaped—so I guess it's fine. As long as it's not run by Norman Bates or anything."

"Let's stay in the car until the rain lets up," he suggested, so Christy put the Corolla in park, ready to wait.

And that was when she looked over at him and saw those piercing blue eyes nearly burning a hole through her.

And time seemed to stop as her heart began to race.

His gaze was so intense that . . . well, usually the gorgeous intensity she saw there made her look away, too shy to meet it—but this time she couldn't *help* but meet it, even as it consumed her, body and soul.

"Jack," she whispered, planning to ask him why he was looking at her so intently. Yet instead all she got out after his name was, "wh . . . wh . . ."

Which was when he said, in the same low tone as her, "Christy."

And she let out a gentle gasp.

"What?" he asked in response to her reaction. "What is it?"

She struggled to swallow back all the inexplicable emotion assaulting her. She just hadn't accurately envisioned what it would be like to be alone with him like this. Or . . . how it would feel to hear him say her name. "You've never called me Christy before."

He blinked, clearly not having realized that. And those blue eyes stayed locked on her as he said, "I guess . . . I feel like I know you now."

And then his warm hand closed over hers where it rested on her thigh, and she looked down, took in the sight of their fingers together, on her leg, and felt the touch moving all through her like some kind of hot, sweet drug coursing through her veins.

And that was when he leaned over and kissed her.

> . . . and her heart began to beat quick
> with excitement as she went on.
>
> Lewis Carroll, *Through the Looking Glass*

Chapter 7

IT, OF course, wasn't the first time she'd been kissed. But it was the first time in a while. And either she'd forgotten just how amazing a good kiss *was*—or this one was more than good. In fact, she thought it was perhaps the most outstanding kiss she'd ever received. It wasn't rushed, nor urgent—no, it was slow and deep and intoxicating, his mouth moving over hers almost as if . . . as if they'd done this before, as if they already knew how each other kissed. And if she'd thought the mere touch of his hand was moving through her veins, his kiss traveled somewhere even deeper within her. To her panties, yes, definitely. But it was even more than that, more than sex. She'd never felt so connected to a guy just from a mere meeting of their mouths.

It was Christy who parted her lips, who pressed her tongue to his until they were circling ever so deliciously. This was like . . . hungering for something for a very long time and then finally getting a taste of it. Like going someplace you thought you never would, or could—like some beautiful garden that had, up to now, lain just out of reach.

As the rain continued to pummel the windows around them, muting everything that existed outside the car, she thought she'd be content to just sit here and kiss him forever in a dark, wet parking lot somewhere in rural Georgia.

It was only when a bright light suddenly illuminated the interior of the vehicle that they both pulled back, ending the kiss. Christy's gaze darted out into the night to see it had been only the headlights of another car passing as it left the motel. But the rain had lightened now, almost stopping—the storm had passed.

Her lips felt wonderfully well used as she dared glance over at him.

He looked a little shell-shocked. "Sorry."

Uh oh. He thought it was a mistake. And of course she understood why, instantly. *Nice guys like him don't get romantically involved with money-grubbing women like me.* "It's okay," she said, the words coming out soft. "I . . . obviously didn't mind."

"Still," he said, "I didn't offer to come on this trip with you to . . . have my way with you or anything. I need you to know that."

She nodded. "I believe you." And she almost wanted to add: *I wouldn't mind if you did*, but instead decided on, "I trust you, Jack."

"It . . . wasn't some big evil plan to take advantage of you," he seemed to feel the need to reiterate—only now it came out sounding more defensive.

And something about his tone almost offended her—he didn't have to act like it was *that* awful. So rather than continuing to put his mind at ease, this time Christy replied by asking a question. "Why did you kiss me?"

The question stood between them like a blunt wall of truth. It was a place in time when she didn't see the need for beating around the bush, even if she herself had been guilty of that with him in plenty of ways. Maybe she was trying to make him acknowledge that he'd liked it, too. She knew he had, but saying it, admitting it, was better than apologies.

He looked away, out into the wet, dreary night where the lights of the motel shone on blacktop, turning it so shiny it glistened. "I don't know— something about the moment, I guess. Maybe something about being in the car together all day, or about the rain." He shook his head forlornly.

And her heart deflated a little. There were so many nicer explanations he could have given, and yet he'd gone with *I don't know*. Just what every girl longs to hear from a guy in an intimate moment.

But Christy bit her lip, swallowed back the little pang of emotion that had just washed over her. Because what did it matter? She couldn't have anything with Jack anyway. As great a guy as he was, he'd entered her life at the wrong time. He couldn't give her what she needed right now—

and apparently had no real romantic interest in her anyway. She felt like nothing more than an available pair of lips when the urge for a kiss had struck him.

"Well," she pulled herself together to say, "I guess we should just forget about it and move on."

"Good idea," he said.

And she tried like hell not to let his eager agreement wound her, but it felt like just that—one more tiny knife being plunged into her heart.

Though she shook it off. She had to. It didn't matter how attracted to him she was—it didn't matter how mind-altering that kiss had been; she needed a different sort of man in her life right now, and Jack obviously was interested in another sort of woman, so forgetting it only made sense.

Be your usual tougher self here. The you life forced you to start becoming the day your parents died. When on earth had she gone so soft, after all?

When you met Jack?

No, don't even think that.

"Ready now?" she asked. Outside, the rain appeared to have stopped completely.

"Yep, let's do it."

And despite herself, her eyes darted back to his. Because of what he'd just said. Because under the circumstances, it had sounded sexual to her—and all too inviting.

"Let's *check in*," he clarified.

"Yes, right," she said quickly—then rushed to put the car back in drive and pulled up to the front doors of the office, where a little orange Vacancy sign glowed in the dampness.

"WHAT kind of candy bar do you like?" Jack asked the moment they walked into the badly-in-need-of-remodeling room and lowered their bags to thin, worn out carpet.

Perhaps understandably, Christy looked confused by the question. "Huh?"

"Candy bar," he repeated. "What kind of candy do you like?"

"Um, Twix or Milky Way, I guess. Why?" She squinted her confusion at him.

"I'll be back," he told her without answering the question. "You can get settled—shower or change or whatever—while I'm gone."

And then he was out the door, back out into the warm, wet, humid Georgia night, a little thankful to be alone. That was what the candy bars were about. Giving her a chance to . . . do whatever she needed to do to get ready for bed. And giving *him* a chance to further recover from what had happened in the car.

He still couldn't believe he'd kissed her that way. And it hadn't been just a little kiss. Nope, it had been a full-blown, like-there-was-no-tomorrow kind of kiss. An I-can't-hold-back-any-longer sort of kiss. It had been a damn long time since Jack hadn't been able to hold back with a girl. Now his groin was uncomfortably tight and his skin literally itched with wanting her.

But he couldn't have her. And so for some reason, the idea of getting them candy bars and soft drinks had popped into his brain. *Because sugar at bedtime is so restful.* He shook his head, wishing he'd come up with some better reason to escape the room for a few minutes. But too late now, so he made his way back to the motel's run-down lobby where he'd seen a row of vending machines tucked into a cubbyhole.

"Pretty little wife ya got there."

Jack turned from examining a candy machine to see the old man who'd checked them in. "She's not my wife," he replied instinctively.

"Even better then," the old guy said with a wink.

Jack just gave a short nod, a halfhearted attempt at a smile, then went back to perusing the candy selections.

The old man meant no harm, he knew.

And what he'd said actually made Jack stop and think. Would it be so awful if something did happen between him and Christy? Was there some reason he was acting like a saint here?

After all, as long as she didn't think he was a competitor in the Rich Man Tournament, and if they were attracted to each other and even really liked each other . . . would it be so terrible to enjoy that? Just for a little while? While they were traveling together anyway? If they both knew that was all it was—fun, just for now—what was the harm?

In fact, maybe, just maybe, it would be good for them both. Maybe it would give them both something pleasurable and easy in their lives right now.

Of course, you'll have to see her afterward, after the trip. You'll have to watch her dating other guys.

But as long as they both understood the situation, and as long as neither of them got attached

. . . well, maybe it would work out okay. Maybe even better than okay.

And maybe that meant it had been pretty silly to go racing from their room the way he had.

Punching the buttons for a Twix and a 3 Musketeers bar, he watched both drop into the metal tray below. Then he bought two cans of Coke from another machine before making his way back outside and up the broken, cracked walkway toward the room.

The truth was, he would normally stay someplace better than the Colonial Inn at this point in his life. But he didn't mind older places, and really had stayed here a few times on guy trips to the beach in college. And even though he'd offered to spring for accommodations on the trip, he intended to make economical choices. A night in a roadside Marriott or Hilton might send the wrong message.

He found an old bench a few doors from their room and settled onto it—he'd told her she'd have time to take a shower, so he shouldn't head back right away. Though the very idea put thoughts in his head. *What if I did go back? What if I knocked on the bathroom door and she told me to come in? Or what if I just turned the knob and went inside without asking? And into the shower* with *her?*

It was difficult not to imagine how she would look beneath the spray of water, soapsuds sluicing down her smooth curves. And it wasn't the first time he'd imagined what her breasts looked like—but it was the first time he'd imagined it in so much detail. He could see them in his mind, could almost feel his hand closing gently around one, squeezing lightly, then more firmly, just before he brushed his thumb across her taut nipple.

As the vision made him go hard—well, harder than he already was—he realized he needed to stop with the fantasizing. Yeah, she'd seemed pretty into kissing him—but then she'd said they should forget it, so who knew if she'd be interested in more.

And he wasn't going to find out by bursting in on her shower. After all, he'd told her he hadn't come on this trip to seduce her. If anything more happened between them, it would have to occur as naturally as that kiss had.

Returning to their room a few minutes later, he tried to maneuver everything he was carrying into one arm so he could dig his room key from his pocket. That was when the door opened from the other side and he found her standing before him in a pair of gray jogging pants and a big faded red T-shirt that said Destiny Bulldogs—and damn, she looked adorable, even now. Damp blond curls curved about her face and shoulders, and she smelled fresh and clean from the shower. Of course, that also brought back to mind that vision of her, naked beneath the spray. "Hi," he said.

"Saw your shadow through the window, trying to juggle everything," she told him.

"Getting settled?" he asked as he handed off a candy bar and a Coke.

"Yeah," she replied, plopping onto the bed

nearest the door. "Shower's a little creepy—kind of screams *Psycho*—but otherwise was fine."

"Sorry about that," he said, suffering a soft pang of guilt.

But she just shrugged, smiling her pretty, innocent smile. "Like you said, it's affordable, so no problem. And I appreciate you paying for the room."

This time the shot of guilt was stronger. Because—damn—she was being so sweet. And this place had really become a dump since he'd last stayed here. But he pushed it away, because if she was okay with where they were, then why should he feel bad about it?

Tossing his own candy bar and Coke can on the other bed, he said, "Guess I'll clean up, too." The fact was, he kind of *needed* a shower, for more than just removing the feel of a long drive.

And he sort of hoped that by the time he came back out she might be asleep.

After a candy bar and a Coke? *Sure, that'll happen.*

CHRISTY sat with her back against the old headboard nibbling at her Twix, thinking through how she'd gotten to this precise place in life. Despite the bad parts, at this moment she somehow remained filled with hope. Going to the beach was always like that for her—something in the journey, and the destination, never failed to fill her with a general sense of optimism for the future.

She still wasn't sure what that kiss had been about—Jack was a guy, and maybe he was just horny—but she had decided to try to do what she'd said and move on from it. And be thankful that he was paying for a lot of this trip, making it much more feasible for her to take it. And also be thankful that she was with someone she liked and who made her feel safe. Yeah, the Colonial Inn was crappy and the kiss was confusing—but at least it had reminded her that there could *be* kisses like that in life, and that when they came along they were wonderful and amazing.

And yes, the kiss had created . . . a feeling of closeness with him she hadn't quite expected. But maybe that was okay. Even if the kiss meant nothing. It had meant something in that moment—it had gone on too long for her to believe she'd been the only one enjoying it—but she could be cool and mature enough to just value it for what it was: a pleasant few minutes that had made her feel a little more connected to him. Her shower had somehow washed away the hurt feelings and helped her appreciate that he was a nice guy not just trying to get her into bed. And there was a lot to be said for that.

Just then, the bathroom door opened and Jack came out in a pair of gray gym shorts, wet hair, no shirt. She looked up—then hurriedly looked back down, at her candy bar. But the vision she'd just seen was branded into her brain.

He looked good with wet hair. And he looked even better without a shirt. She felt it between her legs—a subtle pulsing that hadn't been there a few seconds before. She didn't know why it surprised her that his chest was broad and muscled, his shoulders and biceps just as toned. She just hadn't thought about it, she supposed. But she was thinking about it now. She bit her lip, intent on studying the pattern in her bedspread as if it held all the answers to the universe. Yet she still saw Jack's chest in her mind.

"You're right about the shower—a little creepy," he said.

She glanced back up. Oh God, he looked hot. His grin made her smile back, despite herself. She tried to sound normal when she replied. "Well, looks like we both survived."

After rubbing a towel over his dark hair, he tossed it under the sink outside the bathroom, then plopped on the bed opposite hers. "How's your Twix?" he asked as he picked up his own 3 Musketeers bar.

"Good," she said. "My dad and I both loved Twix bars."

But—ugh, why did she keep bringing up her parents? She was in the habit of *not* talking about them most of the time, because it avoided an unpleasant subject. So what was the deal? A shiver ran through her before she could stop it.

Then she returned her gaze to the bedspread, wishing the moment away. Because that quickly, that was what it had become—a moment. He'd seen her quiver—she knew it, sensed it. And the dimly lit room had grown almost unbearably quiet around them.

"I know it's none of my business," he said gently, "so you don't have to answer if you don't want, but . . . what happened to your parents, Christy?"

Christy drew in her breath, let it back out. She lifted her gaze cautiously to Jack's and dared to peer into those blue, blue eyes. She let herself look beyond the stark beauty of them, beyond the handsome, rugged guy they belonged to; she let herself see the kindness there, let herself feel the same connection as when they'd kissed—only more now.

Yes, she seldom spoke about this—even when people asked—but maybe she could tell Jack. Maybe, for some reason she couldn't quite understand, she *wanted* to tell Jack.

"It was a fire," she said softly. Funny how that word's meaning had changed for her over time. When she said it now, it was no longer about flames or heat—it was only tragedy, and loss; it was something that had obliterated everything she loved. "A house fire. The home I grew up in, outside a little town called Destiny, a couple hours northeast of Cincinnati."

She saw the change in his expression—the horror, the sympathy. Usually, she hated that—it only reminded her how much had been stolen from her and how heartbreaking it was. But somehow Jack's concern, instead, comforted her. She didn't like feeling vulnerable in front of him—but at the same time, knowing he cared meant something to her.

And it was *always* nice when people cared— most people did, she'd found—but why did Jack's care touch her more? Even as he said, his voice low, "That's really rough, Christy. I'm so sorry that happened."

She held eye contact with him. That was slowly getting easier now. But her skin prickled and her voice came out small when she said, "Thank you." Because even if she wanted to open up to him, there was still something . . . raw there. About sharing how much she'd suffered. About letting him know what made her weak—even if it had also, in ways, ultimately made her strong at the same time.

"Were you . . . there when it happened?" he asked tentatively. Clearly wanting to know more but not wanting to upset her.

She gave her head a gentle shake. "I was away at school. At UC. By the time I got home, it was all over. Just ashes left."

Understanding passed over his face. "That's why you don't have the pictures you told me about earlier."

A short nod from her. "Yeah. Lost everything." *Everything.* It was a big word. And it still stung to feel the enormity of it.

"I can't imagine that. Starting over with nothing," he said.

"It's why . . ." Oh crap. She wished she hadn't started the sentence. She was sharing too much now, too fast.

"Why what?" he asked.

She swallowed past the lump that had risen in her throat. "It's why I have so little. There wasn't any insurance. There wasn't anything." Her gaze dropped back to the bed as embarrassment swept over her. She was starting to sound maudlin and pathetic. This was exactly why she didn't talk about this—it made it too easy to start feeling sorry for herself, too easy for weakness to start stealing over her like a dark, pervading shadow. And she liked herself so much better strong.

When an entirely different kind of shadow hung over her—a real one, closing in from her left—she instinctively raised her gaze to find that Jack had come to sit next to her on the bed. His face was suddenly so much nearer, his body, too, and his eyes still held that same care.

"Um . . ." she said, feeling a little overwhelmed by his closeness—and also embarrassed by her uncertain reaction to it.

"Thank you," he said, his voice low, near her ear, "for telling me that. I know it wasn't easy."

She tried to swallow back all her emotions— passion, pain, still a little embarrassment—and whispered, "Thank you . . . for caring. It's a hard thing. And I don't talk about it a lot." Though she'd said little, she felt breathless when she'd finished.

And Jack said, "Christy, I . . ."

And the words hung in the air like a mystery as she waited for him to finish, wondering what on earth he was going to say, because somehow, just from the way he'd begun, it felt big, important.

"You what?" she asked softly.

I have something to tell you, too. The statement sat on the tip of Jack's tongue, on the verge of coming out. She'd just bared her soul to him, after all, and his heart was breaking for her because he hadn't seen anything like this coming. He'd wondered what had happened to her parents, of course, but he'd never imagined she'd lost them in such a sudden, tragic way. And the quietness of her voice as she'd told him—she'd sounded like a little girl. It struck him that perhaps all of us remained children, always, when it came to our parents, especially when it was about losing them. And somehow it all added up to making him want to tell her his truth, too—or at least part of it. About Candy, the divorce. About *his* greatest loss.

It was nothing compared to hers—and yet, it was all he had to share, the thing that had most injured him in life. And he wanted to share it with *her*.

Which was odd as hell. It was his least favorite subject, the thing that . . . diminished him, made his soul feel like it was bleeding out. But maybe he wanted to show her that everybody had wounds, even him. Maybe he wanted to show her he was brave enough to share what hurt him, too. Because he thought *she* was brave as hell. It wasn't easy to bare your soul.

And yet . . . as he looked down into her pretty eyes—especially green just now in the dim lighting—he just . . . couldn't.

Because he couldn't tell her about Candy without it leading in to the whole money talk, and even now . . . it wasn't that he thought she would deliberately set out to use him—but he didn't think Candy had set out to do that, either.

She raised her eyebrows at him and he realized how long she'd been sitting there waiting for him to finish—how long he'd left her hanging. "Were you . . . going to say something?" she asked gently.

So he told her the only truth he could right

now—something else that burned in his soul and, at the moment, seemed more relevant than his own secrets anyway. "I think you're amazing."

At this, her eyes widened and her mouth fell open in the shape of a soft "o" and something about it was more than he could handle. He had to kiss her again.

And so he lifted one hand to her cheek and lowered his mouth over hers. The kiss moved all through him, like something expanding inside him, becoming the biggest part of him. And as he let himself get lost in it, he decided he'd made a damn good decision because making out with her was a lot more fun than confessing a hurtful past. Making out with her, in fact, felt better than anything he'd done in a long time.

She leaned into his kiss, leaned her whole body into his, in fact. He wasn't sure anything had ever felt quite so good as the warm cotton of her T-shirt, the soft globes of her breasts underneath, as they pressed against his chest.

Still kissing her, letting it consume him more with each passing second, he followed the urge to lay her back on the bed. She wrapped her arms around his neck, pulling him down with her, and his hands began to roam her curves.

Between kisses, she sighed prettily as his touch slid upward from her slender waist over the soft cotton. And when he eased one hand over her breast, the turgid peak jutting through against his palm, he found himself deepening the kiss, pushing his tongue into her mouth. She met it with her own and his cock began to harden.

Her feminine breath went ragged as he teased her nipple between his thumb and forefinger through the T-shirt. He wanted to kiss her there. He wanted to kiss her *everywhere.* He'd truly thought he could share a room with her platonically enough when the plans had been made—but now . . . now he couldn't imagine anyplace could feel any sweeter, hotter, than to be making out with Christy Knight in a crappy little motel room in the middle of nowhere.

Soon her legs circled his hips, pulling him to her until the column of stone between his legs—he'd gone rock-hard now—met the soft juncture of her thighs. Though layers of clothes rested between them, they were *soft* clothes, the kind that let him feel exactly how soft *she* was in that particular spot—and he knew she felt how stiff he'd gotten for her, too.

She was panting now as he moved his kisses from her mouth onto her delicate neck—and soon he was kissing his way onto her supple breast, then capturing one beautifully taut nipple between his teeth through the cotton fabric. The moan that echoed from her throat in response nearly buried him, seemed to wrap all around him—and it made him sink his body somehow still deeper onto hers as he began to move, to thrust, almost involuntarily, between her thighs. Damn, he wanted *nothing* between them, wanted to drive himself deep, deeper, deepest inside her.

He wanted her so badly that he could hardly decide what to do next—push up her T-shirt or take off her pants. As his hands eased up under the long hem of the oversize shirt, his fingers curled into her waistband and the decision was made.

He gave a soft tug and she lifted her ass, letting him pull the sweatpants down. Flinging them aside, his eyes landed on the panties he'd just revealed—white cotton with pale pink polka dots. Perfect and sexy and cute as hell.

"You're beautiful, honey," he murmured, his focus still on her hips, then moving more pointedly to the crux of her thighs. He slid his palm upward on one of those silky thighs, stopping at her hip to close his fingers around the pink elastic band, and his voice dropped to a mere rasp as he said, "Wanna take these off, too."

Her quick breath of excitement drew his gaze to her face, where he found her eyes heavy-lidded, her expression passion-filled and ready. "God, I want you, Jack," she murmured.

He followed the urge to bend nearer, to lower a gentle kiss to the skin just above her panties and below her belly button.

In response, another brisk, sexy intake of breath from above.

"I want you, too, honey," he said deeply against her tender flesh.

And as he eased the fingers of his other hand into the pink elastic, ready to rid her of the panties altogether, she lifted her hips slightly to let him, and she said ever-so-softly, "You're only the second guy I've ever done this with."

"And I'll tell you a secret . . ."

Lewis Carroll, *Through the Looking Glass*

Chapter 8

JACK WENT still, everything inside him tensing. He hadn't seen that coming, either—not at all. Christy had told him her age—twenty-four. Young, but not *that* young. Not so young that it had ever crossed his mind that she hadn't had at least a few sexual relationships.

And while, a few weeks ago, he might have questioned whether she was lying, he could feel the truth in her words—and in her body. He could feel it in her physical response. It explained the way she'd clung to him so tightly. And of course, maybe she'd have done that anyway—the chemistry between them was powerful—but now he understood that maybe this was bigger to her than just chemistry. And hell, hadn't he already acknowledged that it was probably bigger to him than just chemistry, too?

And if he was only the second guy she'd been with in this way . . . did this mean she really cared about him? He would worry it was a game on her part if she knew about his money, but she didn't. And yet, even so . . . God, was this wise? This was supposed to be fun, easy—he didn't want to end up falling for her, for so, so many reasons. Not to mention the fact that now he understood Christy was dealing with a great loss and . . . what if she was just grasping at any lifeline?

And all that aside—even if none of that existed . . . hell, he couldn't help feeling in awe of this demure side of her. And when a glance up revealed her biting her lip, suddenly looking a little nervous now that he'd slowed things down, he couldn't deny that maybe he wasn't feeling completely secure, either.

Shit. He wanted her so damn bad. And he knew she wanted him, too.

But it suddenly seemed like a ridiculously reckless move. Maybe for both of them.

"Is . . . is something wrong?" she whispered.

Oh damn. She sounded so . . . vulnerable. Not the Christy he'd come to know.

It reminded him that people weren't simple—they were layered, and complex, and they possessed hidden sides that they seldom, if ever, revealed to others. But Christy had been brave enough to let down her guard with him, and his heart felt bigger for knowing that—so he felt like an ogre when he said, "I don't think we should do this."

Her body went rigid in his arms. "Oh," she murmured. Yep, he was a jerk.

"It's not that I don't want to—believe me, honey,

I do." In fact, what stood ramrod solid between his legs right now began to ache, reminding him just how badly he wanted to.

"Then . . . ?" she began uncertainly.

Hell. He wanted to comfort her, do something to ease her frustration, the same frustration he suffered at the moment, too—but he wasn't sure if it would be better to kiss her or to just pull back and separate their bodies completely. And he owed her an explanation. "It's just . . ."

"That I shouldn't have told you the truth—about only being the second one," she said regretfully.

"But I'm glad you did," he was quick to assure her. "Because . . . it made me feel special. That you would want *me* to be the second guy."

"Well, if you feel so special," she asked gently, still in his loose embrace, "why are you embarrassing me by stopping?"

At this, he let go of her, sat up next to where she lay, and ran a hand back through his damp hair. Distance—he needed to distance himself here. "This happened pretty fast," he pointed out. "And like I said, I didn't come on this trip to seduce you."

"But I'm a big girl, Jack, and I can make up my own mind." Her tone bordered somewhere between put out and humiliated. "And if you're worried this will tie you to me in some way, don't." The longer she spoke, though, the softer her voice grew again. "You know that I . . . well, that I can't have anything serious with you since . . ."

Even though she trailed off, her unspoken words hung in the air as clearly as if she'd said them. *Since I need a guy with money and you don't have any.*

Damn. It was weird. To know he did have money. But thinking he didn't made it so he wasn't relationship material for her. Talk about a twisted situation. And even though he understood her position and had accepted it, it still stung a little to know she automatically counted him out based on cash flow. So much for fun, easy, casual sex.

"Look," he said, regrouping. "Why don't we go to sleep, head to the beach tomorrow, and just . . . ease into this, see where it goes. I, uh, don't want you to make a decision you'll regret just because I wooed you with a fancy dinner and a five-star hotel room."

At this, a loud laugh burst from her throat when he least expected it. And he laughed, too, and was glad he'd managed to lighten the mood.

"If it happens later, at the beach," he went on, "by then we'll both be sure we want it to, you know? And if it turns out I'm meant to be the second guy you have sex with, well, I'd rather give you a better memory than doing it on a crappy old bed at the Colonial Inn."

Sitting up, she tugged her T-shirt down over her hips and sat cross-legged next to him. "It's not so awful here," she said gently.

But he just tilted his head, flashed her a *get real* look.

"Well, okay," she admitted. "It's fairly awful, but . . . I wouldn't have regretted it. I promise." She gave her head a soft tilt, peered up at him. "Though . . . you know what's nice?"

"What?" he asked.

"To know you're a really good guy. In that way."
She pursed her lips, met his gaze, and he sensed
that she was going to confide something else in
him. "The fact is, every guy I've ever said no to
when it came to sex dumped me."

And damn, he hated hearing that. It was so
wrong. And he could only imagine the ways that
had hurt her. He lowered his chin slightly, keeping their gazes locked as he said, "Maybe you're
hanging out with the wrong guys."

By the time they hit the road the next morning, Christy thought it seemed like business as
usual. Jack was back to calling her Alice. "What
do you want for breakfast, Alice?" "Chop, chop,
Alice—we need to hit the road." And as they resumed heading south, she could have almost believed last night had never happened.

Except that she knew it had.

Right after they'd nearly had sex, Jack had
mumbled that he should probably move back to
his own bed. And she'd mumbled a muted sort of,
"Yeah." But he didn't actually do it. And in fact,
at one point she'd awakened in the night to feel
him behind her, his hand curved warmly over her
waist through her T-shirt, his legs mingling just
lightly with hers.

Of course, later she'd woken up to find her bed
woefully empty—at some point he *had* moved.
And she'd felt a little sad about that, but what had
taken place earlier had mostly made her feel . . .
happy.

It was nice—okay, *amazing*—to be touched by him, kissed by him. But even just to look across the space that separated their beds and know things were *happening* between them, that he wanted her the same way she wanted him, that—in spite of herself—the prospect of romance with Jack loomed large . . . that was pretty amazing, too. Passion wasn't all about touching and being touched. There was so much more to it. Maybe more than she'd known up to now.

It made her feel . . . too young, in a way. Naïve. To realize how much she still didn't know about things like romance and passion—and also to have confessed to him what she had. *Why did I say that? Why didn't I just shut up and let it happen?*

But . . . maybe she'd wanted him to understand that, despite his earlier impressions of her, sex wasn't something she took totally lightly. It wasn't just some tool to get what she wanted. It had felt important to make him understand who she really was: a girl who valued her relationships, and a girl who valued *herself.* Maybe she was a little lost right now—but at least he'd learned one important truth about her: that she respected herself enough not to just give her body away to every guy who passed by.

She also wasn't sure why she'd told him the part about getting dumped by guys she'd turned down for sex. After all, she hadn't turned *him* down. In fact, the embarrassing opposite had taken place. But maybe it was just another way of saying to him: *What's happening right now means something to me.* Without quite having to say that.

And even as crazy as her body had been going with lust and frustration, she loved that it had mattered to him, too. Or that at least *she* mattered. How many other guys would have stopped at that point? Until last night with Jack, she would have guessed zero. And the fact that Jack had cared more about making it right, and special, than just *making* it . . . kind of blew her mind. *Oh God, I wish I didn't need a rich guy, I so, so, so wish I didn't need a rich guy.*

But for now, she resolved to put that out of her mind. Jack was behind the wheel; they were going to the beach. They were heading to see Grandpa Charlie. Now was the time to stop thinking about her problems, to just let them go. It was vacation, after all.

And as they passed through Valdosta a few hours after leaving the Colonial Inn, and the Florida state line grew near, that familiar sense of excitement from her younger years began racing through her veins like adrenaline. It was about getting closer and closer to paradise, knowing soon the rest of the world—including your troubles—would be far, far away for as long as you stayed. It struck her just now what a wonderful place it was to run away to if it could really give her all that.

The Welcome to Florida sign had just appeared in the distance when the car began to slow—and she looked over at Jack wondering why as he pulled off into the emergency lane, stopping just in front of the sign.

"What's wrong? Is something wrong with the

car?" God, what if he'd been right to worry about that? She was thankful not to be alone, but she *so* couldn't afford a car repair right now.

"No, just thought we'd take a picture. Of you with the sign. Start rebuilding your collection."

"Oh," she breathed, stunned. That he was so thoughtful, that she'd been lucky enough to meet him. Maybe getting locked out of her apartment hadn't been such a terrible thing after all.

THERE was something about that first view of the ocean, always.

"There it is!" she announced, as giddy as if she were ten years old. The welcoming scent of crisp, salty air wafted through the open car windows as they crossed the bridge that led over a small bay and into the sleepy seaside town of Coral Cove. Hot, tropical sun blasted down, making the water sparkle beyond the sand dunes and sea oats that guarded the beach. "There's a more touristy area up the road," she explained to Jack, "but this is my favorite stretch of beach. It's . . . empty but not lonely." She looked over at him, feeling a bit silly. "Does that make any sense?"

He gave a short nod. "*Perfect* sense. I like it, too," he said. Then he asked, "How long since you've been here?"

"I'm not sure," she replied, thinking back. "High school, I guess. Everything was different then. Life seemed a lot easier."

"Well, try to let it seem easy while you're here," he suggested with a soft grin. "Because that's why you came, right? Vacation."

Now it was she who nodded. "Good point." And there truly was something about the beach that made her cares feel . . . nonexistent. She knew the problems hadn't disappeared, but it was nice the way that simply being here, just coming back to this place she loved, gave her a fresh sense of hope.

North of the gulfside beach lay a small grid of short, quiet streets lined with pastel cottages where many of the community's residents lived, but Jack and Christy followed the beach-lined road south into town.

"There," she said, pointing oceanward once more. "That's the public beach." A small lifeguard tower painted in red and white stripes jutted from the sand, and colorful umbrellas dotted the shore. Families and other small groups congregated beneath them or lay stretched out on towels and in lounge chairs. A few kids played in the surf, and to one side of it all, a large wooden pier stretched from the beach out into the water.

The few restaurants, motels, and other businesses resided across the street from the beach— a clothing boutique and a place selling beach chairs and T-shirts caught Christy's eye as they passed. This part of town was smaller than she remembered—or maybe some of the businesses had just closed over time—but she still found the atmosphere quaint and inviting.

"Where's your grandpa's rest home?" Jack asked.

"Further up the road," Christy explained. "There are a few bigger hotels in that direction, too, past Grandpa Charlie's place. That's where my family always stayed. And there are probably some new ones since I was last here—my grandpa tells me that part of town has grown." She glanced back toward the area they'd just passed through. "Though I guess maybe the older part isn't faring so well."

It was just then that Jack slowed the car as they approached an old row motel painted white with a red roof. According to the big faded sign out front, it was called the Happy Crab—a thin, red tube of neon outlined the smiling crab on the sign. Jack pulled into the parking lot and said, "This looks like a nice place."

And Christy blinked. "It does?"

"Well, a step up from the Colonial Inn at least. And it's right by the beach. I'm betting the price is right, so I think it'll be a good place to stay."

Christy tried to keep the smile on her face— same as the crab on the sign. It wasn't that she had anything *against* the Happy Crab, but all along she'd simply envisioned them staying at one of the bigger hotels near Sunnymeade, Grandpa Charlie's rest home. Only now did it hit her that those places were probably a lot more expensive and that she'd just never thought about that kind of thing when it had been her parents footing the bill for vacation. Which meant she really couldn't complain.

Except . . . what had happened to making things so much more special than they'd been at the Colonial Inn? She glanced over at him, wondering . . . had things changed since last night? Was he calling her Alice again and checking them into another dumpy little motel because he'd decided anything romantic or physical between them was a bad idea?

"Something wrong?" he asked, noticing her expression. Uh oh—she'd forgotten to keep smiling.

But she gave her head a quick shake. "Not at all. I'm sure this place is . . . great."

"And if this part of town is hurting a little, it's nice to give them our business," Jack pointed out. And Christy certainly couldn't argue with that.

After Jack parked the car, they both got out and walked toward the motel's modest front office. Christy appreciated Jack holding the door for her as she stepped inside—then she pulled up short. Holy mother of God—a huge, scaly dragon-like creature lay stretched across the entire length of the front desk! Christy screamed at the sight and, turning, leapt instinctively toward Jack, throwing herself into his arms.

"Don't mind Fifi," a voice said from behind the desk. "She won't hurt you." And only then did Christy see the rather good-looking man sitting there—he'd been completely eclipsed by the horror of Fifi. Whatever the hell Fifi *was*.

"Um, what *is* that?" Jack asked. With one strong arm anchored comfortingly around Christy's waist, he leaned forward to visually inspect the dragon.

"Fifi's a giant iguana. I've had her since she was a baby," the guy behind the desk explained. Getting to his feet to greet them, he shook his head in a playfully tired sort of way. "And she's a handful, let me tell ya."

Christy just continued to stare, aghast.

"A, uh, *big* handful," Jack mused—and the motel keeper laughed.

"Kind of like when you buy a puppy and it gets way bigger than you expected," the guy said with a lazy grin. He struck her as a little scruffy, in the way Jack had at first but which she didn't even see anymore, only with an easygoing beach bum air about him. "But by then they're like family, so whatta ya gonna do, right?"

"Um, sure, right," Jack said. And Christy was beginning to feel more at ease now that the humongous scaled iguana just lay there like a giant stone, but she took her sweet time disentangling herself from Jack. Because it was nice there.

The motel keeper smiled at them from overtop the giant iguana. "So welcome to the Happy Crab. Need a room?"

"Sure do," Jack said.

And the motel guy snapped his fingers and said, "Fifi, down. I gotta do some business."

When the prehistoric-looking blob didn't respond, he stepped closer and gave her a gentle shove. Finally the iguana began to move, seeming to rock slightly from side to side, and then ambled slowly down off the counter to silently disappear somewhere behind it.

"I'm Reece Donovan," the handsome beach bum introduced himself then. "Hope you'll enjoy your stay in Coral Cove. And if I can do anything to make your visit better, just let me know."

And it was after Jack handed over his credit card and stood filling out a guest sheet—because the Happy Crab didn't seem to have anything so fancy or new-fangled as a computer—that Christy looked to Reece Donovan and said, "One question. Fifi doesn't have any . . . brothers or sisters running around here, does she? I mean, she's the only one, right?"

Reece answered in the same easy way. "Nope, she's one of a kind. But don't be surprised if she turns up in some odd places. She gets around." And then he winked—and Christy thought it was supposed to allay her concerns, but it didn't.

Yet after that a funny thing happened. As she and Jack went back out into the Florida heat and walked down to the room they'd been assigned, she began to realize . . . well, the place really wasn't so bad.

And she felt that way even more as Jack used the key on the red plastic crab-shaped keychain he'd been given to let them inside. The room could have used some remodeling, but the colors on the walls were friendly and beachy, and the space possessed unique touches she hadn't expected, like a small glass bowl shaped like a crab holding fruit with a card signed *Reece and Fifi, your Happy Crab staff*.

And unlike most row motels, the rooms contained back windows, which looked out over the bay they'd crossed to get here—and also past a dock where a few boats were tied up. It wasn't the stunning ocean view of a high-rise hotel, but it was pleasant and reminded her with just a glimpse that she was at the beach. As she glanced out, a pelican strolled across the planked dock.

"Hey, look," Jack said with a slightly arrogant grin, "a water-that-leads-to-the-ocean view. Only the best for you, Alice," and then he winked. And she thought—okay, the Happy Crab on its own was a decent place. But the Happy Crab with Jack . . . actually seemed like it might be sort of fun.

JACK had seen the newer high-rises farther up the beach and had figured some of them were bound to be resort hotels. But the truth was, he liked it here. It had character. He liked Reece, the guy who ran the place. And he already felt more at home than he usually did at some upscale but generic name-brand hotel.

And . . . he'd also just thought it was a good idea. To keep things low-key. And inexpensive. Just because he'd nearly lost control with Christy last night didn't mean he was ready to spill the beans about himself. All she needed to know was that he was a nice guy who had come on this trip with her but hadn't wanted to take advantage of her.

He still couldn't believe he'd let that happen. There'd just been something unaccountably sexy about her sitting there in that way-too-big T-shirt and something unexpectedly touching about the things she was saying to him, the way she was opening up.

Like you *should have.*

He barely knew where that little voice inside him had come from, but he silently told it to shut the hell up as they left their room, setting out for dinner and a visit to Christy's grandpa.

An ocean breeze wafted past, lifting Christy's freshly washed hair from her shoulders—left bare by a summery pale pink sundress—and Jack decided to do exactly as he'd advised Christy, to forget his troubles for now. He'd come here for a vacation, he was with a pretty girl, and he was just going to enjoy himself.

The big yellow rain slicker and hat on the sign next door caught his eye. "The Hungry Fisherman," he said, reading the sign aloud. "Sound good for dinner, Alice?"

Her look gave him the impression she was amused by his choice, yet willing to humor him. "Sure." Though as they walked in that direction, she said, "Even if the fisherman looks a little like a lunatic."

Jack studied the sign more closely—it appeared to have been hand-painted, probably a long time ago. She was right. "He has crazy eyes," he observed. "Fisherman by day, psycho killer by night." Then he gave her a wink and a smile. "See, aren't you glad you have me to take you to such interesting places? I mean, if not for me, I bet you'd be out looking for an Applebee's."

Her laugh told him he'd hit the nail on the head.

"If you ask me," he went on, "simple living ends up making life more interesting."

She tilted her pretty head, appearing to think it through. Maybe in the same way she'd thought through asking a stranger to kick her door down or giving names to the alcohol-and-flavor-laced scents that floated through their neighborhood.

He kept discovering there was a lot more to Alice than had met the eye—and he always liked finding that out.

The restaurant was an old, dark, woody place clearly designed to make them feel they were on a large fishing boat—or maybe in an ark. Large fake fish hung on the walls above aged booths sporting torn red vinyl. And a life-size replica of the fisherman on the sign stood at the door to greet patrons. As Christy tried to hide her gasp, Jack whispered, "Little boat of horrors," almost more amused by the Hungry Fisherman than he could stand. "Damn, I love this place so far."

"Name's Polly," said a fifty-something woman in an outdated waitress's uniform dress of burnt orange as she approached a hostess stand. That was when Jack realized how small the dinner crowd was, apparently giving Polly time to be both waitress and hostess. "And that there fella we call the Fish Whisperer. I painted him myself." She pointed at the life-size statue.

"The sign out front, too, I bet," Jack said.

And Polly smiled, clearly pleased. "Sure as shootin'. Sit anywhere that grabs ya. Nice view of the bay on that side," she said pointing.

"Only the best for me," Christy murmured under her breath, casting Jack a sly smile, and he had to work to hold in his laugh.

Despite the plethora of fish on the menu, they both ordered burgers. And Jack marveled aloud that he'd had no idea Coral Cove would be such a quirky place, and she laughed and said she hadn't either, since she'd spent most of her previous time here in the newer, more commercialized area up the road except for days enjoyed on the beach itself.

"Thanks to me," he said with a wink, "you get to see a whole new side to a place you thought you already knew."

"And thanks to you," she said, sounding more grateful than he expected, "I get to see my grandpa. Since I'm really not sure I could have afforded it without you."

But Jack just shrugged. "You could have afforded the Happy Crab."

Yet she gave a much more doubtful shrug in return. "Maybe, maybe not. But it's a big help not to have to worry about that part, so thank you."

It touched him—as so much about her had over the past day or so. And before that, too, if he was honest with himself. There was a reason he'd come on this trip, after all, and . . . aw hell, seemed useless at this point to deny that he'd started caring about her. *But just keep that under control, pal, and everything will be fine.*

They both looked up as an older man walked in the door wearing a fireman's hat but otherwise dressed normally in a polo shirt and dark shorts. He crossed the restaurant toward the seafood buffet table, and a moment later, he called across the room to Polly, "This shrimp fresh? This shrimp doesn't look fresh."

"Of course it's fresh," she said, hands on her hips. "We wouldn't put it out if it wasn't."

"Well, I'm not eating any of it," he snapped

back, then slid into a booth near the buffet, still in his fireman's hat.

"Suit yourself," Polly grumbled—then disappeared to return a moment later carrying two plates.

When she walked over and lowered them to Jack and Christy's table, Jack glanced toward the fireman hat guy and said in a low voice to Polly, "Um, insane asylum escapee?"

"Nah, that's just Abner," she said with an easy shake of her head. She sounded completely relaxed about the guy despite the tense exchange Jack and Christy had just witnessed. "He likes hats. We humor him."

Jack tipped his head back. "He comes in here often then?"

"Well, he kinda has to," Polly replied. "He owns the place. And he's my husband."

Across the table from him, Christy tensed, clearly embarrassed, and her eyes went wide. "I'm so sorry we thought your husband was insane," she said to the waitress in just slightly more than a whisper.

But Polly appeared unfazed as she waved a hand down through the air. "Not to worry—he's pretty wacky sometimes. And damn picky about seafood for a man who chose to open a seafood restaurant. Fact is, though, when you love somebody, you just gotta accept 'em for who they are—flaws and all—and be happy you got 'em."

And it was as they were exiting the restaurant twenty minutes later that Jack held the door for Christy, but looked back to find that she'd stopped to study the fisherman statue by the door. "Um . . . is it just me," she asked, "or does he suddenly look familiar?"

So Jack looked, too—and then he smiled. "Damn, it's Abner. She made him Abner. My God, I love this place."

"I think I could, if I only knew how to begin."

Lewis Carroll, *Alice in Wonderland*

Chapter 9

THE SUNNYMEADE Retirement and Health-care Center sat on a wide swath of ground with views of the water in two directions. Palm trees dotted the well-kept lawn and a winding drive edged with bright pink azaleas and red hibiscus led to the wide sliding glass doors that welcomed visitors. As they approached the doors, Christy noticed picnic tables in shaded areas and some wicker seating under the wide awning to one side of the flat, sprawling building.

"I can see why he likes it here," Jack said. A sweet evening sea breeze wafted past and the calls of seagulls echoed in the distance. "Getting old and being in a rest home isn't my idea of fun, but if I ever have to be in one, I could see picking a place like this."

Yet Christy couldn't help feeling a little more skeptical about the whole concept, and a little sad. "You're right—it's nice. I guess it's just . . . a hard idea for me to get used to. I've never seen him here—I'm not used to it. I'm used to him being my fun grandpa who carried me up the shore on his shoulders when I was little."

"But you said he's happy here, right?" he reminded her.

She nodded. Then tilted her head, remembering how true that was. And why she needed to help him stay here. "Actually, sometimes he sounds far happier here than I can really understand," she admitted.

"Well, maybe you shouldn't *try* to understand," he advised her, "and instead just be glad."

This time her nod felt more content. Sometimes it really did pay not to overthink things. "Good point. Now let's go in—I'm excited to see him."

Stopping at the front desk, she smiled at the slightly overweight thirty-something man sitting behind it in a pair of dark scrubs and said, "We're here to see Charlie Knight. I'm his—"

"Granddaughter," the man said with a big smile, his mannerisms quickly informing her he was gay. "We know all about it. He's going to be thrilled you're here. I'm Ron, by the way, and it's so nice to meet you. We all love Charlie." Then he pushed energetically to his feet, adding, "Follow me."

As they walked down a hall that felt like a cross between a hospital and a hotel—bright and very sterile-feeling yet painted in pleasant shades— Ron said in a low, confiding way over his shoulder, "Visiting hours end soon, but you can stay late as long as you're quiet. No one will mind—we just like to keep it down for the residents who go to sleep early."

"Thank you," Christy said in a hushed tone. "I appreciate that."

Walking into her grandfather's single-room dwelling felt surreal to her. Like the hallway, it was partly about comfort but also partly about care. A flat-screen TV hung on the wall above a small bookcase. Built-in shelving in one corner, near a comfy-looking easy chair and loveseat, held framed photos of her, her parents, her late grandma, and a framed black-and-white shot of her grandparents together when they were young, back in the early sixties. But a hospital bed and medical monitors reminded her that her grandpa couldn't take care of himself anymore.

Though all that flew into the periphery of her thoughts when she spotted Grandpa Charlie seated in a wheelchair in one corner, a dinner tray in his lap. Oh God, he looked old—so much older than when she'd last seen him, at her parents' funeral. She knew their tragic deaths had taken a terrible toll on him, too. And yet . . . his smile when he saw her lit up the room and filled her with a happiness so vibrant that it somehow caught her off guard.

"It's so good to see you," she blurted out. "I'm so glad I came!" Already she could feel that sense of family love—the sense of home that was about who you were with rather than where—all running intensely through her veins.

"My sweet grandbaby's here at last," he said

with a happy laugh. "Come give your old grandpa a hug."

Old. He was. More than she'd realized somehow—more than she'd let herself believe. Part of her wanted to cry, yet she shoved that aside and marveled at how bright his eyes remained as she crossed the room and bent down to wrap her arms around his shoulders. As he embraced her, she drank in a warmth that she'd missed. The beach was nice, but *this* was why she had come.

After they exchanged a few pleasantries about the drive down, Grandpa Charlie said, "Introduce me to your friend."

She looked up to see that Jack had hung back near the door, clearly not wanting to interrupt their reunion. She'd already told her grandpa quite a bit about him, explaining he was a friend who'd offered to come with her to make sure she arrived safely, and who was paying for part of the stay. "This is Jack," she said simply.

Jack stepped up, held out his hand. "Pleased to meet you, sir."

As her grandpa shook Jack's hand, she could sense him quietly sizing Jack up. It reminded her that he'd always bragged he was a good judge of character, that he could tell quickly what he thought of someone, so now she stood watching his eyes, watching the exchange, wondering how he would assess this man she'd so quickly come to trust. "Hear you been helpin' my girl here out with some stuff around her apartment that needed fixin'."

Jack nodded. "Happy to do it."

"What with her bein' on her own, puts my mind at ease a little to know she's got someone willin' to help her out, look out for her some when she needs it."

Jack cast Christy a quick glance she couldn't quite read, then dropped his gaze back to Grandpa Charlie. "Anything she needs, sir, I'm here for her." And Christy's heart melted a little.

"You can ditch the 'sir' and call me Charlie, by the way," he told Jack, and she knew that meant her grandfather had decided Jack was a good guy. And it struck her that no matter what happened—between her and Jack on this trip, with her financial situation and Grandpa Charlie's living arrangements—how fortunate she was to have two such good men in her life. For a girl who sometimes felt she had very little, that alone felt like a lot.

From there, Jack and Christy sat down on the loveseat adjacent to the wheelchair and did a little catching up with her grandpa. She found out that John and Nancy Romo, old family friends from Destiny as well as parents to Christy's friend Anna, had stopped by for a visit earlier. They'd moved from Destiny to Coral Cove years earlier, and it had been Christy's grandparents who had first introduced the little seaside town to the Romos when they'd been looking to make a big life change.

That led Christy to tell her grandfather how she'd recently considered moving back home to Destiny, but that in the end it had just felt wrong to her—too confining. "Maybe it would have been the safe thing to do, but I was afraid if did that, life would never . . . happen to me. That it would just pass me by. And that someday I'd look back and wish I'd taken more chances and relied on myself more."

It was only as she said all this that she became fully aware that she was, in effect, saying it to Jack, too. And she'd never told him anything about that. It seemed like a huge thing to have poured out to him, even if only by virtue of having told her grandfather—and yet it felt . . . okay. Somehow, rather than making her feel vulnerable in front of him, instead she sensed him thinking she was brave, and maybe even admiring that.

After the three of them chatted a while—covering topics like Christy's job, her grandpa's health, and Jack's affinity for restoring and flipping houses—Grandpa Charlie asked her what she did for fun. "All work and no play's not good, my girl," he warned.

In response to the question, her mind first flashed on her kisses with Jack, and on making out with him in bed last night at the Colonial Inn. And then—searching her brain for something she could actually *tell* her grandpa—she thought of things like eating ice cream with Jack on his front porch, and of the unexpected simple pleasure of watching him work, being close to him as he repaired things for her, each act putting some small thing in her life back in order.

But all that seemed too complicated—and too telling, especially with Jack sitting right there—so she said, "I've gotten a lot more involved in reworking old jewelry. I even brought some that I made from the last of Grandma's old pieces to show you." And with that, she opened the yellow straw bag she was using as a summer purse on the trip and drew out a velvet drawstring sack she'd carried the pieces in just for this purpose.

Walking over to his wheelchair, she extracted two bracelets and a brooch she'd created just the week before and held them down so he could see. His eyes lit with recognition. "I remember these pearls," he said, reaching out to touch one. "Paste, but they were all I could afford and she loved 'em. Got 'em for her one Christmas when your daddy was just a boy."

His wistful smile made Christy's heart swell. Even so, she felt compelled to say, "I hope you don't mind that I changed them."

He quickly reassured her with a shake of his head. "No, I'm not one to hold on to material things that way. That's why I gave you the last of the jewelry when she passed. Thought it'd be better for you to . . . give it some new life the way you do." Then he picked up the brooch, a thick conglomeration of transparent colored beads and pale pink pearls. "You make unique pieces, my dear, that's for sure. I wish your grandma could see 'em."

"Thank you," she said. "I wish that, too. I really love doing it. It . . . relaxes me, I guess. Or inspires me. Or something." She laughed softly, not quite sure how to explain the pleasure the jewelry brought her.

"It's good to create," Grandpa Charlie said. "I

used to feel that way back in Destiny when I built barns with my father. Same principle, I guess, as if you're buildin' a sand castle on the beach—feelin' just doesn't go as deep then. But there's a certain satisfaction in creatin' somethin' that wasn't there before. It's like you're . . . changin' the world in your own little way, I guess—addin' to it."

Christy nodded, letting his words resonate through her. "You're right—that's exactly it." Then she looked to Jack. "Do you ever feel that way? When you're restoring a house or repairing something for someone?"

She thought he looked unusually introspective before finally saying, "I know the feeling."

Then she dared to share the idea she'd been considering—though now that she was actually here, it seemed a little scarier than it had back in Cincinnati. "I was thinking," she began softly, shifting her gaze back to her grandfather, "of trying to sell some of my jewelry on the beach. At the Sunset Celebration." She pursed her lips, feeling uncertain. "Do you think anyone there might buy any of my stuff?"

Her grandpa's loving eyes widened in approval. "Now that's a good idea," he said. "And of course they would." And now he was nodding—repeatedly. "Yep—I like that idea a lot. I like the spirit behind it. I like you takin' somethin' you love to do and puttin' it out there in the world, my grandgirl."

She hadn't expected Grandpa Charlie to feel so strongly about her plan, but she found his enthusiasm unexpectedly feeding her own. "I've always wanted to try to sell it, but I haven't had the time to figure out how. Or . . . well, maybe the confidence, either. Because . . . there's no guarantee anyone will buy anything. And I guess . . . I guess . . ." *It would be a huge blow to my ego if I tried to sell the work of my heart and no one thought it was any good.*

She didn't say that part because she realized that, again, she was putting her heart on her sleeve in front of Jack and that she probably shouldn't. She trusted him, but she still didn't know him that well. So he didn't need to be informed of her every hope and dream and fear. At least not yet.

But it was as if Jack had read her thoughts anyway, because that's when he chimed in to say, "You can't go through life being afraid. It's better to put yourself out there, go for what you want, take a risk—whether or not you get it—than to never go for it at all. You never go for it and you always have to wonder. And nobody should live that way."

Christy met his gaze, and she realized that he was, in some sense, sharing something personal, too—with her, and also with Grandpa Charlie. Although she wanted to know more. *What did you go for, Jack? What risk did you take? And did you get what you wanted?*

"Truer words were never spoken," Grandpa Charlie replied. Then he looked up at Christy while pointing at Jack. "This one has a head on his shoulders. Listen to him, my girl—since I think he might be almost as smart as me."

And they all laughed, and despite herself Christy was thankful to her grandfather for lightening what had suddenly begun to feel very serious and profound to her.

She still wondered what Jack might have gone for that required such a bold outlook—but rather than continue to ponder it, she instead decided to just take the advice she was being given. So she shoved aside old fears and doubts and, even if a little nervously, said, "Okay, tomorrow night, I'm setting up at the Sunset Celebration—and no matter what happens, it's better than never being brave enough to try."

And her grandpa reached up to squeeze her hand and give her one more smile. "That's my girl," he said. "That's my sweet girl."

CHARLIE watched his granddaughter and the young man she'd brought with her leave the room. Funny tension between those two—he couldn't quite read it, but he was pretty sure there was more than met the eye there, that at least one of them had feelings for the other, or both of them did. But either way, he wasn't sure it was all out in the open yet, and he suspected at least one of them was fighting it. Which made him a little sad inside.

Christy had already lost so much—love was one more thing he didn't want to see her be afraid of. And yet . . . he understood the fear. People walked around acting strong all the time, but deep inside, most people had sensitivities, tender spots. Some more than others, but there wasn't anyone who couldn't get hurt by love.

Of course, often in life, even love that was entirely returned and requited could still get messed up. So maybe it was none of his concern what Christy and Jack felt for each other. Maybe he should just trust them to take care of their own relationship, their own feelings. He only knew he wanted her to be happy, and to be open to it, brave enough to . . . understand what it was worth. Age and experience had taught him a lot about the value of love.

Just then, the male nurse, Ron, who he'd grown surprisingly fond of, stuck his head in the room. "Did you have a good visit with your granddaughter, Charlie?"

He nodded, grinned. "Better than good."

Ron gave him a smile. "Glad to hear it. She seemed like a sweetheart." With that, Ron dimmed the room's lights. It was a hint, a gentle reminder that Charlie was old and should go to bed. "Goodnight then."

He'd started to leave the room when Charlie stopped him by saying, "Ron? How's Mrs. Waters today?"

Ron just shook his head and chuckled silently. "Same as every day. But it's sweet of you to ask."

Charlie nodded slightly. "It's just that I know she's alone in the world and—"

"And you like her to know somebody cares," Ron finished for him. Yep, all the nurses had heard his reasons for asking, several times over now. And he knew each time he asked that the answer would likely be the same. But he thought it was important to keep asking anyway. He thought maybe, on some level, Mrs. Waters could feel his concern.

"Maybe tomorrow I'll take the walker out for a spin, take myself down to her room and sit with her awhile." He figured it was good exercise, a distance he could reasonably travel without his wheelchair, and he told himself she liked his company even if she couldn't let him know. He just thought it was valuable for her to have visitors. In case it was like people said—in case she was really more aware than anyone could tell.

"You're a good egg, Charlie," Ron said. "Goodnight."

It was dark out now, Charlie realized, another night fallen. He felt the darkness more now in his old age—the awareness that one more day of life lay in the past. Sometimes that left him melancholy, but tonight he let it slide off him; having Christy here had him feeling upbeat, cheerful. There was more to look forward to while she was here—daily visits, maybe some outings, maybe the chance to feel like he was still really living, soaking up life, contributing to the big tapestry of it all even if only in some tiny way just by virtue of saying hello to a waitress or dropping a crumb of food on the beach for a seagull.

Of course, he knew in his heart that the melancholy he sometimes suffered was about more than age or the loss of mobility. He knew it was the emptiness of regret, of decisions he wished he'd made differently long, long ago.

It wasn't that he hadn't had a good life—he had. And he supposed things unfolded exactly the way they were supposed to, so maybe regrets were silly. But he still yearned to do some things over. He thought he could have done things better, could have made someone he cared about happy. Susan. Dear, sweet, frightened Susan.

If he'd made different choices back then, the dark of night would summon better memories—or at least more of the really great ones. And instead, he only had a few all-too-brief recollections of Susan to fall back on. And so he often played them over and over in his head because they were all he had of her.

They'd graduated together from Destiny High in 1953. And by Christmas that same year she'd married Donald King, a saggy-bellied farmer in overalls who chewed tobacco and was more than twice her age. Funny how Charlie had known her his whole life, but he'd never noticed how pretty she was—never taken in the soft, delicate feeling her very presence put in the air—until his father was hired to build a barn for Donald King in the summer of 1954.

Charlie had been sitting in the sparsely furnished living room of the King farmhouse with his father and Mr. King, talking over the plans for the barn, and King had hollered, "Susan, get us some cold Coca-Colas from the icebox."

A minute later, she'd come floating into the room as gently as a girl walking on air—only her mood had felt heavy, hardened. She didn't smile and her eyes held no light. Even so, that was the moment when he'd first noticed her beauty. Long, dark hair pulled back from her face, skin soft and pale as the calla lilies in his mother's flower bed. She'd worn a simple dress of pink calico, but it drew in at the waist and left him taking in her shape in a way he'd never done in school.

"Cold Coca-Colas for ya," she said, handing them to each man. When her fingers brushed his as he took the small bottle from her hand, the sensation snaked right up his arm, same as when he'd been dancing with Della Mae Turner at the younger girl's senior prom last month. Their eyes met, hers a soft shade of blue he was noting for the first time, but she looked away fast, kept her expression grim and sullen.

"Ya'll know my bride, Susan?" King asked.

"Believe we do," Charlie's dad answered.

And Charlie added, "Me and Susan were in the same class—graduated together last year."

"Mmm," King said, his expression nearly as grim as Susan's as he gave his head a quick tilt back. And Charlie felt in the air the weight he'd just accidentally created. It had been easier to act like there wasn't anything wrong with a man his father's age being married to someone *his* age before he'd pointed out exactly how young she was.

"Well then, start next Monday?" King asked, shifting the focus to Charlie's father.

But *Charlie's* attention returned to the girl in the pink dress who stood quietly in one corner now like a quiet little animal, on edge, on guard, but trying to blend in and look invisible. He fought the urge to let his gaze drift onto her—and he lost, letting his eyes go there even though it felt risky somehow. It made sense that he'd want to look at a pretty girl. But it felt forbidden knowing she was another man's wife.

Though King never noticed—he was leaning over now, studying a sheet of paper Charlie's dad had given him with a pencil-scrawled estimate on it. And at first Susan looked away, but he kept his eyes on her anyhow—too bold but feeling daring, somehow driven. And to his surprise, slowly but surely she dragged her own gaze up from the floor and onto him, finally meeting his.

And it was like electricity being zapped through his veins. Just from that. Just from her eyes on his.

Why did you marry him? Why did you marry an old man? He couldn't fathom it. And hell, it wasn't like the man was a looker—he was dirty, paunchy, smelly, and had no personality to speak of. And that's when it hit Charlie—she slept with him. They shared a bed. He couldn't imagine that made her happy—he couldn't imagine it was anything but a torture.

And he began to feel bad, wondering if she could read his thoughts, see them in his eyes—and so he finally looked away, feeling sad for her. Feeling sad for *himself* that she was married. Wishing he'd noticed back in school how pretty she was. Wishing he'd dated her instead of Della Mae, who he'd seen on and off for the past two years but never really fallen for.

On the way home, he asked his father, "Why do you suppose a girl my age would marry Mr. King?"

His father had shifted the gears on their old truck, making it lurch slightly as he said, "Between you and me, son, I don't think she had a choice. Her family doesn't have much, Charlie, and King has more money than you'd think by lookin'. Talk at the General Mercantile is that her daddy pushed her into it, because King can take care of her—and of her folks and brothers and sisters, too, if need be."

"Seems wrong," Charlie said as something in his heart withered.

His father nodded. "It *is* wrong. Have to be blind not to see how miserable that poor girl is. But . . . not a lot to be done about it."

Charlie couldn't argue that, but it had left him frustrated to the point of anger on Susan's behalf. And he couldn't stop thinking how wrong *all* of it was—not just her being married to a much older man she didn't want, but also the fact that she'd never know the simple joys of being able to kiss a boy she liked, fall in love, experience all that the way a person was supposed to.

"You takin' Della Mae to the Ambassador this weekend?" his father asked. "Hear *How to Marry a Millionaire* is finally showin'."

And that's when it hit him that *he* hadn't fallen in love yet either—but at least he could, at least he would, someday. Only not with Della Mae. "Nah, I think we're breakin' up."

His father let out a soft laugh. "Again?"

But Charlie gave a solemn nod. "And probably for good this time."

That decision had changed Charlie's life. For the better. But . . . even now, he wished the choices he'd made soon after had been different.

Though he'd been beating himself up about that for sixty years, and it never did any good. And right now, as he got into bed and turned out the bedside lamp, he tried to think of things that made him happy and would let him rest well. He thought of Christy and her jewelry and how much his late wife would have enjoyed seeing it. He felt thankful all over again for his granddaughter's visit. He said a prayer that his wife and his son and daughter-in-law were in a better place. And he thought of Susan's eyes connecting with his that summer day in 1954 and how it had brought him alive, truly alive, for the first real time, and how nothing had ever been the same after that.

CHRISTY knew there was a lot she could be sad about. Lack of money, an uncertain future, her grandpa's well-being, and a host of other things that stemmed from that list. Perhaps less important—but seeming quite pressing right now—was the fact that Jack hadn't made one single, solitary move on her last night in their room at the Happy Crab.

She'd been going crazy inside as they'd said goodnight, lain down in their separate beds, and turned out the lamps. She'd watched a shadow of light that shone in from the dock out back, wondering if he would suddenly ease beneath the sheets that covered her, ready to give her what she wanted from him so badly. But he didn't.

And then she'd tossed and turned, recognizing the faint, salty scent of the sea that she could smell even indoors here, wondering if she should follow her instincts and be the one who made a move, climbing into bed next to *him*. But *she* didn't do it, either.

And she'd awakened this morning thoroughly frustrated—but happier than she could understand just to see his sexy, scruffy, smiling face as he told her he'd gotten up early and walked to a nearby bakery to get some breakfast. They'd eaten jelly donuts at a picnic table on the dock a little while later, overlooking the water, and Christy couldn't remember ever having a better breakfast in her entire life.

So yes, there were things to be unhappy about, worried about—and some of those things were pretty big. Yet as she stepped onto the pale sand of Coral Cove Beach, the air punctuated with the cawing of seagulls in the distance, she couldn't help feeling that simple sense of joy that had eluded her for so long now.

She glanced over at Jack next to her with a smile. "I forgot how much I love the beach. Something about it just . . . soothes my soul, I guess." Despite the tropical rays of the sun shining down on them from a cloudless blue sky, the sand remained cool beneath her feet and the rush of the surf beckoned.

"There's something extra peaceful here, isn't there?" he said.

And she knew what he meant. He wasn't talking about just the beach itself; he was talking about the whole little town.

"I've always felt better just being here," she admitted. "I'm glad I got the chance to come back." And with that, she reached out and boldly took his hand, squeezing it in hers—a small thank you.

Which also sent an unexpectedly large bolt

of desire shooting into her heart. And to other places, too.

They looked at each other and she was pretty sure he felt it, as well—all of it.

But that was when he turned his gaze back ahead, toward the ocean, and said, "Come on, Alice—let's find a spot to spread out our blanket." And he let go of her hand to trudge slightly ahead of her through the soft sand.

Only . . . the odd thing was that her sense of happiness wasn't dampened by his pulling away from her.

Because there were suddenly things to look forward to. Seeing her grandpa more. Trying to sell her jewelry tonight at the Sunset Celebration.

And, she realized, just being with Jack, spending time with him. Even if nothing else happened. Even if this was all there was.

And for the first time in her life, she understood that caring about someone wasn't about what you could get back from them. It was just about . . . caring.

"The sun was shining on the sea,
Shining with all his might . . ."

Lewis Carroll, *Through the Looking Glass*

Chapter 10

JACK TRIED to take in the sights and sounds on Coral Cove Beach.

Cute little kids played in the surf, and further out the occasional pelican could be seen swooping strategically, diving for fish.

"Look, he got one!" Christy said next to him as he attempted to focus on the pelican's flapping wings and the fish he held trapped in his beak now.

He tried to let the sound of the tide flowing in and out lull him into relaxation. And he worked to let the hot Florida sun make him forget all his worries.

But there were problems.

For one thing, Christy was driving him crazy in an adorably sexy pink bikini. She wasn't *doing* anything to drive him crazy in it—just wearing it. But that was enough. The perfect breasts he hadn't quite gotten to taste swelled provocatively from perfect pink triangles, and her ass—it turned out—was round and gorgeous. Like he needed to add *that* into the mix here. Like he hadn't been frustrated enough already.

Once again he berated himself for the notion that coming to the beach with her was some simple, carefree venture. What had he been thinking? She was hot and he wanted her and it was all he could do by this time not to just grab her and start kissing her again. He'd been half hard since the moment he'd first seen her in that cute little bikini—and sometimes *more* than half.

It was tricky as hell to lie next to her and act normal when he wanted to be all over her. He found himself sneaking glances whenever he could get away with it. Because he couldn't help himself. Because if he couldn't touch, at least he could look.

Last night he'd miraculously managed to keep his hands to himself, but today he felt doubly tortured by having succeeded. Even the coconut scent of her Coppertone was turning him on. Thank God his trunks were roomy.

But maybe it was those other problems that were actually keeping him from kissing her.

Like the conversation that had taken place in her grandpa's room last night. Something about it had felt so . . . real and honest. He'd thought he and Christy had already *done* real and honest, but this had gone deeper. She'd revealed fears he'd not known about before. Fears that had made her seem so unguarded and trusting that he'd suffered the urge to . . . take care of her a little. Damn.

How the hell had *that* happened? Especially given that he was officially out of the taking-care-of-needy-women business.

When he'd encouraged her to go for what she wanted and not be afraid, he'd been thinking about his business. The simplicity of online investment advising done with a personal touch had seemed a bold idea at the time—at least to industry colleagues who thought investment advising was as much about power lunches and glad-handing as anything else. It had taken guts. Especially for someone as young and inexperienced as he'd been at the time.

He remembered that feeling of: *What if this fails? What if I crash and burn?* And what he understood now was that most *everyone* got scared at some point. And that life was a constant battle with putting yourself out there. Success bred confidence, but there were always new challenges, times you had to call upon your courage.

And he'd wanted to tell her all of that and more—but then he'd had to stop, pull back, because there was so much else he *hadn't* told her.

After which he couldn't deny the hypocrisy of advising her to put herself out there—when he was doing the exact opposite with her. Shit.

But what would she think to find out he'd kept all this from her? And there was no rulebook for how soon you shared your deepest wounds with someone—the idea of talking about his divorce, getting into all the ugly whys and hows . . . hell, it sounded like torture. Why would he want to put himself through that?

She told you her worst pains, her greatest weaknesses. She trusted you that much.

But he focused closely on the brightly colored sail of a small sailboat drifting peacefully across the horizon in the distance—and neatly shoved those thoughts aside. *You never asked her to open up to you—that was* her *choice.* And it might be easy to fall prey to Christy's charms, but it didn't change what she was looking for or the problems she was trying to solve.

So go back to taking this for what it is. A trip to the beach. A girl you enjoy being with. Time to unwind, relax. Just have a good time.

In fact, quit sharing your damn deep thoughts on courage and life and risk-taking. Especially since, now that he'd examined it, maybe he wasn't such a great authority on that after all.

Just be her friend here. Maybe more—maybe her lover. But that's all. This wasn't a lifelong relationship they were building—this would be over soon, as soon as she found her rich guy to support her and Grandpa Charlie.

That could be you. You have what she needs.

You could take away all her troubles, make her happy.

And maybe she would make you *happy, too.*

But no, no, no—what the hell was he thinking? He wouldn't fall for someone who was after money more than love—that simple. No matter how amazing she might be in every other way.

CHRISTY felt like someone masquerading as an artist as she sat behind the folding table Reece

Donovan had so kindly loaned her, her jewelry spread out before her in felt-lined trays. When she and Jack had been setting up on the Coral Cove pier, attaching the little price tags she'd made this afternoon, she'd been excited, hopeful, ready for this. But now that she was just sitting here in a folding lawn chair—also on loan from Reece— waiting for something to happen, it wasn't as easy.

All around her on the old wooden pier sat picturesque oil paintings of beach scenes and stained glass sun catchers and delicate water color creations—made by people who were clearly more talented than her. She couldn't help thinking that most of the artists here had created something from *nothing*, whereas all she'd done was taken pieces of old jewelry and mixed them up a little.

Still, she tried to enjoy the atmosphere. A man in a brightly colored Hawaiian shirt painted beach umbrellas on pieces of tile to her left, and to her right an elderly woman dipped homemade ice cream into sugar cones from a metal pushcart. Directly across from her, a thirty-something woman who'd introduced herself as Tamra sold the stained glass pieces Christy had been admiring. Music played from a loudspeaker somewhere— currently Jason Mraz's "I'm Yours"—and on the beach in the distance, colorful kites darted about in the evening air, one shaped like a fish catching her eye as it whirled in circles beneath the path of passing seagulls.

Just then, she flinched at the sight of a dragon-like figure ambling down the pier—on a pink leash held by Reece. Christy was still trying to adjust the idea of Fifi as a pet, but she smiled up at Reece anyway, who pulled off the dark, handsome beach bum look with flair.

After Jack and Reece exchanged greetings, Reece asked, "How are the chairs and tables working out for you?"

"Perfect," Christy said. "Thanks again for the loan—it's a big help."

"Fifi wanted to go out for a walk," he claimed with a wink, "so we thought we'd come down and say hi."

"Well, it's nice to see a friendly face," she admitted.

But Reece just shrugged. "*Everybody* here is friendly." And she realized that was true. Well, except maybe for Abner, but she and Jack had had dinner at the Hungry Fisherman again and this time even he had mustered a hello. Albeit while wearing a suede cowboy hat with khakis.

Just then, Reece glanced over the pier's railing down to the beach below. "Almost time for Fletcher's show. Did you happen to catch it last night?"

She and Jack both turned to look, but Christy couldn't quite make out what she was observing other than a lean, lanky man with a brown ponytail assembling what struck her as a portable clothesline.

"Uh, no," Jack said, appearing just as baffled. "What's he do? Hang his sheets out to dry?"

Reece laughed. "No, it's a little more entertaining than that. He's a tightrope walker. Does it here every night. Be sure to watch—he's a pretty cool dude." And with that the owner of the Happy Crab tugged lightly on Fifi's leash and together they toddled onward.

As the sun sank toward the horizon, the sky began to blaze pink and gold in the distance. And whereas the foot traffic on the pier had been light so far, now more evening shoppers arrived.

A woman in a sundress stopped to check out Christy's jewelry, but she moved on fairly quickly—and despite herself, Christy's heart sank a little as the lady walked away. A minute later, what appeared to be a mother and teenage daughter on vacation showed a bit of interest, but then shifted their attention to the ice cream woman and her array of flavors. And after another couple of such occurrences, Christy turned to Jack, saying quietly, "I knew it. My stuff isn't beachy enough—it doesn't fit here. It's not the kind of thing you want to bring home from vacation."

Yet he merely gave her a scolding look. "Would you relax? It's only been a little while. And whatever happens, at least you're doing what we talked about last night, putting yourself out there." Though she couldn't help noticing that for a guy who always seemed totally at ease, he'd stiffened a bit as he'd said that last part—and she had no idea why.

But a second later it didn't matter, at all, because that was when he reached out to rest his hand on her knee beneath the folding table as he said, "You should be proud of yourself. I am." And the touch tingled all through her.

Jack meant it. He wasn't entirely certain it was

wise to be squeezing her bare knee, all smooth and freshly tanned, but he *was* proud of her. Now that he understood her fears, he also knew that sitting here with her jewelry laid in front of her wasn't as easy as it probably looked to the people on the other side of the table.

"Thanks," she whispered.

And oh shit, I want to kiss her. And that's bad. Even if, at the very same time, it feels so, so good.

"Come one, come all, to the greatest show on earth—or at least on Coral Cove Beach!"

Jack flinched—pulling his hand away and sitting up straighter—at the loud voice suddenly echoing from behind him. But that was probably wise. He looked over his shoulder to see the ponytailed man speaking through a small megaphone.

"Prepare to be stunned and amazed as I, Fletcher McCloud, perform amazing feats of skill and daring from atop the high-wire." With that, he motioned toward what Jack had previously thought a clothesline, then paused to look at it himself. "Okay, so it's more of a low wire," the man added. "But it's the beach, man, so it's the best I can do."

Jack could tell it was a shtick—the guy probably said the same words every single night—but a bunch of kids laughed at the joke and he saw a few of the vacationing adults smile, as well.

Fletcher McCloud continued gathering an audience until the bulk of the evening shoppers had circled around his tightrope on the sand, and most of the vendors watched from the pier despite the fact, Jack supposed, that most had probably seen his act many times before. He caught sight of Reece and Fifi at the edge of the crowd on the beach.

"Are you ready to be stunned and amazed?" Fletcher asked the group. Then he dropped to one knee in the sand, playfully addressing a little boy. "Are *you* ready to be stunned and amazed? *Are* you?" The child nodded enthusiastically and Jack could already see that the guy had an engaging demeanor that worked with his act. He looked like a throwback to the seventies with his long hair and short beard, but his friendliness made him unintimidating.

A few seconds later, he climbed an easel ladder he'd opened in the sand, and stepped, barefoot, onto the thin, taut rope. The crowd oohed and aahed as he balanced there and then began to walk, taking slow, careful steps with his arms held out to each side. Jack couldn't help being impressed—after all, you saw this kind of thing at the circus, but not usually at the beach, and not usually so close-up. He watched the other man's toes bend downward to hug the cord he walked on.

"That's really cool," Christy whispered next to him as they watched the guy walk from one end of the rope to the other.

"Of course, because I don't have a high-wire," Fletcher then said to the crowd, "I realize I might need to do a little more to stun and amaze you. Which is why I need someone to toss me those bowling pins—one at a time please." He pointed to the sand where the pins lay among a pile of props. "That's right! I'm going to juggle while I walk on this tightrope! Feel free to make sounds of awe."

The spectators tittered with laughter, some of them obliging him with "sounds of awe"—and then they watched Fletcher juggle the pins, after which he then upped the stakes to juggling three knives! Throughout the act, Jack and Christy exchanged glances, both clearly impressed.

"For my final act, to make *sure* you leave here stunned and amazed, I'm going to juggle fire!" The audience let out a collective gasp, to which Fletcher responded by laughing and saying, "Nah, I'm just kidding," producing one more chuckle from the crowd.

"Except," he said slowly, holding up one finger while still balanced on the rope, "what if I'm not? What if I'm going to take those very torches lying there in the sand"—he pointed—"and light them and juggle them? Sir, would you be so kind as to hand those torches up to me?"

Once he held he torches, the crowd waited in silence as he pulled a lighter from his pocket and carefully lit each. And then Jack and Christy watched as he did indeed juggle fire! Again, it wouldn't have been a surprise at the circus, but Jack found himself growing curious about Fletcher McCloud, wondering what a guy like him was doing *here*.

When the show ended, Fletcher passed around a large top hat collecting money—and Jack wanted to add something to it but couldn't from up on the pier.

"I wish we could give him something," Christy said.

"I'll walk down and put in a couple bucks," Jack informed her, then headed for the sand.

By the time he reached Fletcher, the crowd had dispersed and Jack opened his wallet and drew out a twenty, adding it to the evening's tips.

"Very generous, my friend," Fletcher McCloud told him appreciatively.

"Your show was great," Jack said in reply.

To which Fletcher answered, "Your girlfriend's pretty."

And Jack balked slightly.

Fletcher just chuckled, and went on. "I've done this show a million times and I'm a skilled multitasker—I can people-watch while I do it. For me, that's the best part."

Now Jack gave him an easy grin since he, too, could appreciate the art of people-watching. Though he felt the need to inform him, "Well, she's not my girlfriend. Exactly." Since at this point, he didn't know *what* she was.

"She *should* be," Fletcher McCloud said as certainly as if he were announcing the sun was about to set.

And Jack blinked, intrigued enough to ask, "What makes you say so?"

Fletcher McCloud narrowed his gaze, looked introspective. "I just get feelings about people sometimes. And my feelings are usually right. Plus you two look at each other a lot. The show's out here, on the tightrope, but you two keep looking at each other instead."

Huh. Jack never would have made that observation, but he couldn't deny it, either. Yet something about the truth in it compelled him to change the subject. So he pointed to the tightrope. "How do you do that?" he asked.

"Balance," Fletcher replied.

And Jack laughed.

But Fletcher said, "No, I'm serious. Life is all about balance. And walking on the tightrope is really just a metaphor for life. It's . . . a balance of putting yourself at risk and keeping yourself upright at the same time. It's about the discipline to teach yourself to do the impossible. Anybody can walk on a tightrope if they're brave enough and dedicated enough. Anybody can learn to do the impossible—if they want it bad enough. I just wanted it bad enough. So what's impossible for *you*?"

"Trust." The word popped out of Jack's mouth before he'd even realized it. Damn, how had this guy drawn that from him so quickly?

Though Fletcher simply responded with a shrug. "The whole world has trust issues. But you know who wins in life? The people who get over it and trust anyway. The question is always—do you want it bad enough?"

And Jack confessed, "That *is* the question."

Jack found Fletcher more than a little intriguing, and easy to talk to—and he considered saying more. But instead he turned to go. Because prolonging this conversation, he suspected, would only have him further examining things he was busy trying to avoid.

Still, he looked back over his shoulder to say, "Mind if I ask you something? What's a guy who can juggle fire on a tightrope doing in Coral Cove, Florida?"

Fletcher laughed good-naturedly. "It's not the hot commodity you might think, my friend," he said. "But the real answer is a long story. I live in a little blue cottage up the beach on Sea Shell Lane. If you're ever up that way, drop by for a beer and I'll tell you what's keeping me here."

Jack walked away even more intrigued. Damn, this little town was *full* of interesting people.

But he forgot all about Fletcher McCloud when he approached Christy's table to find her smiling from ear to ear, holding up a twenty dollar bill of her own. "Look, Jack!" she said. "I sold a bracelet! I really did it! I made my first sale!"

The joy in her hazel green eyes nearly undid him. And damn, he wanted to kiss her again—but instead he just said, "I'm not surprised at all—I knew you would."

Then she bit her lip, looking thoughtful, hopeful, sweet as hell. "Wouldn't it be great if I could ever earn enough money at this to make a career of it? To support Grandpa Charlie and me both?"

"That *would* be great, Alice," he agreed softly.

To which she replied by flashing a deprecating smile. "You don't sound like you think that's possible." She still spoke just as sweetly, and didn't seem hurt or angry—maybe just . . . acceptant.

And he hated like hell that she'd heard the reality in his voice. The last thing he wanted to be was discouraging. "Anything's possible," he told her.

But it's not likely, and it just reminds me that you need someone to take care of you.

Jack had a lot of faith in a lot of things, but he wasn't sure he believed in the impossible. And right now, it seemed pretty damn impossible to figure out a way to be close to Christy without risking *everything.*

Alice rubbed her eyes, and looked again.
She couldn't make out what had happened at all.

Lewis Carroll, *Through the Looking Glass*

Chapter 11

THE FOLLOWING morning, Christy bounded merrily into her grandfather's room, unable to hide her joy. She found him chatting with Ron the Nurse, who looked up and said, "Well, aren't you a ray of sunshine?"

"Of course she is," Grandpa Charlie said. "My day's better already just seeing that pretty smile. Now come give your old grandpa a hug."

Ron excused himself, warning them with a grin, "Now don't you two be plotting any trouble while I'm gone."

And after Christy had given her grandpa a hug in his wheelchair, he said, "What has you looking so happy and glowy this morning, my grandgirl?"

She tilted her head and offered a coy, playful grin. "Maybe it's just seeing *you*."

He laughed and said, "Now, I know ya love me, but this ain't that kinda glow."

And then Christy told him the news she'd been dying to share since last night. "I sold some jewelry at the sunset celebration, Grandpa! Five pieces before the night was through! It started out kind of slow, but then it was just one after another, and I ended up making over a hundred dollars!"

Now Grandpa Charlie smiled, too, big and bold, as a happy laugh left him. "See there? I knew it. And it just goes to show ya—you never know what you can do until ya try."

"That's so true! Thank you for encouraging me. It really was hard to set up my stuff and sit there without knowing what would happen, and at first when people walked right on by, I felt like a big loser. But with a little patience, things got better."

"And ya know, the truth is," he told her, "if you hadn't sold a dang thing that woulda been hard on ya—but you'd still be glad you tried. And you wouldn't be a loser."

Christy thought that through and realized he was right. It would have been disillusioning and heartbreaking, but it would still be better than always wondering what would've happened. And now . . . "Everything feels . . . filled with possibility." And it truly did. Ever since her second sale—which had proved the first wasn't a fluke—she'd felt uplifted, as if she'd discovered the world was a different, better place than she'd come to believe. Her problems seemed smaller. And a halo of hope hung over her every thought.

Just then, Grandpa Charlie squinted, lowered his chin. "Where's your boyfriend?"

And she rolled her eyes. "He's not my boy-friend."

"But you want him to be," Grandpa Charlie said.

Ugh. She let out a sigh. "Is it that obvious?"

"Yes, indeedy, my grandgirl." A warm expression shone from her grandpa's eyes. "And he seems like a stand up fella, so I approve."

This time she held in the sigh, but a great well of emptiness opened inside her. She'd been so happy focusing on her jewelry sales—but when it came to Jack, her emotions were at war. She flip flopped between just being glad to have him in her life and being painfully aware of wanting something more that she just couldn't have. And right now, the suggestion of Jack being her boyfriend had her wanting. "Well, I'm glad you like him, but . . ." She stopped, finally letting out that sigh.

"But what?" her grandpa asked. "What's wrong with him that I didn't see?"

Christy tried to think how to explain. She couldn't just blurt out that she was seeking a rich man in order for him to stay here at Sunnymeade, but . . . maybe he'd understand if she just kept the focus on Jack himself. "Well, Jack's great," she said, "but . . . he's a handyman."

"Honest livin' if you ask me," Grandpa Charlie said without missing a beat.

"Yes, and he's wonderful at it!" she rushed to say. Since clearly she'd come at this the wrong way. "And if I were any other person in any other situation . . ."

"What situation are you in, darlin'?"

Crap. She'd blurted out that last part before thinking, and now she felt . . . shallow. Still, she tried to be honest, and more blunt this time. "I'm dirt poor, Grandpa."

"Well, you don't need to be rich to be happy."

"Oh, I know," she assured him. "And I'm not even sure I'd *like* being rich to tell you the truth." In fact, eating at the Hungry Fisherman the last couple of days and staying at the Happy Crab the last couple of nights had truly shown Christy how much she enjoyed a down to earth lifestyle. And she was forced to realize how much more comfortable—and downright happy—she'd been in places like that with Jack than she'd been in fancy clubs and restaurants back home. "But . . . well . . ."

"Spit it out, girl," her grandpa said.

Oh hell, apparently she would have to put this on the table, like it or not. "Well, between you and me, Grandpa," she said, "you're about to get kicked out of here—and I can't stand to let that happen. Okay?"

And at this, he flinched. "Good Lord, girl, what does one thing have to do with the other, for heaven's sake?"

In response, Christy drew in a breath, let it back out. An open window carried a salty sea breeze in and she let the scent soothe her senses— then forced herself to get even more honest. "I just think . . . if I met the right guy . . . well, maybe he could bail us out. And how can I meet the right guy if I'm . . . with Jack?"

When a troubled look came over her grandpa's

face, she wished she hadn't let the conversation go this far. "My living arrangements aren't your responsibility, honey," he said.

"I know that—of course," she assured him. "But . . . I'm all you have. And ever since you told me about the situation . . ."

Now, though, he was shaking his head. "Well, maybe I shouldn't have done that. It never occurred to me you'd take on my burdens as your own. And if I'd had any inkling you would, I'd have kept my big trap shut, believe you me."

"But I'm *glad* you told me. I'm glad we can be open with each other. We're family and we need to stick together." She reached down to squeeze his soft, wrinkled hand, desperate to take away any guilt or worry she'd caused him.

"Well, be that as it may," he replied, "sticking together doesn't mean goin' so far as lookin' for some money bags type of fella on my account." Then he narrowed his gaze on her more tightly. "Now listen to me, darlin'. I don't want you to worry—because whatever happens, I'll be fine, ya hear? And you're young and beautiful, with your whole life ahead of you, and you need to date whoever you feel drawn to, not whoever has the biggest wallet—got it?"

Christy took all that in. Of course he would say that. Of course he wouldn't want her to feel responsible for him. It only made sense. What she *wasn't* sure of anymore was . . . whether *her* plan made sense. Maybe he was right.

Yet, either way, there was another factor here, more truth to share. "Okay, I got it," she conceded.

"But the upshot is . . . I don't know that Jack wants anything romantic with me anyway. Because he thinks I'm a gold digger."

At this, Grandpa Charlie smacked his hand to his forehead. "You told him about this plot to find a rich man?"

She let out a long-suffering sigh, beginning to realize what a mess she'd created here. "Sort of. Accidentally," she explained. "Before I realized it would matter."

"Well, that's a shame," Grandpa Charlie said. "A damn, cryin' shame. Because that's not who you are, my dear. Not by a long shot. And it pains me to know you've let him think you are."

"It pains me, too—believe me," she said, feeling tired of the whole situation.

"But I guess once you let a cat like that out of the bag," her grandpa said, sounding grim, "it's hard to put it back in."

In the days that followed, Christy and Jack alternated between spending time at the beach and hanging out with Grandpa Charlie. Over the next few nights they sat at the pier during the Sunset Celebration and Christy sold more jewelry. Certainly not enough to pay Grandpa Charlie's way at Sunnymeade, but enough to continue raising her confidence and even help her begin to believe she might somehow build a future in this. And a really wonderful and unexpected by-product of the last few days was that she suddenly felt she fit here now, among the other talented vendors—she believed she was an artist now.

But she'd have to make more than she could at the beach. And now that she knew people liked her creations, it was a matter of figuring out how to turn that into more money.

It was Thursday evening, as the sky blazed a brilliant purple over the horizon in the distance, that a familiar-looking guy with a ponytail and beard picked up one of the necklaces she'd made with her grandma's fake pearls and said, "This is beautiful—I'll take it."

"Aren't you the tightrope walker?" she asked, tilting her head as she peered up at him.

"Fletcher McCloud, at your service," he replied with a grin.

Jack, who'd walked away to get them sodas, returned just then. "Good show tonight, man," he said in greeting. "We watched from up here."

"I know you did," Fletcher said with a small wink that made Jack chuckle as he leaned his head back.

"I forgot," Jack said. Then he dropped his gaze to Christy. "Fletcher here has excellent observational skills from atop his tightrope."

Jack had told her he'd had an interesting discussion with the tightrope guy, and as she wrapped his purchase in tissue paper, she smiled up at him and asked, "Who are you buying this for?"

"My wife," he replied.

She caught the slightly surprised look on Jack's face as he settled in the folding lawn chair next to hers, soda cups in hand. "I don't know why," Jack said to Fletcher, "but you didn't strike me as a married guy."

And Christy thought the other man's slight smile held a hint of mystery as he said, "Do married men act or look a certain way? Still got that beer ready for you. Stop on by some afternoon."

"I might just do that," Jack replied with a nod.

It was only a few minutes after Fletcher had departed that a woman with long, dark silky hair paused to look at Christy's offerings. And as Christy glanced up at her to say hello, she realized she wasn't a stranger. Not at all. But how could this be? "Anna?" she asked, perplexed. To her shock, before her stood her friend, Anna Romo, from back in Destiny.

Clearly surprised to hear her name, Anna flicked her gaze to Christy's and her eyes went wide. "Christy Knight? Is that you? What on earth are you doing here?"

"Visiting my grandpa—he lives here," she explained. "What are you—" But then she stopped, remembering. John and Nancy Romo lived here. Why hadn't she thought about this before. "Oh, you must be visiting your parents!"

"Yes," Anna said with a pretty smile. "Duke and I got here just last night."

As if on cue, Anna's rugged biker boyfriend, Duke Dawson, stepped up behind her and they all exchanged greetings.

And once Christy got over her surprise, she couldn't help feeling some sense of . . . almost *relief* to see Anna here. Anna had been a real friend to her in Destiny, and she couldn't deny that suddenly seeing a familiar face, a girlfriend to turn to and maybe confide in, appealed immensely. "I'm sure you're busy with your family," Christy said to Anna, "but I'd love to get together while we're both here."

"That sounds great," Anna said. "Maybe we can hang out at the beach. My parents aren't big sun worshippers, and while Duke looks hot in a pair of trunks, he gets bored just lying around in the sun."

At this, Duke slanted her a look that made Christy think he was a little embarrassed, but then he dropped his gaze to Jack to say, "You fish?"

"Some, yeah," Jack replied.

"Her dad and I are planning to fish off the pier tomorrow if you're interested. Could let these two do their girl thing."

And though Christy appreciated that Jack did enjoy the beach, she was also pleased when he accepted the invitation so she and Anna could have some alone time. Which was when it hit her. "Grandpa Charlie used to love to fish," she said to Jack. "Maybe if he thinks he could handle it on his walker, you could bring him, too."

"Sounds good to me," he said. "I'd be happy to."

And Christy couldn't help smiling. More and more things seemed to be going right all the time. Yes, she was still heartbroken over the ways she'd screwed up with Jack—letting him think she was only interested in money. And yes, her body ached with wanting him almost all the time now. But maybe if she just quit worrying about that and tried to focus on all that was going well instead, the rest would somehow work itself out.

THE next day Christy and Anna stretched out on towels on Coral Cove Beach, soaking up the rays and watching kids build sand castles and play in the water near shore. It was another beautiful day in paradise and Christy never wanted to leave.

"So you're selling your jewelry at the Sunset Celebration," Anna said. "I'm thrilled to see you moving forward with that!"

Christy smiled in reply. "Thanks—me, too. I was nervous about it at first, but it's been going well." Then she glanced toward the long pier in the distance. It was far enough away that she couldn't see Jack or her grandpa, but she knew they were there somewhere, holding fishing rods over the railing and waiting for a bite. "In fact, if we decide we've had enough sun before the guys are done fishing, I may explore an idea I have for selling even more."

Anna raised her eyebrows. "Oooh, that sounds mysterious and top secret."

"It is," Christy confided. "Kind of. But I'll let you know if it starts looking promising."

Another added benefit of hanging out with Anna was the opportunity to get caught up on all things Destiny.

"Amy and Logan are doing great, and the bookstore is still the town hotspot," she reported.

"I'm so happy to hear that." Amy had been another good friend to her. And Amy's husband, Logan, was a fireman who had felt a lot of unnecessary responsibility for her parents' deaths, so she hoped he was getting over that. "And how are your brothers?"

"Lucky and Tessa are both busy with their businesses, which are doing better than ever." Lucky did custom paint jobs on motorcycles and Tessa was in interior design. "And as for Mike and Rachel—well, my worst fear has come true," Anna announced. "They had their baby and it's a girl! And Mike is so overprotective that I'm about ready to kill him, but I'm making it my personal mission to be sure he doesn't hover over her for her whole life, and to make sure she gets to have lots of fun—whether he likes it or not."

After Anna groused a bit more about her oldest brother's protective ways, Christy asked, "And everyone else?"

Anna tilted her head in thought as she peered out over the ocean. "Let's see. Sue Ann and Adam are always keeping busy with their work and the kids, and—oh—Jenny had her baby, too, an adorable little boy who's going to break lots of hearts someday. She seems so happy to be a mom, and Duke has gotten friendly with Mick and says he seems to be adjusting to fatherhood well."

From there, Anna informed her the bed-and-breakfast she ran was doing a healthy business, but not so much that she and Duke couldn't take a week away to come to the beach. "Duke is building lots of custom furniture and has practically more orders than he can handle," she went on. "Right now he's making new picnic tables for Edna's backyard at the apple orchard. And kitty Erik is still his clingy but lovable self."

Then she took on a thoughtful look and said, "You know, saying all that makes me realize how lucky I am, how happy I am. And there was a time when I couldn't have imagined having such a perfect life. It can happen, you know, when you least expect it."

She tossed Christy a speculative glance, and Christy understood that it was both encouragement and Anna wanting to know how she was doing. But when she didn't begin volunteering information, Anna went ahead and asked, "So, about this Jack guy. He's pretty hot, and he seems nice. But I didn't get the vibe that you guys are a couple. So what's the deal?"

And so then Christy told Anna the deal—all of it, spilling her guts in a way you could only do with a close girlfriend. With Grandpa Charlie, she'd worked hard to sound like everything was fine, like even if she'd screwed up with Jack it was okay—but with Anna she let her emotions flow. "I'm such an idiot!" she said. "Why did I tell him I needed a rich guy? Why did I admit any of that to him at all? Because even though I don't know for sure if that's what's standing between us, I'm pretty sure it is. And I don't know how I can possibly fix something like that."

"You could just tell him," Anna suggested. "The whole truth. Like that you thought you knew what you wanted, but that now you realize you want something else—*him*."

Christy sucked in her breath imagining that and felt a little nauseous. "But I have no idea if he's into me that much, like in a way that sounds so serious. After all, he's done a pretty great job of keeping his hands off me ever since we got here—so maybe it was just a brief, fleeting physical attraction and he's really fine with just being friends. So to just put all that out there without knowing where his head is would be . . ."

"Scary, I know," Anna said, her voice filled with understanding. "I took a risk like that with Duke."

"And it clearly paid off," Christy acknowledged, thinking how happy they were. "Not every risk does, though."

"But . . . what if I hadn't taken it?" Anna asked, looking over at her. "That's why I did, you know? Because things were looking awfully grim between us, but I knew that if I didn't make it really clear to him exactly how I felt that I'd spend the rest of my life wondering if it would have made a difference."

Christy couldn't help being in awe of Anna's courage. To put your heart on the line like that, to risk that kind of rejection, took nerve. "You're so brave," she said. "I envy that."

But Anna just laughed. "You're brave every day. I've known that since I met you. You've gone through so much loss and yet you're out there facing life, moving forward, not letting anything get you down for long. *I* envy that."

Christy took in what Anna had just said. It wasn't new information—she knew she'd been brave, because she'd had no choice—but maybe she'd forgotten that lately. Maybe new challenges made it easy to forget past triumphs. "Somehow, though, with Jack it's harder than some other bravery-requiring things have been. I'm not sure why."

"Because you value him and you're afraid of losing what you already have with him."

Ugh, she was right. When had *that* happened? When had she started valuing Jack so much?

From the start.

She didn't know where the words had sprung from inside her, but it was true. Almost from the moment she'd set eyes on his gorgeous, scruffy face. And then he'd kicked down her door, and been kind enough to repair the very damage she'd asked him to do—and she supposed if she was honest with herself, she'd already been falling for him even then.

"So . . . nothing romantic or physical since you got here?" Anna asked. Christy had told her about their near-sex at the Colonial Inn in Nowhere, Georgia.

"Nope. Though I feel it all the time."

"It?" Anna asked, reaching for a bottle of sunscreen planted next to her in the sand.

"I guess it's . . . tension. And maybe it's just me, not him. But it's just this feeling . . . as we're moving around each other in the room, passing each other coming and going from the shower, or anywhere, this urge to touch. This . . . awareness of his body. I notice *everything*. The way a T-shirt stretches across his chest. The way his hair falls across his forehead when he's just come out of the shower and it's still wet. I even like to watch him brush his teeth—how wacky is that?"

Yet Anna only smiled wistfully as she replied, "Ah, I remember noticing that kind of stuff with Duke early in our relationship. How everything about him—no matter what it was—made me feel all dreamy inside."

Christy sighed because Anna had nailed it—Jack made her feel dreamy. "And in Georgia, when we stopped and didn't do it, and when he said we'd see where things went once we got here, I thought . . . I thought things would go somewhere. But it seems like that's not happening. Maybe I'm the only one of us noticing all those little things."

She bit her lip, thinking it through. "Although I could swear I'm not. And it's breaking my heart to think he really doesn't want things to go any further, because I think we could be really great together in that way. But at the same time, I just try to be grateful for how much fun we have together and how good I feel when I'm with him. I mean, I feel more of that dreamy feeling just sitting next to Jack at the beach or in a restaurant than I have when I was making out with some guy I thought I was crazy about. And really," she stopped, weighing it in her mind, "for a girl who's sexually frustrated and in love with a man I can't have, I'm actually pretty darn happy these days most of the time."

And it was as Anna's eyes widened that Christy realized what she'd just said.

"Oh God," Christy murmured. "Oh wow."

"Yep," Anna said, smiling. "Wow."

"This is what it's like to be in love," Christy mused.

And Anna nodded. "You got it, girlfriend. And it can be a double-edged sword—I remember.

Crazy happy just because he exists and you're with him, but crazy sad because you're not with him *that* way."

"That pretty much sizes it up," Christy said, forlorn. In fact, she experienced the warring emotions even now. And she let out another heavy sigh as the revelation seeped into her soul as intensely as the rays of the hot Florida sun seeped into her skin. She was in love. With Jack.

And maybe she'd never really been in love with Kyle at all—because that . . . that had been nice— even wonderful—but it had felt . . . so much more like a choice than this.

This . . . was a condition. One she already knew she couldn't fight. And even as Anna was advising her to be brave with Jack, she grew more fearful— because she had no idea where this would lead, but it also felt doomed.

Because once you let a man think you were only about money—could he ever really believe you were about anything else?

"And now, which of these finger-posts
ought I to follow, I wonder?"

Lewis Carroll, *Through the Looking Glass*

Chapter 12

JACK LEANED back in a folding chair, the fishing
rod he'd rented balanced on the pier's railing and
held loosely in his hand. It was a damn beautiful
day for fishing, something he'd done a lot of with
his dad growing up, but not much in recent years.
And it was a nice-if-mixed-bag group of men he
found himself out here with. Next to him, Charlie had already caught three healthy-size snook
in just the first couple of hours. And Duke had
pulled in one so far—but John Romo and Jack
were striking out. Even so, it was a peaceful way
to pass the time, and Charlie seemed to be enjoying himself, which made Jack feel good. He liked
the old guy and found him easy to be with.

Until, that is, Charlie looked over at him and
said, out of the blue, "My Christy . . . she's a good
girl."

Oh boy. What was *this* about?

Jack met the old man's eyes, but then felt forced to draw his gaze down—in case he was about to be accused of something. "I, um, know."

"What I mean," Charlie said—though now he looked absently out over the water, "is that she's got a good heart."

"I . . . I—she and I are just friends, Charlie, and I would never do anything to hurt her."

"That I buy," he said. "At least the part about not hurtin' her. I like you, Jack. And that's why I'm tellin' you that . . . if, out of concern for takin' care of me, she led you have any negative beliefs about who she is, they're wrong."

Jack still wasn't sure he understood what they were talking about. But did it have something to do with Chisty's rich man hunt? And was Charlie trying to shove them together? As if Jack weren't already having a hard enough time keeping his hands off her, now her grandfather was giving him the green light?

"I . . . think the world of your granddaughter," Jack answered. "I wouldn't be on this trip with her otherwise." And he decided to just leave it at that.

"Well," the older man said in response, "that's good then."

Jack simply nodded and felt happier when they were quiet again, and happier still when a hard tug came on his fishing line and he could turn his attention to reeling in the bite he'd gotten. A few minutes later, after a slight battle and some encouragement from his companions, he pulled a small black sea bass up onto the pier and was thankful they now had something else to focus on besides Christy.

Not that his mind wasn't still on her. It was almost always on her these days.

But he didn't feel any closer to answers, and so he just tried not to think about it, as much as possible anyway. Which was easier when he had something simple to concentrate on—like this fish.

As for what he'd do later, when he was with her again . . . well, he supposed it would be like every night lately—he'd suffer and wish he was touching her, moving with her. And then he'd roll over and fall into an unsettled sleep fettered with frustration and hope all these complicated feelings just somehow went away.

He knew it wouldn't really be that easy, but maybe at this point he'd begun to think: *If I can just keep myself from taking her to bed until the trip is over, this will fade away. She'll start dating rich dudes again and remind me why it was good I held back. And I'll find a way to get comfortable being only her friend again. And maybe she'll even* marry *one of the rich dudes—and then I'll know for sure it was best not to let myself go any further with her, and she'll be gone from my life.*

But the funny thing was—that whole line of thinking was supposed to make him feel *better*, and in fact, it made him even more miserable than he already was.

"If that bass is ruining your day or something," Duke Dawson said from his place farther down the pier, "I'll take it off your hands."

Jack flinched. Shit. Clearly he was standing there *looking* miserable, too.

"Nope, I'm happy as can be," he claimed, trying to appear more normal.

But he caught Charlie's eye on him just then, and their gazes met for a second before Jack could pull his away, and he knew the old man wasn't falling for any of it.

AFTER Christy and Anna parted ways that afternoon, Christy showered and dressed in a pretty, flowy gauze skirt and a crocheted tank Bethany had given her for her birthday. Then she wrapped up the remaining pieces of jewelry she hadn't sold at the pier and put them in her straw bag. After which she looked in the mirror and said out loud, "You are an artist. You can do this." And she realized, again, that she really felt that way. From the sales she'd made. From her Grandpa's belief in her. From Jack's belief in her. She didn't quite understand it completely, but she saw herself differently than she had before arriving in Coral Cove.

Of course, she also grappled with what she'd figured out at the beach a few hours ago about Jack. She'd known she was pretty wild about him, but falling in love . . . that was a whole other situation. And it meant a huge, monumental change in everything about their relationship—whether he knew it or not.

Peeking back up into the mirror, she realized that now she looked . . . frightened. Shell-shocked. And a little flushed.

Okay, you're in love with him, but you'll just have to deal with that later because right now you're setting out on a very important mission. And you can't let your-self be distracted. Or terrified. Or worried. About him or Grandpa Charlie or anything else. Right now is all about you. And maybe your entire future.

Departing the Happy Crab on foot, she headed north on Coral Street, the main thoroughfare that passed through the small beach town, along the short stretch laden with souvenir stores and ice cream shops. While some businesses like the Happy Crab and the Hungry Fisherman seemed to be suffering from the influx of large resort hotels up the beach, others that were more retail focused continued to thrive—particularly in the evenings, she'd noticed—when the tourists from the large hotels were drawn to this area for the Sunset Celebration.

She'd seen the storefront for Beachtique and thought it looked like a more upscale shop than most in Coral Cove, so now she decided to make it her first stop. She took a deep breath as she walked up and reached for the door handle.

Stepping into the air conditioning brought relief—it was hot if you weren't right on the water this time of day—even if at the same time her stomach swam with nervousness. Looking around the place, she caught sight of sophisticated-looking sundresses and appealing beachwear—as well as a sizable jewelry counter. Pay dirt. Maybe. *Take another deep breath. In. Out. You can do this.*

It was then that an older woman, tall with a rather queen-like air about her, entered the shop through a doorway covered with white curtains. "Welcome to Beachtique," she said as she came up behind the sales counter. Her tone held a certain brashness—like someone who wanted to be nice but didn't quite know how—and Christy knew she had to draw upon her courage even more than she'd expected to. *But I can do it.*

Arriving at the opposite side of the counter, she put on her best smile, the one she'd gotten used to using with shoppers on the pier. And she reached into her bag as she spoke in her most confident voice. "I've been admiring your shop and I'm wondering if you do any consignment."

The tall woman bristled slightly, her back going more rigid as she said, "Oh—no, I'm afraid we're not interested in that type of arrangement."

And normally that probably would have sent Christy on her way right back out the door—but she'd already laid a rolled-up swatch of velvet on the counter and begun to unroll it. So she paused at the woman's words, not quite sure whether to stop or proceed with only two bracelets currently visible on the dark velvet. The woman's eyes dropped there, as well. And as Christy stood waffling between pressing forward and just accepting defeat, the woman said, "But I suppose I'd be willing to look at your pieces."

It felt like a flower blooming in Christy's heart—the sweet relief of suddenly being welcome. "I take old pieces of jewelry and rework them," she explained, then revealed the rest of what she'd brought. "I've been doing quite well at the Sunset Celebration, so I decided to start looking for consignment opportunities, as well. Your shop is the first one I wanted to offer my work to."

"How much have you been selling them for?" the woman asked. "Because I'd need to take at least twenty percent, and I wouldn't feel comfortable pricing any of these any higher than one fifty or two."

Crestfallen, Christy just blinked her disbelief. Was the woman serious? "A dollar fifty?"

And just when she thought the Beachtique lady never smiled, a loud peal of laughter tore from the woman's throat. "No, my dear, of course not," she said. *"A hundred and fifty.* Which would make your profit one twenty." After which the woman went all serious again. "But if you feel you need to make more, then I can't do it."

Christy barely knew what to say. She'd been selling these same pieces for fifteen to thirty dollars apiece so far. And while part of her wanted to let her astonishment run free and ask the woman if she really felt people would pay that for them, instead she just smiled and made a joke. "Well, that's more like it."

Now Beachtique Lady wore a big smile, too. "Of course, I'd also have to ask that you not consign elsewhere within the immediate area. I like to offer unique pieces and I don't want to compete with a neighboring business."

"Of course," Christy said, nodding, still amazed at this turn of events.

"Though," the woman said, leaning closer, suddenly acting like Christy's new best friend, "I'll give you a tip. The shops at the resorts up the beach might be willing to work with you—many of them like to showcase local artisans and handmade goods. And though I do share a customer base with them, my friend Louise works at a shop in the Sand Dollar Resort and we find that the tourists who shop within the resort tend to stay there, on the grounds, for the bulk of their visit. So we don't believe our shops compete directly, and I'd have no problem with you placing some pieces with them so long as you promise to keep my supplies up."

Still trying to hide her shock, and still nodding profusely, Christy said, "Yes, absolutely, and I appreciate the insider info." In fact, she was trying not to sound too excited about it.

A few minutes later, she and Beachtique Lady, whose name turned out to be Lydia, had worked out a deal and Christy left numerous pieces behind to be displayed in the glass jewelry case she'd noticed upon coming in.

And much to her continued joy and astonishment, after taking a cab a few miles up the road to the resorts, she soon had a similar deal with the second shop she visited there, which just happened to be inside the Sand Dollar—and though she didn't meet Louise, the clerk she dealt with acted almost as if she felt the pricing Beachtique had suggested was too low.

Christy spent the cab ride back to the Happy Crab elated. She was an "artisan" now. And though there was no guarantee her jewelry would sell in either spot at the much higher prices, the confidence of the shop people left *her* feeling confident, too. Even if still stunned.

She couldn't wait to tell Jack! And her grandpa! And she'd have to call Anna! *Oh, please please please let Jack be back at the room when I get there.* It was all she could do to contain her excitement over the miraculous turn her day had taken. She'd hoped for a consignment deal or two, but she'd never dreamed her jewelry-upcycling could be as lucrative as now suddenly appeared possible.

Her heart lifted—she could have sworn she felt it rise physically in her chest—when she paid the cab driver, then got out to find her car, which Jack had driven today to pick up Grandpa Charlie, back in the parking lot. It was fairly late—dinnertime.

Digging her room key—attached to the plastic crab-shaped keychain—from her bag, she shoved it in the door and burst in to see Jack standing near the bathroom in a pair of blue jeans, no shirt, wet hair.

"You won't believe what's happened!" she said, letting a big smile unfurl as she gazed on her oh-so-handsome roommate.

His eyes widened in curiosity, even as he teased her. "I was getting ready to say, 'About time?' and 'You could have at least texted me'—but I'll wait and decide how much to scold you based on what you're so excited about."

She kept right on smiling, unable to contain her enthusiasm, as she said, "You're right—I should have texted. But I didn't realize how long I'd be gone. And honestly, I'm not used to anyone caring where I am. But what happened today is—I've arranged consignment deals on my jewelry with two upscale shops, and they both think they can sell my pieces for a couple hundred dollars. Each!"

She appreciated the wonder in his eyes as he blinked. "Seriously? Wow! That's . . . freaking amazing, Christy!"

If it was possible, she got even a little happier then—simply because he was calling her Christy again instead of Alice. "I know," she said, still gushing. "I couldn't believe it. And they both want more than I have on hand, so I'm glad I brought my tools and supplies and can make some new pieces while we're here. Of course, this means no more selling at the Sunset Celebration, but this seems like a much bigger opportunity and like it will be better in the long run, right?"

He nodded. "Absolutely." And he tilted his head a little, and his eyes looked so very blue and so very . . . well, she couldn't think of a word for it, but she saw something in them that seemed deeper than ever before, seemed to show her some new part of his soul she hadn't yet seen. And her heart beat a little faster because of it.

But she kept going, kept talking. "And maybe it's too soon to be this excited, but to have people believe so much in what I create just feels . . . important, you know?"

"I know," he said, and she could have sworn he really understood what she was saying, that he really got it. "And—damn, honey, can I just tell you how proud of you I am? For just going out there and doing this? Because I know that took guts. And I'm sorry if I acted like making a living with your jewelry was too big a thing to shoot for—because maybe you really can."

Her chest contracted, partly in her continued excitement and partly because . . . Jack's belief in her, his approval, meant something to her. More than she would have guessed up until this moment. She wasn't sure why, but somehow it created a whole new bond between them that hadn't existed before.

"Thanks," she said, the word coming out too softly, her breasts heaving slightly within her bra at the effort. Then she bit her lip. Felt a little hot inside. And said, still quietly, "So . . . are you going to scold me?"

"No," he breathed with a slight shake of his head.

"Good," she said.

"I'm going to . . . kiss you," he said. And with that, he let the towel he still held fall from his hand and stepped toward her.

Christy sucked in her breath, her entire body tingling with anticipation. And then his hands were on her, one wrapping around her waist to pull her to him, the other rising to gently cup her cheek.

His mouth, as it came down on hers, was no less than delicious. She knew she hadn't been waiting terribly long for this to happen again—and yet it felt as if she'd craved this for a lifetime. *Because I'm in love with him.*

She'd somehow succeeded in mostly blocking out that still-stunning bolt from the blue as she'd peddled her wares this afternoon. Or . . . maybe the knowledge—both magnificent and horrifying as it was—had somehow added to the confidence she'd mustered as she'd approached the shopkeepers. Because of that funny thing she'd already learned about being in love. That even if it wasn't returned, it still made you feel incredible and full of light inside. It made you see the world through new, brighter eyes.

Either way, she was remembering it now—it was hitting her full force—and she was pretty sure nothing on earth was as amazing as being kissed by a man you loved.

She let her hands rise to his chest, at once shocked and delighted to be reminded that it was bare, his muscled flesh warm beneath her fingertips. She kissed him back with all the passion she'd been storing up inside her—she wanted him to know, to feel, how much she cared for him, how much she wanted him. Being bold had worked for her earlier today and she saw no reason to hold back now.

The longer they kissed, the more fervently their bodies pressed together. It wasn't a decision for Christy, just a thing that happened. And when the hardness behind his zipper connected with the part of her body that most sizzled and longed for him, she felt closer to heaven than she'd ever been before. Even that night in Georgia. Because they'd spent so much more time together now. She'd let him see so much more deeply inside her soul. The way she'd felt she was seeing into *his* just before he'd kissed her.

She didn't fight the heady urge to move against him, to grind the crux of her thighs against that enticingly rigid part of him. She wanted him inside her so badly that she could barely breathe. She kissed him harder, let him know.

Even though surely he already did. Surely he could read every signal her body was sending him. And that maybe even her heart was sending, too. Would it be so awful if he knew? How she felt? Maybe . . . maybe by now he felt the same way, too. Maybe the time they'd spent here at the beach had changed and deepened things for him, as well. *God, please let him love me back.*

When his hand finally rose to one aching breast, she gasped and, without forethought, leaned closer, pushing the soft mound of flesh deeper into his grasp. After a mind-numbingly long round of feverish making out, they finally stopped kissing, and their foreheads came gently together, touching, both of them letting out ragged, labored breath. They stayed that way, frozen in desire—except for Jack's thumb, which stroked across her beaded nipple through her crocheted top and bra. Again. Again. *Ohhh.*

Amazing how intensely she felt it, that one tiny, scintillating touch, as it came over and over. Such a tiny movement—and on that equally small spot on her body. But as they stayed still in every other way, the taut, sensitive tip of her breast felt like the biggest part of her.

Well, except maybe for the area between her legs. It was as if a cord stretched from her breasts downward, each stroke of his thumb tugging at the needy, madly tingling spot that pulsed beneath her skirt.

She'd never felt so comfortable with a man, so ready to connect. Suddenly, her relationship with Kyle seemed so . . . youthful, self-indulgent—even as nice as it had been. But with Jack, it was . . . about Jack. About who he was. About his body, but also about his heart, his mind. It was about things like sharing ice cream with him, or donuts on the motel's dock. It was about the way he listened to her when she talked, the way he made her feel weak yet strong at the very same time. *He's the total package. He's everything I could ever want in a man. Money be damned.*

When his hand dropped to the hem of her top, she was at first disappointed, missing it at her breast—until she realized he was ready to start taking her clothes off. Her breath caught in her throat—and then she pulled back slightly, ready to let him, ready to help him.

"Lift your arms," he rasped deeply—and so she did, feeling gloriously open and eager as he removed the crocheted tank over her head, leaving her to stand before him in her flowy skirt and a transparent pale blue demi bra.

It was her prettiest, sexiest bra, worn today merely because it worked well beneath this particular top, not because she could have anticipated this happening when she'd gotten dressed—but now she was wildly thankful for the choice. She felt so pretty, the curves of her breasts rising feminine and round from the light blue cups, and she could see that reflected in his eyes as he gazed on her bareness. She wanted to bare herself to him even more.

With that weighty desire pulsating through her every pore, she slowly reached up behind her for the bra's hook, even as she kept her gaze locked on him. It hadn't been long ago that she'd struggled to make eye contact with that beautiful blue gaze—but that time had blessedly passed. As had the time for waiting.

And heaven rested a mere heartbeat away as she deftly unhooked the bra, felt it loosen around her, then lifted her hands to her shoulders, ready to pull it off—when Jack said, "Christy, honey— don't."

She tensed. *Don't?* "Wh-why not?"

Because you want to take it off me instead? Please say it's that. Please please please.

She watched him take a deep breath—and felt her heart beginning to implode even before he said, "Because I can't. I'm sorry. I just can't."

"The horror of that moment," the King
went on, "I shall never, *never* forget!"

Lewis Carroll, *Through the Looking Glass*

Chapter 13

CHRISTY STOOD before him frozen in horror.
Of so many kinds. Frustration that bordered on
agony. Embarrassment that—oh God—he was
really turning her down again. And hurt. There
was no other way to describe that part of it—it
simply hurt, so unbelievably much that she wondered how she would survive it.

As her lower lip began to tremble, she bit down
on it, trying not to let him see. Not that that was
enough to help this situation even one iota. She
wanted desperately to rehook her bra, but she
couldn't do it from this angle and could only hold
it helplessly in place over her breasts. She'd never
felt so rejected in her life.

Trying to swallow back her pain, a spark of
anger erupted from her. "Why did you have to
start kissing me? Why did you even start this at
all?" She could no longer meet his gaze—what

had become easy and effortless had now grown impossible again. At some point her eyes had become stuck on his chest because, hot and masculine though it was, it still seemed a safer place to look.

"I'm so sorry, honey," he said. "I . . . didn't mean to exactly. I didn't plan it. It's just that you're . . . really beautiful when you're passionate about something, that's all."

She pulled in her breath, both flattered and bewildered—and Anna's words came back to her. About going for it. About never knowing how things would have gone if you didn't. So even now, even as reckless as it seemed, she didn't hold back. "I'm passionate about *you*, Jack."

He let out a heavy breath. And her heart beat so hard it hurt.

"I'm passionate about you, too, Christy," he said. "Believe me, I am. I just . . ."

"What?" she demanded.

Now it was he who looked away, dropping his gaze to the flowered print of her skirt. "Maybe I'm just worried about . . . attachment."

"Attachment?" she asked.

He spoke more directly this time. "Maybe I'm worried that I'll get attached to you, or you'll get attached to me."

I'm already *attached to you.* But this time she held the words in. Since putting it on the line didn't seem to be working in this case. Who'd have thought getting lucrative consignment deals for her jewelry would be so much easier than giving herself to a man—and getting him to take her.

Somehow Anna's simple story had made Christy believe that if she put her heart out there for him to see, she'd find out he loved her, too. Anna had made it sound . . . hard, and yet at the same time so very simple. Like the happy ending would just come if you willed it to. So where was her happy ending? And why had she been so foolish to believe it could be that easy?

Instead of saying any of that, though—instead of forcing out any more honesty and openness— now she found herself trying to deal in logic. "I thought you said we'd come to Florida and see what happened. That we'd let things take their course, go with the flow. You're stopping the flow."

He looked so pained for her now that she knew her *own* pain was written all over her face. It didn't matter what she said—she'd already made herself as vulnerable as a person could be. And the thing about vulnerability was—once it was out there, you couldn't take it back. *She* couldn't take it back. Anymore than she could rehook her bra.

"That seemed like a good idea at the time," Jack said, eyes still fraught with distress. "But I'm not sure it's that simple now. I mean, it's like I said— I'm afraid . . . one of us will get attached."

"Don't you think," she began desperately albeit still logically, "that *most* sex attaches people? In some way? Even if they pretend it doesn't?" Oh crap, what was she doing? Spilling her heart out onto the floor some more, that was all. And maybe saying things she didn't even really know she felt until this very moment. "And the truth is—I wouldn't want to have sex with anyone I might not get attached to. It's a connection. It's *supposed* to mean something. Even if the whole world has tried to make it into nothing more than a recreational activity." She stopped, sighed, let her gaze drop—because she realized she'd met his eyes again in the course of spewing out all this stupid honesty. And she felt all the more naked, but it had nothing to do with her state of undress.

When she next spoke, her voice went softer. "Or that's how it feels to *me* anyway. So if getting attached sounds so horrible to you, then I guess it's just as well you stopped."

The accusing words hung heavy in the air between them, Christy wondering how her greatest success had been so quickly squelched by the agony of rejection, until Jack said quietly, "It's not that I don't want to get attached to you, Christy. It's that . . . that I'm just not sure it's wise."

Oh. Oh God. She got it now. Finally. How had she been so thick-headed?

She'd forgotten the ideas she'd let Jack have about her. She'd forgotten that maybe these last nice days still hadn't made him see past that. "You still think I'm awful," she said quietly.

"It's not that," he claimed. "I know you now. And I'm not judging you for anything."

"Then why . . ." God, this was hard to ask. Because she wasn't sure she wanted to know the answer. "Why don't you want to be attached to me?"

"Because . . ." He stopped, shook his head, looked exasperated. When she thought *she* was very clearly the one who deserved be exasperated here. "I can't explain."

Oh brother. Was he serious? "Try," she demanded.

He let out a tired-sounding breath. "Because . . . I know it sounds all easy and fun and sexy right now. But what happens when we get back to Cincinnati and you find what you were looking for before we got here? What happens when you find your rich guy?" He shifted his weight from one bare foot to the other. "I just don't want anybody to get hurt here, okay?"

Christy had run out of replies. She was weary of baring her soul to him. She was tired of hearing that he didn't believe in her—since apparently believing in her ability to sell jewelry successfully was a whole different thing than believing in her as a person. Even if it was her own fault he'd ever gotten those ideas in his head, she didn't care— she was tired of letting him see the real her and finding out it didn't matter.

So she was ready to end this conversation and just try to figure out how to push on through the rest of this trip from where they now stood. And despite herself, it turned out that led to her spilling one more piece of heart-baring honesty. As she bent to pick up her crocheted tank, still holding her bra in place with one hand, she said, "I'm going in the bathroom now to get my top back on. But for your information—if you got attached to me, if . . . if I thought you cared for me and wanted something real with me, Jack . . . well, if that ever happened, there isn't a rich guy in the world who could take me away from you."

And with that she stepped into the bathroom and slammed the door.

Jack stood in the middle of their motel room staring at the door that had shut in his face, wondering what the hell just happened. Mainly the last part—what she'd just said. He swallowed back the emotions battling within him and tried to replay it in his mind, make sure he'd heard her correctly.

Because if he had, she was saying . . . she was crazy about him. That this wasn't just about fun and wasn't just about sex. That it mattered to her. That *he* mattered.

And maybe if he was honest with himself, he'd known that all along, or at least picked up on it somewhere along the way. But the totally new part here was . . . she was saying he mattered *enough*. Enough that she didn't care whether or not he had money.

And that—that was . . . huge.

And yet . . . could he trust it? He'd trusted Candy once, and even if she'd had good intentions, she just hadn't been mature enough to know her own heart.

But damn, he *wanted* to trust Christy. With everything in him. He wanted to let go of all his worries, all his fears, and just be *in* this, all the way.

He let out the breath he'd accidentally been holding since she closed herself up in the bathroom. Yeah, what she'd just said was huge, but there was so much else to think about here. He'd just hurt and embarrassed her. She had every right to be angry with him. He'd been all wrapped up in worrying about the ramifications of going forward without considering the ramifications of . . . not. He'd tricked himself into believing that stopping protected them both when, in fact, it had injured *her* pretty damn badly. He'd realized it too late, when there was no way to fix it, no way to rescue her from standing there half undressed and looking like a wounded animal.

Hell, this was a lot to juggle in his head at once. What a fucking mess he'd created. With a girl he really cared about. *Not that anyone would know it from the decisions you make with her.* God, the full measure of what he'd just done to her hit him harder with each passing second.

How was he going to repair things here?

He had no idea.

But he had to do *something.*

So he squared his shoulders and walked closer to the door. "Um . . . did you want to go to the Hungry Fisherman? The early bird special is probably over, but we could get the buffet anyway, my treat."

The sound of her *harrumph* echoed through the door.

God, I'm lame. Trying to make up with cheap seafood. "Or . . . we could go somewhere else. Anyplace you want." That was better.

After a pause lengthy enough to keep him on edge, she finally issued a terse reply. "I'm not in the mood to go out now." *Because you made me feel like shit.* She didn't say that part, but he heard it just the same.

"I . . . can go get something if you want."

And when she didn't answer, he realized he had to say more—he had to get real here and go deeper than talking about food.

"Christy, I'm sorry. I really am. I didn't mean to be an ass. But . . . I'm trying to make up here, and . . . you've gotta eat *something*. So let me take you to dinner—or at least bring something back, okay?"

And just when he'd decided she still wasn't going to answer and that he'd really blown things to bits with her, one quietly spoken word echoed through the door. "Pizza."

And his heart relaxed just a little. "Pizza's great!" he said. "In or out?"

"In," she said. "I just feel like keeping to myself tonight, and I should work on my jewelry anyway."

"That's totally cool," he said. Then he told her once more, "Anything you want."

Of course, maybe he should have taken that simple anything-you-want attitude a few minutes ago. But he hadn't, and despite himself, he still felt the reasons why. Stronger than ever now.

And if you keep passing up sex with a gorgeous, sexy-as-hell girl who wants you like crazy with no promises and no commitments, then . . . it must mean you're pretty damn crazy about her, too.

And that meant . . . he had a lot of thinking to do.

CHARLIE had had a good day. And it just kept getting better. First, he'd gone fishing on the pier with Jack, John Romo, and Anna's boyfriend, Duke. Other than the fact that his knees ached and he was tired as hell from so much distance on the walker, he'd felt . . . downright normal. No, better than normal. He felt alive. Like maybe there was something left and it wasn't all just about waiting to die now.

He and John had split the day's catch, and a few of the evening nurses had taken him and the other patients in his wing out on one of the patios, where they'd grilled them up and made a regular picnic out of it. Mr. Ritter from across the hall hadn't been able to quit talking about how long it had been since he'd tasted fresh fish and how much he envied Charlie the outing today, and Nurse Angie had suggested that maybe they could start organizing more off-premise activities in small groups for the patients who were physically able. Mrs. Glass, a frail-looking and usually silent woman had looked across the picnic table at him several times to say things like, "Good fish," and "This is nice. Real nice." All in all, he felt like his little adventure today had brought a lot of good to a lot of people when he'd least expected it. He'd have to thank Jack again—and Christy, too, for suggesting it.

And if that wasn't enough, after he'd gotten back to his room a little while ago, Christy had called to surprise him with some news—she'd made awfully big progress in her jewelry business today. "I wanted to tell you in person tomorrow, but decided I couldn't wait," she'd said, then filled him in on the details. He told her he couldn't be prouder of her and he'd meant it. She was a resilient girl, but he felt, just in the short time she'd been here, as if he was seeing something new and strong begin to blossom inside her.

Though there had been an odd underlying sadness in her voice. He hadn't wanted to pry, so he'd written it off to her being tired—but now he wondered if it had to do with her feelings for Jack.

He hoped Jack had heard him today, really *heard* him. But it wasn't his place to try to push them together—all he could do was try to make sure both of their heads were in the right place about certain aspects of the situation. Damn, he regretted ever letting his sweet grandgirl know about his financial hardship—he'd never meant for her to take it on as her personal responsibility.

One of the big problems in the world was that people tried to take on too much for other people. All in the name of helping and caring. Sometimes plenty of good came from that, sure. Sometimes people really *needed* help. And there were certain folks who thrived on that kind of giving. But mostly, he believed it was best to let people take care of the biggest parts of their own dilemmas and responsibilities. Because he thought most people were more capable than they realized. And because it was when you started taking care of others that you sometimes forgot to take care of yourself.

He was afraid that was what Christy had done by taking on his burden. He only hoped he'd said enough to fix that. And seeing his granddaughter go after what she really wanted with her jewelry gave him a lot of hope that she'd work things out in her life for the best.

A look out his room's wide window allowed him a last glimpse of a purple sky before it faded entirely to black. And somehow that ethereal purple glow took him back to a particular night in his youth in Destiny, a night that had also been about dilemma and responsibility.

It had started innocently enough with Susan that summer he and his father had built her husband's barn. They seldom saw Mr. King at all—he worked in faraway fields from sunup until dark. But the new barn sat close enough to the house that Susan brought them out sandwiches for lunch, wrapped in gingham cloth in a basket, and more bottles of Coke. Sometimes she would linger, quietly watch them work from a distance. And he'd liked just having her near, feeling her eyes on him, feeling her interest in what he was doing.

Even as innocent as it was, even as wordless and subtle, he'd felt the draw between them, like the powerful pull of a magnet. Something invisible and hard to quantify—and yet so real, so viable, that there were moments he could have sworn you could touch it. He'd almost believed that some cord had stretched invisibly between them and had been tugging them closer and closer, even if he couldn't see it.

He'd felt his own maleness more in her presence. When she wasn't around, he was just him, just a kid hammering nails alongside his dad, working up a sweat, making some summer money, hoping Dad would let him take the truck into town after supper to look for his friends. But when *she* was there, he somehow became aware of the muscles in his arms and shoulders, the way they moved when he worked, because he felt her noticing. When she was there, he felt everything inside him kick into overdrive, like the very cells of his body had suddenly come alive for the first time.

It had been in July, in the middle of a long, hot, dry summer, that his father had hurt his back. And Charlie had started going over to the King place on his own to work on the barn.

The first few days of that had been both easy and maddening. Easy because nothing changed—Susan brought out his lunch, then sat quietly watching him work for a time, then went on her way, both relieving him and breaking his heart as she went.

But then . . . they began to talk.

"See your garden every mornin' when I drive past the house. Looks like you got some tomatoes about ready. Pick any beans yet?"

"Picked a mess the other night and cooked 'em up with a cottage ham. You like green beans and ham?"

He'd nodded, still working. But from the corner of his eye, he'd noticed the way her skin had darkened from chores out in the sun over the past month or so, same as his. The warm glow somehow made her even more beautiful just when he'd thought that wasn't possible.

They'd gone on like that for a while. Talking

about nothing as he labored, but every word still feeling magical.

Until, a day or two later, he'd finally gotten brave enough to stop hammering when they spoke, brave enough to turn and put his whole focus on her, look her in the eye. And Lord, the girl had pretty eyes.

"You like peach pie?" she asked.

"I do," he told her, boldly meeting her gaze.

"Bought some peaches from the General Mercantile. Was thinkin' I might make a pie. Maybe I'll bring ya a slice with your lunch one day."

"I'd like that."

But those were only the words they were saying with their lips. With their eyes they'd been saying much more. About the magnetic pull. About the wanting. About how the relentless summer heat just made it all the worse—and all the better at the same time.

And then had come the day when she'd brought him the pie. And by then . . . hell, he'd spent so many hot, breezeless nights in bed fantasizing about her, and so many hot, steamy days torn between aching for her and trying to fight off the feelings that he guessed the tension had been too much. And things had started to be said. Things he'd known they shouldn't say—and yet, they'd *needed* to be said as badly as he needed air to breathe.

"You like the pie?" she asked. She perched on an old wooden stool in the shade of the barn and he sat on the dirt floor a few feet away, leaning his back against the wall of a stall he'd just built. It had been another blistering hot day in a summer when the heat refused to break.

And he looked her in the eye and said exactly what he was thinking, not trying to hide a thing. "Think it's about the sweetest damn thing I ever tasted."

She'd swallowed visibly. Because he was talking about the pie, but there'd been sex in his answer. He knew it; he'd felt it. He'd gotten tired of pretending it wasn't sitting right there in between them every time they were anywhere near each other.

"Glad you like it," she said, her voice going a little deeper. He got hard in his pants, just from that.

"I like it too much," he told her, still locking their gazes, willing her to keep looking at him, not run away from it. "Wish I could have more."

Her lips trembled and he saw her thinking about what to say. And finally she chose to change the subject. In a way. "You still go with that Della Mae girl from over on Blue Valley Road?"

He shook his head. "Nah."

"Why not?"

"Wouldn't be right when there's somebody else on my mind."

He watched as she drew in a breath, slowly let it back out. Finally, she ventured to ask, "So you got a new girl now?"

He just gave another shake of his head and laid it out between them. "The girl I want is married."

She flinched, and for a brief second he felt bad for being so blunt, for forcing her to face something neither one of them could do anything about. But then he pushed the feeling aside. Because ignoring it didn't make it go away and he was tired of tiptoeing around it. So tired that, hell, he just wanted to get it all on the table, once and for all. "Why you gotta be married to him, Susan? It ain't right."

Unmistakable pain—shame—passed through her pretty eyes. "I don't *wanna* be. Just *have* to be."

He thought again of her sleeping with King and his stomach pinched up. Most of the time he managed to block that out, focus more on the weighty pull between them—but now it snuck in, and it stung bad. "Because he has money?"

She nodded, her face grim. "My daddy said everybody's got a cross to bear and this is just mine. He said there's worse fates in life than lookin' out for your family. He said . . . he said it was the reason God made me pretty. So that Donald King would want to marry me and take care of us all."

Charlie sucked in his breath. And wanted to rip Susan's father to pieces for using her that way, for making her feel it was the whole reason she existed. And he kept right on being honest. "Maybe God made you pretty for *me*."

Another hard swallow from her—he saw the muscles of her throat contract. And though she'd lowered her eyes at some point, now she met his gaze again. Dust floated in a shaft of sunlight angling in between the barn's wooden slats, shining between them like a barrier. "You think I'm pretty?" she asked. She sounded younger than usual, more like a girl of eighteen *should* sound, he thought—and it was the first time he realized that marrying King had aged her, hardened her. He wanted to soften her again, wanted her to be a girl again, like she *should* be.

He wanted more than just that, though.

He wanted *everything*.

"You're all I think about," he blurted.

And the invisible heat between them pulsed for a few long, sultry seconds that felt like hours—until she pushed to her feet and said, "It's late—I should go." Then she rushed from the barn before he could stop her.

And Charlie ached. For himself. For her. For the injustices in life. And he took his frustration out with his hammer and nails the rest of the afternoon.

But it didn't help a thing. In fact, the aches all just got worse and worse. That night he worked until his limbs were as sore as his heart; he worked until the sun set and the sky glowed as purple as a fresh, tender bruise.

CHRISTY sat on her bed, back against the headboard, jewelry tray on her lap, working to attach a delicate glass bead to a clump of others in a multicolored brooch she was creating from a hodgepodge of leftover pieces. An old black-and-white movie played on the TV in front of her and Jack lay on his bed nearby watching it while also looking at the laptop computer he'd brought along—browsing the Internet, she guessed. They'd eaten their pizza in the same fashion—quietly, in front of the TV, and any communication between them had been brief—Jack trying to be nice and her replying as shortly as possible.

She wasn't trying to be mean or to punish him—but she just felt so exposed, and so rejected, that she didn't want to expose *anymore* of herself. And somehow, even just chatting pleasantly would feel like exposure right now. She had the urge to roll up in a tight little ball and bury herself beneath the covers—so compared to giving in to *that*, working next to him while being a little withdrawn felt downright bold.

Refocusing on the brooch, she carefully attached a pink faux pearl and a tiny glass flower of pale green—then smiled, pleased at the way the piece was coming together. When she felt Jack's eyes on her, she did what she'd been doing every time that had happened in the last hour—ignored it and kept her attention on her work, the one thing she could trust to always make her happy, the one thing that was always there for her to run to and immerse herself in.

"All those beads and pearls are your potted plants, aren't they?"

She blinked, looked up at him. "Huh?"

"The way Mrs. Harrington loved her plants, that's the way you love making jewelry."

And despite herself, her heart lifted—just a bit—to hear that he got that without her ever having told him. "Yeah," she said softly. "It's exactly that way."

"I'm glad you have something you love that much," he told her.

And she pursed her lips, trying not to feel too

deeply or respond too warmly, even though the sentiment touched her. Because lots of people had things they loved, things that became their touch-stones in life, but since the death of her parents, Christy had *needed* what this gave her. She could scarcely imagine surviving without it. What would bring her joy, or peace of mind, or a sense of purpose if she didn't have jewelry to create?

"I'm really sorry for ruining your happy news earlier—and for *everything*," he said.

She tried not to look into his eyes—she could see even peripherally that they shone particularly blue and beautiful at the moment. And she didn't want to just be sucked in by them, by him—since she knew the need to protect herself now. "I ap-preciate the apology," she said, accidentally flick-ing her glance to his, then away.

"Think you might forgive me?" His voice held just a hint of playfulness.

But she wasn't falling for playfulness right now. Even if she wanted to. "I don't know. I don't like that you still think I'm all about money."

"I *don't* think that. I promise. Tonight was . . . illu-minating for me. Forgive me, Alice? Pretty please?"

She tossed him one more accidental glance in time to see him raising his eyebrows and looking—oh rats!—cute as hell.

"I'll go find you a Twix somewhere," he offered sweetly, his grin turning almost shy.

Christy sucked in her breath, let it back out. And began to forgive—just a little.

"I guess it's possible a Twix could help," she said grudgingly. "Maybe. We'll see."

> " 'Oh, 'tis love, 'tis love, that makes
> the world go round!' "
>
> Lewis Carroll, *Alice in Wonderland*

Chapter 14

THE NEXT couple of days were quiet.

Christy and Jack spent time at the beach together, but didn't talk much. Because she was still a little embarrassed and still a little angry. And he responded by being patient and considerate.

And to her consternation, she discovered that even amid all those new emotions, she remained—ugh—crazy in love with him. Her heart still lit up when he entered a room. And it beat faster when he emerged from a dip in the ocean looking all tan and hot and wet and sexy as he came toward her in his swim trunks. And—darn it all—she somehow enjoyed his company, his very presence, just as much even when they barely spoke. She'd have never believed it was possible to feel so much pain, heartache, embarrassment, and anger while still enjoying being with the person who'd caused every bit of it.

The evenings were quiet, too—quiet dinners at the Hungry Fisherman, quiet drives to Sunnymeade. Though they both became less quiet around Grandpa Charlie because she wasn't mad at *him*, after all, and she didn't want him to suffer just because things were uncomfortable between her and Jack.

On the third morning after Christy's grand humiliation, they agreed she'd spend the day on her own, making jewelry and delivering new pieces to her two new business partners—and that Jack would simply see which way the wind blew him. "Might fish a little, or take a long walk up the beach," he said over breakfast. "Maybe I'll swing by the rest home and take Charlie some lunch—he liked the place where we all had lunch the other day. Just a little sandwich shop, but he went on and on about the chicken salad."

"That'd be nice," Christy said quietly from across the picnic table on the dock. He still got them donuts, every morning. And damn him for being so sweet to her Grandpa—the man made it hard to keep being mad.

As they parted ways at the door to their motel room a few minutes later, Jack having decided to set off for his walk up the shore, he said, "Have a nice day, Alice."

Though as he began to depart, he stopped, turned back to her.

"What?" she said, meeting his eyes and somehow being a little startled by their gorgeousness all over again.

"You ever gonna forgive me?" he asked.

And she sucked in her breath—unprepared for the question. "Can . . . can you promise me you really don't think I'm all about money anymore?" she asked. "Can you promise me that . . . that you know I'm a nice person with good intentions?"

"Yes, honey, I can promise all of that, and I do." No hesitation.

So she wanted to ask him the next part. *Does that mean you're not afraid anymore? Of something between us? Of . . . getting attached?* But she didn't. Because she wasn't sure how she felt about that now, either. And maybe the only thing that mattered right here, in this moment, was this one step forward. "Okay," she said. "Thank you."

He looked heartened. "So . . . can we maybe get back to normal here now? Get back to enjoying our trip?"

She nodded. Though her boss had allowed her to leave their return date open-ended, she couldn't stay here forever, nor could she expect him to keep paying for their room forever, and maybe it made sense to try to put this behind them and enjoy what remained of their time in Coral Cove.

The smile he cast warmed her heart—and crap, other parts of her, too.

But maybe that was okay. If her heart was telling her to get over this now, maybe she just *should*. Maybe she should forgive and forget, and go forward remembering what a good guy he was.

A little while after Jack left, she took her jewelry and tools out onto the dock. A gentle breeze kept her cool as she strung some chunky, colored beads—and the calls of seagulls and the view of boats drifting past in the bay made her happy she'd come here with Jack, happy she was experiencing Coral Cove all over again, just in a new way this time. Even despite the pain she'd experienced. Maybe things would get better now.

When a scuttling sound drew her attention, she glanced up to see Fifi ambling by in the distance. She wasn't leashed this time, but Reece followed behind her in his usual slouchy khaki shorts and faded T-shirt. The sight of Fifi no longer startled her, proving that a person could get used to anything—even having a miniature dragon for a neighbor.

When the giant iguana paused to sniff at what appeared to be a glob of pelican doo doo, Reece nudged her huge, scaly tail with his flip-flop. "Fi, no," he said gently—same as you might to a puppy or a small child.

"You really do love that thing, don't you?" Christy asked.

Reece looked over, clearly not having noticed her on the dock until now. Then he cast a soft grin. "Found her on the roadside when she was just a baby—she'd been hit by a car. Sometimes when somebody needs you, that's enough right there to make you love 'em." Then he tilted his head, clearly thinking through his own words. "Or maybe it's the being needed part. But either way, yep, this scaly girl has my heart."

Christy replied with a small smile. "Even though she's so . . . ugly?" she dared to gently inquire.

Reece just shrugged. "Eh, you know what they

say about the eye of the beholder. I guess one man's border collie is another man's giant iguana."

Christy laughed.

And Reece smiled, concluding, "Love isn't always pretty."

AFTER walking up the part of Coral Cove Beach where he and Christy had spent time playing in the surf and soaking up the rays, Jack headed beneath the pier and farther up the shore to the much quieter, desolate stretch of sand Christy had pointed out when they'd first arrived. Someone had pulled a rowboat up onto the sand, but otherwise the beach lay untouched and empty, sand dunes and sea oats stretching toward the road in the distance. And as he walked on, the beach curved away from the road, creating an even greater sense of isolation.

Immediately liking the sense of peace, he stopped, sitting down in the soft sand to peer out over the water. He was glad Christy had forgiven him—and he hoped it meant getting back to the way things had been before. He missed the sweet, vibrant girl he'd been getting to know before he'd fucked up so badly with her the other night. And he really did believe her now.

What she'd said before going in the bathroom that night kept playing over in his head. That if he wanted something real with her, no rich guy could take her away from him. In one way, it made him feel . . . well, more special than anything had in a long time. But then he started thinking about the fact that he *was* a rich guy, and that she didn't

know that, and how complex it made all of this—
and that's usually when he pushed the thoughts
away altogether.

*Maybe you should just do what you told her in the
first place, back in Georgia. Have fun. See where it
leads. Don't worry so much.* That had sounded like
a damn good idea when he'd said it—and maybe
it was *still* a damn good idea. Maybe he'd complicated it too damn much, based on his unpleasant
past.

Yep, he could do this—he could get back to
where he should be with her. *I like it here. And I
like her. And the rest of this trip is going to be . . . a lot
easier. Because I'm done mucking it up with my own
shit.*

As he walked on, small pastel cottages came
into view on his right, dotting the higher ground
beyond the beach with structures of sea green
and pale blue, sunny yellow and faded melon.
The sound of wind chimes echoed from somewhere, their music filling the air. Two rows of
slanted white beach fencing created a twisting
trail toward the cottages, along with a sun-washed
signpost that said: Sea Shell Lane.

Jack smiled upon realizing he'd found his way
to Fletcher McCloud's house without even trying.
So he followed the fencing up the sand until
he passed through some sea oats and low sand
shrubs, and then headed up a few weathered
wooden steps to emerge onto the end of the street.

He'd just begun wondering how he'd figure out
which house belonged to Fletcher when he saw a
ponytailed man watering hanging pots of flowers

at the very first house, on a wide side porch overlooking the beach.

As he started in the direction of the little blue cottage, Fletcher spotted him. "Jack, my friend!" he said, a smile unfurling as he stopped watering. "Good to see you. Noticed you and your lady hadn't been at the pier the last few nights."

Stepping up onto the porch, Jack explained about Christy's consignment opportunities—then complimented Fletcher on his home. It was modest but sunny and airy, with French doors that faced the water open to let the sea breeze waft through.

"Come on in," Fletcher said. "It's almost lunchtime—we'll make ourselves a couple of sandwiches, grab some beers from the fridge, then eat outside."

Jack thought the bright colors inside Fletcher's house suited him—maybe they made him think of carnivals and circuses, places Fletcher would fit well.

It was as he passed back through the living room a few minutes later, lunch plate and beer can in hand, that he noticed the little bag in which Christy had placed the bracelet Fletcher had bought for his wife. It lay on a table against a wall with other small bags and boxes, alongside a little stuffed parrot, a glass seahorse figurine . . . and more. Whereas the rest of the house appeared tidy, the pile of small items made this area feel messy—creating question marks in Jack's mind.

So as they sat down at the round wicker table on Fletcher's side porch, Jack asked, "Did you, uh, give your wife the bracelet yet? The one you bought from Christy?"

Fletcher bit into his ham and cheese sandwich, chewing thoughtfully before replying, "No, can't yet. She's not here."

"Traveling?" Jack inquired.

"In a sense," Fletcher said with a light nod.

And Jack raised his eyebrows. "A sense?"

"She's been gone for a while now. Two years this September."

Whoa. Jack had no idea how to reply, so he didn't. Other than an, "Um . . ."

"Used to move the show around," Fletcher began to explain. "We brought it south for the winter—hopping around to different beaches every couple of weeks. Stayed an entire season in Key West once, but mostly we drifted from place to place, wherever the street performers brought out the most tourists. In summer, we headed north, working street fairs and festivals from the Great Lakes to Cape Cod.

"She was my assistant," he went on, offering a wry grin. "Yep, I used to *have* someone to toss me my knives and torches. And we traded banter back and forth, she and I—the crowd *loved* our banter."

He leaned back in his chair, his eyes filled with a certain wistful joy as they met Jack's. "It was a fine life, my friend, a fine life indeed. Walking a tightrope for an hour or two each afternoon or evening—and the rest of my time left for explor-ing the world and making love to my soulmate. Doesn't get much better than that."

Jack had to admit Fletcher made it sound pretty

amazing. And so he almost didn't even want to hear what was coming. Or question how a woman who was Fletcher's soulmate was no longer here.

"Then one afternoon I came back to our motel room and found . . . this." He reached into his back pocket, pulled out a wallet, and from it a small piece of worn paper, folded.

Jack took the slip of paper from Fletcher's outstretched hand, then opened it to read the handwritten message inside.

I'm sorry, Fletch. I love you, but I just have to go. Don't let this hurt too much. Everything will be okay.

                        Kim

"Wow," Jack mumbled, quietly refolding the note and handing it back. He felt the words in his gut—maybe because he, too, had once gotten his heart broken with a shocking jolt.

Then the obvious question finally hit him. "But . . . why did you buy a bracelet for her?"

And that was when he realized Fletcher didn't seem the least bit fazed—by any of this. He'd relayed the whole story in the same matter-of-fact, wisdom-laced tone he always used. "Because she's coming back," he said now as easily as if his wife had just taken a stroll up the beach to look for sand dollars.

"You've heard from her then?" Jack ventured uncertainly.

But Fletcher shook his head, taking another bite from his sandwich.

Whereas Jack had pretty much forgotten about lunch at this point. He squinted slightly, lowering his chin. "Then . . . what makes you think so?"

"She loves me," Fletcher said simply, lifting a napkin to wipe crumbs from his mouth. "And you have to have faith."

Jack fiddled with a potato chip on the plate in front of him, and put forth his next question cautiously. Because he didn't want to be a downer, but . . . "Even in something you have no evidence for?"

"Isn't that what faith is?" Fletcher replied easily. "If you don't have faith in something, if you don't believe things can work out the way you want them to, then what do you have in life?"

Jack took that in. And fought with himself between wanting to explain to Fletcher that perhaps his hopes were unrealistic and impractical—and wanting to believe that maybe his simple sureness would be enough to bring her back somehow. Even though it had been two years. It sounded crazy, of course, but something about his certain attitude made Jack feel bad for doubting him.

That was when it hit Jack that Fletcher had a house here, had made a home here. "So you don't move around anymore?"

"Can't," he said after crunching a chip in his mouth. "We were here when she left. So this is where she'll come back to. If I go anywhere else, she won't be able to find me."

Jack resumed eating at this point, mainly because he needed a minute to quietly absorb all he'd just learned. He continued to feel torn inside—now between pitying Fletcher's sad denial and admiring his calm fortitude. He just couldn't decide which one made the most sense, especially since Fletcher had struck him as a pretty wise dude up to now.

"I know, I know," Fletcher said then, reading his thoughts, "I seem naïve. But whatever it is she's looking for, the road will bring her back to me. She said in her note that everything will be okay, and the only way everything will be okay is when she comes home—so that's how I know she's going to." Then he smiled out over the ocean as if he didn't have a care in the world. "Faith, my friend, that's what life is all about. You have to believe in what you want. Because why would you even want something if it wasn't meant to be yours? That's how I've lived my life and most of the ride for me has been . . . almost effortlessly smooth. This is but a hiccup. A bump in the path. There's something I'm supposed to learn, and when I do, that's when she'll come back and things will be normal again."

"What about . . . a new normal?" Jack dared to venture. "I mean, you have yourself a nice little home here, in a great place. You still have a great life as far as I can see. So . . . do you ever think about just making a new kind of normal for yourself instead of waiting for her to come back?"

Fletcher looked introspective as he considered Jack's words. "I suppose I've done that in a way. But nothing else is as normal as love. Nothing else is as good." Then he lowered his thinly bearded chin just slightly to add, "You shouldn't run from it."

Jack flinched, feeling accused. When had they started talking about *him* here? "Me? Who said I'm running from anything? I'm just on vacation here, man—I'm just taking it easy, trying to unwind."

"Then you shouldn't have come with a girl you're so clearly enamored of. Hard to unwind when you're fighting what your soul wants."

If Fletcher wasn't such a wise-seeming guy— it was something he gave off, almost like a scent, even now, after what Jack had just found out about him—Jack would have started getting pissed at this point. "How are you so sure you know what my soul wants, dude?"

But Fletcher brushed off the inquiry by saying, "The real question here is—why does anyone run from love?"

"Who says I'm running from—"

"Or whatever you feel for her. Because there's *something* there—a blind man could see that."

"Maybe it's complicated," Jack argued.

"I'm sure it is," Fletcher said. "But what if . . . what if you just shoved those complications aside? What if you just pretended they didn't exist? What would happen then? And how good might it be?"

And when Jack started to form a reply, Fletcher held up a hand to stop him, saying, "Don't answer me. Just think about it. Turn it over in your head and let yourself feel it. Because I know how amazing love can be, and if I were in your shoes, I wouldn't pass up the chance to explore that."

Then he pointed up the street. "There's a good ice cream place around the corner. I suggest we go grab a couple cones—what do you say?"

ANNA slid into the cracked vinyl booth at the Hungry Fisherman across the table from Christy. Christy had called her cell and gotten lucky—she was free for lunch. "What's your news?" Anna asked, wide-eyed.

Christy had filled her friend in on her consignment deals by phone a few days ago, so all she had to say now was, "It's selling! My jewelry is selling! Even at those crazy prices!"

And Anna beamed. "That's fantastic, Christy! I'm so happy for you! And you know what? Those prices aren't crazy if people are paying them."

Christy leaned her head slightly to one side, taking in that concept, and began to feel even more fulfilled. Then she told Anna the rest. "I stopped by both places just a little while ago to drop off some new jewelry and each has sold several pieces already, in just these past few days! And they were excited to get more." She stopped, sighed. "It's just so amazing to be appreciated for something I work hard at and love doing, you know?"

Anna smiled in understanding. "I've never been an artist or anything, but I feel the same way when someone compliments some part of the bed-and-breakfast that I remodeled or designed myself. And though he'd never admit it, I know when people love Duke's furniture, it really makes him feel good." Then she gave her head a playful tilt and leaned forward just a bit across the table. "So you're suddenly doing great with your jewelry—that's fabulous. But . . . what's up with Mr. Tall, Dark, and Hot?"

Christy bit her lip. "Well, to be honest, I'm not totally sure." Then she filled Anna in on what she'd missed, leaving out the embarrassing details, and concluding with, "But I guess I'm going to let it all go and just see where things lead. Hope he doesn't hurt my feelings again. Hope he gets that I'm a good person."

"How could he *not* get that?" Anna asked, her eyes softening. "And if he still doesn't, let me know because I might need to beat him up." After which she looked around the Hungry Fisherman. "That said, if I have any criticisms of you at all, it might be that you picked this restaurant." She lowered her voice. "It's kind of freaky. I mean, did you see the scary life-size fisherman at the door?"

Yet Christy just laughed. "It's kind of a wacky place, I know. But I've started getting weirdly attached to it."

Just then, Abner exited the kitchen wearing a plastic king's crown. And Anna silently switched her gaze from him back to Christy as if to say, *Come on, really?*

To which Christy replied by explaining, "That's Abner, the owner. He likes hats."

After they ate and Anna left to go meet Duke at the beach, Christy stuck around the Hungry Fisherman a little longer. The small lunch crowd had dwindled, and over time she'd come to find the rustic, seafaring ambience of the place surprisingly relaxing. Despite the statue of Abner—and, well, Abner himself.

After texting Grandpa Charlie to say hi, she did a search on her phone for local thrift shops, to stock up on her supplies of outdated jewelry. And she found several within easy driving distance. A few minutes later, she said goodbye to Polly near the front door.

Though as she opened it to step outside, a fluffy white cat came slinking in, weaving a path around her ankles. "Oh my—who are you?" she said, staring down at the affectionate kitty.

"Good heavens, shoo," Polly said, waving a hand down at the cat. "She's a stray we've been tryin' to get rid of—or, well, hopin' she wanders away, I guess. But it's hard to drive a cat away from a seafood restaurant, let me tell ya."

"She's certainly friendly enough," Christy remarked as the cat continued rubbing against her ankles, purring slightly.

"We've been callin' her Dinah," Polly said.

And a tingle ran down Christy's spine. "Because of the cat in Alice in Wonderland?" she asked. She recalled Alice owning a white cat named Dinah, and given all the ways her life seemed to echo the story lately, this seemed like too big of a coincidence. Talk about falling down the rabbit hole.

But Polly just shook her head, looking a little bewildered. "No, because she's always tryin' to get into the kitchen. So we named her from that old song—"I've Been Working on the Railroad"—because of the part about someone bein' in the kitchen with Dinah."

And as if to prove that Polly's answer was the more logical one, just then the cat took off like a bullet toward the swinging door that led into the kitchen. After which Polly yelled in that direction, "Cat coming!" and Christy heard a couple of the cooks begin to sing the line from the song.

"They'll grab her and put her out back with some scraps," Polly said, returning her attention to Christy. "Please don't tell people we let a cat in our kitchen. Business is slack enough as it is."

"Oh, I wouldn't," Christy said. "And it's nice of you to feed her."

Though Polly looked doubtful. "Keeps her hangin' around is what it does. But I don't have the heart to throw away food when she's hungry. I tried to get Reece over at the Happy Crab to take her, but he claims cats and iguanas don't mix."

"Well, Fifi seems like a lot to manage."

"Agreed. For the life of me, I don't know what he sees in that creature. A cat'd be a heck of a lot easier if you ask me." Then Polly got a scheming look in her eye, narrowing her gaze on Christy. "Wouldn't *you* like a nice cat?"

And Christy drew back slightly. "Who, me? I'm just here on vacation."

Yet Polly tilted her head. "Nothin' says the cat can't travel. Probably been through worse than a little trip."

Christy still balked, though. "The thing is—I'm broke. I can barely provide for myself, let alone a cat." And even if she was suddenly making unexpected money from her jewelry, she had a million other things to spend it on—like Grandpa

Charlie for one. And for another, a better life for herself.

Even if . . . the idea of having a cat around suddenly sounded kind of nice. She still didn't think a cat could ever complete her, but she couldn't help thinking of Amy back in Destiny—who would be pressing Christy to give the cat a loving home if she were here. If she ever got a cat, though, she wanted to be in a better, more stable position in life, where she could be a good cat mom, but . . . maybe someday.

"Well, you keep an ear out for anyone who might want a nice cat," Polly said, and Christy promised she would.

CHRISTY shoved her key into her door at the Happy Crab, turned the knob, and realized how happy it made her every single time it opened with ease—unlike her apartment door at home. Sometimes it really was the little things in life.

Or . . . maybe she was happy about more than the simple turn of a lock. She suddenly had a lot more to be happy about these days than she had in quite a while. She couldn't help her Grandpa financially yet, but seeing so much of him lately was good for her soul—and his, too, she thought. And she wasn't making a living from her jewelry, but achieving that dream seemed way less far-fetched than it had just a week ago. And she might have gone through a lot of pain and embarrassment with Jack, but . . . maybe that was over now.

"Hey, Alice—how was your day?" Jack greeted

her with a friendly grin as she stepped in the room.

She knew he was hoping to encounter the gentler, kinder Christy she'd been with him until the last few days. And, well, she was going to give him his wish, put the recent unpleasantness behind them. She smiled back—and then couldn't contain her enthusiasm. "It was pretty great. Some of my jewelry sold already! Like—hundreds of dollars' worth! And both shops were happy to get more."

He stood up, his own smile widening. "Wow—that's absolutely fantastic, honey!" And as he stepped forward to give her a warm hug, she realized how naturally he'd done it, that they knew each other so well now that a hug at a moment like this made total sense.

So she let herself hug him back, let herself feel how good and warm it was to be in his supportive embrace. The fact that her whole body tingled—that was just a perk. She still wasn't sure where things would go with Jack now, but she instinctively knew they'd be . . . better.

After that, she told him more about her day. He said he hadn't made it to Sunnymeade for lunch, but had instead ended up hanging out with Fletcher, the tightrope walker. Then he suggested they pick up the chicken salad sandwich for Grandpa Charlie, along with something for themselves as well, and go there for dinner instead. "Thought maybe we could take him out to one of the tables on the grounds, make kind of a picnic out of it."

Christy smiled at his thoughtfulness, and despite trying to be cool-headed about her change in attitude, it made her fall even a little more deeply in love with him. "I'm sure he would love that," she said. "And so would I."

"And after that," he went on, "maybe I can show you the beach I found today. It's near the one you like, but it's beyond where the shoreline twists away from the road. It's private and kind of . . . romantic. I thought we could take a sunset walk there. If you want."

Okay, wow. Jack was suddenly using words like *romantic*? As if romance weren't something to be feared and avoided at all costs lest someone get attached? Maybe things had changed even more than she knew. And . . . well, maybe she should even, realistically, be a little afraid of that herself now, afraid to trust in it, afraid he'd pull back on it again in the end.

But at the moment, it was hard to look into those beautiful blue eyes and do anything but . . . believe. She was learning to have courage, right?

And so, that easily, one more time, she did it— she chose to be brave and have faith. She took a deep breath and stepped out onto her own personal tightrope as she said, softly, "Yeah. I want."

"A pleasant walk, a pleasant talk.
Along the briny beach . . ."

Lewis Carroll, *Through the Looking Glass*

Chapter 15

THE SKY over Coral Cove Beach blazed orange and pink with streaks of purple shot through like threads in a brightly colored fabric. Christy and Jack had walked from the Happy Crab, both in upbeat moods after a pleasant dinner with Grandpa Charlie and the short drive back to the motel. And Christy felt better than she had in a long time. Trusting in her talent, and in her boldness, was making her dreams start to come true—she could feel it in her heart. And maybe trusting in Jack would pay off in the same way.

He truly seemed different tonight—more like the relaxed Jack she'd first met, but also . . . new in a way. The man who walked up the beach beside her now seemed . . . unafraid to let his affection for her show. And it shone in his eyes every time their gazes met—something sweet and wonderful that hadn't ever been there before, or at least not in such an open way.

They walked barefoot at the water's edge, letting the cool gulf surf wash up over their toes before it rushed back out again. They both carried their shoes, and with the same hand that held her beaded sandals, Christy bunched the gauzy fabric of her long skirt to keep the breeze from blowing it too high.

When they came upon the nightly celebration at the pier, they wordlessly bypassed it, staying near the water, walking beneath the wooden structure to continue on their way. Though in the distance Christy spotted a silhouette of Fletcher McCloud balanced atop his tightrope and Tom Petty could be heard singing "Learning to Fly" from a radio somewhere.

"I think you'd like Fletcher's house," Jack said as they ventured onto the more windswept stretch of sand beyond the pier. Christy had always liked walking this part of the beach when she was younger—but with Jack, she already loved it even more. They'd left the small Coral Cove crowds behind that fast and this stretch of sand instantly felt like their own private little piece of the coastline.

"I'm sure I would," she said, peering out over the serene view before her. "His little cottage sounds perfect." Jack had already described it to her earlier.

"I can't decide what I think about Fletcher, though," he said.

"What do you mean?"

"Remember when he bought that bracelet for his wife?"

"Of course," she answered.

"Well, today at his house I found out she left him two years ago."

Christy pulled up short in the sand, stunned. "What?"

"I know—crazy, right?" he said. "And there's a whole pile of things he's bought for her since she's been gone. Because he's absolutely sure she's coming back. And . . . not, like, just *hoping* she is. But he's positive. In this calm way that almost made *me* think she was, too."

Christy tried to wrap her head around this new information. Indeed, there was a quiet sense of insight about the man—it seemed to vibrate out of him. In her brief encounters with him, he'd struck her as someone who had life all figured out and she'd almost envied him. And when he'd bought the bracelet, she'd envisioned him and his wife sharing an easy, fulfilling existence together.

"What do you think?" Jack asked. "Could a guy who seems so . . . at peace with everything around him be wrong about this? Is he just deluding himself?"

"I don't know," Christy replied, "but it makes me sad. That even a guy like him, who seemed so together, has such big problems."

"Guess everybody does," Jack said with a shrug. "Or they've at least come through some."

And Christy turned to look at him. "Have *you* ever . . . had anyone leave you?" she asked. She knew she was prying, but surely they knew each other well enough by now that she could pry a little.

Though he hesitated, kept his eyes ahead as they walked. They'd just passed an old boat that had been pulled high up on the sand, and in the distance a small pier that had seen better days stretched out over the water.

"Yeah," he finally replied. Then added, "Well, in a manner of speaking."

Her next glance over at him revealed a troubled expression, a knit brow. And she didn't want to make that worse, but his answer begged the question. "A manner of speaking?"

His voice came out quieter than usual. "Well . . . she cheated on me. And so we split up. But it *felt* like being left."

Christy nodded, absorbing the hurt in Jack's voice, the gravelly tone that let it leak through. *She'd* shared painful things with *him* before, but it struck her that this was the first truly personal thing *he'd* told *her*. She'd trusted him enough all along to let some personal things out—but now she felt him trusting her in return. Finally.

And good Lord—what woman in her right mind would cheat on Jack? Without weighing the move, she followed the instinct to reach out her empty hand and clasp his. "I'm sorry," she said. "That sounds awful."

He simply nodded, said nothing more—but she could still feel the pain he clearly wasn't comfortable with.

And maybe that explained a lot about his actions with her. And made her feel even more forgiving. Jack just always seemed like such an easygoing guy. She'd never stopped to imagine that anything horrible had ever happened to him.

But maybe *everybody* went through bad things. And some people just wore their scars more invisibly than others.

"It's in the past," he said, implying that he'd left it there. And of course she wanted to know more about what had happened—but if he didn't want to talk about it anymore, that was okay. For now, she was touched that he'd shared even this much.

And she was holding his hand now. And he was holding hers back. She hadn't planned that but couldn't help thinking it was a happy by-product of their conversation. Especially since neither of them seemed to be letting go.

"Anybody ever leave *you*, Alice?" he asked.

"My parents," she said—then flinched, gasped, almost unable to believe the words had fallen from her lips. Guilt coursed through her veins as she rushed to explain. "I mean, I know they didn't leave me on purpose and it's not the same thing as being left in a romantic sense like with Fletcher's wife, but for some reason that just popped into my head. I shouldn't have said it, though," she concluded quietly.

Yet he replied, just as softly, "It's okay."

The beach had curved completely away from the road now, leaving Christy to feel all the more isolated with Jack. But in a safe way. And that was when it hit her. *He makes me feel safe.* And it seemed important. Because she'd felt that way so seldom since the death of her parents.

"Is it?" she asked. The surf was calmer here, the bend of the land creating a small bay, and the water lapped more gently over their feet as they walked. Then she stopped and looked over at him. "Is it okay to feel abandoned by someone who never meant to? Who never would have if they could have helped it?" She swallowed back her fears and voiced thoughts that had perhaps hung in the back of her mind for a long while now. "I mean, I know they loved me more than anything. I know it wasn't their fault. But it's hard to suddenly be left so alone in the world, and with nothing. No money to bury them with. No pictures to remember them by. No answers about why it had to happen this way."

Oh crap. She'd just spilled her guts, big time. She'd said things she didn't even know she felt until now. She'd completely bared herself to him, only in a different way this time—one that was possibly even more revealing.

But that was when Jack whispered, "Come here," and she realized his arms were closing around her, pulling her into a warm, intoxicating embrace. And it felt so good that she simply let herself be swept up in it, let her arms close around his waist, let her face rest against his chest where she could hear the steady beat of his heart. "I don't want you to feel alone, honey."

Though after a moment of comfort wrapped in Jack's arms, she still felt compelled to lift her head, look up at him, and admit, "It was still an awful thing to say, though."

But Jack simply told her, "No. Just no. It really is okay."

And then his eyes dropped from her eyes to her lips, and a familiar heat soared through her just before he lowered his mouth onto hers.

Christy succumbed to the kiss immediately, with her whole heart. No kiss in her life had ever been more welcome. It was at once a sweet escape from life's troubles and a perfect celebration of the things that had been going right lately. So much passion lay stored up inside her that there was no fighting it, only giving in to it and relishing it. She kissed him back with everything inside her, so thankful to be with him in this way again—and yearning for more.

Jack's strong hands roamed her back, the curve of her waist, her hips, caressing and molding her flesh within his fingers. When Jack touched her, she somehow became every inch a hot, desirable woman—no self-doubt, no shyness—and she followed the impulse to press her palms to his broad chest, digging the tips of her nails in just slightly through his T-shirt as their kisses deepened, the want stretching hotly between them.

When Jack's palms curved over her ass and pulled that part of her closer to him, his erection connected with the juncture of her thighs and a small whimper escaped her. It broke the kiss at last, but she couldn't even begin to think about stopping—she looped her arms around his neck and followed her body's urge to grind her hips against his. His grip on her bottom tightened and he hauled her against him harder and she heard them both panting as she sank deeper and deeper into her sexiest cravings.

His breath warmed her cheek and she found herself nibbling at his earlobe. He let out a short groan in response. After another round of fevered kisses, Jack's hands drifted upward, onto her breasts.

A soft sea breeze wafted over them just then, lifting her hair, and she could almost feel it further hardening her nipples, along with his touch. He stroked at the peaks through her tank top with his thumbs, eliciting soft moans each time he brushed across them.

"I want to kiss these," he murmured against her hair.

Every molecule of her body tingled with excitement and lush need. "I want that, too," she breathed. "Please."

The sun had long since set, the sky fading from deepest purple to black, with the moon rising above. And as Jack removed her top over her head, she took in details about the moment: the sound of the rushing tide somewhere behind her, the salty breeze kissing her skin, the sense of blessed seclusion. Her feet sank into soft, dry sand—at some point during all the kissing, they'd moved higher up onto the beach, away from the water.

And then, mmm, Jack's hands came back to her body—one curving around the side of her breast through her lacy bra, the fingers of the other slipping beneath the bra strap on her opposite shoulder. She wanted to give herself to him more than she wanted to breathe.

But then—oh God—something inside her flashed back on the last time she'd gotten this heated up with Jack . . . and she pulled her palms away from where they lightly played at his chest, closing them firmly over both his hands where they touched her. "Jack," she said, her voice coming out ragged.

"What, baby? What is it?" He sounded just as ready as she did. But she still had to be sure. She couldn't put herself at that kind of risk again.

"If . . . if we're . . ." Crap, she couldn't think how to say it. "Just please don't stop this time," she breathed desperately.

"Oh Christy, baby—I'm not. I won't. I swear it. Stopping's the last thing on my mind."

"Because . . . because . . . I just can't take that again. And we don't have to . . . define this. We don't have to put some kind of label on it. We can just see how things go, take it as it comes. The main thing right now is that . . . I don't want to wait anymore. I want to be with you, Jack. I want to know what you feel like inside me."

She heard his low intake of breath, felt his grip tighten slightly on her breast beneath her hand. "Aw honey," he murmured, low and hot. "You're gonna find out. We're *both* gonna find out."

And that was all the assurance Christy needed to let go with Jack one more time. Everything had truly changed now—she could feel that with every beat of her heart. He was with her in this now, not pulling back. And it was an amazing feeling, an amazing place to be with another person.

Jack bent to kiss her again, even as he pushed the bra straps from both of her shoulders. And she wordlessly reached up behind her to undo the hook—this time letting it fall away from her with no hesitation, dropping to the sand at their bare feet.

His eyes caressed her breasts, as potent as any touch, and they practically pulsed with pleasure and desire. "Aw damn, honey—you're beautiful," he said—and no words had ever made her feel more vibrant and alive. Who needed money when you could have this instead? This man, this moment, this feeling.

She tried to form a response, but she was simply too turned on. So only one word echoed from her lips in a soft whimper. "Please." *Please touch. Please kiss.*

And he seemed to know exactly what that one word meant without her saying more because after a scintillatingly hot look into her eyes, he reached both hands up to cup her breasts. A jagged sound of pleasure left her throat as she surged with moisture in her panties.

As he bent to rake his tongue over one beaded pink tip, a moan erupted from her throat and a shiver ran the length of her body. And when his mouth closed fully over her hardened nipple, beginning to suck, her desire soared, expanding outward from her breasts like long, lush fingers, reaching, stretching all through her. The juncture of her thighs ached—heavy, hungry, desperate to be filled. And when he pulled back, the sea breeze wafted over the moisture he'd left on her flesh, making her feel kissed by the wind, as well.

"I want to lay you down," he rasped, and she liked that idea, too. And as his hands closed over her waist, they sank to their knees together in the sand.

She pushed at his T-shirt, whispering, "Take this off." And together they removed the soft fabric over his head, Christy tossing it aside and pressing her palms back into his now gloriously bare chest. She'd been falling in love with that sexy chest and stomach of his every single day she'd been on the beach with him wearing only swim trunks, and to now get to touch it, explore it, felt like finally getting to play with a long-wanted—and very sexy—toy.

When he finally lay her all the way back onto the bed of sand, she went willingly, ever-so-ready for more. And what followed was the closest she'd ever come to heaven.

Jack kissed his way down her neck, onto her chest—and then he kissed his way thoroughly across both breasts even while he sensually kneaded them. His tongue swirled around one nipple and then the other, until finally his mouth closed fully back over her breast and he began to suckle once more, the sensation shooting straight into her panties.

"Oh God," she breathed. "Oh Jack. You make me feel so, so good."

As he sucked and nibbled at her nipples, his hands slid up under her skirt, his touch skimming across her thighs—until he began to tug at her panties. She lifted without hesitation and soon felt the delicious slide of elastic and fabric down over her hips and lower. Even with her skirt still on, having his hands beneath it and her panties gone made her feel gloriously naked with him, for him.

Once the panties had been kicked off into the sand, his warm hands returned, this time more playfully, leisurely grazing her outer thighs, hips. She shivered in his grasp and wanted to be bold enough to reach up, undo his shorts—but somehow, in that way, she still felt a little shy. It was easier to just let him take charge and guide her through this. Despite being undeniably aware of her lack of her experience, putting Jack in control made her feel comfortable, and safe.

He was kissing her again, his tongue pressing between her lips as his fingers sank into her wetness below. A sharp cry of pleasure left her, and then she relaxed into it, beginning to move instinctively against his sure touch.

"So wet, baby," he practically growled against her ear—then lowered a delicate kiss just below it, making her tingle all the more.

"You make me that way," she heard herself say in a near purr, her lips raking across the stubble on his jaw. "All the time."

A guttural sound erupted from him, and even though she hadn't quite planned to admit that, she liked exciting him.

When he stroked more deeply between her legs, she clung to him, giving herself over to every sensation, every response he brought out in her. And she realized that maybe this was one perk of sex with Jack not having happened too fast. Because she knew him now, really *knew* him, she could be even more open with him—another way she felt safe, being so intimate with him.

Soon he thrust two fingers up inside her, ripping another small, heated cry from her throat. Her lips trembled against his neck as she panted her pleasure, and the yearning to connect their bodies in that even deeper way raged within her.

Enough that she finally reached for his belt.

His breath grew ragged again as he helped her undo his pants, and then—oh God—he took her hand and gently pressed her palm to his stretched cotton briefs directly where they covered his incredible hardness. The feel of him, the size of him, threatened to overwhelm her senses. "You feel so . . . big," she murmured without planning.

He gave her a sexy grin to say, "You make me that way. All the time."

She felt her eyes widen on his. But her voice came soft, airy. "Really?"

He nodded, looking unbelievably hot. She took in all of him—those gorgeous eyes, that darkly stubbled jaw, the hair that still needed to be cut. And one more unplanned utterance left her lips. "No more waiting, Jack. Please. Inside me. Now."

A low, lustful groan echoed from him and Christy's desire rose to a fever pitch as she waited for him to urgently extract a wallet from his back pocket, pull out a small square packet, and roll on the condom. She let her eyes drift down to watch, biting her lower lip in anticipation, especially since it was the first time she'd seen that part of him.

And then finally his weight settled between her open thighs, her skirt pushed high around her hips, and she took a deep breath as he began to enter her.

Oh God, she wanted him—but it was tight, and it hurt. She closed her eyes, clenched her teeth, clung to him.

His breath came warm on her neck as he whispered, "Just relax, honey. Relax."

And then he was kissing her cheek, and then her forehead, and then her lips, ever so gently—and she did relax, and her body began to open to him more, allowing him to sink into her until she was full, full, full—filled to the brink in a way that brought tears of joy to her eyes because it felt so very right.

"Oh God, Jack," she whispered softly.

"Is it okay, baby? Feel good?"

"Uh huh," was all she could say at first. But then she managed, "More than good. Amazing. Oh God."

"*You're* amazing," he told her, and something in the low whisper reached down into Christy's soul and told her he truly meant that. And she wasn't sure anyone had ever thought she was amazing before.

When Jack began to move in her, it was jarring at first—though she'd been with Kyle, this somehow felt new all over again. Yet then she relaxed into it once more, shut her eyes, and accepted the pleasure. It grew deeper with every rhythmic thrust he delivered. And for all the pain and frustration she'd endured getting to this point with Jack, now, making love with him on the beach, everything felt perfect. Their struggles to get to where they were, to this astounding place in time, had made it all the more special.

She didn't hold back when his drives into her moisture began to tear hot whimpers and cries from her. She didn't hold back when her body lifted of its own volition to meet his. To connect with him like this was all she had imagined and more.

She'd always heard that sex on the beach was uncomfortable, but she didn't feel that way at all. The soft sand created the perfect pillowy bed beneath her body, and the sound of the surf and the salt-scented air only made the experience all the more wonderful. "I love being with you like this here," she told him. Coral Cove had always been special to her, but now more than ever. No matter what happened between her and Jack going forward, this moment would always mean something to her.

"Aw baby," he murmured deeply, "I love being with you, too." And then he kissed her, slowing his movements, slowing *everything*, and somehow making her feel it even more.

"I'm so glad I asked you to kick down my door," she said, thinking back on how far they'd come.

He cast down a sexy grin. "Mmm—me too, honey."

"And I'm glad you stuck around afterward," she added on a labored breath.

"A damn good move on my part," he agreed.

But then the little smiles they were sharing died away as Jack resumed deeper thrusts into her waiting body and as she rose to meet them. When their eyes connected now it was with the heat of shared lust, the way their bodies were fusing.

"You want to get on top?" he asked, a fresh glint of an animal desire burning in his eyes.

"Huh?" she breathed. She could barely think at this point.

And he said, "I want to make you come."

She sucked in her breath, somehow so replete with pleasure already that she'd actually forgotten that part. "This is enough," she said.

Then watched as his face took on a puzzled expression. "But . . ."

She shook her head lightly against the sand. "Trust me, this is about all I can handle at the moment. Nothing against a good orgasm, believe me—but right now, I just want to keep feeling you inside me, exactly the way we are."

He continued to hold her gaze, and when he began thrusting more deeply into her welcoming flesh again, it felt like a hot, sweet, powerful reward.

They continued that way for a wonderfully long while, until finally Jack said, "God, I'm gonna come in you, Christy." And somehow she opened her heart to him even more, overjoyed to have taken him there as she absorbed his every last stroke.

And when he finally went still, his weight settling gently onto hers, she said, "I love you, Jack."

Oh crap. She'd just put a label on it. A really big one! It had just somehow slipped out! Because it was so undeniably true. But she hadn't meant to tell him, for God's sake! "Oh Lord, pretend I didn't say that," she rushed. "It just snuck out. Please don't let it ruin this."

Jack stayed painfully quiet for a long, still moment. They no longer looked at each other—his head rested near her shoulder and she peered up at the stars millions of miles in the distance, wishing she could snap her fingers and suddenly be that far away, too.

Oh God, how had she let herself say that? Her heart beat faster in panic and she wondered if he could feel it or if he was too busy still being as horrified at her words as she was.

And then, finally, he said, "Did you mean it?"

Oh God, what to say? Now her heartbeat tripled. And with no time to think, she simply opted for the truth. "Yes, but . . ."

"Good," he said. " 'Cause I love you, too, honey. I love you, too."

Alice was so astonished that she
could not speak for a minute: it quite
seemed to take her breath away.

Lewis Carroll, *Through the Looking Glass*

Chapter 16

As UTTER astonishment flooded Christy's expression, Jack realized what he'd said. He'd more
been thinking it, feeling it, than actually meaning to say it. But he understood that she'd been in
the same boat and so he'd just let it out—without
much consideration for what this meant, for the
questions it opened up.

But now it was out there, for both of them, and
Jack reached another conclusion: He had no regrets. He loved her. And he was finally ready—to
believe in her, to let himself go there. He was finally ready to do the thing he'd feared he'd never
be ready for again—trust.

And if she loved him, too, well . . . how freaking
amazing was that? He hadn't really seen any of
this coming, but now that it was here, he thought
it seemed almost like . . . destiny. After all, he'd

been fighting it from the start—he'd harbored doubts, he'd stayed wary, he'd pushed his feelings away time and again. So if he'd managed to get through all *that* and change his mind, and if she'd stayed patient and forgiving all this time and still wanted him . . . hell, giving in to it felt good. And not just the sex, but the rest of it, too. The part that made the sex . . . more than sex. And what they'd just done had definitely been more than sex.

Finally, he let out a laugh. "Don't look so surprised."

She just blinked up at him, looking pretty and flushed beneath him in the moonlight. "It's hard not to. I mean . . . you haven't *seemed* like somebody who loves me."

The next short chuckle that echoed from his throat was a little more self-deprecating. He lifted a hand to her face, gently brushed a wavy blond tendril from her cheek. "I'm sorry, honey—I know I've been . . . fighting this. And . . ." He lowered his chin, raised his eyebrows teasingly. "You know I actually had a pretty good reason." He didn't mean to make her feel bad, but it was the truth and he wanted to keep things real here.

She lowered her gaze, but then met his again, her expression soft and sweet—just like all of her. "Yeah—it was bad timing for me to meet you at the one moment in my life when I was doing something that didn't seem totally . . . aboveboard." Then she bit her lip and peered up at him more pointedly. "But you aren't worried anymore? About . . . getting attached."

He nodded.

"Why?"

He tilted his head, still thinking through it. "It's just . . . getting to know you. And learning about your life, and who you are. I liked you from the start, Christy. A lot. You were . . . all I could think about," he admitted.

Her eyes widened on him prettily. "Really?"

Another short nod. "But . . . I've been burned before. Trusting somebody. And it made me wary. Can you understand that? And forgive me for . . . everything I've done wrong up to now?"

Now it was she who nodded—and said, "I'm sorry someone hurt you, Jack. Is it . . . something you want to tell me more about now?"

And for the first time tonight, Jack hesitated. Because . . . how could he tell her all of it? Beyond the simple part about having been cheated on— where would he even begin? And yet he knew he owed it to her—after all, hadn't he just told himself he wanted to keep things real? "Well, you've probably already figured out . . . it's not the easiest thing for me to talk about."

She nodded once more, her eyes brimming with compassion, and pressed her palm softly to his bare chest. "You can tell me anything and I'll understand."

And he felt that. Yet still his gut churned. This night was too damn good—he didn't want to ruin it. "How about not tonight?" he whispered. "How about tonight . . . we just enjoy each other?"

And—aw God—he loved hearing her soft little intake of breath in response; it moved all through him.

And no matter what she claimed, he still wanted to make her come.

So without waiting for a reply, he lowered his mouth to hers for more long, slow kissing. Her light, delicate moan reached all the way into his soul, urging him onward—and soon his kisses left her sweet lips to move down onto her slender neck and then to the smooth skin of her freshly tanned shoulders.

As he rained still more kisses across the curves of her pale breasts, outlined in tan by the shape of her bikini top, he paused to suck on their puckered tips. Her impassioned sighs made him harder than he'd already gotten, and everything in his body tightened with hunger. Damn, she was beautiful. And when her fingers began to thread through his hair, grazing his scalp, he suckled all the deeper, harder, and one hand drifted instinctively between her thighs.

He loved when she parted them automatically— loved that he could feel her giving herself to him completely, wanting the same things *he* wanted. He'd spent too long resisting this—and it was nice to be on the same page now, both opening to the desire together.

Heady whimpers and hot little cries rose from her throat, fueling his need as he stroked his fingers through her wetness, focusing on the swollen point he knew brought her the most pleasure.

But he didn't want only his hand there—he wanted to *kiss* her there, wanted to love her with his mouth. And so he left her breasts, dropping tender kisses across her tan stomach and next to her navel, and it was just as he pushed two fingers up inside her moist warmth that he raked his tongue across the parted flesh between her legs.

She yelped, jerked, but he pressed his other hand warmly to her hip to still her, calm her.

And then she relaxed into it. And he licked that sensitive spot again, again, until her pelvis began to rise against the pressure of his mouth in rhythm with his ministrations, moving against his eager tongue more and more fervently.

His cock had grown rock hard again now, his whole body responding to her pleasure. He wanted to make her feel so damn good—he wanted to make her feel better than she'd ever felt in her life. And it filled him with a masculine pride he hadn't expected to know he was only the second man to be with her and that, in fact, he probably *was* making her feel better than she ever had. And he intended to do a lot of that.

"Oh . . . oh God, Jack," she murmured in a haze of excitement he could feel wrapping around him. It set every nerve ending on edge, made him hunger still more to make her explode into orgasm.

Now her fingers practically clawed at his scalp, but he didn't mind—he liked it. His own fingertips dug into her ass as he used both mouth and tongue on her, and she moved faster and more powerfully against him until finally she tensed, then cried out as she came. Hot satisfaction flowed through Jack—after all the frustration he'd put her through, somehow this felt like a way to make up for it.

When finally the orgasm finished, she said, "Jack, please," and—mmm, God—she sounded desperate, her voice heated.

"Please what, baby?" he whispered against her skin, then lowered a soft kiss to the spot just below her belly button.

"In me again. Now."

Oh. Okay. Definitely. And he didn't waste a second before sliding up alongside her body, using his hands to firmly spread her legs once more, and sliding smoothly into her, all the way to the hilt. Aw, God, yes—she was so snug, warm. Her deep gasp told him it felt just as good to her as it did to him.

And funny—but he felt like their bodies had been apart longer than they really had, like he'd been waiting for this, aching for her. Maybe it was just soothing the ache he'd been trying to push down all along, all over again. *Maybe it'll always be that way. Maybe we'll always be filled with that hungry need. Maybe with her, it'll never get normal, never get average.*

He didn't know where those thoughts came from—only that he liked them. And that he believed with Christy maybe he could really have that, and it made him glad all over again that he'd finally given in to what he really wanted.

This is the real thing. And the past doesn't matter. This is safe. This is special. And . . . this time it can last.

Following his animal urges, he moved in her hot and wild, thrusting hard, hard, hard. Until the time came when he needed to go slower, to rest a little and rebuild his strength—and that's when he whispered more sweet things to her about loving her, loving to be inside her, loving to kiss her and touch her.

She whispered back that she loved him, too. And then she told him this was the most amazing night of her entire life. And that "you take away everything bad."

And then he couldn't hold back anymore and he came inside her, thinking it might just be the most amazing night of *his* life, too. When he'd least expected it. But then it hit him that was when most of the important stuff usually came along.

Only then something *not* so good hit him. "Aw shit. Honey, I'm so sorry—I was so excited that I forgot a condom." Damn, he'd never done that in his life. "But I promise I'm safe. You don't have anything to worry about."

And she simply said, "I know. I trust you."

And he trusted her, too.

And as he eased away to lie beside her in the sand, the cool sea breeze wafting over them, he thought he could easily stay here like this with her forever.

For Christy, the following days and nights were blissful.

In addition to relaxing with Jack on the beach, they spent time in a variety of other ways, too.

One afternoon, they drove to area thrift shops and Christy found some amazing old pieces of costume jewelry, cheap. And in between other activities, she found time to make some new items for consignment, usually working in the evening, in the room, while Jack looked at his laptop.

They hung out with Grandpa Charlie at Sunnymeade and he told them funny stories about Christy's dad as a kid that she'd never heard before. Twice they picked up dinner and had an evening picnic with him, one night even inviting Ron the Nurse to join them out on the lawn for fried chicken. When Jack broke out the camera and started taking pictures, he reminded her, "New pictures for new memories," and she smiled. Seemed all kinds of new memories were being made on this trip.

Another evening John and Nancy Romo invited them to their cottage near the ocean for a cookout, allowing them to spend more time with Anna and Duke. And it turned out the Romos lived only a couple of streets away from Fletcher McCloud. Jack was right—Christy adored all the little pastel beach houses Jack had told her about, and after grilling out, they sat in white Adirondack chairs around a fire pit on the beach roasting marshmallows for s'mores.

She and Jack snuggled, sharing one of the big white chairs, and later, Anna pulled her aside to quietly say, "Seems like things are going well with him now, yes?" And Christy assured her they were, and couldn't help thinking it seemed like almost *everything* was going well for her these days. And she wasn't sure exactly how that had happened, but she wasn't complaining.

Christy asked Mrs. Romo if she wouldn't like a nice white cat, and Anna joined her in prodding after she heard about Dinah at the Hungry Fisherman, but Nancy declined. Christy also asked several of the nurses at Sunnymeade, along with the stained-glass artist, Tamra, when they saw her the following night at the Sunset Celebration. And she asked Fletcher, too—who said, "I like cats, but I can't. My wife's allergic."

When, in response, Christy exchanged looks with Jack, Fletcher just laughed and said, "I know, I know—but she'll be home soon." And Christy saw what Jack meant—something in the easy way he said it almost convinced her it was true.

Reece Donovan invited Christy and Jack to go out on his catamaran snorkeling in the small bed of coral about a half mile offshore that gave Coral Cove its name. Christy had seen the vessel docked behind the motel, but hadn't realized it belonged to Reece until he explained that he sometimes took tourists snorkeling, and that Happy Crab guests went for free. "Since you're the only guests right now, you'll have the coral and the fish all to yourselves."

Although Christy felt bad that business seemed lacking at both the Happy Crab and the Hungry Fisherman, she and Jack enjoyed a great day with Reece on the water, complete with lunch.

Of course, the best parts of those days for Christy were actually the nights, usually after they returned to "the Crab," as they'd started calling it. They now shared the same bed, and Christy loved that Jack couldn't keep his hands off her. Sex, sleep, sex, sleep—that was how most nights went, and Christy always found herself sleepy but happy the next day. Fortunately, it was easy to squeeze in a nap on the beach.

Late Friday afternoon, Christy paid a visit to Grandpa Charlie on her own to drop off the paperback mysteries he'd requested she get for him. She'd pushed his wheelchair out onto the lawn and now sat on a wrought iron bench next to the chair. "I'm so happy, Grandpa," she told him. Then she let out a replete sigh of joy, just basking in it.

"I can't tell you how glad I am about that, my grandgirl," he said on a laugh. "You and Jack have gotten past your differences and moved things along to where they *should* be—am I right?"

She hadn't told him that—she hadn't talked to him about her relationship with Jack since explaining she'd let Jack think she was only interested in money—but she guessed her grandfather had seen the two of them together enough this week that it was obvious. "Yes, you are," she informed him with a smile.

Another chuckle echoed from Grandpa Charlie's throat. "I knew that Jack was a good egg and would come to his senses."

But then she bit her lip, remembering the only downside to the whole situation—well, the only downside to her whole life right now. "I'm just sorry I can't figure out a way to help you stay here, though. Somehow I thought if I could make money selling jewelry that it would help you as much as me, but now that it's happening, I'm realizing that even at the high prices its going for, the earnings just can't add up quick enough."

He raked a hand down through the air, absolving her. "Was never your problem and I regret ever lettin' you feel it was. It'll work out however God intends," he said. "But nothin' could make me happier than to see you in love with a good fella. That's more important than money any day of the week, darlin'."

And though Christy's heart still ached for her grandpa, she understood now how true that was. Or . . . well, she'd always understood it. But she'd just gotten sidetracked for a little while. And it would be easy to blame Bethany for that, but Christy knew her friend had meant well, and she *had* let herself be talked into the ill-fated plan.

As for Grandpa Charlie, she decided she had no choice but to look at it the way *he* did, only with a more optimistic spin. "I'm just going to believe," she told him, reaching out to squeeze his hand, "that some kind of miracle will happen and fix everything. Because miracles don't seem so impossible to me lately."

CHARLIE watched Christy exit the room, aware how much brighter her presence made the place. He'd never seen his granddaughter so elated. And he hoped her happiness lasted. It could be fleeting, that kind of joy, based on being in love. People changed. People had secrets. And . . . some people could have the best of intentions but manage to ruin things by thinking they knew every damn thing.

He wasn't usually a cynical man. Or a self-deprecating one, either. But that last thought took him back once more to that long, hot summer in

Destiny that he'd so often revisited in his mind lately. How smart he'd thought he was at eighteen. How wise and practical. But maybe he was too hard on himself. The life he'd led up to then—humble parents, farm life, small town far away from anything exciting—had *taught* him to be practical. *Too* practical, it had turned out.

Yet there had been those few sweet, sultry days that summer of 1954—those few short, wholly glorious, wholly frightening days—when he hadn't been practical at all.

His father's back hadn't healed quickly. And the heat wave of all heat waves continued to bake the Midwest. In Destiny, the heat had come with drought.

Susan's husband spent his days in distant fields attempting to irrigate as best he could. And Charlie had gone on laboring on the barn by himself, sawing and hammering from sunup 'til sundown, sawing and hammering until his hands were blistered from extra hours and trying to work hard enough to make up for his father's absence. And also trying to keep his frustrations at bay.

Everything inside him burned for Susan, hotter and hotter, seeming to rise right along with the temperatures. When he saw her, those were the worst moments. And—at the same time—the best ones, too.

The tension between them when she brought his lunch each day was palpable. And now that he worked such long hours, she'd taken to bringing him dinner, and cold drinks throughout the day as well. She didn't say much, but she didn't have to. When their eyes met, everything they weren't saying was plain to see—and feel.

By the start of August, the structure was coming together, beginning to look like a barn. A few more days and he'd be ready to start putting on the roof.

He stood back surveying his own work late one afternoon when her voice came from behind him. "I told him it should be red."

He turned to look at her. She wore a yellow gingham dress and was as beautiful as ever, her hair drawn up into a ponytail, likely due to the heat—but he liked the way it allowed him to see her slender neck. He wanted to kiss it. Though he had no idea what she was talking about. "What should be red?"

"The barn," she replied. "I said you should paint it."

He tilted his head, still not understanding. "Don't believe paintin' it was part of the estimate."

She hesitated, and he could feel her weighing her next words, deciding how much to say. "I know," she told him. "But you'll be done soon. If he pays you to paint it, you'll have more to do."

He kept his gaze steady on her. "And . . . ?"

"And . . . I could still bring you lunch each day. Watch you work. For a while longer."

Charlie had trouble catching his breath as he absorbed her words. He didn't know how to reply. Because she'd been the one to run away when he'd tried to talk about whatever invisible thing lay between them. But now she wasn't running.

When he didn't answer, she added, "I'll be sad

when you're not here anymore. You make me less lonely, even if we don't talk a lot, and . . ."

"And . . . ?" he asked her once more.

"And . . . I think about you. At night." Now her voice came hushed, like *she* was having trouble breathing, too.

And in the course of a few short seconds, a million things raced through Charlie's mind. *Life is short. He's miles away. It's hot as hell. She looks fresh as a breeze. I need to kiss her more than I need air in my lungs. Maybe it's wrong. But it's wrong that she's with him, too.* She was talking about red, but he saw shades of gray. And progressed to other questions. *Will she slap me? Will she run again? Or will she take me to heaven?*

And then there seemed nothing else to do but follow his instincts, the urge that had been burning him up from the inside out, consuming him for weeks now. It only required two steps forward. After which he reached out, grabbed her hand. So soft. Or maybe his had just hardened from all the work this summer.

But either way, everything about her struck him as soft and perfect and feminine as he boldly curved his other hand around the nape of that lovely bare neck—and kissed her.

It wasn't a sweet kiss—it wasn't the slow, romantic meetings of mouths you saw at the picture show. It was wild and hungry, rough and real— and she was kissing him back. Sweet baby Jesus, she was kissing him back.

That set off even more untamed need inside him, to know she was in this with him, feeling every bit of it, too, and giving in to it—and it spurred him to pull her closer. He felt all the more connected to her, forgetting where he was, forgetting the hot sun that blasted down on them, forgetting she had a husband and that this was surely the most illicit thing either of them had ever done. There was only the hot kissing, the touching, the hands that began to roam, explore. There was only the yearning he couldn't push down and had quit trying to anyway.

There was nowhere in the world Charlie would rather have been than standing on the baked brown earth on a farm outside Destiny, Ohio kissing Susan for all he was worth. And despite that, despite the fevered heat of it all, he was trying his damnedest to be a gentleman, not move things too fast here, not push her. But fighting the urges grew useless—he'd been fighting them for too long already. And when he could no longer resist the desire to slide his palm over the gingham print that covered her ripe breast, she gasped—soft, pretty, excited—and let him. Let him squeeze and mold her in his hand as they kissed some more.

Though a sound—the distant hum of a tractor from somewhere far enough away and yet still too close—brought back their reality.

"Aw, God, Susan," he rasped between kisses. "You don't belong with him. You belong with . . . somebody like me."

He held her in a gripping embrace; her hands pressed deliciously onto his chest. To be touched by her was to be branded—he'd never stop feeling it. "Somebody *like* you?" she asked, sounding confused. "Or . . . you?"

It gave him the courage to just say it, as he should have the first time. "Me," he said. "You belong with *me*."

Her dark gaze went desperate with longing and he brought his mouth down on hers again, unable not to. He'd never experienced such animal responses—but Susan brought something alive in him, awakened some new part of him he'd never known before.

With one hand he molded and stroked her breast—the other he clamped possessively onto her rear through the dress and hauled her even closer up against him, wanting her to feel his hardness. She let out another heated, startled gasp—and then began to move against him, writhing like liquid heat in his arms.

But then it came again, the sound of the tractor on a distant ridge. It might not even be King's; it could be from the next farm up the way or the Dilly place, its dented silver mailbox situated right across the road from Susan's white metal one. Susan's and King's. It was *his* name on the box, after all. His name on . . . her.

And she must have felt all that, too, because the second he stopped kissing her, she pulled back, anguish now painting her expression. "What are we doing?" she exclaimed. "Where on earth can it lead? We have to stop, Charlie—we have to stop!"

And before he quite knew what was happening, she was breaking free from his grasp and darting away. He turned and watched her go, watched her racing toward the farmhouse up the short dirt lane like she was running from the devil himself. And Charlie had to ask himself—which one of them was the devil here, him or Donald King?

JACK and Christy walked hand in hand up the beach—the isolated part again—after having consumed corndogs and funnel cakes at the Sunset Celebration and then watching Fletcher's show.

When the phone in the back pocket of her shorts buzzed, Jack let go of her hand so she could check it. Peering down, she smiled and announced, "A text from Grandpa Charlie. I texted him earlier, told him what we were eating, and now he wants us to smuggle him in a funnel cake some night soon."

"Smuggling funnel cake won't be easy, but we can give it a try," Jack said on a laugh. Then he added, "It's cool that your grandpa texts."

"The nurses taught him just a couple of months ago," she replied with a smile. Then she raised her eyebrows at him. "Hey, let's take a picture of ourselves to send him."

They were near the old rowboat they'd seen on the beach before, so now they sat down on one of the seats inside, and Jack held Christy's phone out and snapped a shot.

"It's a good picture," she said, checking it out, and then proceeding to send it to Charlie.

"Another new memory," Jack told her.

It was a few minutes later, as they headed farther back up the beach, that Christy ventured, "So, are you ever gonna tell me about . . . you know?"

Jack glanced over at her. Damn, she looked so pretty, her hair blown back by the wind, a fresh touch of sun on her face. She wore white shorts and a colorful tank, the outfit showing off her tan—somewhere along the way she'd transformed from Alice in Wonderland into the perfect blond beach babe.

And, of course, he knew what she was talking about. She hadn't asked him about it again, not once, between the first night they'd made love and now—but he knew. And still he heard himself asking, "What?"

"About . . . the girl who hurt you," she said.

"You promised to tell me your history,
you know," said Alice.

Lewis Carroll, *Alice in Wonderland*

Chapter 17

"*I* DON'T like bringing up something unpleasant," she went on, "but I feel like there's so much I don't know about you. And I guess I'm curious. I mean, you always seem so sturdy, so strong . . . it's hard for me to imagine you being hurt."

Jack sighed, took in all she was saying.

In a way, what Candy had put him through had begun to seem a lot further in the past since Christy came along. So maybe this should be easier to talk about now. But hell, where did he begin? How would she take knowing he'd held back something so big from her as an entire marriage?

"It . . . happened around three years ago," he said.

They still walked, the calm surf tonight just barely lapping at their feet when it came flowing up onto the sand, and beside him, he sensed her waiting patiently for him to go on. And when he didn't—when he struggled to find the next words, the next *safe* part of the story to tell her, she asked, "What was her name?"

"Candy," he said. That was safe.

But she waited for more.

And he finally heard himself telling her again the one part she already knew. "Like I said before, she cheated on me."

He felt Christy's compassion pouring out in her heavy sigh. "I'm so, so sorry that happened to you. I can't imagine how that kind of betrayal feels."

And shit—he didn't like this already. Of course she was going to be sweet, sympathetic; it was her nature. But he didn't like admitting that he wasn't always that guy she saw, the strong, sturdy one. He didn't like revealing his weaknesses. Hell, who did?

And hadn't their time here in Coral Cove been tainted with enough unpleasantness already? The last week or so since everything had changed, since they'd had sex and started saying *I love you*, had been phenomenally good. Fun. Happy. The way it was *supposed* to be with a girl you were crazy about. He hadn't had that in a long time. He'd thought he might never have it again. And couldn't Christy use some happy, easy days, too, without worry or angst? Was it wrong to want to keep being strong and sturdy in her eyes? Was it wrong to just want a little happiness for them both?

He'd tell her about his divorce soon—he just didn't want to get any deeper into this now.

"But enough about that," he said easily, trying to blow it off.

He felt her draw back slightly to look at him, pausing their steps. "Enough? You haven't told me anything about it yet."

Her surprise was perfectly understandable, so he was honest. About this anyway. "It's a nice night, Alice. I'm having fun with you. I don't feel like ruining that by traveling back down that particularly ugly path in my life tonight. I'd rather focus on the present. Which is pretty good, right?" He glanced over, gave her a grin.

And she smiled back. "Pretty *great*," she corrected him.

And he liked that correction. She was amazing, and he wanted things to *keep* being amazing between them. So he asked, "Can you understand why I'm not up for telling you the whole unpleasant story tonight?"

She gave a soft nod.

And his heart warmed as relief flowed through his veins.

He squeezed her hand, a silent thank you for letting him off the hook again.

JACK left Christy by the side door they now usually came in at Sunnymeade. Ron the Nurse had quietly called it the "after hours door" with a wink to Christy soon after their first couple of visits. Jack had a funnel cake to deliver and he didn't want it getting any colder before Charlie could dig in to it.

So he walked into the older man's room carrying the paper plate full of fried dough that Christy had covered with napkins—and as soon as Charlie looked up, Jack used his free hand to whisk the napkins away and quietly say, "Surprise. One funnel cake, just like you ordered."

As Jack expected, a smile lit up Charlie's whole face. "Holy Toledo," he murmured, "bring that here to me."

It was late—after ten—and he sat in bed watching TV, so Jack drew closer and passed him the plate, its contents laden with powdered sugar.

"Mercy, forgot how messy these are," Charlie said, tearing off the first bite and putting it in his mouth, just before letting out an "Mmm, mmm, mmm." Then he laughed. "I'll have to be sure I don't have any of this sugar on my face before Angie makes her next rounds."

Jack gave Christy's grandpa a grin. The fact was, he had a lot on his mind at the moment, but Charlie usually put him at ease. So he tried to forget his worries and asked, "As good as you remember?"

"Maybe better," he replied. Then he leaned slightly forward, looking past Jack. "Where's my grandgirl? You lose her?" Another good-natured chuckle left him.

And Jack pointed vaguely over his shoulder, down the hall. "She got a phone call right as we were walking in." Though the mere mention of Christy brought back Jack's discomfort. It had been with him all day, despite repeated attempts to shake it off. Because it was silly—it wasn't like he was committing a crime here. He just hadn't found the right time to tell her a few things, that was all.

But maybe having had her actually *ask*—*again*—had left him feeling different. Like what before had mostly seemed like self-preservation now felt . . . a little more like keeping a secret.

"Why do you look so antsy?" Charlie asked then, his eyes narrowing suspiciously.

Aw hell. Jack tried to blow it off. "Well, I just smuggled contraband food into this place—how do you expect me to look?" He even ended with a short laugh—which sounded wooden to him.

Charlie didn't smile. "There's not trouble with Christy?" he asked.

"No, Christy's great," Jack promised.

"Then . . . trouble at home—with family? Friends?"

Damn, since when was Charlie so nosy? "Nope—everything's fine," Jack insisted.

And Charlie said nothing—but he continued casting a critical glare Jack's way even as he shoved another bite of funnel cake into his mouth. And his look was so pointed that . . . hell, even without saying another word, the old man had Jack feeling like he was being interrogated under a bright light. Or . . . maybe that was guilt setting in.

He just wasn't convinced he had anything to feel guilty *about*. Exactly. Because he had every intention of telling her about his divorce. He just hadn't done it *yet*.

Still, that imaginary bright light and Charlie's probing gaze compelled Jack to speak, almost against his will. "Let's just say I like it when life is nice and easy, like things have been *here*, with Christy, lately. And I'd rather forget the complicated parts." He shoved his hands in the front pockets of his khaki shorts, trying to look like he had the situation completely under control. Since he did. More or less.

Yet Charlie's critical expression didn't fade. "There isn't . . . some reason you can't be with her?"

"No. No, nothing like that," Jack replied quickly. Though he flinched slightly—and he didn't even know why.

"But you're holdin' somethin' back from her, aren't ya?"

Shit—did the old guy have ESP or something? Now it was Jack who narrowed his gaze on Charlie. "You're a little too insightful tonight."

Charlie swallowed another bite of sugary funnel cake, appearing to carefully consider his next words. "It's none of my business," he finally began, "but . . . relationships are about a lot of things, and honesty is one of 'em. So I'd advise you to come clean with her. Not much can't be fixed with honesty. And faith."

For some reason, the last part threw Jack off. Charlie had talked about Christy having faith in *herself* when they'd first arrived here, but this was different. And God knew Jack didn't want to prolong this conversation, but . . . "Faith?"

"In her. In you. In the truth makin' everything right. You ask me, most everything in life is about havin' faith."

It was like a conversation with Fletcher, he realized—all this talk about faith and believing.

And yet . . . Jack wasn't sure why, but it was actually the word *truth* that rang out to him right now, and that he suddenly felt hanging over his head. *The truth is . . . this isn't just about wanting to enjoy this time with her. The truth is that you're worried she won't understand, worried she'll see you differently, worried you'll ruin everything with her by revealing the secrets you've kept.*

But maybe you're making way too much of this. And Charlie was right. Maybe if he was just honest with her, it would be okay.

Before Jack could conjure a reply, though, Christy came whisking into the room, her pretty face fraught with distress. Charlie tuned into it immediately, too. "What's wrong, darlin'?"

She let out a sigh, her hazel eyes downcast. "My boss called. Someone quit at the store this week and she needs me back by Monday."

No one said anything for a moment, absorbing the news. And then Christy went on. "Silly, I guess, to be so bummed. I mean, it's a vacation, and most people aren't lucky enough to have one as long and open-ended as this one has turned out. But I guess somehow it had started to seem . . . like something that didn't have to end. So now that it suddenly does, I'm just caught off guard. And sad that it has to be over."

Christy had just echoed Jack's feelings about the trip perfectly—and he had a feeling Charlie probably felt the same. With no clear conclusion to their stay in sight, it *had* been all too easy to feel almost like it could go on forever.

Jack watched as Christy stepped forward

toward Charlie's bed. "It's been so nice spending time with you. I . . . don't like leaving you alone here."

Jack saw the sorrow etched in Charlie's eyes—but the old man forced a smile to say, "I'm not alone, sweetheart. I have lots of friends here. Ron, Angie, Mrs. Waters down the hall . . . and lots of other people, too."

"But it's not the same as with me and you know it."

Charlie let out a small laugh. "You're right, it's not. But I was fine before and I'll still be fine. And I'm thankful we've had such a good, long visit—and I'm more grateful than I can say to Jack here for helpin' to make it possible."

Jack barely knew how to respond. He'd long since forgotten that he had, in fact, done that. And he couldn't help thinking about how if he'd known then what he knew now how he'd have handled everything differently—how he'd have happily insisted on paying for the whole trip, and offered Christy her choice of the resorts up the road.

And the idea of that didn't appeal so much because of the level of luxury he could have offered her—since he thought they'd both enjoyed the Happy Crab more in some ways than some big, upscale hotel—but it appealed to him, he realized, because . . . honesty was just easier. And because—hell—maybe *dis*honesty had taken more of a toll on him with Christy than he'd understood until this moment.

"Well," he finally said, "it turned out to be a great trip for me, too, in lots of ways." First he made eye contact with Charlie, and then Christy, to whom he also gave a loving smile.

When she smiled back, his heart expanded in his chest.

And shit—he needed to tell her the truth.

And he would.

And everything would be better then. Much, much better.

UPON returning to the room that night, they made love. Christy thought of it that way now. It sounded dorky to her in a way—so old-fashioned—but there was no other term for it that encapsulated what she felt when she and Jack had sex. And it wasn't that it was all quiet and serene—it wasn't. Sometimes it was wild, and letting Jack guide her in that direction, as well as opening up to him that much further, made her feel all the more intimately tied to him.

In fact, after round one in bed, she'd taken a quick shower while Jack fell asleep and she'd been standing at the sink outside the bathroom, naked, running a cool cloth over her face, when she glanced into the mirror to see him behind her, his eyes warm and sexy and overflowing with fresh desire.

And when his hands closed over her waist, then glided smoothly down over her ass, she sensed what was coming. She bit her lip, sucked in her breath, met his gaze in the glass. And their eyes stayed locked as he eased his magnificently stiff erection inside her. Now that was openness. That was intimacy. And Jack somehow made that easier and more natural than she ever could have imagined.

She let out a little cry at the entry—and moaned as he slid deeper, deeper. She'd never had sex standing up before and it sent a startling sensation down her legs while delivering a fullness that stretched far beyond the spot between her thighs. "Oh God," she whispered. "I feel you so much."

He lowered a kiss to her shoulder, and then followed it with a little nibble of his teeth that—when added to everything else—nearly shattered her.

I think I love you more every minute. But she couldn't say that. Maybe she should be able to say anything to him now—that was what this kind of closeness was about, after all—but they were leaving soon, and she didn't know how that would change things and it was scary. What if she'd gotten too comfortable in Coral Cove? Jack had turned this into her own personal paradise, and she wasn't sure what life would be like after this—when they weren't in paradise anymore.

But when he began to move in her, to thrust, she let go of the thoughts—because the pleasure was too consuming. There was nothing to do but surrender to it. Cease thinking, cease worrying. It filled her completely and left room for nothing else.

Each drive he delivered extracted a hot cry from her throat. Behind her, Jack groaned, gripped her hips tighter.

And suddenly . . . she needed to show him. How much she loved him. That there was nothing ordinary about this. That it wasn't a vacation fling. That she wasn't afraid to open herself to him all the way.

And it wasn't about fear, or the uncertainty of leaving. It was about . . . giving. And growing. And being brave enough to let herself get even closer to him—even if she didn't know exactly what returning home would bring.

And so when he stopped, pulled out of her, turned her around, ready for a new position, she pressed her palms to his chest and pushed him backward, toward the bed.

He pointed vaguely over her shoulder. "Um, I wasn't done with you in there," he said, his voice deep with lust.

"But I want . . ." she began—then shoved him again so that he fell back to sit on the mattress.

"You want what?" he asked, peering up at her.

And she wasn't sure how to answer. She was ready for it, but maybe not good at putting it into words just yet. So instead of saying anything more, she simply dropped to her knees before him. Let her eyes fall to the prominent column of flesh between his legs. Then raised her gaze to his.

"Oh," he murmured.

And then, unexpectedly, she founds words. "I want to make you feel good. With my mouth." The last part came out in a whisper.

"Aw baby," he rasped.

And it was with a surprising amount of comfort and total trust that Christy calmly reached out, ran her fingers over the smooth silkiness of him, then wrapped her hand full around him. She'd touched him there before, of course, but not with this intent. And then she bent and tenderly kissed the tip of his erection, pleased by her boldness and fueled by the low moan that left him.

The rest was easy, too. Parting her lips, sliding them down over him, was easy. Taking in the unexpected pleasure of the way he filled her mouth was easy. Being bold enough to begin moving slowly up and down on him was easy.

More than easy. It was . . . amazing. To listen to the sounds that echoed from above, to know how good it felt to him. To feel his hands in her hair, grazing her scalp. To make herself that vulnerable to him, to be that fully trusting, to want to be that close to the powerful part of him that brought her such pleasure. To feel his very maleness moving between her lips.

There came a time, though, when she needed even more, when she needed to kiss him, and to feel him everywhere. And so she finally released him from her mouth, enthusiastically climbed up to straddle him on the bed, and kissed him for all she was worth.

And then he was grabbing her hips, pushing his way up inside her again, and she was whimpering her pleasure, and riding him, and soon coming in a blazing climax more powerful than she'd ever experienced.

After he came in her, too, they lay side by side, kissing softly—tired but still wanting to kiss— and Christy rolled to her back afterward with a heady sigh.

Only . . . then she remembered. That they were leaving. That everything was still uncertain.

Even if it changes, even if he doesn't want things to keep on this way, at least you have this. She would never regret opening herself to him this way, ever.

Still, a lamp burned low across the room, and Jack must have glanced over and caught her pensive expression. "Um, what we just did is supposed to make you happy," he said. "And you look anything but. This is bad for my confidence."

She laughed softly—oh God, she loved him.

And as much as she didn't want to be some needy, worried chick, she decided to be honest. After all, what was the point of letting herself feel this close to him if she couldn't say what she was thinking. "I guess I was just wondering how things will be when we get home. Because life isn't a permanent vacation. And we kinda went into this with a no-strings-attached agreement. Only then things changed and seemed more serious. But I don't want to assume anything, and if you still want to leave things . . . casual or whatever, I understand. I just—"

"Christy, stop," he said, shutting her up. And she realized she'd started rambling like . . . well, like a girl scared to death she was about to lose this good thing she'd found. Which was exactly what she was.

She drew in a deep breath, met his gaze beside her in bed, then drew it away again, suddenly nervous. She'd tipped her hand. He knew she was emotional about this now. Ugh.

"I'm hoping things will stay . . . like they are now," he told her. "If . . . if you're up for that."

She blinked. Stunned, relieved. If she was up for that? Was he kidding?

She replied by pretty much lunging on him, twining her arms around his neck, and kissing him wildly.

And when finally she stopped, relaxing into his loose, comfortable embrace, he let just the hint of a grin sneak out as he said, "I take it you're up for that."

THEY'D returned to that quiet, secluded area of the beach where they'd first had sex. Jack supposed it had become their favorite place to be together. When he'd suggested another sunset walk tonight, twenty-four hours since Christy had gotten that phone call from her boss, they'd wandered in this direction, hand in hand, without ever discussing their destination.

Now the last vestiges of a neon pink sunset turned deep purple on the horizon and they'd stopped at the old green rowboat on the shore to sit and look out over the water. They kissed for a few minutes—damn, it had gotten hard to be near her without kissing her—and afterward Jack watched as she exited the boat, found a stick, and proceeded to draw a big heart in the sand. Then she wrote JD+CK inside it.

Afterward, she looked up at him, a playful yet slightly self-deprecating expression painted on her gorgeous face. "Does this make me seem like I'm about twelve?"

And he laughed. "No, I like it. I think it's cute as hell."

"I guess we have to head home Saturday," she said, sounding sad. Jack knew neither of them had really wanted to start talking about leaving all this behind, but it was Thursday night and she needed to be at work on Monday morning, so he supposed it was time to make those plans.

"Guess so," he said. "I'll let Reece know we'll be checking out."

She nodded. "Maybe we can spend part of the day at the beach tomorrow and part of it with Grandpa Charlie," she suggested.

"Sounds good," he told her. "And maybe one last dinner at the Fisherman?"

She smiled, tilted her head. "Is it weird that I'm gonna miss that place?"

He laughed and made a confession of his own. "Probably not nearly as weird as it is that I'm actually gonna miss Abner and his hats. Did you see him in that full length Native American headdress the other day? It went all the way to the floor!"

When discussion died down about Abner—and the fact that they were also going to miss Fletcher, Polly, Reece, and maybe even Fifi in some strange way—they both went silent for a few minutes, wordlessly lamenting leaving Coral Cove behind as the darkness gathered around them.

Then it hit Jack. "I should have taken a picture of your heart."

She raised her eyebrows, clearly not understanding.

"In the sand. For your 'new adventure' pictures." Together, they'd both done a pretty good job, Jack thought, of taking enough photos on the trip to give Christy lots of brand new good memories to look back on through pictures later. "It's too dark now." He could still see the heart with his eyes but he knew his phone's camera wouldn't be able to capture it. And a moonless night made it darker on the beach than usual.

"Maybe we can come back sometime tomorrow," she suggested. "After our Hungry Fisherman dinner—one last sunset walk up the beach?"

He smiled, winked. "You got it, Alice." Then he decided this conversation had become too much about saying goodbye to the place, too much about endings. "And it's not like we can't ever come back. We can. We will. And next time it'll be nicer."

She continued to play absently in the sand with her stick, even as darkness swallowed the last light of the day, but he could see the silhouette of her pretty head tilting to one side. "Nicer? How could it be nicer?"

He had to smile. She really was a down to earth girl, his Alice. And knowing that made what he was about to do easier. Because it made him know everything would be all right. "Well," he said, "I dig the Crab and Reece and all, but on the next trip we can stay at one of the bigger places with the fancy lagoon pools—maybe the resort that's selling your jewelry."

She moved back toward him, climbed into the

shallow boat, sat down next to him again on the wooden seat. "That's sweet, Jack, but not necessary. Unless one of us is suddenly rolling in dough or something," she added, sounding tongue-in-cheek.

And Jack took a deep breath and said, "I've got something to tell you, honey. A couple of things, actually."

Another head tilt—he could see her a little better now that she was closer to him again, but more the shape of her than her expression. "Really? What?" She sounded interested, curious.

Jack knew he'd had plenty of time to figure out how to say this, but not having wanted to think about it more than necessary, he hadn't planned anything out. So now he winged it. "Remember I told you about Candy, who cheated on me?"

"Of course." Next to him, Christy sat up a little straighter, and even in the dark, he sensed her eyes widening. She was actually happy he was going to tell her more about that now—good. This really *would* be easy.

So just say it. "Well, the reason I didn't want to talk about it before now is because . . . I was married. *We* were married. When she cheated on me. That's why it was . . . well, pretty fucking devastating, to be honest. It ruined my life. It pretty much destroyed my faith . . . in everything. Until you," he told her. And then he went quiet. To give her a chance to respond.

She stayed silent for a long moment, and then finally she said, sounding calm but a little astonished, "You were married?"

"Yeah," he said. "For about two years when it happened. It was . . . the worst time of my life."

And he was sitting there, still waiting for her to be as sympathetic as she'd been the last time they'd started discussing this—when instead she said, *"You were married.* And you're just now telling me?"

Jack took a deep breath. Shit. This wasn't going as smoothly as he'd hoped. He'd really convinced himself it would be simple. Because Christy was so sweet. Caring. Forgiving. So if he explained some more, that would straighten this out. "The reason I didn't—couldn't—is because ever since then . . . I've been pretty sure that, whether she really knew it or not, she married me for my money. So you see why, when I met you, I wasn't comfortable letting you know about that."

He sensed her tensing even further beside him. "Money? What money?" She shook her head, clearly confused.

And Jack took a deep breath. *Keep going—this will be all right.* "Honey, I'm not really a handyman. I really do flip houses—as a hobby. But I also run an online investment advisory firm. And the truth is, I'm kinda loaded. And—"

"Wait," she interrupted, holding up both her hands to stop him. "Let me get this straight. You're telling me you've been married. And that you're loaded."

"Yeah," he answered softly.

And after a few seconds, she said, "Oh my God, Jack. I can't believe you. And . . . I wish I never had to see you again."

With that, she got up, stepped out of the little boat, and began to trudge up the beach. And as Jack watched after her, dumbfounded, he realized the heart she'd drawn in the sand was completely invisible to him now, hidden by the darkness.

"And here I must leave you."

Lewis Carroll, *Through the Looking Glass*

Chapter 18

CHRISTY WISHED there were more moonlight so she could see where she was going. Instead she followed the shoreline with the help of the water where it rushed up onto the sand and then flowed back out—she trundled along recklessly, just wanting to be away from him, as far away as she could get. She walked as fast as possible, in disbelief, her heart beating like a drum in her chest.

She didn't know him at all. She'd given herself to him entirely—she'd opened herself up in ways she hadn't even known she could—and she hadn't really known him at all.

He'd been *married*? And he was freaking *rich*? She could barely even wrap her mind around either one of those concepts at the moment, let alone getting hit with both at once. All she knew was that Jack wasn't . . . Jack now. He wasn't the guy she'd come to know. He wasn't the guy she'd bared her heart and soul to. He was just . . . somebody else. Some liar. Some deceptive jerk.

"Christy! Christy, wait!"

Oh Lord. He was following her. Following her up the beach. When she wanted—*needed*—to be alone. She didn't want to let him explain because how could you explain a lie?

She kept walking only to hear him call again, his voice closer now. And then a few seconds later his hand closed over her shoulder, stopping her—but she pulled away from him and continued up the shore. "Leave me alone," she said.

"You're really that mad? About *this*?" he asked, having the unbelievable nerve to sound perplexed.

Okay, *now* she stopped walking. And looked him in the face. It was dark, but she could still see the glint of his eyes and make out the hint of a bewildered expression. Seriously? He was bewildered?

"Of course I'm that mad! You lied to me! About huge things! You led me to believe you're some entirely different guy than you really are! And okay, maybe I get why you didn't come clean about the money in the beginning. But by now?" She stopped, took a breath, rolled her eyes. "I can't believe you're actually *rich*. I mean, the irony of it! And you don't *seem* rich."

"Because I'm a nice guy," he said. "A nice, normal, down to earth guy. I wasn't *always* rich. I made money by being smart and ambitious. And I really want to tell you about it. I've wanted to tell you—lots of times. But it was confusing to know when."

"Yes, that's one of the problems with lies. They're confusing. Not to mention hurtful." She trudged on.

And he followed behind her, catching up. "Look, it's not like you don't know *why* I lied. It's not like I'm just some guy who just lies at random."

"No, your lies were very well thought out and effectively executed. In fact, I'm guessing you were dealing with more important stuff than social networking every time you've had your laptop open, right? You should be very proud of how convincing you were."

"Is it really any different than what you were planning to do to any rich guy you dated?" he asked, his tone a little harsher now. "You were going to keep information back. Not let them know money was a requirement and that you wouldn't be dating them otherwise. How is it you're suddenly the innocent one and I'm the bad guy?"

She pulled in her breath. That stung—because it was true in a way. But there were big distinctions between the two situations. "It's different," she said pointedly, "because it turned out I sucked at pulling that off. Because it felt wrong and I figured out I couldn't go through with it. Because I wanted actual *love*. And I thought I'd found it. But now I have no idea *what* I've found."

"Christy, be reasonable. Just because I didn't tell you everything doesn't mean this isn't love, that it isn't real. It just means I made a mistake, that's all."

"That's all?" she repeated back to him. Easy for

him to say. And as she stopped for a second, as she weighed it, she knew *exactly* when he should have given her the whole truth. "You said you loved me, Jack. You said you loved me, but you still didn't tell me. You kept right on lying even after that. And love is *trust*. Love is *honesty*. So this *can't* be love."

She almost felt the large *whoosh* of breath that left him at the weight of her words and he stood speechless before her for a long, heavy moment. Until finally he said, "It's not as easy as you're making it sound. It's not that cut and dried, that absolute."

Which she thought was ridiculous, and so she said, simply, "It is to me."

"Christy," he beseeched her, "you have to understand. I was just so damn afraid to trust anyone after what happened with Candy."

"And now you've paid it forward," she explained to him, "because now *I'll* be afraid to trust anyone after what happened with *you*."

Next to her, he let out a low, frustrated-sounding sort of growl. "Don't be crazy," he said. "This isn't as bad as you're making it out to be, honey."

"Don't call me crazy," she snapped. "And don't call me honey, either—I'm not your honey anymore."

Now it was he who stopped walking and she could tell something about that particular reply had knocked the wind out of him. Well, good. Because she'd meant it. Her heart broke a little more with each step she took. She'd actually been

. . . happy. And she'd started trusting in that—believing it was okay to finally feel happy again, after all she'd lost. And now this.

And to top it all off . . .

She came to a halt now, too, and turned back to face him. The only sound was the surf rushing in and out a few feet away. "Do you have any idea how foolish I feel, Jack? To have thought you were being generous by paying for our room at the Happy Crab? To have thought you and I were alike, that we were in the same boat in life? And to find out that we aren't?" There was so much to absorb and sort through, and at the moment, this was the one particular facet of it hitting her. "You must have thought it was so silly of me to be excited to sell that first piece of jewelry for twenty dollars when you probably drop that much on a fancy glass of wine. You must have been laughing at me inside."

"Never, Christy," he said, his tone gone somber. "I understood why you were excited—I was happy for you. Having money doesn't make me a snob. And . . . we *are* in the same boat in life."

"How do you figure?" Even though he couldn't see it, she rolled her eyes.

And he said, "We both lost what mattered to us most. And with it we lost our sense of security."

"Oh . . ." she breathed softly, not liking the fact that the comparison made her unwittingly understand where he was coming from a little better, made her remember that he'd been through something, too—something painful and hard. She didn't want to empathize with him right now, though—

she was too angry, too hurt by the deceptions. She thought it easier to forgive almost anything else.

"And I do know what it's like to feel foolish—on top of all the other kinds of pain, I felt pretty damn foolish to find out my wife was having a full-blown affair with another guy and that I'd had no idea. And I'm sorry. I never thought about you feeling foolish. There's nothing to feel foolish about, I promise."

Still, it didn't help. It stung too much to think of every single time he'd pretended not to be much better off financially than her. It stung to think of how long he'd let the lie stand between them. And the fact that he'd been through an entire marriage and divorce and thought it was okay to get this deeply into a relationship without telling her about it was upsetting in a whole different way. The result of *any* lie to someone who trusted you was to make a fool of them—that simple.

And as she stood there staring at him, glad the lights of the fishing pier shone in the distance yet also wishing they'd already reached it, wishing they were already back to the more populated part of Coral Cove and closer to the Happy Crab, it hit her what it all boiled down to. "I was real with you. I was honest with you, always. And the better I got to know you, the more honest I got. I opened up to you. I talked to you about things I don't talk to many people about. Because I trusted you. And you . . . you just shit all over that, Jack.

"You got to see parts of me that are private, special. I gave you parts of myself that I've never given to anyone else. And the fact that, the whole time, you couldn't even be honest with me about the biggest parts of your life . . . well, it tells me how much you really valued me and the time we've spent together here."

Jack let out a breath she could hear. She felt the heaviness of her words covering them both like a thick, smothering blanket. When he spoke, his voice came out solemn, quiet. "That's not true, Christy," he said. "It just isn't."

"It is for me," she told him. "And it's nothing you can fix or change. So you may as well not even waste your time trying."

And with that, she trudged onward—both relieved and perhaps a little unexpectedly disappointed when he didn't follow this time.

She really *didn't* want him to waste his time. She saw no point in continuing to go over this. But maybe, deep down, some tiny part of her had been secretly hoping he *could* find some miraculous way to change everything and magically make it all right again. And the fact that he wasn't following, wasn't trying, made her realize that even *he* could see that it would take a miracle. And that he didn't have one to give her.

JACK hadn't chased her the second time she'd run away from him. He'd been tired, and out of ways to try to repair this. He knew he'd screwed up—he'd just truly trusted enough in her sweetness to think she'd understand, and forgive.

Was it dumb of him to have thought she'd actually be happy to find out he had money? After all, wasn't that what she'd wanted? Wasn't he exactly what she'd been looking for when they'd first met?

But he supposed she couldn't see beyond his deception right now. And he didn't know how to show her that he really *was* a good guy—even if he didn't seem like one right now.

He walked slowly up the beach, watching her jog away from him. The bright yellow tank top she wore showed up better than most things in the dark, but just like that heart in the sand, it grew vaguer and harder to see in front of him until it was completely gone.

Reaching the pier, quiet and empty at this hour, he walked out onto it, to the very end, then leaned against the railing to peer out over the ocean. And he thought about trust. It came in a lot of different shapes and sizes. He'd trusted Candy and she'd broken that trust. And so by trying to protect himself, he'd been dishonest with someone else— and ended up losing her because . . . he'd done the same thing Candy had done to him. The offenses were very different, of course, but in the end he supposed trust was trust. And that being sorry didn't bring it back.

He'd never actually thought about how his deceptions would make Christy feel. He'd weighed the chances of her being forgiving—but he'd never stopped to really think about how it felt to learn you'd been fooled, to learn that what you thought you understood you actually didn't. Maybe if he'd ever really taken the time to consider her part in this instead of just worrying about himself, he'd have been honest a lot sooner. And everything would be fine now.

But he hadn't, and it wasn't.

He thought of Charlie's advice to him. Come clean. And have faith. "I had faith," he said quietly to the sea, "but so much for that. So what now?"

When the sea didn't answer—not a big surprise—he finally turned and began making his way back to the Happy Crab. And he thought about going to Fletcher's house instead, or maybe seeing if Reece was still up—he lived in an apartment behind the motel's office—but he didn't actually think talking about this would help anything.

He used his key to quietly open the door to the room. Inside, all was quiet and mostly dark. She'd left the bathroom light on, presumably so he could see, but she was already under the covers and fast asleep—in her old bed. She'd been sleeping in his since the first night they'd had sex. And the mere sight of her back in the other one was like one more blow to the gut.

"I can't believe she's back in her old bed, just like that," he murmured to himself, then started across the room.

"Of course I'm back in my old bed," she said softly, apparently not so fast asleep after all. "We're over, Jack. You ruined it. You ruined everything. So don't act like it's my fault."

And since she was awake, he took another stab at talking about this. "I'd fix it if I could, Christy. I honestly thought you'd understand. Because you're an understanding person. I never thought you'd be this upset." And then the agonized words she'd shared with him a little while ago came back to him—and he got real with her, as real as he could possible get. "And what you said about opening up to me, I *love* that you were open with me. It's what made me fall in love with you. It's what made me brave enough to finally tell you all this."

In response, she flipped the covers back, sat up in bed. And God, even in the dim lighting, she looked so sad that it ripped his heart out. How had he been so careless with something so valuable? "But you told me too late," she said.

Jack sat down on the foot of her bed and met her pretty gaze. He peered into her eyes and wondered if there was anything he could do to make her believe in him again. "What if I opened up, too?" he asked her. "What if I told you everything I should have already told you? I'm not good at being open like you are. But . . . what if I try?"

He couldn't read her eyes, even as he looked deeply into them. Yet it was only then that he realized the skin around them was red and a little puffy, and that she'd been crying.

"I'm so sorry I hurt you, Christy," he told her, feeling like the biggest clod alive. He shook his head. "I swear I never meant to. And maybe I've been selfish here, but I never meant to do that, either. Maybe I don't know . . . where the line is between selfishness and self-preservation."

"It's a thin one," she admitted, sounding about as spent as he felt. And finally she added, "I appreciate what you're trying to do here, Jack. I know you're sorry and trying to make up for it. And you can tell me about the things you held back from me if you want to. But . . . I honestly don't know if it'll make a difference."

"Fair enough," he said.

And then he began to tell her. Everything.

Because it was his only shot, all he had to offer her at this point. And as hard as it would be to talk about some of this stuff, it would be worth it. Even if it didn't work. Because he had to try.

First he told her about his business. How he'd started it. The reasons why. How it let him do what he was good at without compromising who he was.

Which led to talking about his family, and how glad he was that he could help his parents out financially when they needed it. "I was thinking about my dad," he told her, "when I was fishing with Charlie, Duke, and John at the pier—thinking how much he'd have enjoyed it and that I wished he were there with us. I really need to make a point of doing things like that with him more often."

"That's nice," she said softly—and he could feel that they weren't just words, that she really got what fishing with his dad meant to him. Even though he hadn't said all that much about it. "I like hearing about your parents, Jack. I wish you'd told me more about them before now."

He nodded. She was right. It wouldn't have been so hard to share a little of his life with her, just things like that. "Me, too," he confessed.

"And . . . the rest?" she prodded timidly.

"Yeah, the rest," he said. And . . . hell, all those emotions from when he'd found out about Candy's affair came rushing back over him. But if he could tell anybody about that, if he could trust anyone with his feelings, it was Christy.

And so he told her. How he'd met Candy when she had a flat tire in the rain and he'd stopped to help her. And how it had seemed like a fairy tale romance . . . until suddenly it hadn't. "There was no warning," he said. "It came out of nowhere. One day I was happy and thought I had a clear view of my life and my future—and the next it was all blown to bits."

He was glad the room was dim and shadowy. Because he didn't often let himself go to the places he was going right now. It was one thing to know it happened, but another to relive the memories and feel the pain all over again. And it was hard as hell to admit to himself or anyone else exactly what he'd felt in those days, and maybe for quite a while after.

"Candy was . . ." Hell, how could he explain it? "I thought we'd have kids together, and grandkids, that we'd grow old together. I trusted her completely. I loved her with my whole heart. And . . ." Maybe he should just shut up now, not tell her the rest, the parts that had wounded him the deepest.

But no—no, he *had* to tell her. And maybe . . . maybe somehow it would even be good to get it off his chest. Because he'd never told *anyone* about this.

"After I found out, she said . . ." He stopped,

swallowed past the hurt. "She said she'd never really known what love was until she hooked up with Scott, our neighbor. She told me she'd thought she loved me, but that she never really had—that she'd just been blinded by the money, by the fact that I seemed like a good catch." He caught his breath, remembering that moment. No, more than remembering—living it all over again. His chest tightened.

But he went on, tried to do what he'd promised—open himself up to her. "It ripped my guts out," he told her. "It made me feel like . . . like I wasn't worth loving." Aw hell. Had he really just said that? His throat threatened to close up at the confession.

And Christy said softly, "Oh Jack."

And he knew he could shut up now—he'd bared enough of his soul. But for some reason, he kept going. Maybe he wanted to purge it from himself now, every bit of it. "To top it off, after that I overheard her on the phone with a friend, saying she hoped she'd get a good settlement, because she was going to miss my money a lot more than she'd miss *me*."

And—shit—now he was reliving *that* moment, too, the harsh reality and humiliation that everything he'd loved about their life together had truly been one-sided. Maybe not always. Maybe not in the beginning. But to learn that his wife had honestly lost all affection for him and just considered him a bank account had decimated whatever had remained of his soul.

At some point, he'd dropped his gaze to the

bedcovers, but then, without planning it, he lifted his glance to Christy's—some uncontrollable urge to see her face, her reaction, if any—and their gazes held. And her eyes looked glassy, wet. And he realized she was crying a little. For him.

"Come here," she whispered.

And he murmured, "Huh?"—but then she was reaching out, tugging him toward her, and he crawled up beside her in the bed, and her arms closed around him in a gesture not of passion, but simply of comfort.

And he thought how amazing she was—that even now, when she was angry with him, hurt by him, that she would comfort him. Turned out she was even more selfless than he'd ever given her credit for.

He hugged her back, smelled the scent of the salty sea breeze from earlier lingering in her hair, on her skin. And it hit him that when he'd found out about Candy, there hadn't been anyone to provide that kind of support, to simply hug him. His parents had been on a trip out west at the time. And he had guy friends, but they didn't do that.

He whispered in her ear, "I wish I'd been there to hug you when your mom and dad died."

And she embraced him a little harder in response, and he tightened his hold on her, too.

"I'm sorry I ever thought you were anything but perfect, honey," he murmured near her ear. "Because you are. Absolutely perfect."

And when he heard her sniffle, he knew she was crying a little more, and he wanted to take her tears away, kiss them away. It wasn't so much a decision as an impulse that led his mouth to her cheek. And even as he kissed her, his heart broke a little more—over Christy's loss, and over what *he'd* lost by not being honest with her.

He delivered another inelegant kiss high on her sun-pinkened cheek, then leaned his forehead against her temple. He could feel her breathing—and began to hear it, as well, gentle yet a little ragged. Everything inside him hurt for her, and for him, too—and he just ached to get back to normal.

And he was trying not to kiss her, but then his mouth found its way to her cheek once more. And then to her mouth.

Christy knew she couldn't kiss him back. She couldn't. Because it would be madness.

And yet her body and soul yearned for him. And despite what all the logic and reason inside her was saying, she couldn't resist returning his hot, tender kiss.

It was agonizing and sweet at the same time. Pleasure and pain. Because she kept trying to stop and simply couldn't. They were slow, deep kisses that came from her soul and threatened to swallow her.

She suffered a familiar fire between her thighs, in her breasts—and the kisses went from being desperate to wild and hedonistic. Complete surrender. Because it felt so good. *He* felt so good. And letting herself go with him had become all too easy. *Dangerously* easy, it turned out.

Yet when Jack's hand rose to her breast and the thick pleasure shot through her and a hot moan rose from her throat—she realized she truly couldn't. No matter what her body craved. No matter what her heart wanted.

It was possibly the hardest thing she'd ever done to press her palms to his chest and push him away. "No, Jack—no. We can't," she said raggedly.

"Why not?" he asked, breath labored, his grip tightening on her, tempting her. "I love you, Christy. And I'm sorry."

Her heart contracted at the words. And also at the truth they didn't change. "Because . . . even if we love each other, it doesn't make me suddenly able to trust you again. It's . . . it's kind of like breaking a plate," she said, trying to explain.

He looked understandably confused. "Huh?"

"If you drop a plate," she explained sadly, "it shatters into bits. And no matter how sorry you are . . . it's still broken."

> . . . she made up her mind to go on:
> "for I certainly won't go back,"
> she thought to herself.

Lewis Carroll, *Through the Looking Glass*

Chapter 19

SLEEPING IN separate beds that were side by side was awkward. Waking up the next morning was even more so. And Christy felt bad when she saw the sorrow and uncertainty in Jack's eyes, but now *she* was the one who had to worry about self-preservation.

She couldn't help thinking that breaking trust with someone was just one big self-perpetuating cycle. You trust, you get hurt, then you try to protect yourself by closing yourself up—and someone else ends up getting hurt because of *that*.

But she couldn't lament all that right now. There was too much else to think about. That's how Christy handled loss—by dealing with the practical ends of life. When her parents had died, she'd focused on just those very things. There'd been funerals to plan. And then there'd been moving, and leaving school, and finding a job—a thousand ways to keep busy.

Now, with Jack, she had to do the same thing. And she couldn't control the choices he'd made, but she would concentrate on the parts of her life she *could* control. Just since getting to Coral Cove, she'd shown herself that she was capable of much more than she'd ever realized, and now she wanted to keep right on proving that.

"Still going to the beach today?" Jack asked cautiously, hopefully, from the other bed.

"No," she said softly. Then pushed back the covers and got up, committed to getting a start on her day and ending this particularly awkward part of it. She began tidying the bedcovers slightly, just for some semblance of order. "I'm thinking we should leave early tomorrow and drive straight through. That way we'll get home late tomorrow night and I'll have Sunday to unpack, do some laundry, and get caught up on things before work on Monday."

As she kept talking, she walked to the drawers beneath the TV and selected a pair of shorts and a top to wear. "So today I want to do some more practical things—I'm going to stop by the shops where my jewelry is consigned and make plans for sending them more. And I'm going to talk to the administrative people at Sunnymeade about Grandpa Charlie's situation—just to see what options there might be that I don't know about, if any."

"Sounds like a plan," he said—even if his voice came out a little wooden. And she was glad he didn't argue with her about driving straight through. It meant one less night in a motel room with him, which seemed wise.

"I'd be happy to go with you on your errands today," he offered kindly. "If you want some company."

Oh God, Jack, stop being so sweet and nice and tempting. It threatened to rip her heart out. But she calmly kept her eyes on her current task—checking her cell phone for overnight messages and finding none. "Thank you," she said, "but this is stuff I'd rather do myself." *Because I'm a self-sufficient chick. And I need to get better at that, once and for all. I need to face it boldly and bravely and with more optimistic expectations.* When she'd approached selling her jewelry that way, after all, it had paid off. No more feeling sorry for herself. And no more wishing for a rich man to rescue her. Because if one thing had become startlingly clear to her last night, it was the fact that it would take more than a rich man to make everything right in her world. She had one sitting right here in front of her, after all, wanting desperately to be in her life, and she understood now that life and love were far more complex than that. Money didn't solve everything.

"Okay," he said. "But if you change your mind, or need me for anything, I'm just a text or a call away."

Funny—Jack had never offered that kind of support before. And she knew he was just being nice, trying to make her feel less alone in the world—but right now maybe she *needed* to feel alone. Because life was no longer about wishing for someone to bail her out. It was about making her own way. She had to quit wishing for miracles or waiting for someone to depend upon.

"Thanks," she said anyway, and just left it at that.

"Don't suppose you'd be up for our usual breakfast?" he ventured, still in bed.

And a lump rose to her throat. It had become an everyday thing she loved—donuts on the dock behind the Happy Crab. The fresh morning ocean air, the sights of tall masts and crisp white sails in the bay, fresh donuts and juice . . . and Jack. "Thank you," she said again, "but I'll just grab something on the way. Mind if I take the car?"

"Of course not," he said. "I'll just hang at the beach." He sounded disappointed but acceptant about breakfast.

When she came out of the shower a little while later, the room was quiet, Jack gone. But she found a white bakery bag containing two of her favorite donuts sitting on the room's small table, a little bottle of orange juice next to it, and her heart constricted. He'd understood that she just hadn't wanted to eat with *him*. *Oh God, why does this have to be so hard?*

But she had to be tough, stay strong. Because of the whole broken plate thing. Once it was broken it was just . . . broken.

Upon leaving, she was all business—and she planned to stay that way. *No more silly emotions for* this *girl.* Those things only created trouble, and weakness. And she'd be far better off without them. Even if Sinead O'Connor singing the old but still wrenching "Nothing Compares 2 U" on the car radio threatened to make her cry. She reached down and changed the station.

Her first stop was Beachtique, where she found her pieces still selling well, and Lydia was eager for more. A stop at the Sand Dollar Beach Resort netted the same results—a request for more jewelry. And as she got back in the car, new thoughts formed in her head. Mission 1: When she got home, she needed to devote some serious time to scouring thrift stores and estate sales to stock up on supplies again, and then she needed to dedicate more time to her craft since her work was selling faster than she could make it. Mission 2: If she found she could keep up with demand, maybe she could find additional places for consignment deals. And recommitting herself to her craft was going to be a great way to get over Jack.

Of course, there would be the issue that he lived across the street—but he'd flip the house soon enough, right?

And then . . . a really big idea hit her. With her jewelry selling in the local shops . . . could she possibly move here? It would be a complicated undertaking, of course, but . . . well, she'd just tuck that thought away in the back of her mind for now. And maybe she'd pull it back out sometime down the road.

And so what if the idea of Jack *really* leaving her life made her feel like something was clawing at the inside of her stomach, trying to get out? That would get better over time. *For now, just keep pushing forward.*

She picked up the chicken salad sandwich Grandpa Charlie liked on her way to the rest home, but before going to his room, she stopped at the front desk and asked to speak to someone in billing. After sitting with a nice woman named Adrianne for half an hour, she'd learned that there were payment options available, but the payments were hefty—more than Christy could afford, even with the influx of jewelry money—and that there probably wasn't much she could do at this point to help her grandfather out financially. Still, she took the paperwork and numbers Adrianne gave her and figured she'd study it further when she got home.

And as she walked down the corridor that led to Grandpa Charlie's room, she thought it rather ironic to know that Jack would probably be happy to pay for her grandpa to stay here—if only they'd had a normal relationship that had developed the normal way. If only she hadn't wanted to be rescued. If only he hadn't been dishonest. But as much as she wished she could fix her grandfather's living situation, she couldn't use Jack to do it.

Her grandpa's face lit up when she walked in the room—and she smiled back, trying to hide the sadness of knowing she wouldn't be seeing him like this anymore.

"Brought your favorite sandwich," she said brightly, holding up the bag. Maybe she could hit up Ron the Nurse to occasionally stop for the sandwich now that she and Jack no longer could.

"Then I get two treats at the same time," he

said, "it and you." After which he looked around. "Where's Jack?"

And Christy sighed. She didn't want to talk about this, but she knew she had to. She'd just keep it as brief as possible. "I asked him not to come with me. He and I are over, Grandpa."

Her grandfather's eyes went wide. "Good Lord, girl—why? What happened that I missed?"

Keep it simple. "He was dishonest with me about some stuff. Big stuff."

"Hmm," Grandpa Charlie said, taking that in. He looked introspective. "And that can't be forgiven? Because he's crazy about you. I'm old but my eyesight's still good, and you'd have to be blind not to see that."

"I can forgive," she said. "But that doesn't mean I could ever trust him again. Counting on people too much just seems . . ."

"What?"

"Like a way to be let down," she said. "Or maybe . . . abandoned is closer to how I feel."

"Like when your folks died," he said matter-of-factly, surprising her.

And she stiffened at the very suggestion. "No, not like that at all. That wasn't their fault."

"Still, you thought they'd always be there, and then they suddenly weren't. And even though I know you forgive them, too, they did leave ya without any money. I'd say it's hard not to feel abandoned after that, even if you don't blame 'em for it."

She knew there was some truth in what he was saying—she'd acknowledged as much to Jack, after all. But she still wasn't completely comfortable accepting that, so she just said, "Regardless, maybe it was just too big a letdown too close on the heels of losing them." She stood up a bit straighter, ready to be strong and secure. "The upshot is that I've realized I just have to be tougher now, less softhearted. I have to really grow up and let go of being emotional."

"Emotions have nothin' to do with age, my grandgirl. And if you ask me, people in touch with their emotions are the mature ones. As for givin' 'em up, I'd be careful with that."

She looked at him guardedly. "Why?"

"They might not be as easy to outrun as ya think."

Then she narrowed her gaze on him. "Are you speaking from experience?"

Grandpa Charlie tilted his head. "I'm just sayin' there might be a time for toughness and strength, but runnin' away from what you feel will most likely lead you down a path to nowhere. And you deserve to be someplace far better than nowhere, darlin'. So do what you need to do to be in charge of your life, but also remember that bein' happy has to factor into that. Just promise me you'll think about it, okay?"

"I will." And she meant it. Then she admitted, "I'm going to miss this."

"This what?"

"Your grandfatherly wisdom."

He leaned his head back for a laugh. "Wisdom might be a generous term."

But she shook her head. "No, you *are* wise and

I like getting your insight on things. I'm really sorry I have to leave. For both our sakes."

He gave her a warm smile that she tried to embed into her heart so she could remember it. "Well, you know how much I'll miss seein' ya every day, my grandgirl, but don't you worry about me. I'll just get back to spendin' more time on my mystery novels, and my crosswords, and visitin' with Mrs. Waters down the hall."

Christy squinted. "Who *is* Mrs. Waters?" He'd mentioned the woman the other day, but never before, and now she was curious.

In response, his smile lightened into something that struck her as . . . almost youthful, but she couldn't say why. "Oh, she's just a sweet lady in a coma. Doesn't have any family, so I like to sit with her, just in case she needs the company."

Hearing that this was all her grandpa had to do when she wasn't here almost made Christy sad—but then she remembered that lighthearted smile of his. And she hoped Mrs. Waters somehow knew he was there with her and what a special man she had sitting by her side. "That's sweet of you, Grandpa."

He shrugged, let out a chuckle. "Probably does me as much good as her—or more."

It had been thundering for a week that August in Destiny. Thundering but never a drop of rain would fall. Clearly it wanted to, but the skies just kept teasing them with that promising rumble.

And so by the middle of the month the sound of thunder no longer excited anyone, least of all

Charlie, who was beginning to think this god-forsaken summer would never end. His father was still laid up, leaving a man's job on a boy's shoulders. And Susan had become like a ghost, a shadow he would catch a glimpse of leaving the barn after placing a covered plate atop a work bench or ducking into the house in the distance if he looked in her direction when she was out tending the ailing little vegetable garden she'd picked the wrong year to try to grow.

Of course, not seeing her was just as torturous as when he'd seen her every day but not been able to have her. Worse in a way. Like thunder, perhaps the tease of something you want, the possibility, was better than having it taken away entirely.

In the late afternoon of another hot scorching day, Charlie nailed a crossboard onto a wide barn door laid across two sawhorses. He barely noticed the sound of thunder in the distance or the fat billowing clouds overhead, other than the fact that they brought with them a little blessed shade. But he did notice Susan—her blouse a small dot of white in the garden. He tried not to look—after all, he could see very little—but he kept glancing in that direction anyway. If he had to guess, he thought she was kneeling in the cucumber patch, likely seeking any big or ripe enough to pick.

And that was when the skies burst open. It came without warning or fanfare, no grand thunderclap or lightning strike—it just rained. And it felt like heaven falling wetly to the ground.

Rain, during a summer like this one, was probably one of the few things that could steal his attention from Susan, but steal it it did. Charlie leaned back, turned his face skyward, and just laughed. Because this was no small drizzle—it was pouring. It was the kind of rain that would normally send a person running for cover, but he just wanted to bask in it, soak it up, the same as you soak up the sun on the first warm day of spring.

"It's raining! It's really raining!"

He turned and saw Susan—who hadn't run for cover either, and who smiled from ear to ear, equally as overcome with joy. He smiled back—it never occurred to him not to; it was the kind of moment that made you forget what's come before and just want to share the splendor of it. And caught up in the happiness and relief of it all, Charlie followed the next impulse that struck him—he threw his arms around her, picked her up, and spun her around.

When he lowered her to the ground, both of them were laughing, soaked through—and that's when the obvious hit him. Their clothes were drenched. The thin, sleeveless white blouse she wore with a pair of pedal pushers clung to her skin and nothing of her white lace bra was left to the imagination. The darkness of her nipples shone through the fabric—and he went instantly hard at the sight.

And suddenly he wasn't smiling anymore—nor was she. But their gazes stayed locked. The rain still fell in a deluge as his breath grew short and her chest began to heave slightly. *This is happening. This is really happening.* And he couldn't have held back if his life had depended on it.

What took place after that wasn't about any sort of decision, any thought about which moves to make, where to touch, how to kiss—no, it was about pure animal instinct. His hands cupped her face and he kissed her wet lips for all he was worth. To feel her kiss him back, just as fervently, was like . . . the rain itself. No longer a thing yearned for, waited for—it was finally here, consuming him. And he wanted to drown in it.

He knew with his whole soul that he'd never seen anything more beautiful than Susan in the rain, her dark hair clinging to her skin, her shirt soaked through, her face alight with passion. And maybe he never would again. She was that lovely, that real. Hiding nothing now. Letting him see her every response and emotion as it traveled across her face.

It was, again, pure instinct that led his hands to the front of her blouse, to the buttons. They came undone easily beneath his fingers, and as he pushed the blouse from her shoulders, she shoved his dingy white T-shirt up over his stomach, his chest. Her touch left trails of fire on his skin, even in the rain.

And as the fever of his desire escalated, along with the hardness in his pants, he grabbed for the shoulder straps of her bra, yanking them down. And then he was reaching behind her, struggling with the hook, but soon the white lace fell away from her as easily as the blouse had, baring her full breasts before him.

He wanted to take in the sight of those perfect porcelain mounds of flesh—remember what they looked like, lock the vision in his brain—but he also wanted to kiss them, suckle her, and so he didn't hold back. He took her once more into his arms, drew one hardened nipple into his mouth, and knew paradise as she arched, moaned. This was surely the closest to heaven he'd ever been and he wanted to go all the way.

And so he reached for the waistband of her pedal pushers.

And then suffered possibly the most miserable shock of his life—when she suddenly shoved him away.

He stood frozen for a second, getting his balance. And realizing the downpour had slowed to a heavy drizzle now.

"What's wrong?" he asked, lifting his gaze to hers.

She looked startled by the question. "This!" she said. "Everything!"

And he understood—but he just didn't want to let it stop them. "It doesn't have to matter," he said. Even though, in fact, he *knew* it mattered—he just didn't want to let himself believe that right now. Right now he just *wanted* her, everything else be damned.

"I have to go back into that house tonight," she reminded him. "I have to keep on with this life I'm living. I can't just run away from it afterward."

And he understood all that, too. But he still didn't want to think about it. He didn't want reasons to stop. And his frustration made him angry. "This is impossible! You shouldn't come out here if you don't want this, want *me*."

He regretted his tone the second he saw her wounded expression. "Of course I want you, Charlie—I just can't have you. Not really."

"Then . . . hell, maybe we should just keep our distance from each other. Maybe you shouldn't come back out here." More words spoken in anger and frustration. And yet he didn't take them back. He meant them. Because he couldn't be in this halfway. Either this would happen or it wouldn't, but he couldn't bear to play around with it, flirt with it, let it tease him the same way the thunder had been.

She looked crestfallen as she snatched up her bra, blouse—turning her back and rushing to put them on. And he shut his eyes, feeling her pain— God, he'd made her ashamed. He hadn't wanted that. He wasn't sure *what* he'd wanted . . . except just some easy answer, some way to make this be okay.

That was when she took off running toward the house in the still falling rain.

"Susan!" he called after her.

But she didn't stop. And he didn't chase. He didn't want to make this any worse. And the fact was, she belonged to another man.

"I'm sorry!" he called behind her. She still didn't look back. And he guessed he couldn't blame her.

That night he went into town with his parents— his father had had a good day and felt up to treating Charlie and his mother to dinner out at the diner on Main. The streets of Destiny were wet and people were upbeat and smiling. He'd never seen rain make people so happy.

Only *he* wasn't. He didn't know *how* to feel. Angry. Sad. Desperate. Heartbroken. All he knew was that he was pretty damn far from happy.

"Might be able to start comin' back over to the barn with you next week, son," his father said over slices of fresh cherry pie at the diner.

"Good, I could use the help," he said—and then his father told him how proud he was of him for handling so much on his own these last weeks. *Would he be so proud if he knew I'd taken Mr. King's wife's top off today in the rain?*

When he drove the old farm truck up to the barn on the King place the following morning, the sun was shining but the air was softer and more inviting than it had been for a while. He glanced at the house as he drove past, wondering what Susan was doing right now. How was she feeling after yesterday? Did her loins ache the way his did? Was her heart hurting the same as his? Had she had to have sex with King last night, right after Charlie had touched her and kissed her? Had he made her feel even more ashamed?

Slamming the truck's door, he walked toward the barn—surprised as hell when Susan stepped out from it looking as perky and fresh as the day itself, wearing a dress the color of pink lemonade. He didn't think he'd ever been so glad to see anybody in his whole life.

"I'm sorry about yesterday," he told her quickly. "About the way I acted."

But she didn't even respond to that, instead racing ahead to say, "I done some thinkin' last night."

"Yeah?" he asked.

And she said, "Run away with me, Charlie."

And his heart began to beat harder, faster. He sure as hell hadn't seen this coming. He'd never even thought about it before. "Huh?"

"We can run away," she said. "Just the two of us. We can be happy, be together."

Charlie blinked, still caught off guard. "But what about your family? About King takin' care of 'em. With his money and all."

But she shook her head, vehemently, and he could see she'd really thought about this. "God will provide for them. Better than I can." She let out a heavy sigh. "I can't keep livin' like this. I thought I could because I thought I had to—I thought there was no other choice in the world for me. But there is. I lay in bed nights thinkin' of you and me, of how things could be—and then I suddenly just thought, why can't that be real? Why can't we *make* it real? You've made me see that there's more, Charlie. You've made me *want* more."

When he said nothing, trying to simply digest the idea, she said, "Unless it's just sex. Unless you don't care for me the way I care for you. If that's how it is, I understand. And I won't ask more of you. But I care for you, Charlie. I yearn for you."

"It's not just sex," he said quickly, her words moving all through him. "I've never felt anything like this. I know we don't know each other real well, and yet . . . it's like we do."

Her eyes went wide and beautiful. "Yes! I know! I feel that way, too!"

And he started toward her, instinctually—but then he stopped. Remembering yesterday. Remembering she had to go back into that house tonight.

"Will you take me away from here, Charlie?" she asked, her eyes fraught with desperation beneath a blue Destiny sky. "Will you take me someplace where we can do what we want? Where we can be happy? Without anybody else to answer to but each other?"

"Yes," he said. Just that.

And that seemed to be enough. Just the promise. Because now it was *her* coming toward *him*. Now it was her arms sliding around his neck; it was her pressing her curves up against the straighter lines of his body. "You make me want everything," she whispered in his ear. "And you make me think I can actually have it."

And when Charlie kissed her, *he* thought they could have it, too.

But when a moment later Susan took his hand and led him inside the barn to a soft pile of work tarpaulins lying there, he forgot about thinking altogether. Kissing, they sank to their knees, and then she was on her back and his hand was beneath her dress. And soon her legs were wrapped around his hips and they were making love.

"Donald is taking his mother to church on Sunday," Susan said afterward as they lay in each other's arms. "I'll pretend to be sick and stay home. We can leave then."

Charlie thought through it and agreed that would be enough time—three days from now—

to make plans. They could take his family's farm truck. He'd think of a place to head to between now and then. He could empty his small savings account at the Bank of Destiny Saturday afternoon and hopefully word from the bank wouldn't spread before he took off on Sunday. And it wouldn't be forever, they decided. He could call his parents, let them know he was okay. And she would call her own when the time felt right.

"We're going to be so happy, Charlie," she said, smiling up at him. "So, so happy. I can feel it."

CHRISTY walked in the front door of the Hungry Fisherman to find the white cat, Dinah, suddenly swirling around her ankles again. The place was empty at the moment, thank goodness, and Polly came running from behind the counter to shoo the cat away. "You, out," she said, holding the door open and shoving the cat with her shoe. Christy couldn't help feeling a little jarred on the cat's behalf.

"Sorry," Polly said. "I know it's my own fault. I feed her at the back door and expect her to know she can't come in the front. But I can't seem to bring myself to just quit takin' care of her completely."

Christy smiled. "She's lucky to have you."

But Polly just shrugged. "Still need to find her a home. Cat hair in the buffet might be enough to kill what's left of our business. And you can bet Abner's none too happy about this, either."

Christy took a seat at what had become her usual booth and ordered a piece of key lime pie.

She knew she and Jack had planned to have a last dinner here tonight, but like the rest of today's plans with him, that was off. So she told Polly, "We're leaving in the morning, so I just thought I'd stop and say goodbye."

"Well, I'm real sorry to hear that," Polly said, then tilted her head. "And it's none of my business, but you don't seem like your usual perky self today, honey. Sad to be endin' your vacation?"

She nodded. "Something like that."

Polly put her hands on her hips and narrowed her gaze. "Or . . . is it man trouble?"

Christy sat up a little straighter, her fork paused in midair. "Why do you ask?" Did it show?

"Well . . . maybe I overheard part of your conversation about that hunky Jack when you were in here with that pretty dark-haired girl a while back," she confessed. "Seemed like there were ups and downs there."

Christy thought it over for a few seconds and decided there was no reason not to come clean. "Well, it's completely down now, and there won't be any more ups."

Polly looked disappointed as she took a seat on the cracked vinyl across from Christy. "He did somethin' that bad?"

Christy gave another nod. Then said, "Is it wrong to expect someone to treat you the same way you'd treat them? With things like . . . honesty?"

"No ma'am," Polly said. "Sure isn't. But I'll admit I'm surprised. Jack didn't seem like the sort to lie."

"Don't I know it," Christy said on a sigh. "That's why it caught me off guard. And I don't think he hurt me intentionally. He's been through some things that made him want to be . . . less than open. And he was apologetic. But we all have our troubles, right? That doesn't mean it's okay to treat people poorly."

"No, it doesn't. Though . . . if he wants to make amends, you're not open to that?" Polly leaned forward and spoke conspiratorially. "Because I'm just sayin', if I had a fine specimen like that warmin' my bed, I'd have a hard time kickin' him out of it. And there's a lot to be said for forgiveness. And for overlookin' somebody's flaws." Then she laughed. "I mean, take Abner. There's a lot to look past there, believe me. Most folks around here think I'm married to a crazy man. But I chose to look past that a long time ago. Because he makes me happy. He won't quit paradin' around in those damn hats, but he makes me happy. And I decided that was more important than the rest of it."

Christy appreciated Polly's point of view, but she didn't have the heart to suggest that Jack's offenses were possibly tougher to get past than Abner's. Not that Christy thought life married to Abner would be easy—but it was comparing apples to oranges.

Polly gave Christy her pie on the house, and when Christy exited back out into the hot sun, she found Dinah still loitering near the door. Stooping down to pet the kitty, she said, "I wonder what will become of you. And of me, too, for that matter."

JACK sat on Fletcher's porch, drinking a beer and peering out over the ocean. He was going to miss it here. And yet, in a way, he *already* missed it here—because part of what had been so great about being here was enjoying the place with Christy. Without her, everything felt a little empty.

"You can get her back if you want to," Fletcher said matter-of-factly.

Jack glanced over at his ponytailed friend. "And how is it that I go about that?"

"Just have faith," Fletcher told him.

And Jack couldn't help rolling his eyes. "Oh, you mean like how your wife is going to come back. All you have to do is wish for it and it happens?"

Fletcher gave his usual, easy shrug, clearly unoffended. "It's not so much about wishing as it is believing, expecting. Knowing that's how the story will end because nothing else makes any sense."

Jack liked Fletcher—in fact, he was a downright interesting dude—but he felt the need to try to reason with him. "What about times in life when the story ends in a way that *doesn't* make sense?"

"Then whosever story it was didn't believe it would make sense in the end. Or the story wasn't really over and it only seemed like it was."

When it came right down to it, Jack *liked* Fletcher's way of looking at life. And he wanted to believe it was all as simple as Fletcher claimed. But the trouble was that he just didn't. Because Christy had every right to have lost faith in him, to have stopped trusting him. And he couldn't think of a way in the world to change that.

When Jack stood up to depart a little while later, he said goodbye to Fletcher for the last time.

"I'll miss you, my friend," Fletcher told him.

"Same here," Jack replied. And as he neared the edge of the porch, ready to return to the beach, he looked over his shoulder to add a last thought. "I hope she comes back, man."

And Fletcher smiled the same calm, sure smile as always to say, "She will."

Jack considered suggesting they keep in touch, if only because he would always wonder—and if she came back, he would want to know. But then he thought better of it—because if she *didn't* ever come back, well, then maybe he'd rather just stay in the dark about it.

Heading toward the wooden steps that led through the shrubbery and down into the sand, he glanced across the way to see the woman he remembered meeting at the Sunset Celebration—Tamra, he thought was her name—sitting on another big, open porch, working on her stained glass. He hadn't realized she was Fletcher's neighbor.

And then he spotted a For Sale sign in the quaint little green cottage next door to her and directly across from Fletcher's, also facing the ocean. And he couldn't help thinking that it would be a nice place to live.

The fact was, he really had no ties—he could live wherever he wanted. He could stop flipping houses, find some new hobby to take up his spare time. And maybe after Christy, a whole new place would feel good, fresh, like a new beginning.

But . . . that could never really be. Because,

as he'd already realized, being here without her would be . . . empty. And maybe being *anywhere* without her would be empty now.

Early the following morning, Reece and Fifi came out to the parking lot to say goodbye.

"How is it possible I might actually miss you?" Christy said, peering down at the giant iguana.

Reece winked. "See, I told you she was lovable in her own way."

Jack had already walked to the bakery to get some donuts for the road, and Christy was glad. She had a feeling it was going to be a long drive home—for many reasons.

A quick last stop at Sunnymeade allowed her to give Grandpa Charlie one last hug goodbye, and she stepped out in the hall and worked to hide her tears as Jack and her grandpa said so long, as well.

They stayed quiet as they started on the journey. Jack was driving and it didn't surprise her when he pulled off the road to let them both look for a moment at the stretch of secluded beach in the distance that they'd noticed on their drive in. It had been merely a pretty view then. Now it was a place where so much had happened. Maybe *too* much. And her heart broke all over again just peering out over it.

Goodbye, Coral Cove.

". . . but it's no use going back to yesterday,
because I was a different person then."

Lewis Carroll, *Alice in Wonderland*

Chapter 20

CHRISTY SAT on her sagging couch piecing together jewelry while Bethany got ready for a date
in the next room. It was hot and the windows
were open—they couldn't afford A/C—and the
particularly odd scent of lime whiskey wafted
through the room.

In some ways, the trip to Coral Cove felt like a
dream. One which, like all dreams, had eventually ended. And brought her back to where she'd
started. And it was hard not to feel sad. Not only
about the end of the dream about Coral Cove, but
also the end of the dream about Jack.

The drive home a few days ago had felt pre-
dictably long, fluctuating between lengthy, heavy
stretches of silence and Jack occasionally taking
another stab at "trying to make her see reason."
And by the time they'd arrived home, it was clear
he thought she was just being stubborn.

Finally, as they'd crossed the bridge over the Ohio River back into Cincinnati, she'd said to him, "Do you remember what it felt like to have the rug yanked out from under your whole life when you found out about your wife cheating?"

"Of course," he'd said. "It was horrible. But this and that are two very different things."

"I'm not suggesting they're the same," she told him. "But I've already had the rug yanked out from under my life when my parents died. And then . . . then . . ." Oh yuck, she'd started feeling more emotional than she'd wanted to. But she'd pulled herself together and kept going. "You came along and I started feeling happy again. And what happened in the end just reminded me . . . I don't ever want to feel that way again, that blindsided, that abandoned or that flipped-completely-upside-down without warning. And to trust someone who's already shown me they can't be trusted would just be . . . setting myself up for another big fall. And I just can't risk another big fall, Jack."

"Christy, I could give you everything!" he'd exclaimed from the opposite seat. "I *want* to give you everything. And yeah, I fucked up. Everybody does sometimes. But you know I'm a good guy, you know I never meant to hurt you. Why can't you just try to get past this?"

And her answer had come out simple and sure. "Because you showed me that even a good guy can hurt me. Without even meaning to. And that doesn't make me feel . . . safe. And what's the point of a relationship if it doesn't make you feel safe?"

Now she thought about what he'd said, that he could give her everything. Though he'd never gotten specific, she'd known what he meant. That he could take care of all her money woes, and Grandpa Charlie's, too. And maybe, even if only for her grandpa's sake, she should be jumping all over that—doing what Jack said, getting past it, letting it go.

But everything had become so much more complicated now. Or maybe it had always been complicated and she just hadn't realized it. Or maybe it was the things she'd learned about herself in Coral Cove that had turned things more complex.

But what it boiled down to was this: Despite how Jack's lies had hurt her, she also really admired all he'd made of himself, the way he'd built his business from nothing, on his own terms, and she liked how humble and down to earth he remained in spite of his success. And now . . . well, maybe she wanted that, too. Maybe she wanted to prove to herself that she could do this on her own, make her own money, become a success at something she loved. Maybe she didn't *want* to take the easy way out anymore. And even if part of her loved Jack for wanting to give her everything she'd been looking for from the moment she'd met him, she also wished . . . that *he* wanted that for her, too.

Up until her parents' death, her life had been too easy—she'd been spoiled and fawned over. And then it had instantly become too hard—and nothing had worked since. And somehow, having her heart crushed just made her yearn, more than ever, to make her life *work*. To move on, move forward. To quit living in the remnants of something old and instead create a new sort of existence for herself.

Just then Bethany walked into the room. So Christy looked up and said, "I think I've just figured out the secret to a perfect relationship."

Bethany's eyebrows shot up in anticipation. "Let's hear it."

"It's feeling safe with someone . . . without wanting them to save you."

"That's deep," Bethany said.

And Christy laughed. Jack would probably say the same thing.

Then Bethany asked, "Does this skirt make me look slutty?" She did a turn in a pink leopard print mini she'd picked up for just a few dollars on a clearance rack.

"No," Christy assured her. "More cute than slutty."

"Crap," Bethany replied. "I was going for slutty tonight. Back to the drawing board." Then she retreated again into her bedroom.

And Christy thought about how much she loved Bethany and always would, but somehow she'd gotten to know herself a lot better on her trip to Coral Cove, and the result was that she'd felt a little less connected to her roommate since returning home. It was almost as if . . . she'd gone away and changed, grown, and coming back made everything different. Even things that were entirely the same felt completely different now.

And so it *hadn't* been a dream. Because even

if she'd come home to the same life, the things
that had happened to her there had changed her.
You just miss the things you felt there, that's all. And
maybe that meant . . . she should try to get them
back, feel them again. Well, at least some of them,
the things she could feel *safely* again.

A few minutes later, as Christy continued her
work, her mind spinning with fresh ideas and
possibilities, Bethany came back out, this time in
a tight red micro-mini and matching red heels.
"Well?" She held her hands out.

"Nailed it," Christy said. "Much, much slut-
tier."

Bethany smiled. Then came to join Christy on
the couch, her expression softening as she asked,
"Should I be worried about you?"

Christy looked over at her, surprised by the
concern. "Why?"

"Well, ever since you got home and told me
about this whole Jack fiasco, you've just seemed
. . . not depressed exactly, but . . . you've seemed
more like *me*."

Christy let her brow knit. "Like you how?"

Bethany tilted her head, clearly thinking it
through. "Just . . . more practical, I guess. More
matter-of-fact. And . . . less romantic."

"What do I have to be romantic about?" Christy
asked on a sigh.

"Maybe that's my point," Bethany replied.
"You've never had *much* to be romantic about, but
you always were anyway. Just in general. You believed in true love, happily ever after and all that.
And I'm worried you don't anymore."

Christy took all that in, thinking it over. Maybe everything Bethany was saying was true. And maybe that was the saddest part of all. But if even a guy like Jack let you down in the end, what chance was there for true love? And at the moment, she couldn't imagine letting herself even *begin* to go there again, to believe in that, to put herself at risk again believing in it, yet secretly—deep inside— just waiting for the other shoe to drop. "If that's so," she finally told Bethany, "maybe it's good. Wise."

Bethany tilted her head, cast a sad smile. "But I love that about you," she said. "Because . . . if *you* don't believe in happily ever after anymore, what chance do the rest of us have? What chance do *I* have? I guess I've come to count on your heart to be open enough for both of us."

Unexpectedly moved, Christy said, "I didn't know that."

"Well, it was kind of a secret," Bethany admitted quietly. "Us jaded, slutty girls don't like to go that soft, you know?" She winked, trying for another grin that didn't quite make it to her eyes.

"To be honest," Christy said, "I'm not sure *what* I believe right now—except for one thing. That I need to show myself I can stand on my own two feet. So that's what I'm going to focus on doing. And I'm going to be fine." She squeezed Bethany's hand, a silent promise. "Just fine."

Of course, just then she thought of Jack. In better times. Times when she trusted in him completely and he'd touched her and kissed her and made her feel more whole than she'd known she could. And just when she was so committed to being strong and sturdy, the memory cut like a knife into her heart.

So she pushed the sweet memories away and kept on being who she needed to be right now. Strong Christy. Not romantic Christy. Or weak Christy. Or Alice in Wonderland wandering this way and that, helpless and lost. Those old versions of herself didn't exist anymore. She wouldn't let them.

And she would only cry over Jack late at night, in the dark of her bedroom, so that it would be like a tree falling in the forest—if no one saw it, maybe it never really happened.

THE following day Christy didn't go in to work until the afternoon, so she used her morning aggressively. She called the nice lady, Adrianne, at Sunnymeade and asked more pointed questions this time. Would they be willing to defer some of the payments if Christy could give them a chunk of money up front? Could they work with her if she made regular payments to them, even if small? The answers she got gave her more hope about the situation than she'd had up to now.

Then she got online and started looking at apartment rentals in Coral Cove. Because wouldn't moving there really make sense? She could be with Grandpa Charlie. The people were nice there. She'd fallen in love with the quirky little seaside town and if she really wanted a new start, wouldn't Coral Cove be a great place for that?

And maybe she could even adopt the cat at the

Hungry Fisherman. For some reason, the friendly stray had stayed on her mind and she almost even wished she'd brought Dinah home with her.

But then it suddenly hit her why she'd felt an attachment to the white kitty. Dinah was an orphan, just like her—doing her best, scraping to get by. And she probably needed somebody to love her. But maybe a new start for Christy in Coral Cove would make it so neither one of them felt like an orphan anymore.

And the idea of moving, which had once seemed so monumental as to be overwhelming, now felt . . . less so. More doable. A lot of things felt more doable.

If she really did it, though, the hard part would be leaving Jack. Even the last few days, just knowing he was across the street had made her feel a lingering connection with him.

But on the other hand, if she knew she couldn't forgive him, what did it matter if he was close or far away? And he'd left her alone ever since they'd arrived home, so maybe he was getting over her more easily than she was getting over him. Maybe he didn't miss her. And maybe he was realizing she hadn't been all that special to him anyway.

Next, she'd left early for work. And she'd taken a huge step. She'd stopped at her bank to apply for a loan large enough to keep Grandpa Charlie at Sunnymeade for now and also help her establish her jewelry business and move. She knew it was a huge risk, but she was willing to take it. Her recent success with her jewelry had given her a belief in herself she'd never had before. And *that* was what had changed in her at Coral Cove.

And as she'd exited the bank out into a hot summer Cincinnati day, something hit her. Something big.

If Jack had told her the truth all along, if she'd gone to Coral Cove thinking: *Hooray, I've found a guy I'm crazy about who can also bail me out financially* . . . she wouldn't have learned *any* of this about herself. She wouldn't have worried about selling her jewelry and then been bold enough to pursue it. She wouldn't have figured out that having a guy she loved made money seem so much less important. She wouldn't feel so good about her talents right now, or her courage, or about taking care of herself. She wouldn't have figured out that she didn't want to be saved. And though she'd never thank Jack for lying to her, she supposed everything happened for a reason, even the really bad, hurtful stuff—even if you couldn't see why right away.

She went through her work day with a new sense of confidence. She felt older, wiser—though it had nothing to do with age—and she felt more in control of her existence and her future.

And as she returned home that evening, she glanced at Jack's house—quiet in the June heat— and she suffered a familiar pang of loss, but also a thankfulness for the happiness he had brought her, however brief. For the first time since their breakup, she was able to look at it with a bit of distance and be glad she'd experienced such closeness and bliss with a man. And she decided not to worry about if she ever felt that way again but to instead just have faith—like Grandpa Charlie had taught her—that everything would work out in her life for the best. Even if her heart hurt like hell right now.

And then, getting out of the car, she glanced up the street to the Harrington house, where a For Sale sign had been posted in the front yard. Another happily ever after that hadn't turned out to be happily ever after. *But maybe they'll both find happiness elsewhere. I hope she finds someone who sees how her plants are her soul and would never, ever break them.*

CHARLIE couldn't sleep. And he wanted to blame it on a pain in his knee or worry over his living arrangements . . . but he knew it was about Christy and Jack. His granddaughter's love life was surely none of his business and he should stay out of it. But ever since they'd left, it had been eating at him.

People squandered love too easily. He thought it the greatest sin of life. But the big joke of it all was that maybe you couldn't see that until you were old, until long after you'd squandered it. He just didn't want Christy or Jack either one to wake up one day when they were old and have regrets over what they'd done or hadn't done *right now.*

Rolling over, he looked at the glowing red numbers on his bedside clock. Nearly midnight. Too late to call.

But he reached for his cell phone anyway, and he pulled up Jack's number, having gotten it when they were making plans for their fishing day. He already knew what he'd say because it had been burning in his gut for days now.

"Hello? Charlie?" Jack sounded groggy, like he'd been asleep.

"Sorry to wake you, Jack, but this couldn't wait."

"Are you okay?"

"Me—I'm fine. It's you I'm concerned about."

Jack hesitated on the other end. "How's that?"

"You and my grandgirl, you're good together. Too good to let a mistake or two blow the whole thing."

Jack hesitated only briefly before he answered, "Yeah, try telling *her* that. Because *I* have and she's not buying it. Stubborn as a mule, turns out."

Charlie chuckled softly. He'd once been stubborn, too. As had his son. "Family trait, I'm afraid. But you have to get her back, my boy, no matter what it takes."

"I do?" He sounded understandably baffled by Charlie's sudden insistence.

But Charlie simply said, "You do. Because love is rarer than people think. And she doesn't know that yet. She doesn't know yet about compromise and sacrifice and forgiveness. And I'd never ask her to sell herself short, but I know that life isn't black and white, cut and dried. And you have to show her who you really are, you have to show her that you understand her, value her. You have to make her want to take another shot at happiness more than she fears it. You have to make her look *past* fear."

On the other end, Jack sighed audibly. "That all

sounds good, but, uh, kind of like a tall order. So how exactly do you suggest I do that?"

"Simple," Charlie said. "Figure out the one thing she needs from you that nobody else is givin' her. Dig down deep, under the surface, and find it."

More hesitation from Jack. "Simple, huh?"

But Charlie just chuckled. "Once you figure it out, it'll seem like it was the simplest thing in the world."

"Huh," Jack murmured, sounding tired and perplexed.

However, Charlie had said what he'd intended to say and now the rest was up to Jack. And Christy. So he told him, "I'll let you get back to sleep now. And maybe *I'll* be able to sleep now, too. Goodnight, my boy." And then he hung up.

And he rolled back over to a comfortable position. But he still didn't fall asleep.

Instead he thought about regrets. He felt them in his heart. And he said a prayer to God that his granddaughter would end up happy.

And after that, he thought of Susan. On a sunny August Sunday, a flowered scarf tied beneath her chin and an old suitcase in her hand. Her eyes had sparkled with hope. It was, he realized looking back, probably the happiest he'd ever seen her. And yet, ironically, that vision of her, seared into his brain, had always been a painful memory.

She'd stood in front of the old farmhouse, waiting for him. When he'd pulled up in the truck and gotten out, slamming the heavy old door, she'd said, "He'll be gone 'til at least three. We can be far away by then." Her voice had come out sounding part nervous, part excited. And something in that had broken his heart. Because he was about to break *hers*.

"Susan, I can't. *We* can't," he said.

She'd blinked. "Can't what?"

"Go."

Horror and disbelief etched themselves onto her face. "What?"

He hated himself in that moment. He hated himself in a way he never had before—or since. It was the only time in his life he'd ever willingly destroyed someone's hopes and dreams. But he'd swallowed back the emotions as best he could and tried to explain. "I have nothin' to offer you." He shook his head. "I don't have any money. I don't have a job. At least King can provide for you." He'd lowered his eyes while he'd spoken—unable to face the despair in hers. "I don't know that *I* can. And it just seems too risky."

She instantly stepped forward, beseeching him. "But I'm not afraid, Charlie! I know we'll be fine. I know it!"

Yet her words didn't change anything. The more time that had passed since he'd agreed to run away with her, the more practicality had set in. He didn't want to hurt his parents; he didn't want Susan to hurt hers, either. They'd both be going from situations where they had only a little to one where they'd have even less. Charlie was truly in love with Susan, and he didn't want her to have regrets in a week, or a month, or a year. "Susan, I love you. And it's because I care for ya that I won't let you do this. I'd be okay no matter what happened, but I'm not sure *you* would."

"What do you mean?"

"You don't really know what you want, or how serious this is. You don't know what's good for ya right now. You'd be sorry down the road and there'd be no comin' back. So I just can't let you do it."

"I know what I want, Charlie!" she insisted, yelling at him in her front yard. "I hate it here—I hate it! And with you, I'm happy. So, so happy."

"But what about . . . everything? Your family? What if one of 'em got sick and needed some expensive treatment or surgery? What if I can't give you the things ya need and you end up hatin' me for it and wishin' you'd never left?"

She shook her head vehemently. "That could never be."

"I know you *think* you know," Charlie said to her. "I know this seems like the answer. But I'd never forgive myself if somethin' bad happened—to you, or any member of your family—and because of me it couldn't be fixed."

The truth was, he wanted nothing more than the opportunity to try to make her happy. But the further truth was . . . deep down, he just didn't have faith in her to be strong enough, to transcend her current life, to look beyond the rose-colored glasses he feared she was wearing and face the realities their new life together would bring.

"I know you can't see it now, but one day you will," he assured her.

"See what?" She shook her head, looking completely bereft.

"That I'm only doin' what's best for you."

She'd just stood there staring at him, sad and desperate.

And then she'd broken his heart even a little more. She'd dropped to her knees on the cracked front walk that led from the farmhouse to the drive. And she'd clasped her hands together and begged him. "Please. Please let's go away from here. Let's forget this conversation. Let's forget everything bad. If I stay here, Charlie, I'll die inside. *Please*."

That almost got him. Almost. To see and hear her utter despair made his heart hurt physically.

But despite being the same age as her, today he felt called upon to be the older one, the responsible one who looked beyond the moment. And so he said, yet one more time, "I'm doin' what's best for you, Susan, I promise. Trust me." And then he lowered his eyes again, unable to keep seeing her that way, as he muttered, "I'm sorry. So sorry."

Then he turned and walked back to the truck. He left her there, on her knees, tears rolling down her cheeks. Because if he stayed even a moment longer, or if he let her see that his own heart was crumbling to dust inside his chest, maybe he'd do the wrong thing and leave with her. And ruin her life.

He was only eighteen. He didn't know how

to take care of her and he didn't want to let her down. Above all else, he wanted her to be safe. And with King, at least she had that. And it was more than *he* could promise her.

And that was it.

And life went on.

He and his father finished the barn—though there never came a request to paint it, and he was glad.

Susan never again brought a sandwich or a bottle of Coca-Cola out to him. In fact, during the final two weeks of work, Mr. King mentioned that his young wife was sick in bed. He confided with a laugh that he was secretly hoping to find out it meant she was in the family way. And Charlie had kind of wanted to vomit, even though he knew it was a different kind of sickness altogether she was experiencing. Heartache.

Although it was difficult at times in a town as small as Destiny, he and Susan kept their distance from each other as much as possible, resulting in only fleeting glimpses here and there—a chance sighting at the General Mercantile from time to time, occasionally passing each other on the road, a near head-on physical collision once at the Ambassador Theater nearly three years after that hot, passion-filled summer. She'd been with King; Charlie had been with his brand new fiancée and had wished for the theater floor to open up and swallow him whole.

He'd gone on to marry a good woman. He'd loved her, he'd raised a nice family with her, he'd had a pleasant life. But deep inside, he'd always pined for Susan and felt a passion for her he'd never experienced with anyone else.

And as for Susan, she'd never gotten in the family way. She and King had lived on that farm alone together for twenty years until a heart attack took him. Months later, Charlie heard she'd met a man from Portsmouth and that she'd sold the farm and was moving away.

But on the very day after his wife's friend Edna Ferris had told him this when he'd stopped to buy a bushel of apples at her orchard, he'd been walking across Destiny's town square—when he'd looked up and found himself face to face with Susan herself.

She'd matured from a pretty girl into a beautiful lady—though her eyes looked far too tired for a woman of thirty-nine. And they stood close enough to each other—frozen in place actually— that it was impossible not to feel it all over again. That same magnetism. That same yearning. Good Lord, all those years later and it still hadn't died.

"Heard you sold the farm," he said. He wasn't sure *what* to say, so that was what had come out.

"Finally getting away," she told him.

He'd just nodded. Already out of words.

And an awkward silence stretched between them until she said, "You were wrong."

"Huh?"

"Back then. When we were young. You were wrong. I knew what I wanted. I would have been happier with you than with him. Nothing as good has ever happened to me as when you were building that barn."

His heart had plummeted. "I'm . . . sorry," he said. Lost for words even more now. Surprised at her boldness. Apology was all he had.

"Are you happy?" she asked.

For a moment, he couldn't catch his breath. But then he managed . . . the right answer, the easy answer. "Yes."

Yet she seemed completely unconvinced. And so confident about it that it made him feel caught in a lie. "But not as happy as you would have been with me, if you'd let yourself."

"No," he agreed simply. It suddenly felt useless to deny it. Then he said, "You? Are you happy? With the man you're marrying?"

"Yes. But not as happy as I would have been with you."

He let out a heavy breath. It was too painful, thinking about what could have been, what he'd ruined. "I hope that'll change. I hope it'll turn out that you find more happiness with him than you can even imagine."

She'd seemed resentful up to now, but this appeared to soften her, letting him see in her the girl he'd first fallen for twenty years earlier. "Thank you," she said quietly. "It won't happen—you'll always have my heart, Charlie—but thank you anyway."

And like the last time they'd parted, life went on. But that meeting had stayed with him for a long time. Just being close to her had turned his heart inside out, making him happy and sad all at once, in that way only love can.

But what it came down to was that he'd made a

huge mistake—he hadn't known what she needed; he hadn't trusted her to be capable of more than he saw. And that was when he'd realized the greatest thing you could ever do for someone you love is have faith in them. That was all. Just have faith.

And somehow it seemed like the same thing was going on with Jack and Christy. And if Jack could figure out what Christy needed—hell, it wouldn't fix Charlie's past mistakes; it wouldn't fix the pain he'd caused or the love he'd ruined, but at least maybe it would fix something for somebody else.

Despite himself, sleep still eluded him. Susan, Susan, Susan. He'd thought that call to Jack would clear his mind of the past, at least a little, but it hadn't.

And so at long last, despite the odd hour, he slowly hauled himself up out of bed with the help of his walker. He started to head toward his wheelchair, but then thought better of it. He'd been more active when Christy was here, resulting in the nurses encouraging him to use the walker more, the wheelchair less. This was a good opportunity to do so.

Soon he moved slowly down the quiet, dark corridor outside his room until he reached Mrs. Waters' door. Gently, he pushed it open and studied her from a distance, a soft shaft of moonglow shining through the window to light her face.

She hadn't changed so much. He could still see in her the beauty she always had—even if she was always asleep now, and hooked to machines.

More slow steps led him to the bedside chair

he often occupied these days. Reaching up, he touched her arm, rubbed it softly. "Life is funny, isn't it?" he mused in a whisper. Then he gave his head a soft shake. "Still a miracle to me that we both ended up here together, my sweet Susan. Of all the rest homes in all the world, they rolled you in to mine." He gave a quiet chuckle, and prayed she could hear him, that somewhere inside her she could feel happy to have him near her, could silently smile at his little Casablanca joke.

"One day soon you'll wake up." He knew that with his whole soul. He finally had the faith in Susan that he should have had when they were young. And he needed to be there—for her, and for himself—when she opened her eyes and re-joined life again.

And that was the *real* reason he couldn't bear the thought of leaving Sunnymeade.

JACK barely slept that night. Charlie's words kept haunting him. They'd haunted him all damn night. And all damn day after he'd woken up the next morning.

Now he sat out on his front porch swing eating a bowl of ice cream. It was hot out—the thick of the Cincinnati summer was upon them—and it seemed like as good a dinner as any. *That's what I like about being single—no one can yell at you if you feel like eating ice cream for dinner.*

He'd kept to himself since getting home—he'd caught up on work, he'd resumed fixing up his house . . . and he'd finally packed away that old honeymoon picture. Now, of course, brand new heartache had taken the place of the old, so also on his to-do list since returning home was doing his damnedest to get over the girl across the street.

He'd felt nearly as alone as he had in the early days after finding out about Candy's disloyalty. But he'd tried to ignore that and be the guy he'd been before Christy had come along. The guy who closed himself off from feeling very much. The guy who focused on his business and home renovations. The guy who had everything all under control. And he'd figured he could keep right on doing that until it became real and not just a matter of shoving the hurt away. But Charlie's phone call had changed that.

On one hand, he didn't know what the hell to make of it. He liked Charlie and thought the old guy had a lot of good insights on life—but on the other hand, for all he knew, that call was the result of some medication he was on or something. And maybe he should just regard it as an old man's ramblings.

Because by the time they'd gotten home, Christy had finally convinced him they were really through. And maybe it was just healthier to accept that than to keep fighting it, keep wanting and wishing for something he'd lost and wasn't getting back.

Life, it seemed to him, was a delicate balance of hope versus acceptance, and it could be difficult to know when the best thing to do was to just cross that line. Accept loss. Try to make peace with it and move on. And right now, Charlie had him screwed up on where the line was.

Forget about it. Forget the call. Forget getting Christy back. If she doesn't think you're worth forgiving, then why do you want her anyway? You don't need any more hurt. Maybe the best thing for both of you really is to just accept that this is over.

Even if the mere thought of her still makes you happy, sad, crazy, and wildly hot for her body all at the same time.

He rolled his eyes at the thought. *I'll get over her. I really will. Starting now.*

He set his empty ice cream bowl aside as Christy's car pulled to the curb across the street. She didn't look up as she got out—in fact, she appeared rushed as she hurried to her front door. He wondered what was up. But then he stopped. *She's not your business anymore.*

Well, he *tried* to stop. But he kept watching. He watched her slide her key into the lock, then turn it. Then jiggle the knob. Then cuss. "Damn it." Her voice echoed across the street.

Two minutes later, she still struggled with the door.

And even Jack felt her frustration. He was mad at her and sad at her and lots of other things, too, but he still wanted her to be able to get in her front door. And without quite planning it, he found himself standing up and walking across the street.

Stepping up onto her porch behind her, he realized he hadn't been this close to her in days and that it felt strange—and desperately good. But he didn't want to feel that. He wanted to feel surly and bitter instead. So he said, "Big date?"

She flinched, then turned to him with a sneer. Understandable, he supposed. And it made her no less gorgeous. "If you must know, I'm waiting for an important phone call and I forgot my cell today."

Jack shifted his weight from one foot to the other. He almost knew what they were both thinking, even if he hesitated to say it. It seemed an odd road to go down again. But he still finally said, "Want me to break the door down, Alice?"

. . . and the fall was over.

Lewis Carroll, *Alice in Wonderland*

Chapter 21

CHRISTY CONSIDERED the offer. It was all too tempting to say yes. But . . . it suddenly seemed like an irrational move. It was a phone call, after all, not . . . a date with a rich guy. And for the first time, her original decision to have him bust the door down suddenly seemed irrational, too. Funny, at the time that date had seemed so all-important. *That was before you were brave enough to depend on yourself and just wanted someone to rescue you.* She was glad those days were over because she felt so much stronger inside now—even if not all that much had really changed.

"It's not a lock I don't have a key to this time," she explained. "It's just that the regular lock always sticks. Let me try it one more time."

And looking down with fresh determination, she shoved the key back in the lock, then pulled it back just a smidge, then gently turned the doorknob and key at the same time with just the right finesse—and the lock finally clicked open.

She gasped in wonder as she lifted her eyes to the man next to her and they both let out happy laughs. "Life's little miracles," she said.

And he replied, "They come along when you least expect them."

"Thanks for the offer, though," she told him. "It was sweet of you to be concerned."

"I'm a sweet guy," he said, their eyes meeting briefly again. But then he blew it off with a wink and a joke. "Just don't let that get around."

As he followed her up the stairs to the apartment, he asked, "So what's this phone call you're stressed about? Something about Charlie? Is he doing all right?"

She looked over her shoulder at him as she entered her bedroom, making a beeline for her phone on the rickety bedside table. "He's fine as far as I know," she said. "I'm expecting a call from my bank."

"Oh?" He sounded surprised, which she could understand. She was still pretty surprised at her own boldness, too.

And she didn't mind telling him about it—though the words came out more quietly than intended. "I applied for a loan," she said as she grabbed up her phone to check it. And sure enough, she'd missed a call and had a voice mail.

"A loan?" he said behind her. "To take care of your grandpa?"

But she was already dialing the voice mail, so she held up a finger to ask Jack to wait a minute.

"Ms. Knight, this is George Donner, your loan officer. We've thoroughly reviewed your loan application and would be happy to extend to you the amount you've requested—however, given your short credit history and your current income, it'll be necessary to have a co-signer on the loan." From there, he went on to explain what she already knew—that a co-signer bore the responsibility of making payments on the loan if she failed to.

This was just what she'd feared and hoped against. She didn't want to make anyone bear her burden. And besides, the only person she knew who even had the means to co-sign for her was the guy standing behind her right now, the guy she didn't want to ask for any financial favors. She knew he would probably do it, but she didn't want to be the girl he'd originally thought her, the girl who would use him for his money.

"You don't look happy," he said. "They turned you down?"

"Not exactly." She continued looking at her phone in order to avoid looking at *him*. "It's just that they want . . ."

"A co-signer," he guessed.

"Yep," she confirmed, tossing her phone on the bed in discouragement.

"Tell me about the loan, Alice. Is it to take care of your grandpa? How much is it for?"

Christy was torn. Because she knew he was going to offer. And she almost didn't even want to let him. And yet . . . she *knew* she could make the payments; she just knew it. Her jewelry was selling so well and there were no signs of it stopping. And she would save as much of her money as possible in case lean times came, like after tourist season ended. And then maybe she could get into some boutiques further south, where tourist season *didn't* really end, or maybe she could try to get some sort of foothold selling her pieces online, and then it wouldn't even be about location.

So she took a deep breath and told him the amount. "And mostly, yes, it's to support Grandpa Charlie. But also to help me get my jewelry business more firmly established now that I've seen such promising results."

"I'd be happy to co-sign for you," he said. "If you'll let me."

Christy pulled in her breath. She remained torn—but tempted. If she did this, if she let this happen, she had to make sure they were both on the same page about it. "If I were to accept your offer, Jack, it wouldn't mean I want your money."

"I know that, Alice," he said very calmly.

"And I'll make the payments, come high or hell water. I'm not looking for a bailout anymore—I promise. I need for you to understand that and to know how serious I am about it."

Jack peered down into her pretty hazel eyes, so desperate and wild at the moment, and longed to put her at ease. He didn't like her feeling she had to justify herself to him. And he was sorely tempted to tell her he could just pay for Charlie's care at Sunnymeade himself, and that he'd be happy to give her whatever additional amount she needed for her business.

But even as he opened his mouth to say all this, he realized . . . it was the wrong answer.

She didn't want a bailout. She didn't want his money.

And he instinctively understood that she didn't even necessarily want to be put at ease right now.

She wanted something else entirely.

She needed . . . for him to believe in her as much as she'd come to believe in herself. She needed him to believe that she was capable of making smart decisions and growing her jewelry business.

What he'd had in life that she didn't were people who had always believed in him and supported him—his parents, teachers and professors, friends and co-workers—and only in this moment did he realize how much their encouragement had mattered when it came to following his dreams and striking out on his own.

So instead of offering her the money, he offered her something else. He said simply, "I have faith in you. All the faith in the world."

And when an unexpected light sparked in Christy's eyes, he understood—that was what Charlie had meant. He'd found the thing she needed from him. Just simple faith. That was all.

Christy looked up at the man with whom she'd traveled such a strange and twisted and passion-filled road. She hadn't expected this, and something in the simple words touched her more deeply than she could have anticipated. "Jack," she said, "after everything, you don't know how much that means to me."

And then she followed the instinct to throw her arms around his neck in gratitude. And, of course, wrapping her arms around him, having his body pressed up against hers, made her feel far more than just gratitude—and when Jack enclosed her in a warm embrace, then said near her ear, "I know you can do this, honey," it buried her. It erased every last ounce of her resistance. And it made her kiss him.

She never meant to—it just happened. And to have her lips pressed against his warm mouth, to have his body molding so snugly against hers, felt like coming home.

She knew it was crazy to be kissing him under all the circumstances, and yet she couldn't stop. He kissed her back, just as feverishly—until together they sank to their knees on her bedroom floor.

And then he stopped kissing her just long enough to whisper, "Have faith in me, too, Christy. Please."

The words stole her breath, made her pull back, look into those sexy blue eyes.

"Have faith in me to never hurt you again. Have faith in me to always be honest with you, to always trust you. Have faith in me to be the man you deserve. Have faith in me to love you and make you happy. Because I'll do all those things if you'll only let me."

Christy knew a moment of truth when she

saw one. And she also knew there were plenty of good reasons she'd walked away from Jack that night on the beach. And she knew that even if she wanted to trust him again, it wouldn't happen automatically—trust had to be earned, and that would take some time, some caution. It came back to that whole broken plate thing—being sorry didn't instantly repair it.

But what if protecting herself was the wrong thing to do here? What if protecting herself meant never again opening herself up to real happiness, to a real, loving connection with someone?

And didn't she know that, despite his deceptions, Jack was the most amazing guy she'd ever met? And that she loved him?

And so if she was ever going to open her heart again, shouldn't it be to the man she loved? And to the man who had faith in her?

If he believed in her, was it so much of him to ask that she give him the same in return?

"Real trust," she said cautiously, "won't happen overnight."

But she could instantly see that her words had given him hope, told him she was opening the door, just a crack.

"I don't mind proving myself," he promised her. "For however long it takes."

Christy weighed it all in her head—and in the end, she realized it came down to taking a risk, and believing. Just like when she'd set up that table at the beach that first night, nervous and afraid she wouldn't sell any jewelry. And look how that had turned out.

She didn't want half a life. And how on earth could anyone live a whole life—a real life, a happy life—if they weren't willing to take chances and believe in the things, or people, they cared about?

"I love you, Jack," she said, being brave enough to open the door a whole lot more. "And I want us to go back to where we were, back to being happy, back to loving each other."

"I never *stopped* loving you, honey," he assured her, and her heart swelled in her chest.

"I didn't stop loving you, either. I tried, but I couldn't."

"Thank God," he murmured, then kissed her again.

But a blissful moment later, she stopped them with a gasp, pressing her palms to his chest. "Only . . ."

"What?" he asked, clearly worried.

"I . . . kind of decided that if I got the loan I would move to Coral Cove. Because it makes sense to be near Grandpa Charlie. And that's where the heart of my business seems to be. And, well, because I grew a lot there, and I was happy there, and so I just thought it made sense."

"You're right," he agreed with her, "it does make sense."

She blinked. "But what about us?"

"I can't think of a nicer place than Coral Cove for us to start over together, Alice."

Christy drew in her breath, amazed. "Really? You'd do that for me? You'd move to Coral Cove?"

"In a heartbeat, baby."

And as she got lost in more warm, sweet kisses, she knew already that she'd made the right choice about Jack. And she suddenly had all the faith in the world in him, too.

> "She tried the little golden key in the lock,
> and to her great delight, it fitted."
>
> Lewis Carroll, *Alice in Wonderland*

Epilogue

"*I* LOVE you, too, Grandpa Charlie," Christy said, then pushed the disconnect button on her phone, leaned back in the white wicker chair on her porch, and peered out over the ocean. It was a clear, sunny, blue-sky day and the surf was calm and the view never got old. Just one more reason, of many, to be happy.

She could scarcely believe the conversation she'd just had with her grandpa. Soon after she and Jack had moved down here to Coral Cove a few months ago, he'd spent a long afternoon on the pier with her and Jack telling them about Susan, his first love who had amazingly ended up at Sunnymeade with him, but in a coma. And just now he'd called to tell her of one more miracle—this morning Susan had opened her eyes. And she'd said his name. And she'd been aware of all the time he'd spent at her side. Christy had never heard her grandfather sound more giddy or youthful.

She couldn't wait to tell Jack, but he was inside, in the office they'd created from a spare bedroom in the little green cottage they'd bought on Sea Shell Lane, directly across from Fletcher's place. He was making calls to clients this afternoon, so she'd promised to leave him alone. But it had been a big day already, and she was having trouble containing herself.

In addition to Grandpa Charlie's incredible news, she'd gotten some other phone calls, too.

Bethany had just been given the art showing she'd been dreaming of, at a downtown Cincinnati gallery. And Christy had talked her into coming down for a celebratory vacation in a few months.

And Anna had called to tell her Duke had just proposed! They were planning a simple wedding on the lawn of their inn in Destiny, the Half Moon Hill Bed and Breakfast, next spring, so Christy and Jack would definitely need to make a trip home for that. She couldn't have been happier for her dear friend.

And last but far from least, she'd confirmed two new consignment clients today, an upscale clothing and jewelry shop on Clearwater Beach and a hotel gift shop in St. Petersburg. Meanwhile, sales continued to soar, and she was having no trouble making her loan payments and sending payments to Sunnymeade as well. Of course, having combined households with Jack made finances a lot easier—there was no denying that—but she still truly believed she could have done this on her own if she and Jack hadn't gotten back together.

All in all, life in Coral Cove was amazing. She loved living at the beach, and she and Jack had returned to the secluded spot where they'd first made love more than once to recreate the moment. It was wonderful being so close to her grandpa, and close to other friends they'd made here, too. They still frequented the Hungry Fisherman, and tomorrow Reece was taking them out for another snorkeling trip. Tonight, after the Sunset Celebration, they had plans to meet up with Fletcher, Tamra, and some of the other residents of Sea Shell Lane for a bonfire and marshmallow roast on the beach.

She loved their little beach cottage and—oh, the simple joy of being able to turn the key in the lock and always be able to get inside!

"And then there's you," she said, glancing down at the fluffy white cat who had just trotted up to weave a figure eight around her ankles. She bent to heft Dinah up beside her in the chair. "You don't have to scavenge for fish remains anymore, and Jack and I get to have a furry friend around the house. I think that worked out well for all of us, don't you?"

Dinah meowed, and Christy scratched behind her ears the way the kitty liked. Dinah, it turned out, was the perfect last piece of the puzzle, the final ingredient in her joyful new life that made it . . . perfect.

Though of course the best part of her life in Coral Cove was Jack. A little faith between them had gone a long way. So far that it wasn't even necessary to think about it anymore—it was simply this soft but solid thing that floated all around them.

And with Jack she'd already found what she'd declared to Bethany made for the perfect love: He made her feel safe without saving her. She'd saved *herself*. And she'd fallen in love with a great guy in the process. What more could a girl want?

Well, the beach maybe. But she had that, too.